英美文学教程与作品赏析

屈平 编著

中国原子能出版社

图书在版编目（CIP）数据

英美文学教程与作品赏析 / 屈平编著. ——北京：
中国原子能出版社，2020.4 （2021.10 重印）
ISBN 978-7-5221-0518-5

Ⅰ．①英… Ⅱ．①屈… Ⅲ．①英国文学－文学欣赏－
教材 ②文学欣赏－美国－教材 Ⅳ．①I561.06 ②I712.06

中国版本图书馆 CIP 数据核字（2020）第 051271 号

英美文学教程与作品赏析

出版发行	中国原子能出版社（北京市海淀区阜成路 43 号　　100048）	
责任编辑	刘东鹏	
责任印刷	潘玉玲	
印　　刷	三河市明华印务有限公司	
经　　销	全国新华书店	
开　　本	787mm×1092mm　　1/16	
印　　张	14.75	**字　　数** 241 千字
版　　次	2020 年 4 月第 1 版	2021 年 10 月第 2 次印刷
书　　号	ISBN ISBN 978-7-5221-0518-5	**定　　价** 68.00 元

网址：http://www.aep.com.cn　　　　E-mail：atomep123@126.com
发行电话：010-68452845　　　　　　版权所有 侵权必究

前　言

为了帮助大家更好地理解英美文学原著，在较短的时间内洞察这些经典作品的奥妙所在，掌握赏析文学作品的方法，作者编写了这本《英美文学教程与作品赏析》。

本书由英国文学和美国文学两部分构成，共十二章。每一章都详细介绍了文学背景知识、文学思潮、文学特色、主要作家与作品等内容，其目的是让读者从宏观上把握本章的学习内容。第二部分是作家与作品简介，包括所选作家及主要作品的简短描述、选读作品的赏析等，其目的是让读者从微观上把握本章的内容。

为方便读者更好地理解本书的内容，并运用所学知识正确地回答问题，本书使用汉、英两种语言撰写。各章概述和作家作品简介用汉语表述；选读作品赏析等用英语表述。通过本书的介绍、分析，希望一方面能为高校学生和广大英语爱好者打开一扇认识和了解英美文学作品的大门，激起他们热爱英美文学、阅读英美文学作品的兴趣；另一方面，又能为他们欣赏和阅读英美文学作品提供一些有效的方法指导。

在本书写作过程中，充分采用了学界最新的研究成果和一些新观点，吸收了一些现代教学理论和教学方法，教师可重点讲解，加强课堂互动，以拓宽比较视野，加强英美作家与世界作家的比较与分析。任何一个国家的文学，只有放在世界文学范围内才能独显其魅力，才能显示各国文学之间的相互交流、发展与繁荣。

本书在写作过程中，参考了国内外出版的多部文学史及选读方面的书籍。但由于作者水平有限，书中错谬之处在所难免，恳请读者和专家们批评指正。

作者

2019 年 8 月

目　录

第一章　中古时期的英国文学解读与作品赏析

一、主要文学特色

来自北欧的日耳曼部落带来了盎格鲁·撒克逊语，即古英语，同时还带来了一种恢弘而又哀婉的诗歌传统。盎格鲁·撒克逊时期的诗歌大体上分为两大类：其一是源于北欧的故事，称为世俗诗歌；其二是有关基督教的故事，称为宗教诗歌。宗教诗歌主要围绕圣经这一主题。世俗诗歌主要关注盎格鲁·撒克逊人在苦寒之地的生活；北海的恶劣气候对诗人的情绪和诗歌的语调影响巨大。

中世纪的英国文学涌现出了像杰弗利·乔叟这样杰出的作家。和古英语时期的文学相比，中世纪的英国文学描写的对象更加宽泛，风格、语调和体裁更加多样化。民间文学在这一阶段占有重要地位，虽然缺乏思想的原创性，但它对生活的描写不仅准确，而且丰富生动。骑士文学是这一时期较为流行的文学形式，它以叙事诗或散文的形式来歌颂骑士的冒险经历或其他英雄事迹。

二、主要作家与作品

《贝尔武夫》，一首典型的古英语诗歌，被认为是盎格鲁·撒克逊最伟大的民族史诗。

《高文爵士与绿衣骑士》，英国最好的骑士文学之一。

《罗宾汉民谣》，中世纪最重要的民谣之一。

《坎特伯雷故事集》，杰弗利·乔叟的代表作。

第一节　杰弗利·乔叟

一、作者简介

乔叟，宫廷诗人，他一生接触广泛，从宫廷贵族到资产阶级、普通百姓都有深入了解。通过观察，乔叟创造出了富有个性色彩的各式各样的人物形象，开创了英国文学的写实主义传统。乔叟艺术风格的特点是幽默和讽刺。他的诗歌语言生动，既注重刻画人物的外貌特征，又不忘深刻、细腻地展示人物的内心世界。乔叟把东部的方言（伦敦方言）作为自己文学写作的语言，从而为现代英语的发展打下了基础。乔叟学习并吸收了法国和意大利诗歌的艺术风格，并借用它们来丰富和提高英国诗歌的艺术表现力。《坎特伯雷故事集》中的不少故事是用十音节"双韵体"写成的。这种诗歌形式逐步演化成了"英雄双韵体"，并为后来的英国诗人所广泛采用。乔叟也因此被誉为"英国诗歌之父"。乔叟的《坎特伯雷故事集》，无论在内容和技巧上都达到了他诗歌创作的顶峰。

二、主要作品简介

（一）《坎特伯雷故事集》

这是一部诗体故事集。乔叟原计划创作 120 个故事，但他只完成了 24 个故事。《坎特伯雷故事集》题材广泛，人物来自社会的各个阶层，展现了广阔的社会画面，其中以骑士女修道院长、巴斯妇等人讲的故事最为有名。《坎特伯雷故事集》深刻反映了资本主义萌芽时期的英国社会生活，揭露了教会的腐败和教士的伪善、贪婪，谴责了扼杀人性的禁欲主义，并肯定了世俗的爱情生活。因此，该作品的艺术成就很高，远远超过了同时代其他作品，是英国文学史上写实主义的第一部典范。作品将幽默和讽刺结合，喜剧色彩浓厚，对后来的英国文学产生了深远的影响。

（二）选读作品赏析

Excerpts from the General Prologue of The Canterbury Tales

In April, with the beginning of spring, people of varying social classes come from all over England to gather at the Tabard Inn, preparing for a pilgrimage to Canterbury to receive the blessings of St. Thomas a Becket, the English martyr. Chaucer is one of the pilgrims. That evening, the Host of the Tabard Inn suggests that each member of the group tell tales on the way to and from Canterbury in order to make the time pass more pleasantly. The person who tells the best story will be awarded an exquisite dinner at the end of the trip. The Host decides to accompany the party and appoints himself as the judge of the best tale.

The Canterbury Tales is more than just a collection of stories. It is a pageant of 14th century life. Every class variation is represented except the highest and the lowest. These people act their parts in a way that reveals their private lives and habits，their moods and dispositions，and their good and bad qualities. In the General prologue Chaucer sets up the general structure of the tales and introduces each of the characters.

The General Prologue in essence serves as a guide for the tales，giving some explanations for the motivation behind each of the tales. The Canterbury Tales begins with the imagery of spring and regeneration. Then Chaucer veers into some spiritual territory. In springtime these travelers make a religious，pilgrimage to Canterbury. He gives relatively straightforward descriptions of the characters and has some inclination to show their best qualities. Each pilgrim is described as an exemplar and a number of these pilgrims are described as "perfect" in some way or another.

Subtle criticism and sly wit are also taken into consideration by Chaucer. The description of the Prioress is obviously flattering，yet it also sharply criticizes her foolish sentimentality and oppressive attention to manners. Although she strives to be polite and refined，she speaks French with the vulgar rural pronunciation compared to elite Parisian French. Furthermore，she weeps at the mere sight of a dead mouse. The wife of Bath is among the travelers low on the social scale. Chaucer describes her as lewd and boisterous. Her clothing is ostentatious，meant to attract the attention from others. She is quite promiscuous-she has been married five times and has an undetermined number of lovers.

第二节　民间歌谣

一、"The Three Ravens"

Three ravens discuss a slain knight as the main course of their breakfast. But the knight is guarded by his hawks and hounds and they cannot get close to him. Later on his mistress finds his body and helps to clean his wounds. Then she carries the dead knight to an earthen cave and buries him there in the early morning. After that she lies down beside him and dies in her grief. Moved by the scene, the ravens, as by standers, forget about their food and pray to god.

This ballad concentrates on the most dramatic part of the tale. The images are simple and direct. All background detail is cast aside in favor of the actions of the knight's hawks, hounds, and mistress. There are elements of love, loyalty, supernatural and eternity. It is one of the most beautiful of the old chivalry ballads.

二、"Get Up and Bar the Door"

The wife wants her husband to bar the door because the wind blows in and disturbs her cooking. The husband doesn't want to do it. Then they agree after an argument that the first person who speaks will have to bar the door. If neither speaks, neither will go and bar the door. At night, two strangers enter through the open door and eat the food. The wife has prepared. Neither husband nor wife says anything. However, when the strangers propose to cut off the husband's beard and kiss the wife, the husband rises up in a rage and shouts at the thieves, at which the wife rejoices. She then asks her husband to get up and bar the door.

The basic conflict in this ballad is one that is easily recognized: man vs. woman, or more specifically, husband vs. wife, a battle of the wills. The setting of this story is mid-November, in the home of a couple. The most direct lesson from the ballad is that not barring the door has led them to trouble. Several literary techniques help to heighten the drama in this ballad. "Get Up and Bar the Door" follows the traditional four-line stanza and abcb rhyme scheme found in ballads. It also makes use of repetition of variations of the phrase "Get Up and Bar the Door". This seems to suggest the urgency of shutting the door and the danger the inhabitants of the house confront by letting the darkness of the night into their house. If any adjectives describe the man and wife, it is "stubborn" Though humorous, the ballad has a serious theme One's stubbornness can inadvertently cause harm to himself or others.

第二章 文艺复兴时期的英国文学解读与作品赏析

一、主要文学特色

受到人文主义思潮和宗教改革的影响，英国文艺复兴时期的思想家、艺术家和诗人们在文学作品中表达了对人性美和人类成就的向往这一新的感情，与神学感情形成了鲜明的对比。在英国文艺复兴的繁荣时期，其文学的主要特色是：

（1）古典文学、意大利和法国文学作品翻译的流行；

（2）伊丽莎白时期兴起的民族感情催生了许多有关历史主题的作品；

（3）游记、新发现和远征探险历程的作品；

（4）诗歌风格多样化，抒情诗，尤其是十四行诗开始盛行；

（5）戏剧的发展与繁荣。

二、主要作家与作品

开创英国文艺复兴时期诗歌新风的两个重要作家是菲利普·锡德尼和埃德蒙·斯宾塞。在他们的抒情和叙事作品中，展现出一种辞藻华丽、精雕细琢的文风，如斯宾塞的《仙后》。到 16 世纪末，诗歌又出现了两大流派。其一是以约翰·邓恩为代表的玄学派诗人，其二是本·琼森为代表的骑士流派。英国文艺复兴时期的最后一位大诗人是约翰·弥尔顿，他的诗歌具有惊人的震撼力和优雅的韵致，同时传达出深邃的思想。其代表作为《失乐园》和《力士参孙》。戏剧是英国文艺复兴的文学主流。最具才华的大学才子克里斯托弗马洛冲破了旧的戏剧形式，创作了《帖木儿》《浮士德博士》等剧作；而这一时期造诣最高的剧作家和诗人则是威廉·莎士比亚。他的剧作思想深刻，艺术表现手法精湛，历经几个世纪，长盛不衰。此外，作为英国早期的人文主义者，托马斯·莫尔的《乌托邦》批评了当时的英国和欧洲社会，设计了一个社会平等、财产共有、人们和谐相处的理想国，开创了英国哲理幻想小说的先河；散文家弗朗西斯·培根的《随笔》题材广泛、文笔典雅、略带古风而又明白畅达，他将散文艺术发展到一个新的高度。

第一节 埃德蒙·斯宾塞

一、作者简介

埃德蒙·斯宾塞（1552—1599）被称为"诗人中的诗人"，对后来的英国诗人弥尔顿、拜伦、雪莱、济慈和坦尼森等产生了巨大的影响。在宗教上，斯宾塞深受宗教改革的影响，始终站在新教的立场，激烈抨击天主教的虚伪与腐败。他崇尚自然之美，同时严守道德准则。在其作品中，他有效地将古典文学的传统与基督教的教义融为一体，并表达出强烈的爱国主义情感。他创造的斯宾塞诗节成了英国诗歌发展史上重要的诗歌形式。他的诗歌极富想象力，语言精致优雅，富有强烈的音乐节奏感。他在诗歌技巧的处理上也比前人的作品更加灵活。

二、主要作品简介

（一）《仙后》

《仙后》是斯宾塞的代表作，每一卷都有一个英雄骑士为光荣的"仙后"（意指伊丽莎白一世女王）执行高贵的任务。每位骑士代表着一种美德，如圣洁、温和、贞洁、友谊、正义和谦恭等。这首长诗是一个延续的寓言，也是文艺复兴时期英格兰民族的浪漫史诗。以亚瑟王为代表的骑士传统象征着正义的英国，而那些以不同面貌出现的魑魅魍魉则是她的敌人的邪恶形象。

（二）《牧羊人日历》

《牧羊人日历》是斯宾塞的第一部主要诗作，由 12 首牧歌组成，每一首对应一年中的一个月份。诗中不同的人物均以天真、纯朴的牧人形象出现，用对话的形式谈论人生和爱情，对当时的社会和宗教问题发表严肃的、带讽刺性的见解。

三、选读作品赏析

"Sonnet 75"

Sonnet 75 is about the authors attempts to immortalize the love of his life. It happened in a summer day at the seaside. The poet writes his love's name in the sand at the beach，but the oceans waves wipe it away over and over again，just as time will destroy all man-made things. Nevertheless he feels confident that he is able to immortalize his love by a different kind of writing，his poetry，no matter how short life on earth may be. At the same time the writing of the lady's name，which is the central image of the poem，is transferred from earth to heaven. Love，poetry and religious belief are closely associated.

Technically，Spenser's poetry is at a very high level. He skillfully uses simple words to create a complete，harmonious picture. After the action of the first quatrain he switches to the dialogue in the second and third，to conclude with the couplet which summarizes the theme of the sonnet. Spenser's perfect handling of vowels and the wavelike rhythm of his poem can only be appreciated when the sonnet is read aloud so as to bring out its melody. His frequent use of alliteration binds the poem together. What distinguishes Spenser's poem from earlier poetry is the personal note it strikes. The poet places himself in the center of the poem telling us about his personal situation emotions and convictions. During the Elizabethan age，love sonnets generally told the story of men in love with unattainable women. However，Spenser's sonnets defy such a pessimistic view and give an optimistic look towards love.

第二节　克里斯托弗·马洛

一、作者简介

马洛（1564—1593）是英国戏剧的先驱者，他首次运用无韵诗（不押韵的抑扬格五音步诗）作为英国戏剧创作的主要手段。他自由地借鉴古典戏剧的典范，在戏剧舞台上创造了反映时代精神的巨人性格和"雄伟的诗行"，为莎士比亚的艺术创作铺平了道路。

二、主要作品简介

马洛最好的戏剧作品有：《帖木儿》（1587）、《马尔他的犹太人》（1592）

和《浮士德博士》（1588）。这些作品反映了文艺复兴时期新兴资产阶级对于知识的追求、自尊的渴望和永无止境的探索精神。马洛戏剧的主题是歌颂从中世纪教条和法律桎梏中解脱出来的人的个性，弘扬人类永无止境征服宇宙的信念。其作品中的主人公大体上都以其坚韧的性格、对于传统教条的嘲笑和压倒一切的激情而著称：在《帖木儿》中是野心，在《浮士德博士》中是对于知识和权力的欲望，在《马尔他的犹太人》中是对财富的贪婪。这些典型的人物形象展现了马洛作品中极端的个人欲望，个人主义的雄心壮志给世界，甚至他们自身，带来了破坏和毁灭。

三、选读作品赏析

"The Passionate Shepherd to His Love"

This short poem is considered to be one of the most beautiful lyrics in English literature. It derives from the pastoral tradition. In this poem, the shepherd enjoys an ideal country life, cherishing a pastoral and pure affection for his love. It describes the life in the fairyland, and strong emotion is conveyed through the beauty of nature. First the shepherd glorifies the natural beauty of the hills, fields, waterfalls and birds singing love songs. Then he promises his love gifts made from nature. Finally he offers the community as a gift by saying that shepherds's wains will dance and sing for his beloved. He will give her what he thinks she'll need once she falls in love with him and would want to live with him in the romantic rural setting together they will all the pleasure prove and he would show her a world where birds sing, the sun shines, and everything is serene and perfect.

Its theme is the rapture of springtime love in a simple, rural setting. Implicit in this theme is the motif of carpe diem—Latin for? "Seize the day," which urges people to enjoy the moment without worrying about the future. The shepherd does not worry whether his status makes him acceptable to the maiden; nor does he appear concerned about money or education. He courageously courts her through poetry, and sincerely believes that love is all one needs to have a good life. The future will take care of itself. What matters is the moment. The significance of the poem lies mainly in the imagery presented in the poem-hills, valleys, birds singing love songs, beds of roses, a cap of flowers, a belt of straw with ivy buds. Through the description, the author conveys a kind of inexpressible emotions.

第三节 沃尔特·拉雷

一、作者简介

拉雷（1552—1618）是伊丽莎白时期一位才华横溢并极负探险盛名的爵士。他也是一名战士、政治家、海上旅行者、诗人和历史学家，因被不公平地指控犯有叛国罪而被处死。他曾组织多次航海探险，并在美洲拓展殖民，并将烟草和马铃薯引进英国。他的一生是这一时期英国展示野心和探索精神的典型反映。

二、主要作品简介

拉雷的作品有探险游记《发现圭亚那》、在狱中创作的《世界历史》以及一些短小的抒情诗。他创作的诗歌充满了想象力。其特点是在彼特拉克式的爱情主题中，掺入自己对人类生活环境的思考，表达了对生命无常和时光短暂的感慨，带有伤感、抑郁之情。"仙女对牧羊人的回答"是对马洛的《痴情的牧羊人致意中人》所做的回应。诗歌从仙女的角度来创作，提出如果爱情和世界永远年轻，她就愿意和牧羊人一起生活，然而世间万物是不断变化的。仙女执着于自己的信仰，一再阐明物质的享受无法吸引自己；青春易逝，爱情不会永恒，并以此拒绝了牧羊人的求爱。从诗歌中可以看出拉雷的态度，他不贪恋尘世的虚假爱情，而是追求真正超越凡俗的爱情。

三、选读作品赏析

"The Nymph's Reply to the Shepherd"

The Nymphs Reply to the Shepherd is a witty and well-written reply to Marlowe's more innocent "The Passionate Shepherd to His Love". Raleigh uses the same meter and references to present "mirror images" of Marlowe's poem. The nymph in the poem sets up a hypothetical set of questions that undermine the intelligence of the shepherd's offer because all that he offers is transitory. Time does not stand still; winter inevitably follows the spring. The rocks grow cold, the fields yield to the harvest, the flocks are driven to fold in winter, the rivers rage and the birds complain about the winter. So do the gowns, shoes and beds of roses. And the nymph cares nothing about the stuff like the belt of straw or the ivy buds. Only if youth last and love always thrive would she agree to live with the shepherd. It shows the nymphs realistic view on love. This poem is more like a criticism to Marlowe's original poem. After all, we are not in Eden but in a fallen world. The seasons pass, so does time.

The use of imagery and figurative language not only brings the poem to life, but it also sets a tone, a mood, to which the poem lives by. The Nymph's Reply to the Shepherd "has a rather daunting mood, as the nymph cuts the shepherd's proposal to shreds. Yet, towards the end, the mood gains a slim hope when the nymph offers that if the shepherd were able to prove his love for her then maybe their union could be possible. Like the shepherd, she longs for such things to be true, but like Raleigh, she a skeptic, retaining faith only in reasons power to discount the" folly of "fancy's spring". The nymphs reply debunks the shepherd's fanciful vision.

第四节　威廉·莎士比亚

一、作者简介

莎士比亚（1564—1616）是英国文学史上最具影响力的剧作家和诗人。作为人文主义者，他描写了国内战争的残酷及其反自然的特点，但并不彻底反对封建统治。他反对宗教迫害和种族歧视，反对社会不平等和金钱至上的社会风气。对于被压迫者他给予同情，但是带有一定的局限性。他也找不到解决社会问题的出路。他唯一能做的只能是逃避现实，在梦想中寻求慰藉。

莎士比亚接受了文艺复兴的观点，认为文学集真、善、美于一身，应该反映自然与现实。他借哈姆雷特之口，指出戏剧创作的目的就在于真实地反映当时的社会现实状况。同时，他认为那些能真正反映自然与现实的文学作品是不朽的。同时代的戏剧家本·琼森称赞"他不属于一个时代，而是属于永远"。

二、主要作品简介

莎士比亚一生共创作了 154 首十四行诗、2 首叙事长诗和 38 部戏剧。他的十四行诗采用的是通俗的英国形式——三个四行诗节和一个对句。对句通常将一首诗与整组诗的某个主题加以联系，而四行诗节则可自由发挥诗歌的艺术魅力，从而使单个的每一首诗都让人惊叹叫绝。他的十四行诗所倾诉的对象为一青年男子而非女子，主题往往涉及时光流逝、岁月无情、物质世界的迅速衰败以及美貌、青春与爱情的短暂等。虽然这些诗篇赞美生活，却对死亡有着敏锐的感知。更重要的是，其中所包含的道德和审美意识远比伊丽莎白时期其他人创作的同类作品更为深刻。

莎士比亚的戏剧内容更多的是关注现实生活，通过剧作真实而生动地反映了那个时代的主要社会矛盾。他笔下的主要人物往往具有多重特质，代表了现实生活的复杂性。莎士比亚的戏剧也因其巧妙的构思而著称。他常常从古老的戏剧或故事，或古希腊罗马文化中借用素材。剧作故事通常贯穿多条线索，从而产生紧张的戏剧效果。悲剧和喜剧要素的结合以及戏剧反讽手法的巧妙运用使其作品的情节和结构更加丰富。剧中剧的手法也在某些作品的结构方面发挥了重要作用。莎士比亚还是一位真正的语言大师。他通过使用头韵、夸张、暗喻、双关等不同修辞手法，别具一格地展示作品的思想内容。他继承、发展了马洛开创的无韵诗体，使之适应不同的戏剧氛围，极大地丰富了英语的表现形式与技巧。

莎士比亚最著名的四大喜剧是《仲夏夜之梦》《威尼斯商人》《皆大欢喜》和《第十二夜》；最著名的四大悲剧是《哈姆雷特》《奥赛罗》《李尔王》和《麦克白》；另外，他的悲喜剧《罗密欧与朱丽叶》和传奇剧《暴风雨》也极负盛名。

三、选读作品赏析

"Sonnet 18"

This sonnet starts out with a rhetorical question："If I were to compare you to a day in the summertime，would that be an adequate description of how beautiful you are?" Then it answers its own question："No，because you're lovelier and milder than that." Then it goes on to discuss some of the ways in which the beauty of a summer day is not perfect and does not last - "The rose buds get bruised by the wind；the sun shines too hot，and often its golden face is darkened by clouds；and everything beautiful stops being beautiful，either by accident or simply in the course of nature. —Then it concludes by saying，"You will never fade and die，because by writing this poem about your beauty，I am making you immortal." So the poem praises the beauty of someone the poet loves，who will live on forever in the words. In this sonnet Shakespeare deals with the traditional themes of time，beauty and poetry and expresses his feelings towards the addressee. The poem is a comparison between the man's eternal beauty with summer's temporal beauty，between the inconstancy of nature and the timelessness of poetry. Shakespeare poses the idea that though poetry，beauty gains immortality. his image of transience and eternity is used throughout the poem.

The Shakespearean sonnet has three four-line stanzas (quatrains) and a two-line unit called a couplet. The meter of this sonnet is iambic pentameter. The thyming lines in each stanza are the first and third and the second and fourth. In the couplet ending the poem，both lines thyme. The beauty of this poem is tied to the strict structural rules that a sonnet is bound by.

第五节　弗朗西斯·培根

一、作者简介

培根（1561—1626）是英国第一位论说文作家。他晚年致力于哲学著述和科学研究。其哲学思想强调人是自然的奴仆和解释者，真理不是来自权威，知识是经验结出的果实。培根也是现代科学的奠基人，马克思称他为"英国唯物主义及现代实验科学之父"。

二、主要作品简介

培根的作品有总结前人科学成果的《学术的推进》、阐述归纳推理法的《新工具》和"乌托邦"性质的作品《新大西岛》。培根也以他的《随笔》而著名。1625 年再版时他的《随笔》已经收录了 58 篇论说文。这些文章清晰准确，短小隽永，题材涉及政治、人情、处世、修身、真理、爱情、青春、财富，等等。其中许多言简意赅、充满哲理的精辟语句已成为格言名句。

三、选读作品赏析

"Of Studies" from Essays

Of Studies is one of the most popular essays by Bacon. The main focus of the essay rests on explaining to the reader the importance of study knowledge in terms of its practical application towards the individual and its society. At first, it analyzes what studies chiefly serve for delight, ornament, and for ability ". Then it presents the different ways adopted by different people to pursue studies, and how people from all walks of life approach the idea of studying" Crafty men contemn studies, simple men admire them, and wise men use them... After that, it offers some pertinent advices but to weight and consider. At last, it shows us how studies exert influence over human character.

The text employs many devices of connectivity, including grammatical devices lexical cohesion, logical connection, pragmatic and semantic implication, and even prosodic associations. Of all the grammatical devices utilized in the text, the most striking are perhaps ellipsis, parallel construction and antithesis. The lexical cohesion of the text is achieved mainly through reiteration and collocation. Devices of other types add much to the coherence of the text, which is achieved by the combination of all types of devices of connectivity, not only at the levels of the text and the paragraph, but also at the level of many rhetorically forceful sentences. This essay, as many readers agree is distinguished for its incisiveness, terseness and clarity. Unlike many of his contemporaries, Bacon makes full use of so meager a vocabulary to explicate his great Theme.

第六节　约翰·邓恩

一、作者简介

邓恩（1572—1631）的诗歌以爱情、讽刺、宗教等为题材。诗歌中许多

"别出心裁的比喻"十分奇特，让人初读觉得不可思议，掩卷细想又觉得颇有道理。他的诗歌在语言形式上不拘一格，在情景意象上独具特色。在文学史上，邓恩被认为是 17 世纪玄学派诗歌的创始人。玄学诗是情感与灵巧智慧的融合，其特色便是"奇思妙喻"和"巧智"。它较少关注情感的表达，更多地注重对情感的分析，以及探索诗人意识的最深处。

二、主要作品简介

邓恩的作品大致可以分为两类：早期创作的爱情诗和讽刺诗，如《歌与十四行诗》。这些诗歌充满了奇思妙喻，意象奇特、语言晦涩。他主张爱的本质是灵与肉的完美结合。理想主义和玩世不恭的态度共存于他的爱情诗中。后期接任圣职之后，其作品则以圣诗和认诚诗为主。邓恩的布道文最能显示他卓越的散文才华。这些布道富于理性和机智，具有强烈的感染力；它们探讨基督教的基本教义，而不是沉湎于神学的争论。邓恩布道文的魅力来自它们强烈的戏剧性、坦率的个人启示、富于诗意的节奏，以及特色鲜明的奇思妙喻。

三、选读作品赏析

A Valediction：*Forbidding Mourning*

A valediction is a farewell statement. The poem is autobiographical as John Donne wrote it before he was going to travel abroad for months or maybe years. In this poem the speaker explains that he is forced to spend time apart from his lover, but before he leaves, he tells her that their farewell should not be the occasion for mourning and sorrow.

The nine stanza of this poem are quite simple compared to most of Donne's, poems which utilize strange metrical patterns overlaid jarringly on regular rhyme schemes Here, each four-line stanza is quite unadorned, with an abab rhyme scheme and an iambic tetrameter meter. Besides its simple form, the poem might also be one of donne's most direct statements of his ideal of spiritual love. Here anticipating a physical separation from his beloved, he invokes the nature of that poem is essentially a sequence of metaphors and comparisons, each describing a way of looking at their separation that will help them to avoid the mourning forbidden by the poems title .

First, the speaker says that their farewell should be as mild as the uncomplaining deaths of virtuous men, for to weep would be "profanation of our joys." Next, the speaker compares harmful "Moving of th' earth" to innocent "trepidation of the spheres," equating the first with "dull sublunary lovers' love" and the second with their love, "Inter-assured of the mind." Like the rumbling earth, the dull sublunary (sublunary meaning literally beneath the moon and also subject to the moon) lovers are all physical, unable to experience separation without losing the sensation that comprises and sustains their love. But the spiritual lovers "Care less, eyes, lips, and hands to miss," because, like the trepidation (vibration) of the spheres (the concentric globes that surrounded the earth in ancient astronomy), their love is not wholly physical. Moreover like the trepidation of the spheres, their movement will not have the harmful consequences of an earthquake.

The speaker then declares that, since the lovers' two souls are one, his departure will simply expand the area of their unified soul, rather than cause a rift between them. If however, their souls are "two" instead "one", they are as the feet of a drafters circle.

The compass (the instrument used for drawing circles) is one of Donne's most famous metaphors, and it is the perfect image to encapsulate the values of Donne's spiritual love, which is balanced, symmetrical, intellectual, serious, and beautiful in its polished simplicity.

Like many of Donne's love poems, A Valediction: Forbidding Mourning "creates a dichotomy between the common love of the everyday world and the uncommon love of the speaker. Here, the speaker claims that to tell the laity", or the common people, his love would be to profane its scared nature, and he is clearly contemptuous of the dull sublunary love of other lovers. The poem is more like a promise or oath from donne to his beloved wife not to mourn him or grieve during his absence.

第七节 乔治·赫伯特

一、作者简介

赫伯特（1593—1633）作为玄学派的圣徒，创作了大量的宗教诗歌来歌颂上帝的荣光，其特点是用词严谨、韵律多变，巧妙地运用了玄学诗派所崇尚的意象与奇想。美国作家爱默生曾评价说："赫伯特的诗是一个虔诚心灵以诗人之眼和圣徒之爱来探索世界之谜的表现。在这里，诗歌有了最高尚的用途。"

二、主要作品简介

赫伯特一生所创作的160多首诗全部收录在他的宗教诗集《圣堂》中。他通过把各种各样的意象用在教堂的宗教仪式和信仰上来阐释他自己虔诚的沉思冥想。他以象征的方式描述自己的思想和感情。《圣堂》中大部分的诗歌是他对于上帝和自己灵魂之间精神冲突的诉说。"美德"是一首语调舒缓但蕴意深刻的诗。诗人用白日、玫瑰，春天和干木这四个意象烘托了主题，告诉我们，世间万物，无论怎样绮丽芬芳，总不免消亡，唯美好有德的灵魂永存。诗歌语言直白平易，意象清晰。在简单中蕴藏复杂，却又表现出复杂的简单。

三、选读作品赏析

" Virtue"

George Herbert employs the device of anaphora by repeating the word " sweet in each stanza of this poem to describe the transitory beauty of the nature. The three things he lists- the day, a rose, the spring, stand for youth, beauty, and pleasure, which all last only a short time, but virtue endures forever. The structure of the poem is carefully crafted, like the first three quatrains; and the content is sensuously perceived, like the depictions of the day, nightfall, a rose and spring. It is a typical metaphysical poem consisted of the bold metaphors and colloquial language that struggle with and illuminate each other. Herbert contrasts the passing glories of the mortal world with the eternal glory of the immortal soul, and thereby distinguishes between momentary and eternal value. Though the whole world turns to coal, the virtue still lives.

Virtue is a poem that combines meaning. emotion language and images. It contains rhythm and sound with sight and ideas. All at once it appeals to the senses feelings and the mind. It works together even when the parts seem to exist separately.

First we approach a poem simply and add the complexities one at a time to see how the parts work Generally, we can say that Herbert's work is more private, subjective but modest in its aim. his tone is more conversational. and his art is directed to achieve a sense of naturalness and simplicity. What is striking about Herberts style is its clarity and directness; Herbert regularly defends his plainness or commends a commonplace expression of praise. The notion of restraint, temperance and self-discipline in the argument of many of the poems is reflected in their structure.

第八节　安德鲁·马维尔

一、作者简介

马维尔（1621—1678）是 17 世纪英国著名的玄学派诗人。他不但继承了伊丽莎白时代爱情诗中的浪漫主义传统，成为一位具有浪漫主义气质的诗人，而且开启了 18 世纪古典主义的"理性时代"。古典派诗人偏重意象的完整优美，喜以哲理入诗；浪漫派诗人则偏重情感的自然流露。前者重形式，后者重实质。在马维尔的诗中，常能体现二者的完美结合，理性令他的诗寓意深刻，浪漫则使他的诗情境优美。

二、主要作品简介

安德鲁·马维尔曾创作不少政治讽刺诗和小品文，抨击政府的腐败和宗教的迫害。同时，他以诗歌来阅读并解说"大自然的神秘书籍"。在"致他的娇羞的女友"一诗中，马维尔将激情和理智并置，用优美的语言表现"及时行乐"的主题。整篇诗作音律优美，结构严谨，气势磅礴，充满了奇思妙喻，具有独特的艺术魅力。"花园"一诗文字绮丽，音韵优美，意象生动，将田园诗的风格和玄学诗的特点融合在一起，形成了马维尔诗歌特有的风格。

三、选读作品赏析

"To His Coy Mistress"

This poem is a lyric poem, while some scholars also consider it as a metaphysical poem. It presents a familiar theme in literature carpe diem, or "seize the day". Here is the gist the speaker of the poem is telling his mistress that it would be alright to wait for her if they were immortal or if they were going to live for hundreds or thousands of years—— "Had we but world enough, and time; This coyness, lady, were no crime. But since they are both going to die ——" But at my back I always hear, Time's winged chariot hurrying near, she should stop being coy and seize the moment being with him to enjoy life.

Marvell skillfully uses the third-person possessive pronoun "his" to refer to the young man in the poem. He enters the mind of the man and reports his thoughts as they manifest themselves. The word "coy" in the title tells the reader that the lady is playfully hesitant and artfully demure; while the man is impatient and straightforward. His motivation appears to be carnal desire rather than true love: passion rules him.

Seduction is the theme of nearly all carpe diem poems, and time is used to emphasize the importance of acting now. What makes Marvells poem unique is the careful combination of time and seduction. The poem is also notable for its playful, explicit treatment of sex its total control of tone and pacing, as well as its conciseness and precision in wording And there is no end to how far this poem can be understood.

If we look beyond the limited perspective of the speaker himself, we can see that Marvell is making a statement about how all of us should savor the pleasures of the moment. For the poet, there are two kinds of attitude toward the present: activities in the present are judged by their impact on the future; and there is no future state activities occur in the present and can only be enjoyed or evaluated by their impact at that moment. Marvell is not suggesting that unbridled lust is preferable to moral or ethical restraint; sex is the subject matter, not the theme of the poem. Marvell's actual point here is that instead of dividing our lives or our values into mathematically neat but artificial categories of present and future, we should savor the unique experiences of each present moment; to convey this theme, the poet uses irregularities of rhyme、rhythm, and meter to undermine the mathematically neat but artificial patterns of the poem.

In this poem, Marvell makes use of allusion, metaphor, and grand imagery in order to convey a mood of majestic endurance and innovatively explicate the carpe diem motif.

The images invoked by the speaker are by no means ordinary in their description. They rouse feelings of urgency and longing. From the grave where none do there embrace to oneness "roll our strength into one ball" all conjure a vast array of emotion that the speaker feels. This poem is indeed persuasive in nature but subtly so. He makes his argument with valid facts to support that argument. They will grow old and gray; while they watch their youth slip slowly away. There is no denying this. In his final appeal he makes his young mistress a promise though we cannot make our sun. Stand still, yet we will make him run. One can almost see the smile on a young mans face as he craftily petitions a girl to sleep with him. This persuasiveness would not be as affective without Marvels superb use of imagery.

第九节 本·琼森

一、作者简介

琼森（1572—1637）是莎士比亚之后最主要的剧作家。他在当时的文坛上颇受推崇，成为作家中的领袖人物，围绕他活动的文学圈被称为"琼森派"。他是一名多产的剧作家，其作品以气质喜剧见长，即剧中不同角色均具有特定的气质、性情和举止。他的剧作遵循古典主义原则，并有强烈的道德倾向。琼森是英国文学史上 18 世纪古典主义的先行者。

二、主要作品简介

琼森的剧作包括悲剧、喜剧和假面剧。他的悲剧的特点是对历史事实学术般的精确描写和对古典悲剧艺术规则的严格坚持；而假面剧只为宫廷娱乐而作；喜剧才真正奠定了他在文学史上的地位。他最好的喜剧有《个性互异》《狐狸》《炼金术士》《巴梭罗缪市集》等。琼森的戏剧以伦敦正在膨胀的经济和商人阶层为背景，用尖锐讽刺的手法指出贪财几乎总是压倒其他一切的偏好，而愚蠢也比比皆是。他的诗歌语言朴素精练，富于音乐美。

三、选读作品赏析

"Song：To Celia"

Ben Johnsons "Song To Celia" is a highly polished poem，which has two stanzas each of eight lines. In the first stanza，the speaker opens with a plea for the lady to drink to him with her eyes，or to leave a kiss in the cup while drinking. Thus，he would prize it more than nectar of the gods. This wish shows the speaker wants a pledge more than an expression of her love. Her kiss will intoxicate him more than any alcohol could and the wine would be an inadequate replacement for her love. In the second stanza，the speaker sends a garland of roses to the lady for the hope that the garland shall never wither once being under her spell. Though the lady has sent it back，he is quite pleasing because it smells not only of the roses but also of his dearest love Celia.

The poem is a short monologue in which a lover addresses his lady in an effort to encourage her to express her love for him. Johnson smoothly integrates the images of eyes，wine and roses in the poem，which reinforce and heighten the speakers expression of a powerful feeling，erotic love and longing. The poem is written in what is known as the ballad meter，that is，in alternate eight-syllable and six-syllable lines of iambic meter and with a rhyme scheme of abcb. The use of figures of speech，the pleasing sound and rhythm，make this poem memorable。

It is interesting to note that this perfect lyric was pieced together from sentences in five different love letters of Philostratus. However，Jonson makes a good combination of the classical tradition and the world of seventeenth-century England，thus subordinating both tradition and contemporary milieu to the authors sensibility. This subordination，which effectively proposes the authorial consciousness as a master-text encompassing and assimilating all others，comprises a typical Jonsonian literary gesture. It is called a masterpiece in its purely lyric composition and individuality.

第十节　罗伯特·赫里克

一、作者简介

赫里克（1589—1674）是一位骑士派诗人，其作品多为描写山野、田园风光、自然景物以及恬静、安逸的生活。作为本·琼森的门生，赫里克的诗歌也充满了古典主义的元素，但他的诗歌简洁精练、辞藻华丽，更能刺激感官。他经常把鲜花的短暂跟人类生命和爱情的短暂性联想到一起，主张享受生活，及时行乐，但在其轻松快乐的表象之下往往隐藏着光阴消逝、末日来临的预感。

二、主要作品简介

赫里克约有 1400 首诗歌传世，分别收入《雅歌》和《西方乐土》中。《雅歌》主要是宗教诗；而《西方乐土》长久以来一直为人们所推崇，原因就在于诗集中所体现的清新、抒情的风格。他最著名的诗作是抒情诗"为请惜时致少女"。这首诗虽然短小，但主题明晰，含义深刻，意境飘逸。诗中反复吟唱的主题在于劝诫年轻的少女"莫负好时光""及时行乐"。诗人用玫瑰、时光、太阳等作为喻体，烘托"青春易逝，抓住时光"的主题。

三、选读作品赏析

To the Virgins，*to Make Much of Time*

To the virgins，to Make Much of Time is also one of the most famous poems to extol the notion of carpe diem. In the first two stanzas, the poet compares the flower to a maiden, the sun to a lamp，to say that the virgin should grasp the opportunities to win a husband. With images from nature, including flowers dying and the sun setting, he reinforces his point with the reason in the last two stanzas time is quickly passing; ones youth is the best time in life, and the ladies should not waste their prime time because they cannot get it back. The poem finishes by encouraging these young virgins to make good use of their time and pursue opportunities for marriage before time turns you into old maids. Echoing Ben Jonson's poem, Song: To Celia, the speaker of the poem underscores the ephemeral quality of life and urges those in their youth to actively celebrate life and its pleasures; however, the speaker does not urge the virgins simply to frolic adulterously, but to seek union in matrimony.

第十一节 约翰·弥尔顿

一、作者简介

弥尔顿（1608—1674）是17世纪中期最伟大的革命诗人、政论家、清教徒文学的代表和真正的民主斗士。弥尔顿以其对自由意志的强烈信仰，对知识的热忱追求和对真理的尊重而被归入人文主义者之列。他的人文主义思想尤见于他对《圣经》创作素材的处理方式。他认为这些素材可以根据个人判断加以诠释，并对它们进行自由、大胆和富于想象力的加工。弥尔顿的上帝不仅是力量和爱的象征，同时也代表统驭宏观宇宙和人类灵魂的理性原则。他强调宗教与美德在提升道德判断力方面的重要性，这和基督教人文主义的主要目的相符。弥尔顿也尊重求善求真的直觉本能，他希望"为促进真实和实质性的自由之进步做贡献，这种自由不应从外部而应从人的内心去寻求"。

二、主要作品简介

弥尔顿的创作生涯可分为三个阶段：早期的诗作，其中比较优秀的有《利西达斯》；中期以散文和议论文小册子为主，最出名的是《论出版自由》；后期的伟大诗篇包括《失乐园》《复乐园》和《力士参孙》。其代表作《失乐园》与荷马的《伊利亚特》、但丁的《神曲》并称为西方三大诗歌。《失乐园》以《旧约圣经·创世纪》为基础创作。主要描述撒旦引诱亚当和夏娃违反神的禁令，偷尝禁果，最后被逐出伊甸园的故事。弥尔顿以平行和对照的手法安排情节，突出善与恶的矛盾，在光明与黑暗、秩序与混沌、爱与恨、谦卑与骄傲，以及理智与情感之间的冲突中强化主题。《失乐园》的伟大还体现在其纵横驰骋的想象力、包罗万象的渊博学识，以及雄浑有力的庄严史诗风格。《力士参孙》讲述了参孙在遭妻子黛利拉出卖和被菲利斯人弄瞎双眼后，与敌人同归于尽的故事。晚年的弥尔顿同样双目失明，他的国民饱受奴役。通过这个旧约故事，弥尔顿力图激励遭受挫败的英国清教徒不怕牺牲，去争取胜利。古典式的严谨风格在这部作品中得到了突出表现，诗歌语言跌宕起伏、铿锵有力，极富表现力。

三、选读作品赏析

（一）An Excerpt from Book I of Paradise Lost

Satan and his troops have been defeated in the war in Heaven, and now Satan awakes to find himself chained to the burning floor of Hell. His desperate situation is even more intense than that which precipitated his rebellion in heaven. Breaking the awful silence, Satan speaks to his second-in-command, Beelzebub, acknowledging the shame of succumbing to the heavenly forces. Although being cast down into Hell, Satan does not repent of his rebellion against God, suggesting instead that they might gather their forces for another attack. beelzebub is doubtful. he now believes that god cannot be overpowered. Satan does not contradict Beelzebub's assessment, but he does suggest the possibility of perverting Gods good works to evil purposes. The two devils rise up and fly to the dry land next to the flaming lake. Once out of the lake, Satan becomes more optimistic. He calls to his fallen angels who followed him in defying God and have so become devils. The fallen angels obey Satan immediately, joining him on land despite their wounds and suffering. Satan is choked with emotion, for so many have fallen in following his cause and yet still look to him for leadership. After some debate, the now fallen angels resolve to continue their revenge against God by turning against Man. Satan himself makes the hazardous journey out of Hell.

In the first part of Paradise Lost, Satan seems to be the hero of the poem. This is partly because the poem focuses entirely on him and partly because the first part establishes his struggle and casts it in a sometimes sympathetic light. Satan finds himself defeated and banished from Heaven, and sets about establishing a new course for himself and those he leads. Learning about Satan struggle makes us see Satan as the protagonist, for typically the hero or protagonist of any narrative is the character who strugglesto accomplish something.

The classical epic hero is someone for whom the supreme virtue is courage in battle the desire to gain a kingdom or empire, or the quest for honor or immortality. The earliest epic hero known to world literature is Gilgamesh; this hero of ancient Sumeria and Babylonia fought, but failed, to gain immortality from the gods. Later epic heroes such as Achilles and Odysseus fought for military honor, riches, and even the simple privilege of returning home. One thing these heroes have in common is their struggle with and against the gods. With this in mind, it is easy to see how Satan fits the pattern of classical epic hero. Satans themes in his opening speech are the glory of the failed attempt to overthrow God, his determination "never to submit or yield", and his declaration that it is Better to reign in Hell, than serve in Heaven.

Milton introduces the main subject matter of the poem in Book I: the fall of the humankind and the loss of the Garden of Eden. Miltons use of enjambment helps the poem flow from one line to the next. The metaphors and images that he uses are related to his contemporary history or religious background. Milton also reveals the central theme of the work in Book I: to justify the ways of God to man. "Justify" here means to explain and defend and ultimately to vindicate, Gods course of action in dealing with Adam and Eve after they succumbed to the temptation of Satan and ate the forbidden Fruit.

(二) "When I Consider How My Light Is Spent"

This poem starts with the speaker, Milton, reflecting upon his blindness and how God expects him to make full use of his ability as a writer, if he cannot even see the paper on which he writes. The talent of the "poet is useless now that he is losing his sight", even though he wishes to serve God with his writing now more than ever. After stating this problem, he wonders if God wants him to do smaller tasks since he can no longer see light or use his talent. Miltons own patience answers his question as foolish that god does not need man to do work for him and those obedient to him bear his mild yoke. Patience continues to tell Milton that God is being continuously served by thousands of people and the natural world. Most importantly Milton understands that waiting can be its own kind of service. When expressing this, Milton expresses it in a tone of depression and frustration.

This poem is a sort of argument going on in Miltons mind. Milton places huge emphasis on his relationship with God. He thinks that God will punish him for his blindness. The word "light" refers to his blindness and also his inner light. Many references are made to monetary exchange within his thoughts on his blindness and duty to God. Along with the words that have monetary diction, are his Biblical references When "talent" is used, it can refer to the story of a master giving three servants coins to hold for him. The master rewards the two that spent them wisely and cast into darkness the servant that has buried it. If Milton buries his talent to use at a later date, it might become hidden forever, and no good will come of it. Then he will be cast into Gods

darkness. Again Milton makes reference to the bible when he says Who best/ bear his mild yoke, they serve him best. The yoke, ox harness, represents the will of God Patience is capitalized in the eighth line and becomes more clearly personified when answering Miltons question.

This is an Italian sonnet. Its rhyme scheme is abbaabba cdecde. It has an octave that poses a problem, and a sestet that offers an answer. The turn is usually contained in the ninth line, but Milton places it in the middle of the eighth, which helps convey a feeling of impatience. The enjambments also make the poem seem hurried and the last line stand out by contrast; in some sense they help the last line perform what its theme is, to stand still and wait. The iambic pentameter makes the poem balanced There are four main themes in this sonnet. One is limitation. Milton believes that his blindness will ruin his chances for using his talents as he once could have done. Without his sight, it becomes even more difficult to create poetry, or even write it down for others to read. The light in the poem becomes another theme. The reader only needs to notice the importance that he put on light after his sight was gone to see what it meant to him. Not only does it represent the light that is seen with the eyes, but also the spiritual light and the light of life. The day can be a metaphor for life and our lives are limited and once night comes that day is gone forever. Though Miltons life has not expired, his life of poetry has died. Duty and submission are the last two themes. His duty is to make use of the "talents" that have been given to him. At the end, he realizes that God does not need man to do work for Him and that he will be able to serve God in another way other than how he had served him before.

第三章 新古典主义时期的英国文学解读与作品赏析

在斯图亚特王朝统治期间，国王与代表新兴资产阶级利益的议会矛盾日趋激烈，政局动荡。1642 年终于爆发了反对封建君主制度的英国资产阶级革命。1649 年国王查理一世被处死，英国成立了共和国。克伦威尔去世之后，资产阶级革命阵营内部发生分裂。1660 年，查理二世返回伦敦登基，开始了封建王朝的复辟。当詹姆士二世企图恢复天主教时，资产阶级和新贵族联合起来推翻了复辟王朝，迎来威廉三世与玛丽二世共同即位，从而建立了君主立宪体制，确立了议会高于王权的原则。这就是史上有名的"光荣革命"。从此英国进入了一个相对安定的发展时期。18 世纪的英国见证了史无前例的工业技术革命，使得社会的生产、生活方式发生了巨大的变化。随着经济的迅速发展、政治党派的诞生以及科技的进步，英国文学也得以繁荣发展。

一、启蒙主义运动

启蒙主义运动是一场进步的知识分子运动，兴起于法国，后来席卷整个欧洲。启蒙运动的宗旨是用当代哲学与艺术思想的晨光启迪世界。启蒙主义者把教化民众看作改造社会的基本途径；他们赞颂理性、平等与科学。他们认为理性是衡量人类行为与关系的唯一准则。启蒙主义者们反对阶级不公，反对僵化偏见以及其他的封建残余。他们试图把科学的各个分支同人类的实际需要联系在一起，从而使科学为整个人类服务。

二、主要文学特色

在文学领域，启蒙主义运动带来了对古代经典作品的重新关注。这种倾向也被称为新古典主义，其特点如下。

（1）新古典主义文学奉古希腊、罗马的经典作品和当代法国作品为创作之圭臬。

（2）新古典主义作家自觉地追求均衡、统一与和谐表达的优雅，从而形成了雍容、雅致、诙谐、睿智的文风。

（3）这一时期的文学说教意味浓厚，成为流行一时的大众教育的手段。

（4）各种文学体裁均遵循某些固定的条律和规则。

（5）包括当时流行的模拟史诗、传奇、讽刺诗在内的各体诗歌结构工整，遣词雅致，语气庄严，注重说教。小说则不同于传统的贵族传奇文学，以现实的笔触摹写普通人的生活。18世纪中后期，还出现了感伤主义这一文学潮流。一些诗人和小说家厌倦了新古典主义者们的矫揉造作和对理性的绝对推崇，力图在文学作品中寻找更为自然、更富有真情实感的表达方式。

三、主要作家与作品

新古典主义推崇理性，强调明晰、对称、节制、优雅，追求艺术形式的完美与和谐。这一阶段的诗歌，以亚历山大·蒲柏、约翰·德莱顿及其他诗人为代表，力图创作在音韵节律上具有规律性的完美文学作品。18世纪英国的散文开始繁荣，其风格建立在新古典主义美学原则之上。其中包括英国文学史上最伟大的讽刺散文作家乔纳森·斯威夫特，他的文风淳朴平易而有力。在《格列佛游记》中，他通过对众多虚构国度的描写，以理性为尺度，尖锐地批评和抨击了英国社会各领域的黑暗和罪恶。而人文主义文学批评的巨擘塞缪尔·约翰逊的散文风格自成一家，集拉丁散文的典雅气势与英语散文的雄健朴素于一体。《莎士比亚戏剧集序言》和《诗人传》是他对文学批评做出的突出贡献。

18世纪中叶，还兴起一种崭新的文学形式——英国现代小说，这种文学与传统贵族的骑士文学相反，着重描写英国普通百姓的生活。《鲁滨逊漂流记》被认为是现实主义小说的创世之作，为丹尼尔·笛福赢得"英国小说之父"的称号。亨利·菲尔丁的《汤姆·琼斯》则让现实主义小说得到了进一步的发展。此外，资本主义工业化还导致了以大自然和情感为主题的感伤主义作品一度流行。比如，托马斯·格雷的《墓园哀歌》表达了诗人对时代纷乱状态的厌恶和对自然简朴生活的向往；罗伯特·彭斯的抒情诗自然生动，感情真挚，讽刺诗尖锐锋利，妙趣横生；而威廉·布莱克的诗歌意象鲜明、语言清新，极富个性。理查德·布林斯利·谢利丹的风俗喜剧《造谣学校》则表达了他对于上流社会和感伤主义的嘲讽。

第一节　约翰·德莱顿

一、作者简介

德莱顿（1631—1700）出生在一个清教徒家庭。他集诗人、剧作家、文学评论于一身，曾被封为"桂冠诗人"。在那个风起云涌的特殊年代，德莱顿紧随潮流，不断改变自己的政治和宗教信仰。在文学创作中，他遵从古典主义准则，将英雄双韵体作为主要的诗歌形式之一。他还身体力行，开拓出简洁、明朗的英国散文新风。同时，他通过《论戏剧诗》等文学评论作品来阐述自己的文学观点，极大地推动了英国文学批评的发展。

二、主要作品简介

约翰·德莱顿热衷于戏剧创作和文学批评，作品产量颇丰。他以古典主义的原则将莎士比亚的悲剧《安东尼与克莉奥佩拉特》改写成《一切为了爱》。德莱顿把戏剧冲突控制在安东尼对克莱奥帕特拉的爱与对自己的现世考虑之间的内心挣扎上，情节紧凑，诗体优美流畅。除了抒情诗之外，他还创作了大量的长诗，如《押沙龙与亚希多弗》。德莱顿的诗歌大都采用英雄双韵体，即两行一押韵，每行五个音步，每个音步采用抑扬格形式。他最著名的散文作品当属《论戏剧诗》，该文以对话的形式表达了德莱顿对新古典主义戏剧原则的崇尚和对英国戏剧的偏爱。

三、选读作品赏析

An Excerpt from An Essay of Dramatic Poesy

In An Essay of Dramatic Poesy，Dryden takes up the subject set forth by Philip Sidney in his Defence of Poesie（1580）. Dryden attempts to justify drama as a legitimate form of "poetry" comparable to the epic，and he deals in his criticism with issues of form and morality in drama.

Dryden wrote this essay as a dramatic dialogue with four characters representing four critical positions，which deal with five issues. Eugenius（"well born") favors the moderns over the ancients, arguing that the moderns exceed the ancients because of having learned and profited from their example. Crites argues in favor of the ancients they established the unities, which are esteemed and followed by French playwrights and Ben Jonson, according to Crites, followed the ancients' example by adhering to the unities. Lisideius argues that French drama is superior to English drama; for the French writers closely adhered to the classical separation of comedy and tragedy. Neander thought to be represented by Dryden favors the moderns, but does not disparage the ancients. He also favors English drama, and takes a critical eye on French drama.

Neander thinks that tragicomedy increases the effectiveness of both tragic and comic elements by way of contrast. Neander criticizes French drama essentially for its smallness its pursuit of only one plot without subplots; its tendency to show too little action; its servile observations of the unities… dearth of plot, and narrowness of magination are all qualities which render it inferior to English drama. Neander extends his criticism of French drama into his reasoning for his preference for Shakespeare over Ben Jonson. Shakespeare "had the largest and most comprehensive soul", while Jonson was "the most learned and judicious writer which any theater ever had". Ultimately Neander prefers Shakespeare for his greater scope, his greater faithfulness to life, as compared to Jonson's relatively small scope and French/ Classical tendency to deal in the beauties of a statue but not of a man.

Crites objects to rhyme in plays and says Rhyme is incapable of expressing the greatest thought naturally. Even though blank verse lines are no more spontaneous than are rhymed lines, they are still to be preferred because they are" nearest nature Neander responds to the objections against rhyme by admitting that "verse so tedious" is inappropriate to drama. "Natural" rhymed verse is, however, just as appropriate to dramatic as to non-dramatic poetry the test of the naturalness of rhyme is how well chosen the rhymes are.

Dryden was obviously making a compromise between the rules of Neoclassicism in drama and the practice of the great English dramatists of the late 16th and early 17th centuries. However, the main point of the essay seems to be a valuation of becoming (the striving, nature imitating, large scope of tragicomedy and Shakespeare) over being (the static perfection of the ideal imitating Classical/French/Jonsonian drama).

His "Shakespeare vs. Jonson" comparison contrasts the formers appeal to nature as a model for his characters with the latters use of classical models. Famous is Dryden's praise of Shakespeare for having the largest and most comprehensive soul. William Shakespeare to sympathize with and represent anything in nature, but it is a nature he found when he "looked inwards". This reminds us of Sidney's Sonnet I in Astrophil and Stella, and the notion that human nature is grounded in some unmovable knowledge which it is sin or folly to deny, to ignore, or to seek to improve.

Shakespeare's comedy is faulted for its "clenches" (puns), but he is generally praised as the best of his generation in their one judgment. Jonson is praised as one who was best when a satirist, and whose classical knowledge was wholly digested in his art rather than merely decorating it He has done his robberies so openly, that one may see he fears not to be taxed by any law but he invades authors like a monarch; and what would be theft in other poets is only victory in him. This passage commonly is used when distinguishing poetic adaptation of the tradition from mere plagiarism. Also, Dryden faults Jonson's attempt to romanize our tongue "with Latin loan words In conclusion, Dryden says" If I would compare him (Jonson) with Shakespeare, I must acknowledge him the more correct poet, but Shakespeare the greater wit.

Shakespeare was the Homer, or father of our dramatic poets; Jonson was the virgil, the pattern of elaborate writing; I admire him, but I love Shakespeare.

第二节　约翰·班扬

一、作者简介

班扬（1628—1688）是个虔诚的基督徒，一个坚定的不信奉国教者。他主张按照圣经的律条而不是按照教会牧师的解释来生活，而每个人都有权按照自己的方式来理解《圣经》。他认为人只有通过自己的精神奋斗才能获得最终的救赎。在政治上，班扬对腐败、虚伪、靠强取豪夺致富的富人阶级怀有深刻的仇恨，其作品表达了英国资产阶级革命前后底层人民的呼声。

二、主要作品简介

班扬的主要作品有《天路历程》《上帝赐予最大罪人的无限恩惠》和《圣战》（The Holy War）。其中《天路历程》采用寓言的形式讲述基督的精神历程，给读者呈现了一幅 17 世纪现实主义的图景。班扬的作品语言通俗简洁，内容朴实，细节生动，因而作品受到了广大民众的欢迎。

三、选读作品赏析

"The Vanity Fair"：*"An Excerpt from The Pilgrim's Progress"*

The Pilgrim's Progress tells of the experience of a devout Christian in a world full of vice and wickedness. Through the allegorical journey made by the christian pilgrims from the doomed worldly parts of the country to the Celestial city, Bunyan condemns the vices of sloth, hypocrisy, arrogance, indulgence in pleasure-seeking, falsehood, and so on but eulogizes such virtues as perseverance, firmness in belief, unyielding will and unfading courage.

In this episode, the two pilgrims, Christian and Faithful, had walked out of the wilderness and arrived at a town where a fair called vanity Fair was kept. At the fair, the sellers displayed items like houses, trades, titles, countries, as well as delights like whores, blood, bodies, pearls, gold, and so on. The history of the fair could be traced back to 5000 years ago, when three devils, Beelzebub, Apollyon, and Legion were traveling through this place, they decided to set up a marketplace for luxuries to tempt Jesus Christ and other pilgrims. As Christian and Faithful passed through, everybody stared at them because of their clothes and their speech. They were offered to buy something of the "vanities" on sale, but they showed no interest in the wares and claimed they would only "buy the truth". The pilgrims' behavior irritated the sellers and sparked chaos in the marketplace. They were taken to the judges, who judged them to be madman and sentenced them to be beaten and put into a cage as a spectacle for the men of the fair. They patiently sustained all these and then caused disputes among the people of the fair themselves.

The Vanity Fair is a well-known section of The Pilgrim's Progress. Here the writers condemnation of the vices of his society is most strongly expressed. The Vanity Fair contains all manners of material goods to tempt men. It is a canal feast masterminded by Beelzebub. This allegorically refers to the real world where people have become so degenerated that all they are concerned about is to buy and sell everything they can. What they care about is the "possession of goods and money", that is, the material wealth. They have lost the sense of honor, uprightness and conscience. In a word, they are spiritually lost. In this part, Faithful and Christian are pious enough to shun the worldly goods in favor of more permanent riches from heaven. This is an indication of the need for people to reform their lives for a spiritual rebirth or salvation However, their selfless determination to avoid the trappings of sin only causes the people of Vanity Fair to resent and mistrust them, and they suffered greatly at the hands of these people. Through this, Bunyan implies the prevalent political and religious persecution of his day, the hard lot of the simple, honest people, their spiritual sufferings at a time of great changes, and their aspiration for a better life.

第三节　乔纳森·斯威夫特

一、作者简介

斯威夫特（1667—1745）在政治上既不保守也不激进，更不热衷党派政治。他认为人性中有严重的缺陷，因此有必要对人性和人类制度加以改造和革新。斯威夫特思想开明，终生为真理、正义、平等和自由而斗争，他抨击一切形式的虚伪、罪恶、战争、欺诈、腐败、对宗教信仰的滥用以及剥削和压迫，同情广大劳动人民，经常利用他自身的影响来帮助别人。

二、主要作品简介

乔纳森·斯威夫特的主要作品包括《一个木桶的故事》《书战》《一个温和

的建议》和《格列佛游记》。斯威夫特的语言简单明了、充满活力。在不动声色的平静下面常常潜伏着辛辣的讽刺。《格列佛游记》以第一人称的叙述方式讲述了格列佛在旅行当中的种种奇遇。

该作品对于作者所处时代的恶习进行了无情的讽刺，表现了斯威夫特对英国的政治、经济、宗教等方面所表现出来的种种丑陋现象深恶痛绝，以及他对底层民众的深切同情。

三、选读作品赏析

An Excerpt from Chapter 3, Part I of Gulliver's Travels

The first part of the book is about Gulliver's adventure in Lilliput. He hopes to be set free, as he is getting along well with the lilliputians and earning their trust. The emperor decides to entertain him with shows, including a performance by Rope-Dancers, who are Lilliputians seeking employment in the government. For the performance, which doubles as a sort of competitive entrance examination, the candidates dance on ropes slender threads suspended two feet above the ground. When a vacancy occurs candidates petition the emperor to entertain him with a dance, and whoever jumps the highest earns the office. The current ministers continue this practice as well, in order to show that they have not lost their skill. As another diversion for Gulliver, the emperor lays three silken threads of different colors on a table. He then holds out a stick, and candidates are asked to leap over it or creep under it. Whoever shows the most dexterity wins one of the ribbons. Then Gulliver builds a platform from sticks and his handkerchief and invites horsemen to exercise upon it. The emperor greatly enjoys watching this new entertainment, but it is cut short when a horse steps through the handkerchief, after which Gulliver decides that it is too dangerous for them to keep riding on the cloth. Some Lilliputians discover Gullivers hat, which washed ashore after him, and he asks them to bring it back. Soon after, the emperor asks Gulliver to pose. like a colossus, or giant statue, so that his troops might march under Gulliver. Gullivers petitions for freedom are finally answered. Gulliver must swear to obey the articles put forth, which include stipulations that he must assist the Lilliputians in times of war, survey the land around them, help with construction, and deliver urgent messages. Gulliver agrees and his chains are removed.

Gradually, Gulliver gets to know more about Lilliputian culture, and the great difference in size between him and the lilliputians is emphasized by a number of examples, many of which are explicit satires of British government. The travel in Lilliput is a mini-picture of modern English society. For instance, Lilliputian government officials are chosen by their skill at rope-dancing, which the Lilliputians see as relevant but which Gulliver recognizes as arbitrary and ridiculous The would-be officials are almost literally forced to jump through hoops in order to qualify for their positions. Clearly, Swift intends for us to understand this episode as a satire of England's system of political appointments and to infer that England's system is similarly arbitrary. Swift mocks the selection system of English government. The articles that Gulliver is forced to sign in order to gain his freedom are couched in formal, self-important language. But the document is nothing but a meaningless and self-contradictory piece of paper: each article emphasizes the fact that Gulliver is so powerful that, if he so desires, he could violate all of the articles without much concern over his safety.

第四节　亚历山大·蒲柏

一、作者简介

蒲柏（1688—1744）在政治上是一个保守者。他钦慕贵族阶级的传统价值观，宣称"一切存在都是合理的"。在文学创作和批评上他坚持新古典主义原则，宣称文学作为才智的表现和大众教育的媒介不应降低其标准，强调应以新古典主义的秩序、理性、逻辑、有节制的情感、品位和得体等标准来评判文学作品。作为新古典主义的代表，蒲柏对于"英雄双韵体"诗歌的创作技巧达到了炉火纯青的地步。另外，他擅长使用讽刺和警句，但作品缺乏想象和情感抒发。

二、主要作品简介

亚历山大·蒲柏的主要作品有：《卷发遇劫记》《群愚史诗》《人论》和《论批评》。其中英国史上最优秀的仿英雄体讽刺诗《卷发遇劫记》确立了蒲柏在英国诗歌语言和讽刺文学方面的大师地位。该诗根据一个真实的故事创作而成。蒲柏采用荷马史诗的宏大叙事模式来讲述为一缕秀发而引发的两个世交家族之争，辛辣地讽刺了 18 世纪英国贵族阶级愚蠢、无聊的生活。《论批评》是以英雄对偶句体写成的教诲诗。该诗追溯了从亚里士多德到布瓦洛的文学批评史；详尽列举了文学批评中存在的种种问题，赞扬了古典主义的创作原则，从而对 18 世纪的英国文学批评产生了巨大影响。

三、选读作品赏析

" Ode on solitude"

This poem sets a very peaceful mood. The relaxed language that Pope chooses to use makes the calm, routine lifestyle of a farmer seem more appealing than usual. He focuses on the idea of using only one's own means to survive while living completely alone but he does not make it seem boring or melancholy. The various techniques that he uses, such as uniform stanzas, a predictable rhyme scheme, and simple language makes it seem as if the speaker is not some poet that is trying to take on a foreign voice describes the farmer in the same language that he would most likely use . The first stanza starts off with the word "happy" . While Pope could have used a more complicated word, the simplicity and commonness of his choice immediately sets the mood for the reader. This stanza describes how the man in the poem is only concerned with what happens within his inherited land. It doesn't mention anything about the man wishing to break free of this lifestyle, but states that he is content to breathe in his own ground.

In the second stanza, Pope once again uses uniform language to emphasize the regularity of this farmers life. He lists where the farmer gets his resources to live in simple language with very little hidden implications. The mention of how the trees are useful both in winter and in summer reassures the reader that this farmer, though alone is provided for by nature.

The third stanza seems to express Pope's wish to experience this kind of solitude because he refers to this man as "Blest" . Pope's eventful lifestyle, constantly ridden with conflict, seems to be a complete opposite of this simple man. In the city, it is early impossible to find this kind of peace, and then to enjoy it without being reminded of what lays outside of that safe zone. He also mentions that this man is in health of body, something that Pope will never be able to achieve because he was burdened with health problems since early childhood.

The third and fourth stanzas seem to mesh together with the line Quiet by day because it can be recited as part of either. While it rhymes with the stanza that it stands in, it could also be fluidly integrated into the next stanza because of its juxtaposition with the phrase "sound sleep by night". This meshing of stanzas reflects, once again, the uniformity of this type of lifestyle. Each day is so similar to the next, that the man may not be able to distinguish where one week ends and another begins simply because of how repetitive his life is.

The last stanza expresses the farmers acceptance of his life. He understands that he is unknown and does not attempt to fight it. He also understands that like all of the seasons he experiences, he will die as well. In most poetry, the idea of an unlamented death seems very depressing, yet to this farmer, it is a perfect ending to a quiet life.

This stanza also implies that this farmer has no living family. It seems as though this man is so used to being alone that he makes no effort to change that because it has worked for him for so long. This solitude could also be an allusion to Pope's own love life because he never got married during his life.

Pope used very simple language, structure and ideas in this poem to communicate the thoughts of a solitary, but not lonely, farmer. He also subtly expresses his own desire to experience some of life the way that this man does. Additionally, heintentionally leaves out certain statements that would make this description of a farmer's life complete, such as mention of other family, to demonstrate the degree of interesting secrecy that draws Pope to thinking about this kind of lifestyle. He effectively implements a variety of simple elements to successfully communicate the meaning of "Ode on Solitude".

An Essay on Criticrːsm is an attempt to mediate between a wide range of traditional and contemporary critical thoughts and arrive at an acceptable synthesis of the two. The poem is the nearest thing in eighteenth-century English writing to what might be called a neo-classical manifesto. It comes very close, perhaps, to being a guide to the critic's orthe poet's art. It is accordingly of great value to us today in understanding what Pope and many of his contemporaries saw as the main functions of criticism in eighteenth-century England.

The poem is built upon a series of maxims, such as "To err is humane; to forgive, divine", or "For fools rush in where angels fear to tread". Pope's ability to sum up an idea tersely and memorably in a phrase, line, or couplet, of imaginative clarity is a hallmark of An Essay on Criticism. The polished couplets encapsulate points that reverberate in the manner of conversational repartee.

One of Pope's most distinctive achievements in An Essay on Criticism is his ability to make his ideas striking and memorable through the graphic quality of his imagery. The allusive range of Pope's creative imagination is apparently boundless as he shifts the are as of reference from natural history to entomology, from science to theology, and from politics to military and territorial campaigns. His fertile imagination draws on image upon image to establish and expand his ideas and secure his argument.

The poem falls into three parts. Part Ⅰ deals with true taste and judgment in a critic; Part Ⅱ with some of the causes of false taste and judgment; and Part Ⅲ with the true conduct of manners in a critic, concluding with a brief survey of the history of criticism. Pope moves across the stated demarcations, just as he moves backwards and forwards over ancient and modem criticism, offering a polished, conversational view of his conception of the critic's function and duty.

Pope holds that critics need to be good judges, but the true taste necessary for good judgment is as rare as the true genius necessary for good poetry. Most men, says Pope are born with the seeds of good judgment, and yet good sense is all too frequently spoilt by false education. Most critics strive to be wits, but succeed only in becoming pale copies. True critics, on the other hand, know, and operate within, their own reach They work within the limits fixed by nature rather than launching themselves beyond their own depth.

The first great rule for true critics, therefore, is to "follow nature". Pope's appeal to nature is complex it is an appeal both to nature as empirical reality and to nature as the artist, s perception of an ideal order and harmony revealed in God's creation. It is an appeal to the actual and to the ideal, and to the fusion and intercourse between the two Unerring nature is presented as a fixed point in a turning world, a "clear, unchanged and universal light". It is at once "the source, and end, and test of art" and is crucial to the spirit and vigor of a work of art, like " the informing soul" in " some fair body".

The rules of the ancients are useful guidelines for the true critic for they are "nature methodized". Pope charges that more recent critics, however, have made a fetish of the rules, without understanding their source, and applied them mechanically. True critics should therefore study the ancients, especially Homer, Virgil and Aristotle, but always be prepared to allow for exceptions, for there's a happiness as well as care. There are some beauties, which no rules teach, and true geniuses will always be prepared "to snatch a grace beyond the reach of art". Prudent critics will take account of this, but the ancients remain immortal heirs of universal praise.

Part Ⅱ shifts direction to discuss the causes hindering good criticism and immediately focuses on the most powerful of the deadly sins, pride, as the greatest cause conspiring to misguide the mind. Next comes imperfect learning, "a little learning is a dangerous thing", followed by failure to survey the whole. Such failure leads to the formation of judgments based on some small fault in the parts rather than on the overall effect.

Part Ⅱ deals with the conduct of manners necessary for a true critic and begins by urging such a person to "let truth and candor shine". Pope encourages diffidence and modesty; good breeding and tact; sincerity and freedom of advice.

Pope's poem remained popular throughout the eighteenth century, receiving the highest accolade from Dr. Johnson, who said that if Pope had written nothing else, An Essay on Criticism would have placed him among the first critics and the first poets, as it exhibits every mode of excellence that can embellish or dignify didactic composition selection of matter, novelty of arrangement, justness of precept, splendor of illustration and propriety of digression.

第五节 丹尼尔·笛福

一、作者简介

笛福（1660—1731）是个反封建、反传奇文学的现实主义作家。他的思想开明，观念前卫，崇尚清教伦理观，信奉勤奋、自立、坚韧。他的作品反映了他对所处时代的关注，即人为了生存和发展与大自然和社会环境的斗争。此外，他在生意场上的盛衰和宦海沉浮使他洞悉世情，心胸开阔，对所有的人，包括为法纪所不容的人，都怀着包容之心，并以增进大众福祉为己任。笛福的写作风格简朴、通俗却不粗俗，语言清晰、直白，毫无矫揉造作之气。四十多年的新闻写作经验使得他的作品素材丰富、细节逼真、想象丰富，并具有极强的趣味性。

二、主要作品简介

笛福最引人入胜的作品包括《鲁滨逊漂流记》《大疫年日记》和《摩尔·弗兰德斯》。

《鲁滨逊漂流记》取材于一个真实事件。通过对鲁滨逊独自一人在荒岛上同无情的大自然成功斗争的客观描述，主人公性格中最为优秀的品质得到了完整的体现：他在工作方面不可思议的能力，他在克服艰难险阻方面不屈不挠的毅力，他同大自然展开了艰苦的斗争且从未低头。作品旨在歌颂 18 世纪西方物质文明的胜利及人类征服自然环境的理性力量。

三、选读作品赏析

An Excerpt from Chapter 4 of Robinson Crusoe

Robinson Crusoe is an adventure novel presented as an autobiography by the fictional character Robinson Crusoe. The story is about a man who is stranded on a desert island for 28 years. With the supplies he's able to salvage from the wrecked ship. Robinson Crusoe eventually builds a fort and then creates for himself a kingdom by taming animals, gathering fruit, growing crops, and hunting. The book contains adventures of all sorts: pirates, shipwrecks, cannibals, mutiny, and so on. Robinson rescues Friday from the cannibals, who turns out to be a loyal companion of Robinson.

Robinson Crusoe，s story is also Biblical in many of its themes and discussions. It's the story of the prodigal son, who runs away from home only to find calamity. Throughout the ordeal, he eventually makes peace, and goes on with his solitary existence. In the end, Robinson makes his escape when a ship of mutineers sails to the island. He and his companions help the British captain to take back control of his ship. He sets sail for England on December 19 after spending 28 years, 2 months, and 19 days on the island. He arrives back in England, after being gone for 35 years, and finds that he is a wealthy man.

Chapter 4 is about the day after the shipwreck. Awakening the next morning refreshed, Crusoe goes down to the shore to explore the remains of the ship. Swimming around it, he finds it impossible to climb aboard until he finds a chain hanging, by which he pulls himself up. Crusoe conceives the idea of building a raft out of broken lumber on which he loads provisions of bread, rice, goat meat, cheese, and other foods. He also finds clothes, arms, and fresh water. He sails his cargo-laden raft into a small cove where he unloads it. He notices that the land has wildfowl but no other humans, how to survive on the island has become crusoe s main concern In Robinson Crusoe, Defoe celebrates the eighteenth-century Western civilizations material triumph and the strength of human rational will to conquer the natural environment. In describing Robinson's life on the island, Defoe glorifies the bourgeo is nan, since the protagonist is just one of them who have marvelous capacity for work boundless energy and persistence in overcoming obstacles. The character of Robinson Crusoe is representative of the English bourgeois middle class at the earlier stage of its development.

Defoe uses the simple, direct, fact-based style of the middle class. His language is smooth, easy, colloquial and mostly vernacular. His sentences are sometimes short crisp and plain, and sometimes long and rambling, which leave on the reader an impression of casual narration. What's more, he presents facts in order, and the meaning is clear. He had a gift for organizing mi-

nute details in such a vivid way that his stories could be both credible and fasci-
nating. The preface of the book even pretends that the account of Crusoe's adventures is nonfiction, saying, "The Editor believes the thing to be a just History of Fact; neither is there any appearance of Fiction in it."

第六节　亨利·菲尔丁

一、作者简介

菲尔丁（1707—1754）热衷于社会改良，对劳动人民的同情，英国社会的
种种丑恶行径——政治的肮脏腐败、法律的不公平、上流社会的腐化堕落和宗
教迷信都激起了他对反动统治阶级的愤慨。

菲尔丁是英国现实主义小说的奠基人。他的小说建立在对于真实生活的精
确观察和描述的基础之上。他抛开主观叙事法，采用"第三人称叙事"来发展
情节，突显人性。拜伦曾经精辟地称菲尔丁是"刻画人性的写散文的荷马"。
同时，菲尔丁持有启蒙家的观点，认为小说的目的不仅是娱乐，而且是教育。
他创作的目标是真实地展示社会生活，寓教于乐。他运用语言的能力令人叹
服，语句富有逻辑性和节奏感。小说总是精心构架，结构平衡。

二、主要作品简介

菲尔丁的主要作品包括《约瑟夫·安德鲁斯传》《大伟人江奈生·魏尔德
传》《汤姆·琼斯》和《爱米莉亚》。《汤姆·琼斯》是菲尔丁最为杰出的作品。
小说以调皮轻率却又本性纯良的汤姆·琼斯为主人公，描述了他在流浪生活中
的冒险与灾难故事。故事在乡村、路途及伦敦三个不同的背景下展开，全面呈
现了18世纪英国社会风貌的全景，中间夹杂着对人性的深刻理解，对社会罪
恶的无情鞭笞。小说人物形象丰满、语言诙谐精练、结构独特。

三、选读作品赏析

An Excerpt from Chapter 2, Book Ill of Tom Jones

Tom Jones is a novel that centers on a likable hero who romps through a
series of adventures while growing up and pursuing the girl he idolizes. The

novel is divided into three sections of six books each, which reflect Toms journey: those taking place at home in the country, those on the road, and those in London. The third part concludes with Tom coming home to the country. These three sections also roughly correspond to the three movements of the romance. In the first six books, Tom and Sophia fall in love; in the second six they are separated; and in the third six they meet again and Sophia is slowly reconciled to Tom. The culmination of both the journey and the romance is the couple's marriage and return to the country.

In Chapter 2, Tom is introduced with an unfortunate anecdote. Young Tom is naughty and wild. He has been caught robbing the orchard and stealing the duck and picking Master Blifil's pocket of a ball. Another instance of Tom s vice comes when hunting with Black George, he and the gamekeeper trespass beyond the all worthy estate and are caught poaching from their neighbor, Squire Western. As punishment, Tom is beaten severely by his tutor. Toms vices appear all the worse contrasted to Blifil's virtues. Blifil was a lad of a remarkable disposition; sober, discreet and pious, beyond his age, qualities which gained him the love of everyone who knew him, whilst Tom Jones was universally disliked, But in fact Tom robbed the orchard and stole the duck from a generous motive: to help his friend the impoverished gamekeeper, Black George. That Tom covers up for Black George in the poaching incident is also to protect George, because George would lose his job if discovered.

The kinds of obvious, public vices Tom has the very ones that society often judges most harshly are really less serious than the hidden vices of vanity, hypocrisy selfishness, and greed that lie at the core of Blifil's character Prudence, one of the cardinal virtues of Western culture, essentially means thinking ahead, considering the likely consequences of one's actions, and acting accordingly. The failure to do this is Toms downfall over and over, until the very end of the story Although Tom has many virtues -he is kind, good-hearted, generous, brave, loyal, and forgiving- his lack of prudence gives his adversaries opportunities to harm him, Throughout the novel, Squire All worthy, usually with great patience and kindness admonishes Tom that he must be more prudent and wise in his actions. It takes years and many misadventures for Tom to learn the lesson, but he does learn it Tom Jones is one of the most elaborately plotted, highly structured novels ever written. Fielding tries very hard to reveal the social evils: cruelty, moral degeneracy deceit, and hypocrisy The style of Tom Jones is one of its greatest pleasures. Witty and ironic, Fielding is the master of the epigram- the brief, clever, pointed remark. He calls Tom Jones "a comic epic poem in prose". To achieve that comic epic effect he often employs the mock-heroic style, which uses the grandiose similes found in epics not to make characters seem heroic but to make fun of them.

第七节　塞缪尔·约翰逊

一、作者简介

约翰逊（1709—1784）是一个爱国主义者，他主张维持现状，反对变革政治制度。他曾撰文攻击那些以爱国之名行损害国家利益之实的政客。在文学上，约翰逊是一个古典主义者。他的文学评论散文大多依照古典主义的准则写成。他坚决主张作家应反映普遍的真理和经验，即自然；作家写作不仅应使人愉悦，还应使人获得教益；作家不得冒犯宗教或宣扬不道德的东西；作家应用传统的规范和原则指导创作。

二、主要作品简介

1747 年约翰逊致信内阁大臣切斯特菲尔德，提到了他的"英语辞典计划"，并且为这项工程辛苦工作了 8 年。除《英语辞典》外，约翰逊的主要作品还有《诗人传》和哲学小说《阿比西尼亚王子拉塞勒斯传》等。《诗人传》是一本传记体的论文集，讨论了 52 个诗人的生平和作品。每篇论文首先叙述每位诗人的生平事迹，描述他的个性，然后对他的作品进行评价。有关密尔顿、德莱顿和蒲柏的论文写得最好，但有关小诗人的较短一些的论文也写得很有力度，妙趣横生。该书不仅是约翰逊的杰作，也是最优秀的古典主义里程碑式的作品，虽然在选择诗人和对他们的作品的评价方面尚存明显的缺陷。

三、选读作品赏析

To the Right Honorable the Earl of Chesterfield

In 1747, at the suggestion of Robert Dodley, a book-seller, Johnson decided to compile a dictionary of the English language. The plan of the dictionary was written and addressed to the Earl of Chesterfield, a distinguished "patron of literature". During the seven long years of hard labor on the dictionary, Lord Chesterfield had offered neither aid nor encouragement to the poor lexicographer. But on the eve of publication of the dictionary, the nobleman wrote two papers for The World, a famous periodical, highly recommending the dictionary to the public and expecting that Johnson would dedicate the work to him, as was the common practice at the time. Johnson, enraged and disgusted by the false, hollow, honeyed words, wrote this letter to the fame-fishing Chesterfield In this letter to the lord, Johnson declared that he did not feel obliged to anyone and that he was not "accustomed to favors from the great". He reminded the Lord how he was treated with total indifference and contempt years ago when he visited him in hope of getting some help for his work, and how, over the past seven years, he had toiled and suffered working on his dictionary without any help from any patron.

As he had relied solely on himself in this gigantic task, he did not want the public to think that he had received help from a patron. He condemned the fame-fishing act of Chesterfield by hinting that the lord was such a man who looks with unconcern on a man struggling for life in the water, and when he has reached ground, encumbers him with help.

Although the letter is written in a refined and polite language, it carries a bitter undertone of defiance and anger. With seemingly peaceful retrospection, reasoning and questioning, the letter actually expresses the authors strong indignation at the lord's fame-fishing to the best satiric effect. It also expresses his firm resolution not to be reconciled to the hypocritical lord. It expresses explicitly the authors assertion of his independence, signifying the opening of a new era in the development of literature hnson's style is typically neo-classical. His language is characteristically general often Latinate and frequently polysyllabic. His sentences are long and well structured interwoven with parallel words and phrases. No matter how complex his sentences are the thought is always clearly expressed; and though he tends to use learned words they are always accurately used.

第八节　托马斯·格雷

一、作者简介

格雷（1716—1771）是一位腼腆寡言的学者，生活中规中矩，从不公开表明自己的政治、艺术观点，但其作品显示了他对地位卑下的人们真诚的同情，对权贵们的强烈蔑视。他颇有些感伤，但能用古典艺术的克制、从容观念加以约束。他敏于感受大自然的美丽，但并不像浪漫派诗人那样认为自然美与人性密不可分，他以生命短促、死神的力量不可战胜、人类的生存与奋斗毫无价值、人类的虚荣无意义等作为探讨的题材。他也为人类的不幸命运哀叹，思考有关人类生活的哲学问题。

二、主要作品简介

格雷一生作诗不多，仅十余首传世，其中以《墓园挽歌》最为著名。此诗创作长达8年之久，堪称感伤诗派的代表作。此外，还有《春天颂》《伊顿学院远景颂》等。格雷的诗总是带着一种绝望的悲愁情绪，具有一种其他人难以达到的古典美。诗歌情感深沉、节奏适度，用词讲究，语序多倒装，且格式独特，思想复杂，富有暗示性。《墓园挽歌》是格雷最著名的诗。诗人在一个乡镇的教堂墓地对四周贫穷之人的坟冢进行苦思冥想。通过想象叙述了他们在世时贫穷俭朴生活中的欢乐，由此展开对死亡、生命的悲哀、人生的神秘的思索，思索中带着一点淡淡的个人痛苦。诗歌洋溢着诗人对于英国乡村的浓厚兴趣以及对普通劳动人民的真挚同情，加上对暮色中大自然的描写和诗歌本身感伤的情调，使这首诗充满了浪漫主义色彩，同时又不失古典主义的精确与优雅。

三、选读作品赏析

An Excerpt from "Elegy Written in a Country Churchyard"

Its title describes its function: lamenting someone's death, and affirming the life thatpreceded it so that we can be comforted. One may die after decades of anonymouslabor, uneducated, unknown or scarcely remembered, one's potential unrealized, Gray's poem says, but that life will have as many joys, and far fewer ill effects on others, than lives of the rich, the powerful, the famous. Also, the great memorials that money can buy do no more for the deceased than a common grave marker. In the end what counts is friendship, being mourned, being cried for by someone who was close Its solemn cadence, its majesty of diction, and its vivid though melancholy pastoral imagery have garnered it many admirers. But such does not obscure the fact that the sociopolitical message is mixed, and not altogether benign. While on the one hand the poet tries to celebrate the simple lifestyle that these rural people lived, even at the expense of reputation or wealth, on the other hand he also claims that they have been spared from the excesses of power and corruption. The poem rests, then, on the traditional Tory justification of the plight of the poor; they may have been deprived, but it is, after all, for the best, since their poverty kept them out of trouble.

The poem's theme that the lives of the rich and poor alike lead but to the grave would have been familiar to contemporary readers. However, Gray's treatment, which had the effect of suggesting that it was not only the "rude forefathers of the village" he was mourning but the death of all men and of the poet himself, gave the poem its universal appeal.

The speaker considers the fact that in death, there is no difference between great and common people. He goes on to wonder if among the lowly people buried in the churchyard there had been any natural poets or politicians whose talent had simply never been discovered or nurtured. This thought leads him to praise the dead for the honest simple lives that they lived.

In this poem, Gray creates a process by which laborers come to symbolize the perfection of the pastoral through their daily toils. These people come to represent the ideal form of pastoral life. In this poem, however, Gray consigns these people and their lifestyle to darkness and death in order to save them from a world whose changing ideals support their idyllic lifestyle.

These peasants were very important to the economic cycle of every day, as all peasants are. They may not have contributed very largely as the nobles had, but their contributions, as moderate as they were, had a positive effect on the rest of society. For this reason gray says that the lower class should not be looked down upon or even mistreated by the upper class. The peasants work just as hard and probably harder than the nobles to earn a living. The peasants' difficulty is that they were never given a chance financially and had no possible means to make their way into the upper class. Gray spoke of how death is the greatest equalizer of all. No man can escape death, be he rich or poor. Everyone is equal as humans, upon death.

Gray wrote the poem in four-line stanzas. Each line is in iambic pentameter. In each stanza, the first line rhymes with the third and the second line rhymes with the fourth as abab. For poetic effect, Gray frequently uses inversion (reversal of the normal word order).

第九节　罗伯特·彭斯

一、作者简介

彭斯（1759—1796）生于苏格兰民族面临被异族征服的时代，因此，他的诗歌充满了激进的民主、自由的思想。彭斯也曾公开支持法国大革命，这在他的作品中也有所体现。彭斯是苏格兰的国家诗人，他的诗歌是彻头彻尾的苏格兰乡村主题。他的巨大成功很大程度上也归功于他的农民出身，以及他对苏格兰古老歌谣的熟知和适当把握。通过诗歌能看到彭斯对自己身心最恰当的、最真实的，也最完整的诠释。

二、主要作品简介

罗伯特·彭斯的诗歌作品多使用苏格兰方言，并多为抒情短诗，如歌颂爱情的名篇《一朵红红的玫瑰》和离别歌谣《往昔时光》等。他还创作了不少讽刺诗，如《致谄媚者》，以及叙事诗《欢乐的乞丐》。彭斯的作品自然生动，感情真挚，尤其表达了平民阶级的思想感情。对苏格兰乡村生活的生动描写使他的诗歌作品具有民族特色和艺术魅力。除诗歌创作外，彭斯还收集整理大量的苏格兰民间歌谣，编辑出版了 6 卷本的《苏格兰音乐总汇》和 8 卷本的《原始的苏格兰歌曲选集》。

三、选读作品赏析

"A Red，Red Rose"

This poem is written to be sung. Robert Burns based it on a folk version of a song he heard on his travels. He completed the poem in 1794 in an English dialect called Scots Burns clearly states the theme：The speaker loves the young lady beyond measure "A Red，Red Rose" is a lyric of genius，made out of the common inherited material of folk song. It is an example of something that is very old but which seems startlingly new because it manages to convey deep feeling without qualification.

The poem begins with a quatrain containing two similes. Burns compares his love with a springtime blooming rose and then with a sweet melody. These are popular poetic images and this is the stanza most commonly quoted from the poem. The second and third stanzas become increasingly complex，ending with the metaphor of the "sands of life"，or hourglass. On the one hand we are given the image of his love lasting until the seas run dry and the rocks melt with the sun，wonderfully poetic images. On the other hand Burns reminds us of the passage of time and the changes that result. That recalls the first stanza and its image of a red rose，newly sprung in June，which we know from experience will change and decay with time. These are complex and competing images typical of the more mature Robert Burns. The final stanza wraps up the poems complexity with a farewell and a promise of return.

The author used the poem to express his yearn towards a woman. There were only two people in this poem，the author himself and the woman he's in love with. There's no truth in the story，however he used modified scenes comparing to his situation，at line eight，nine and ten. Till the seas gang dry. Till a'the seas gang dry，my dear，and the rocks melt with the sun. There were no events happening in the story, just a man expressing his feeling when he's in love.

In "A Red, Red Rose", traditional similes and comparisons perform a serious function. The rose, the melody, the drying seas, the melting rocks and sands are symbolic. Burns imagination and his ear gathered these inherited comparisons and metaphors together, altered them, however slightly, purged them of all vulgarity and created in the end one of the loveliest lyrics of all time. It is a masterpiece of technique rather than of passion. It is by the superb blending of the various units into one harmonious whole that the song achieves its beauty.

There are many literary features in the poem, perhaps one of the most symbolic ones are simile and hyperbole. O my Love is like a red, red rose. This is a simile used in the first verse of the poem; it is effective because he compared the woman's beauty to a rose.

Another smile he is used in O my Love is like the melody, that's sweetly played in tune. The author is comparing her love to a melody, a melody usually makes people joyful, so his love is making him joyful whenever she is beside him.

The poem is written as a ballad with four stanzas of four lines each. Each stanza has alternating lines of four beats, or iambs, and three beats. The first and third lines have four iambs, consisting of an unstressed syllable followed by a stressed syllable. The second and fourth lines consist of three iambs. This form of verse is well adapted for singing or recitation and originated in the days when poetry existed in verbal rather than written form.

第十节　威廉·布莱克

一、作者简介

布莱克（1757—1827）是一位虔诚的基督教徒，常在作品中描述基督的仁慈和博爱，但他反对教会的禁欲观点，肯定生活和人生的美好。在政治上，布莱克深受资产阶级民主革命的影响，痛斥封建专制，要求人类平等。他批判资本家的残酷剥削，反对英国殖民主义政策。他对法国革命寄予极大的期望，把它看作通向《圣经》所预示的千禧年所必经的一个阶段。在文学上，布莱克是18世纪首次宣称应该将想象放置在理性和物质主义之上的作家，他的诗摆脱了古典主义教条的束缚，以清新的歌谣体和奔放的无韵体抒写理想和生活，有热情、重想象，开创了浪漫主义诗歌的先河。

二、主要作品简介

布莱克早期作品简洁明快，中后期作品趋向玄妙晦涩，充满神秘色彩。他的主要作品包括抒情短诗集《天真之歌》和《经验之歌》，布莱克最著名的诗歌《老虎》就是《经验之歌》当中的作品。而预言诗《天堂与地狱的婚姻》则因表达了布莱克对于压迫的反抗精神而倍显重要。《天真之歌》表现了一个欢乐而纯真的世界，而《经验之歌》则对人民的贫困生活、不幸遭遇与愁苦心绪进行了淋漓尽致的描写。《天真之歌》中的许多诗篇在《经验之歌》中都能找到对应的诗篇。例如，"婴儿的欢乐"与"婴儿的悲伤"相对应；纯洁的"羔羊"与燃烧的"老虎"相配对。两部诗集拥有相似的主题，但格调、重点和结论则迥异。这种对比意义重大。它标志着诗人人生观的发展进步。早期的诗集中几乎没有阴影的存在，诗人所见到的是一个充满光明、和谐、平静与慈爱的世界；但在人生的后期，经验使诗人对于邪恶力量和人生苦痛有了更为清醒的认识。

三、选读作品赏析

（一）"The Chimney Sweeper"（from Songs of innocence）

The speaker of this poem is a small boy who was sold into the chimney-sweeping business when his mother died. He cleaned chimneys with other orphan boys. They lead a hard and depressing life："chimneys I sweep"，"in soot I sleep". The speaker recounts the story of a fellow chimney sweeper, Tom Dacre，who was upset that the people he works for cut his hair. The speaker comforts Tom，who falls asleep and has a dream of several chimney sweepers all locked in black coffins. An angel arrives with a special key that opens the locks on the coffins and sets the children free. The newly freed children run through a green field and wash themselves in a river, coming out clean and white in the bright sun. The angel tells Tom that if he would be a good boy, God would be his father. When Tom awakens, he and the speaker gather their tools and head out to work somewhat comforted that their lives will one day improve.

This poem comprises six quatrains, each following the aabb rhyme scheme, with two rhyming couplets per quatrain. The first stanza introduces the speaker, a young boy who has been forced by circumstances into the hazardous occupation of chimney sweeping. The second stanza introduces Tom Dacre, a fellow chimney sweep who acts as a foil to the speaker. The next three stanzas recount Tom Dacre's dream of the chimney sweepers "heaven". The final stanza finds Tom waking up the following morning, with him and the speaker still trapped in their dangerous line of work.

There is a hint of criticism here in Toms dream and in the boys subsequent actions however. Blake decries the use of promised future happiness as a way of subduing the oppressed. The boys carry on with their terrible, probably fatal work because of their hope in a future where their circumstances will be set right. This same promise was often used by those in power to maintain the status que so that workers and the weak would not unite to stand against the inhuman conditions forced upon them. As becomes much clearer in Blake's Songs of eaperience, the poet had little patience with palliative measures that did nothing to alter the present suffering of impoverished families. What on the surface appears to be a condescending moral to lazy boys is in fact a sharp criticism of a culture that would perpetuate the inhuman conditions of chimney sweeping on children. Tom Dacre whose name may derive from Tom Dark reflecting the sooty countenance of most chimney sweeps is comforted by the promise of a future outside the "coffin" that is his life's lot. Clearly, his present state is terrible and only made bearable by the two-edged hope of a happy afterlife following a quick death.

(二) "The Chimney Sweeper" (from Songs of Experience)

This poem parallels its namesake in Songs of Innocence. Like Tom Dacre of the earlier poem, the chimney sweeper is crying. When asked where his parents are, he replies, They are both gone up to church to pray. The boy goes on to explain that his appearance of happiness has led his parents into believing that they have done no harm in finding him work as a chimney sweeper. He says they taught him to "wear the clothes of death" and "to sing the notes of woe". The boy finishes with the damning statement that his parents are gone up to praise God his priest King/ Who make up a heaven of our misery.

When compared structurally to the companion piece from Songs of Innocence, it is obvious that this poem is half as long as its counterpart is. In addition, many lines are much shorter by one or two syllables. The voice of the young chimney sweeper is similar to that of Innocence, but he clearly has little time for the questions put to him (hence the shorter lines). This poem starts with the aabb rhyme scheme characteristic of innocence and childhood, but as it delves deeper into the experience of the Chimney Sweeper, it switches to cdcd efef for the last two stanzas. The final stanza, in fact, has only a near rhyme between "injury and misery", suggesting an increasing breakdown in the chimney sweeper's world, or the social order in general.

The entire system, God included, colludes to build its own vision of paradise upon the labors of children who are unlikely to live to see adulthood. Blake castigates the government (the "King") and religious leaders (Gods "Priest"), decrying the use of otherwise innocent children to prop up the moral consciences of adults both rich and poor. The use of the phrase "make up a Heaven" carries the double meaning of creating a Heaven and lying about the existence of Heaven, casting even more disparagement in the direction of the Priest and King.

（三）"London"

The speaker wanders through the streets of London and comments on his observations. He sees despair in the faces of the people he meets and hears fear and repression in their voices. The woeful cry of the chimney sweeper stands as a chastisement to the Church, and the blood of a soldier stains the outer walls of the monarch's residence. The nighttime holds nothing more promising the cursing of prostitutes corrupts the newborn infant and sullies the marriage hearse. The poem has four quatrains, with alternate lines rhyming. Repetition is the most striking formal feature of the poem, and it serves to emphasize the prevalence of the horrors the speaker describes.

The poem's title denotes a specific geographic space. Everything in this urban space even the natural River Thames-submits to being chartered, a term which combines mapping and legalism. Blake s repetition of this word reinforces the sense of stricture the speaker feels upon entering the city. It is as if language itself, the poet, s medium experiences a hemming-in, a restriction of resources, Blakes repetition, thudding and oppressive, reflects the suffocating atmosphere of the city. But words also undergo transformation within this repetition thus "mark", between the third and fourth lines changes from a verb to a pair of nouns- from an act of observation which leaves some room for imaginative elaboration, to an indelible imprint, branding the peoples bodies regardless of the speaker's actions.

Ironically, the speakers "meeting" with these marks represents the experience closest to a human encounter that the poem will offer the speaker. All the speaker's subjects- men, infants, chimney sweeper, soldier, harlot - are known only through the traces they leave behind the ubiquitous cries, the blood on the palace walls. Signs of human suffering abound, but a complete human form is lacking. In the third stanza , the cry of the chimney sweeper and the sigh of the soldier metamorphose into soot on church walls and blood on palace walls- but we never see the chimney-sweeper or the soldier themselves. Likewise, institutions of power - the clergy, the government-are rendered by synecdoche, by mention of the places in which they reside. Indeed, it is crucial to Blake's commentary that neither the citys victims nor their oppressors ever appear in body Blake does not simply blame a set of institutions or a system of enslavement for the city's woes; rather, the victims help to make their own mind-forged manacles, more powerful than material chains could ever be.

The poem climaxes at the moment when the cycle of misery recommences, in the form of a new human being starting life: a baby is born into poverty, to a cursing prostitute mother. Sexual and marital union- the place of possible re-generation and rebirth- are tainted by the blight of venereal disease. Thus Blake's final image is the marriage hearse，a vehicle in which love and desire combine with death and Destruction.

第十一节　理查德·布林斯利·谢利丹

一、作者简介

谢利丹（1751—1816）曾涉足政坛，成为英国国会辉格党议员。在政治上，他思想开明，反对与正在争取国家独立的美国人进行战争，反对国王乔治三世对国会和政府的控制，反对法国革命期间的对法战争。他十分关注道德问题，强烈谴责当时社会上的种种恶行，诸如诈骗、放荡、造谣中伤、矫情、自私自利、虚荣、贪婪、虚伪、阴谋诡计、飞短流长等。在戏剧创作上，谢利丹把传统的戏剧技巧发挥得淋漓尽致，对隐匿身份、误认身份和戏剧反讽等手法运用得得心应手。他的作品情节组织合理，人物刻画鲜明。特别值得注意的是剧中妙趣横生的对话、独创性的喜剧场景和灵巧、雅致的语言。

二、主要作品简介

谢利丹的代表作是风俗喜剧《情敌》和《造谣学校》。这两部戏精妙地讽刺了上流社会的物质主义、流言蜚语以及虚假伪善，也传达了作者对于感伤主义的嘲讽。《情敌》对上层社会青年妇女的多愁善感和矫情的胡思乱想进行了讽刺。《造谣学校》是英国戏剧中最杰出的经典作品之一。这部喜剧尖锐地讽刺了英国18世纪的贵族—资产阶级社会的道德堕落、无所事事的富人间恶毒的造谣中伤、上层社会不计后果的放纵生活、追逐异性的钩心斗角，以及在尊贵的生活和高尚的道德原则面罩下的不道德和伪善。

三、选读作品赏析

An Excerpt from Act I of The School for Scandal

Richard Brinsley Sheridans The School for Scandal is a comedy of manners, a play satirizing the behavior and customs of upper classes through witty dialogue and an intricate plot with comic situations that expose characters' shortcomings. The school refers to the living room of Lady Sneer well, where the scandals come from. It is a story about two brothers: Joseph Surface and Charles Surface. Charles is in love with Maria while Sir Peter Teazle is loved by Lady Sneer well. The lady instigates Joseph to pursue Maria for her money. Joseph secretly seduces Lady Teazle, Sir Peter Teazle's young wife. The play ends with great disgrace for Joseph, and Charles wins his love and the inheritance of his rich uncle. It is a sharp satire on the moral degeneracy of the aristocratic-bourgeois society in the 18th century England.

School for Scandal is a five act play. Here is the plot of Act one, Scene one: Lady Sneer well and Mr. Snake are discovered on stage in her dressing room, discussing planting scandals in a scandal sheet, possibly The Morning Post or the Town and Country Magazine, and starting rumors about others of their acquaintance. They want a story to reach a gossiping acquaintance, Mrs. Clackitt, so that she will spread the rumor. Snake does not understand why Lady Sneer well is so involved in the intrigue between the two Surface brothers Joseph and his younger brother Charles and Sir Peter Teazle and his new wife. He says it is known how much Joseph admires her, but she tells Snake that Joseph is only interested in Sir Peters ward, Maria, for her money but Maria is in love with Charles, with whom Lady Sneer well is also in love. Lady Sneer well reveals that, while Joseph appears to be "man of sentiment", he is in fact a hypocrite who has fooled everyone apart from her.

Joseph is shown up, and expresses remorse at the dissipation of his brother, until Lady Sneer well reminds him that he is among friends and does not need to express any moral sentiments with them. When Snake leaves, Joseph expresses doubt in his deity to the cause of scandal he has spent too much time talking to Rowley, formerly his fathers steward. Maria arrives, trying to avoid her "lover" Sir Benjamin Backbite ("a poet and a wit") and his Uncle Crabtree. They discuss whether wit can be really funny unless it hurts someone. Maria thinks it is only funny when it doesn's hurt anyone Lady sneer well states that it is not funny unless it is cruel. Mrs. Candour, a woman who does more harm to people's reputation by defending it, arrives to spread more gossip, while saying how she hates people who spread gossip. She spreads more rumors about Charles and sir Peter Teazle (Maria's guardian and his wife. Sir Benjamin Backbite and his Uncle

Crabtree arrive in pursuit of Maria. They tell stories, spread gossip, and humiliate Charles about his spending and his ridiculous borrowing of money. Maria leaves in distress, and Mrs. Candour, Sir Benjamin and Crabtree go after to cheer her up Joseph and Lady Sneerwell worry that Maria is still too much in love with Charles for their plans Underlying the comedy is a serious theme condemnation of the odious practice of slander and, in the case of the written letters, libel. Spreading scandal was commonplace in London's high society of the 1770s, when conversation-in drawing rooms, at balls, in spas, and across card tables- was a form of entertainment. People are hypocritical and deceitful. Lady Sneer well pretends to be a warm-hearted hostess Joseph Surface pretends to, be a paragon of honor and rectitude while attempting to sabotage his brother and marry into a fortune. Mrs. Candour and others of her ilk pretend to oppose gossip but delight in spreading it. When Maria tells her that it is strangely impertinent for people to busy themselves with the affairs of others, Mrs Candour says, Very true, child but what's to be done? People will talk- there's no preventing it. That may explain everything.

第四章　浪漫主义时期的英国文学解读与作品赏析

一、浪漫主义运动

浪漫主义运动是法国大革命、欧洲民主运动和民族解放运动高涨时期的产物。它反映了资产阶级上升时期对个性解放的要求，是政治上对封建领主和基督教会联合统治的反抗，也是文艺上对法国新古典主义的反抗。在英国它出现于 1798 年，以《抒情民谣集》的出版为起点，以 1832 年瓦尔特·司各特爵士的逝世和第一个改革法案在议会通过为终点。

浪漫主义运动是在人们对启蒙运动"理性王国"的失望、对资产阶级革命中的"自由、平等、博爱"口号的幻灭和对资本主义社会秩序的不满的历史条件下产生的。因为浪漫主义作家都经历了封建主义社会的腐朽与不公，以及资本主义社会的经济、社会和政治势力的非人性特点。浪漫主义有意将自己的注意力从外部世界的社会活动转移到人文精神的内心世界，旨在把个人看作所有生命和一切经验的中心。

二、主要文学特色

在文学上，浪漫主义者把他们关注的焦点从理性移向直觉与情感，认为本能与情感作为个人独特感情的表达方式，是文学最宝贵的因素。其主要文学特色如下。

（1）特别注重想象力的创造作用。

（2）认为自然界中能见到真理显现，崇尚自然。

（3）表现手法大胆夸张。

（4）注重抒发强烈奔放的主观感情，偏好描写内心反应和情绪。

三、主要作家与作品

浪漫主义时代是诗歌的时代。代表诗人有华兹华斯、柯勒律治、拜伦、雪莱和济慈。他们发起了对新古典主义的反叛，这就是后世所称的"诗人革命"。其中华兹华斯和柯勒律治所代表的"湖畔派诗人"歌颂大自然，语言清新活泼。例如，华兹华斯的《水仙花》。拜伦的诗歌创作倡导热情和想象，他的诗作被世人赞誉为"抒情史诗"，具有作者本人的思想性格特征的叛逆者，被称作"拜伦式英雄"。例如，长诗《唐璜》。雪莱是第一个表现了空想社会主义理想的诗人，被恩格斯称为"天才的预言家"，代表作有《西风颂》和《解放了的普罗米修斯》。与拜伦和雪莱齐名，才华洋溢的诗人济慈主张"美即是真，真即是美"，留下了《夜莺颂》等名篇。浪漫主义时期小说的代表作家是简·奥斯汀。她继承和发扬了英国 18 世纪优秀的现实主义传统，创作了一系列以爱情和婚姻为主题的作品。其最著名的作品是《傲慢与偏见》和《理智与情感》，以细致入微的观察和活泼风趣的文字著称。

第一节　威廉·华兹华斯

一、作者简介

华兹华斯（1770—1850），英国浪漫主义诗人，"湖畔诗人"的代表。其与柯勒律治合作发表的《抒情歌谣集》是欧洲浪漫主义诗歌的开端。华兹华斯的文学思想对后世影响巨大，1843 年被英国女王任命为"桂冠诗人"。他认为诗歌真实性的源泉来自感官的直接体验；主张日常生活和平民百姓的言语都是诗歌创作的原始材料；他的诗歌形式及格律自由舒展。他最主要的贡献是开创了现代诗歌的先河（关于内心自我不断成长的诗歌），并且通过倡导回归自然，运用平实、朴素的语言，改变了英国诗歌的发展方向。

二、主要作品简介

（一）《序曲》

《序曲》是他最具有代表性的作品，是华兹华斯的自传体诗歌，由 14 卷组成，记录了他从儿时到剑桥读书的人生轨迹、在伦敦生活的经历和法国大革命期间对革命的印象。虽为自传诗，这部长篇关注的焦点实际上是诗人对这些事件的真实反应和感触，像是折射出他思想、情感和想象力的感性旅途。

（二）《丁登寺旁》

《丁登寺旁》描写了诗人重游丁登寺废墟附近怀河的情景，呈现了一幕荒凉古寺的美妙奇观，表现了诗人感受到大自然灵感时的状态，并用神秘主义解释了大自然安慰人类灵魂的奇异功能。诗歌反映出诗人对当年怀河风光和少年生活的怀念，折射出他对现实中污浊肮脏的城市文明的不满和厌恶，抒发了他对大自然的深厚热爱。语言朴实自然，口语化的风格得到集中体现。同时，诗歌的韵律轻盈活泼而具有流动感，打破了当时统治诗坛整齐刻板的英雄双韵体。

三、选读作品赏析

"Wandered Lonely as a Cloud"

In this poem, the speaker recalls a day when he was out walking and saw a host of daffodils. He is looking back on how much of an impression it has had on him In the first two lines of the poem the speaker applies the image of a cloud to himself, which symbolizes his integration with the natural world. Both he and the cloud are aspects of the world, which is subject to the laws of nature but they can still retain their freedom in spite of this. Other images in the poem reinforce this- the dancing flowers, the lake, the breeze and the continuous stars and they are associated with self-joy and contented solitude.

The speaker expresses feelings for nature through these symbolic objects. He personifies the daffodils as dancers, dancing gaily as part of the beauty of nature, and compares them to the stars, which reflect the beauty and consistency of nature. The speaker centers on the role of the imagination in the interplay between the mind and environment and it is only after he has experienced this scene does he turn to contemplation of it and it thereafter becomes a reflective and restorative memory for him. He realizes the full extent of the wealth the scene has given him in a spiritual way and it stays with him always as an inspiration.

The first three stanzas show the speaker moving from a state of feeling alienated and isolated in the universe to a state of feeling connected; another way of expressing the change is to say he moves from perceptions of fragmentation and direction lessness to a vision of harmony and correspondence.

We can trace the change by thinking about motion ("wandered" and "floats" become " dancing" and " danced"); about number (" lonely" is countered by " crowd", "host", " ten thousand" and " company"), and about relation (the isolated image of a single cloud is replaced by the doubling, echoing images of fluttering daffodils, twinkling stars in the milky way, and sparkling, dancing waves) . The sense of correspondence here develops not just because the poet connects with nature (after all, to say "lonely as a cloud" is already to connect with nature); a new state emerges because the speaker perceives a world of interconnecting relationships and sees the universe as a harmoniou whole, in which parts mirror and echo other parts.

In the fourth stanza, memory recreates the scene in the imagination; the eye sees an inner landscape. The first emotion ("gay") seems to be ceca ("pleasure") . But this is a kindred not an identical emotion. The first emotion took the poet out of his loneliness; this second emotion arises out of something like, but not identical to. loneliness. Think about the difference between loneliness and solitude . Then, what does the poem tell us about the experience of time? The first experience, the experience of the first three stanzas, is recorded all in the past tense.

This experience is past; it is over; it functions in the mode of time that is subject to loss. The second experience is conveyed to us in the present tense ("lie", "fash", "fls", " dances") . Then, most important, note that little word of often. This second kind of experience is not subject to loss because it can be repeated because it recurs. The imagination, the inner landscape, is a permanent possession; it takes us beyond our mortality to connect us with immortal things.

The four six-line stanzas of this poem follow a quatrain- couplet rhyme scheme: ababcc. Each line is metered in iambic tetrameter. The plot is extremely simple depicting the poet's wandering and his discovery of a field of daffodils by a lake, the memory of which pleases him and comforts him when he is lonely, bored, or restless The characterization of the sudden occurrence of a memory is psychologically acute, but the poems main brilliance lies in the reverse personification of its early stanzas. The speaker is metaphorically compared to a natural object, a cloud, and the daffodils are continually personified as human beings, dancing and " tossing their heads "in" a crowd host.

This poem discloses the relationship between nature and human beings: how nature can affect ones emotion and behavior with its motion and sound. Wordsworth uses various natural phenomena, such as clouds, daffodils, stars and waves, as devices to characterize his speakers different stages of emotion and feeling. The poem also marks the attainment of a balance and harmony of mind wrested from the tension between daytime awareness and the influences of subconscious proclivities. The poem might also be understood as a quest to overcome the rift between the worlds of inner and outward reality.

第二节　塞缪尔·泰勒·柯勒律治

一、作者简介

塞缪尔·泰勒·柯勒律治（1772—1834），英国诗人和评论家，他一生是在贫病交困和鸦片成瘾的阴影下度过的，诗歌作品相对较少。尽管存在这些不利因素，柯勒律治还是坚持创作，确立了其在幻想浪漫诗歌方面的主要浪漫派诗人地位。政治上他坚持政府必须建立在有产阶级的意志的基础上，而且是有产者从上至下强行对其他阶级进行统治。宗教上他是一个虔诚的基督教徒，把自然、诗歌和信仰看作人性恢复的源泉。在艺术上，柯勒律治认为艺术是人与自然的媒介，诗歌是所有人类知识、思想、激情和感觉的精华，而想象力则是将思想与情感联结起来的手段。他相信艺术是现实自然的永恒启示，在不损害领悟力的前提下，诗人应该意识到那种来自无意识的模糊亲和力。

二、主要作品简介

（一）《古舟子咏》

《古舟子咏》是一首象征性的，或是关于宗教、哲学、心理学或伦理学的诗。在叙述中，柯勒律治刻意渲染复杂的氛围，用心地描绘时间与背景以及道德教化的意义。他用一种十分个人化的方式改造了旧式民谣的形式和修辞技巧，将其写成了英国摄政时期（1810—1820）的名篇。古体的词汇、头韵、反复及民谣诗节，这些技巧的运用使该诗更加成熟，使之能支持诗中最主要的罪恶与救赎的伦理结构。

（二）《忽必烈汗》

《忽必烈汗》历来被奉为浪漫主义诗歌中具有丰富想象力的代表作，典型地表现了浪漫派神奇瑰丽的特色。该诗描述的是梦中之境，一个片段，但表达的远不止一个纯粹的梦境。诗中梦幻般的视觉魅力、独特的想象和神秘的感觉，尤其是富于节奏的音乐美给读者带来神奇的感受。

（三）《午夜霜降》

《午夜霜降》被认为是一首最成功的对话体诗歌。该诗一开始表达了诗人一种与周围世界隔离和异化的感觉，继而通过想象与自己的婴儿对话，共同参与到自然的美景之中。诗人的精神成长分三步在一个复杂结构的时间序列中发展：他的思绪从现在的情景回忆到过去，又通过想象进入可以预见的将来，而这个将来让他既能抓住过去又能回到现在。这首诗是一个顿悟记录。它把一个固执的、迷信的、带有压抑感的唯我论的思想活动戏剧化了，在潜在信仰的基础上，以友善的形式去理解新生的同伴。这也是一首宗教诗，描绘了如何通过可见的世界洞察不可见的世界。诗歌以霜的"冰冷严酷"开始，也以此结束。

三、选读作品赏析

" Kubla Khan"

This poem describes Xanadu, the palace that Kubla Khan, a Mongol emperor orders to be built. The place he chooses for its construction is where the holy river runs across and then flows into a vast underground sea.

The speaker of the poem tells of the area in which the pleasure-dome is being built It measures ten miles in length and contains fertile fields enclosed by walls and battle turrets. The gardens are bright with flowers. Many small streams water it. Sweet smelling trees grow everywhere, together with ancient cedar forests. The speaker emphasizes the magical quality of the land. The chasm into which the river plunges is said to be "romantic". The forests are made up of cedar trees. The place is "savage" and yet "holy" and "enchanted", where you might find a woman wailing for her demon lover.

The place is also in a state of great physical unrest. A mighty fountain of water jets up from the chasm in gusts as if it is panting. Within this water are huge fragments which are flung into the air and then, falling back, bounce around the ground like hail, or like wheat which bounces around when being hit by the threshers flail. From there the river meanders for five miles until it reaches the caves, where it falls in a great cataract into the underground sea. Into this cacophony of sound Kubla Khan hears the voices of the ancestors prophesying war.

There seems to be a change in the poem at this point. The speaker tries to pick up the threads by speaking of the shadow of the dome falling on the river. He says the dome was a miracle, and yet there is the paradox of a sunny pleasure-dome but in caves of ice Then in the fourth stanza, a very clear break occurs as the speaker moves away from this landscape. He now speaks of yet another vision in which he sees a young Abyssinian woman playing music on her dulcimer. Her song is of Mount a-bort, a mountain in Abyssinia (or what is today Ethiopia) . The vision, however, is fading quickly now. Yet the speaker believes that, if only he could remember the dream, it would rekindle the excitement of it all. Then he would attempt to rebuild the pleasure-dome in his Imagination.

Toward the end of the poem, the speaker describes past visions, which bring him to a final image of a terrifying figure with flashing eyes For he on honey-dew hath fed And drunk the milk of paradise.

The structure of "Kubla Khan" is really in two parts. The first, which contains three stanzas, describes Xanadu as if Coleridge is actually there, experiencing the place first hand. The second part of the poem is filled with longing to be in Xanadu, but Coleridge is unable to capture the experience again.

The first stanza has a definite rhythm and beat and describes the beauty and sacredness of Xanadu with rich sensual and exotic images. The second stanza depicts the savage and untamed violence of life outside of the pleasure dome. The disorder and primitive cycles of nature are mixed with images of evil and the threat of war are also introduced in the second stanza. In the third stanza, the life forces are entwined together to prove that beauty and danger cannot be separated from each other, despite what the ruler Kubla Khan wants. Coleridge believes that it is Kubla Khan who controls the land of Xanadu, a sunny pleasure dome with caves of ice. The dome itself is a contrast with sun and ice, the sun symbolizing all things good and the ice symbolizing death and destruction.

There is a definite change of tone between the third and fourth stanzas. The fourth stanza no longer describes Xanadu, but Coleridge's. desire for control over his imagination, to be able to reconjure up the feelings and ideas of Xanadu. The two parts may initially seem unconnected, but the ideas in both parts of the poem link these sections together by showing that even the ruler cannot have control over the forces of nature, and the writer over his imagination.

Both parts of the poem deal with the attempt to create Kubla Khan has built a pleasure dome and Coleridge is trying to use language to recreate the perfection of his dream with words. The poem is conveyed to the reader with the use of language and the structuring of the poem plays an important part in this.

In this poem, Coleridge uses contrasts in the images he presents to his audience. Xanadu is idyllic, but also "savage". The image of a woman wailing for her demon lover brings the dark side of the supposed utopia to light. The peace and serenity is contrasted by the violent disorder of the river and the threat of war.

The poem is a good example of appearances being deceptive. The pleasure dome may be beautiful with its bright "sunny" gardens and "blossoming incense trees" but it is an enchanted eye of the storm. The garden is surrounded by savage destruction caused by the " ceaseless turmoil seething".

第三节　乔治·戈登·拜伦

一、作者简介

乔治·戈登·拜伦（1788—1824），是英国 19 世纪初期伟大的浪漫主义诗人。他不仅是一位伟大的诗人，还是一个为理想战斗了一生的勇士；他积极而勇敢地投身革命，参加了希腊民族解放运动，并成为领导人之一。政治上，拜伦向往自由而痛恨一切独裁专政。艺术上，拜伦继承了 18 世纪启蒙主义者所倡导的古典主义传统。他歌颂 18 世纪的启蒙主义者，而对他同代诗坛的保守派则给予抨击，表达了他对"湖畔诗人"平庸之态的蔑视。

二、主要作品简介

（一）《恰尔德·哈罗德游记》

这首诗主要描写英雄哈罗德。由于对现代文明感到失望，他决定离开自己的祖国去国外，到更朴实的人当中去生活。该诗反映了当时世态的全貌，从对民族风俗习惯的记述、自然风光的描写，到作者的哲学思考及大胆的政治见解等方面均有涉及。

（二）《该隐》

这部作品是拜伦最有成就的诗剧，讲述的是逐出乐园后的亚当、夏娃及他们的两个孩子——亚伯和该隐——的故事。根据基督教传统的阐释，《圣经》中，亚伯是一个好人，是上帝的忠实仆人，后来被邪恶的该隐所害。但拜伦笔下的亚伯是一个懦弱的奴隶；第一个反叛上帝并谋杀人的该隐却被拜伦塑造成一个伟大的英雄，其原因就是该隐是一个敢于质疑上帝对人类万物有恩的反叛者，是一个拒绝盲从上帝的人。同样，拜伦笔下的撒旦也是一个不愿做奴隶而起来反对上帝的高傲的反叛者。拜伦表达了他对撒旦反叛的认同，从而暗示魔鬼是自由的伟大热爱者。

（三）《唐·璜》

这是一首伟大的讽刺史诗，是基于西班牙传统中一个多情公子的故事改编而成的，诗中拜伦把现代社会所忽视的，诸如勇敢、慷慨、坦率等伦理美德都赋予了唐璜。另外，通过描写唐璜的探险经历，拜伦表现了各种社会的全貌，描绘了人生不同阶段所经历的爱情、欢乐、痛苦、憎恨和恐惧。连接《唐·璜》各部分的纽带是其最基本的反讽主题，即现实与现象之间的冲突。诗中汇集的各种不同素材和各种情感的冲突都因拜伦深刻地洞察了生命现象与本质之间的区别而变得和谐起来。

三、选读作品赏析

"Song for the Luddites"

The early 19th century in England was a bleak time for the poor and destitute. Social injustice is hardly descriptive of the general situation. As for the working poor conditions in the textile mills and putting-out shops were hostile to the many children who were compelled, of economic necessity, to work there.

In response to conditions in a specific industry, machine-breaking was a more common and effective tool for workers to express discontent. The Luddite riots began in Nottingham in November 1811, and spread to Yorkshire and Lancashire in early 1812. The main feature of the riots was the organized destruction of stocking frames by small bands of workmen. They warned the masters to remove the frames from their premises. If the masters refused, the Luddites smashed the machines in nocturnal raids, using massive sledgehammers. It is widely agreed that the Luddites leader, known as "King Ludd", did not actually exist. The name is said to derive from one Ned ludd, a apprentice weaver, who some years earlier smashed a loom in a rage at his master who had beaten him.

Observers closer to that time, such as lord Byron, identified with the revolutionary elements in the Luddite movement. However, the Luddites were severely punished by the ruling class in England.

This is one of the two poems written by Byron to show his consistent support of the Luddites for whom he made his famous speech in the House of Lords in 1812. The Luddites were workers who destroyed the machines in their protest against unemployment and were severely punished by the ruling class in England. The poets great sympathy for the workers in their struggle against the capitalists is clearly shown The word "cheaply" here is used ironically, meaning dearly. The phrase tree of liberty is used metaphorically, referring to the democratic movement of the working people fighting for their own freedom and liberation that will develop prosperously like a growing Tree.

This short poem contains three five-lined stanzas of anapestic, movement. The lines are of irregular lengths. The rimes in each stanza are abba.

第四节　波西·比希·雪莱

一、作者简介

波西·比希·雪莱（1792—1822），英国浪漫主义民主诗人、第一位社会主义诗人，受空想社会主义思想影响颇深。政治上，雪莱是一个民主革命者，他一生都反对暴政、不公独裁、制度化的宗教以及富人的种种虚伪。他认为他所生活的时代是被压迫者与压迫者对抗的时代，并坚信尽管大革命失败了，自由的力量会再次在欧洲获得胜利。文学上，雪莱极力推崇想象力、高度赞扬诗歌的作用，认为只要有了诗歌就会使人类获得自由，并让人对诗歌的魅力有更全面的了解。诗歌是"我们内心活动和情感的更直接的表现"，通过语言想象力可以更充分地理解真理的完美秩序。

二、主要作品简介

（一）《解放了的普罗米修斯》

雪莱根据埃斯库罗斯的《被缚的普罗米修斯》改写而成的一部四幕剧。原剧中普罗米修斯最后与暴君宙斯妥协了，而激进的革命者雪莱却做了完全不同的解释，把妥协变成斗争，只有斗争才能使受压迫者得到解放。在他的母亲"大地神"和新娘亚细亚的大力支持下在德谟各根和赫喀琉斯的帮助下，宙斯被赶下了王位，普罗米修斯获得了解放。该剧是赞颂人类潜在能力的杰作，表达了民主自由和博爱的主题。

（二）《西风颂》

这是雪莱最著名的抒情诗。雪莱在西风意象下为自己的狂想与雄辩找到了合适的主题。秋风一边埋葬逝去的一年，一边又迎接新春的到来。就像雪莱希望的，秋风变成了他自己的意象，具有它那样的自由，它那样的毁灭与重建的潜在力量，以及它的宇宙性。整首诗具有一种逻辑感，一种难以分析的运动感，它导向胜利的、有希望的和有信念的结语："如果冬天已到，难道春天还用久等？"在这首诗中，雪莱借用了但丁的隔行押韵的方法，雪莱与自然界互动从而产生的精神上的激动通过艺术和想象的力量，都转化为一种强大的、有预见性的力量并渴望与之相融合，希望生命的气息吹入他的心田。

（三）《阿都力斯》

这是一首田园式的挽歌，即哀悼某人的去世，体现了牧歌传统。正如弥尔顿的《利西达斯》强烈地批判圣职一样，雪莱的《哀歌》是对评论者的一种尖锐的控告，因为雪莱认为是这些无端的评论者让济慈走上了绝路。这首诗讨论了有关荣光与死亡的主题和诗人对自己生命的畅想，同时涉及其他诗人的作品，以及促使世上万物复苏的精灵。所有这些汇合成部交响乐曲。前 38 个诗节表达了一种哀悼之情，而后 17 个诗节抒发的则是一种告慰之一。

(四)《诗辩》

这是雪莱最重要的文学批评。《诗辩》明确地指出了诗人和诗歌的教育意义和社会功用。他认为诗人是社会的立法者、生活的导师。他应当为人类指出正确前进的道路，不仅要争取自由主义，而且要保证新社会的实现。他在这部作品中重点探讨一切伟大诗歌，作为想象力的结晶，所共同拥有的永恒而普遍的形式、性质和价值观。他把诗人一词引申为所有打破自己时代禁锢从而接近永恒价值观的作家群。

三、选读作品赏析

" *A Song：Men of England* '"

This poem was written in 1819, the year of the so called Peterloo Massacre. It is empowering anthem for the workers of England. In this poem, the poet used a lot of common nouns like "robe", "food", "shelter", "weapon", "plough", "spade", "hoe", "loom", ete., and verbs like "plough", "weave", "feed", "wear", "drain", "drink", "forge", "keep", etc. Through all these images, the speaker is really pointing out the way things are. He recognizes the absurdity and unfairness of things. "Drones" and "bees" are metaphors used by the poet to indicate the exploiters, who, like the drones, would do nothing but enjoy all the fruits, and the exploited, who, like the bees would work all day long, but could get nothing. This is also an address to the working people, pointing out the intolerable injustice of economic exploitation.

In the middle part of the poem, he tells the workers how it should be: Sow seed, -but let not tyrant reap; Find wealth, -let no impost-er heap; Weave robes let not the idle wear: Forge arms in your defense to bear.

The last stanzas delivering the final repetition of the initial imagery are so dark and urgent with a hint of insult that it stirs the emotion of the reader. A worker reading the poem would have been angered by the last stanza and be stirred to follow true message of the poem in order to prevent the ending from becoming a reality. The poem is not just a simple cry of empowerment but an urgent, stirring call upon all working people to rise up against their political oppressors.

The poem consists of eight stanzas, each with four lines. There is an aabb rhyming scheme and a rhythmic scheme that gives it a nice flow. The tone of the poem is an imperative one. The tone of the speaker is condescending, almost daring his readers to rise up to his challenging call to action. Thematically, Shelley wants the rest of England to see the country the way he sees it: a tyrannical, imbalanced usurper of the people's power, where the rich reap all the fruits of the poor's hard labor.

第五节 约翰·济慈

一、作者简介

约翰·济慈（1795—1821），出生于 18 世纪末的伦敦。他的诗篇被认为完美地体现了西方浪漫主义诗歌的特色，被推崇为欧洲浪漫主义运动的杰出代表。济慈相信诗歌能给痛苦以安慰，是通向天堂的工具。他认为，诗歌的崇高使命是为人民的福利效劳。他诗歌中的主要思想和情感可以这样来概括：自然的世界是美丽的；艺术、诗歌和想象的王国是精彩绝伦的；但现存的社会却有着难以逃避、无从解脱的痛苦。他的主要诗歌作品均流露出如何将理想与现实、想象与真实联系起来的关注。在诗歌中，他善于用敏锐的观察捕捉创作的对象，并能针对不同的对象用不同的形式和格调创造出美的诗篇。他在诗歌中特别强调"美真统一"的思想，认为"美即是真，真即是美"，认为"想象所见的美的即真"。

二、主要作品简介

（一）《恩底弥翁》

这是一首基于希腊神话的诗，讲述了关于恩底弥翁与月亮女神的故事。济慈在令人陶醉的氛围中写下了自己的所思所想——在一个月光如水的夜晚，人间的爱情和理想的美融为一体。这代表了济慈诗歌当中传统的一面。

(二)《拉弥亚》《伊莎贝拉》《圣爱尼亚前夕》及其他

这是济慈的第三集，也是他最优秀的一部诗集。三首标题诗都以古代、中世纪和文艺复兴时期的神话传说为主题。这些诗中都浸透了济慈对理想与现实、想象与事实、男人与女人如何融合的关注。这部诗集当中还包含了他最伟大的四首"颂诗"：《忧郁颂》《希腊古瓮颂》《夜莺颂》和《心灵颂》；他的抒情诗代表作《秋颂》以及未完成的长诗《海披里昂》。

(三)《颂诗》

一般认为颂诗是济慈最重要也是最成熟的作品。它们的主题是诗人对想象与优美如何融合所给予的特别关注。在这些伟大的作品中，他也对伴随狂喜所产生的潜在幻灭感给予了关注，并暗示人类的痛苦会不断地质疑因艺术而获得的想象超越感。

(四)《十四行诗》

济慈一生写了六十四首十四行诗。他早期的十四行诗基本上都是意大利式，尽管他对亚格的韵律总是引进各种变化。他也写过一些莎士比亚式的十四行诗。他最著名的十四行诗包括《记首次阅读查普曼的〈荷马〉》《记重读〈李尔王〉》《记蚂蚱和蟋蟀》及《当我害怕我会死时》。

三、选读作品赏析

" *To Autumn* "

In this poem Keats describes autumn like as if it was a person and expresses his love for the season. The three-stanza poem seems to create three distinct stages of Autumn growth, harvest, and death. The poem also describes a progression through the season from the late maturation of the crops to the harvest and to the last days of autumn when winter is nearing. Parallel to this, the poem depicts the day turning from morning to afternoon and into dusk. These progressions are joined with a shift from the tactile sense to that of sight and then of sound, creating a three-part symmetry. As the poem progresses, Autumn is represented metaphorically as one who conspires, who ripens fruit. who harvests who makes music.

In the first stanza Keats describes autumn with a series of specific, concrete, vivid visual images, which allow the audience to actually see and feel the joy of what he is describing ripening grapes and apples, swelling gourds and hazel nuts, and blooming flowers. In the second stanza, Keats describes the wonderful activities of harvest threshing, reaping, gleaning, and cider making. He uses personification to give human characteristic to the season. Autumn is a thresher sitting on a granary floor, a reaper asleep in a grain field, a gleaner crossing a brook, and, lastly, a cider maker. In the concluding stanza, the poet puts the emphasis on the sounds of the season. Autumn is seen as a musician, and the music which autumn produces is as pleasant as the music of spring-the sounds of gnats, lambs, crickets, robins and swallows. The sounds are not only those of Autumn but essentially the gentle sounds of the evening. As night approaches within the final moments of the song, death is slowly approaching alongside of the end of the year.

In this poem Keats celebrates autumn as a season of abundance, a season of reflection, a season of preparation for the winter, and a season worthy of admiration with comparison to what romantic poetry often focuses upon- the spring. Although Keats describes Autumn as a time of warmth and plenty, yet it is perched on the brink of winters desolation, as the bees enjoy later flowers, the harvest is gathered from the fields, the lambs of spring are now "full grown", and, in the final line of the poem, the swallows gather for their winter migration.

Thematically, "To Autumn" may be seen as an allegory of artistic creation. As the farmer processes the fruits of the soil into what sustains the human body, so the artist processes the experience of life into a symbolic structure that may sustain the human spirit. This process involves an element of self-sacrifice by the artist, analogous to the living grains being sacrificed for human consumption.

The poem uses powerful language to achieve effect. Its rich imagery, exaggeration and onomatopoeia create a rather sweet and peaceful atmosphere of the English autumn It emphasizes the harmony of autumn and this effect could also be a metaphor for the slowdown of life during autumn, and the imminent death of the season.

In terms of rhyme scheme, each stanza is divided roughly into two parts. In each stanza, the first part is made up of the first four lines of the stanza, and the second part is made up of the last seven lines. The first part of each stanza follows an abab rhyme scheme. The second part of each stanza is longer and varies in rhyme scheme: The first stanza is arranged cdedcce, and the second and third stanzas are arranged cdecdde.

第六节　简·奥斯汀

一、作者简介

简·奥斯汀（1775—1817），是英国著名女性小说家，她的作品主要关注乡绅家庭女性的婚姻和生活，以女性特有的细致入微的观察力和活泼风趣的文字真实地描绘了她周围世界的小天地。她是一位属于早期现实主义流派的作家。她的作品中透出一股坚定的信念——理性战胜情感，理性与常识的价值战胜感伤的、哥特式的、浪漫的倾向。她在作品中对生活给予鲜明而严肃的批判，揭露人类的各种陋习与幻想。通过巧妙的讽刺，她表达了对愚蠢、势利、笨拙、世故、庸俗等陋习的蔑视。在写作风格上，她是一个新古典主义的倡导者，她笃信秩序、理性、精确与优美。

二、主要作品简介

（一）《傲慢与偏见》

《傲慢与偏见》写成于1796年，原书标题为《第一印象》，后经过作者改写并于1813年用现名发表。该书是她最成功的，也是最受欢迎的作品。故事围绕女主人公伊丽莎白·本尼特和男主人公费兹威廉·达西及另一对人物简和查尔斯·宾利展开。主要人物平凡的感情生活——喝茶、访客、散步、舞会、聊天以及其他，既是意料之外又在情理之中的插曲最后导致了两对主要人物的幸福结合。

（二）《爱玛》

《爱玛》是简·奥斯汀一部优秀的反讽基调格外浓厚的小说。《爱玛》中反讽手法的运用不同于《傲慢与偏见》。这部小说没有像伊丽莎白和达西那样的才智过人、语锋犀利的讽刺主体。应该说女主人公爱玛是作为一系列反讽的对象或牺牲品而存在的。小说通过爱玛的一个个主观臆想在现实中一次又一次挫败，演绎了爱玛从幼稚走向成熟，最终得到幸福的故事。由此可以看出，这部小说的反讽特色不是体现在语言上（或不完全如此），而主要体现在小说的结构中。因此，结构反讽手法的运用在小说中占突出地位。

（三）《理智与情感》

《理智与情感》是简·奥斯汀富于幽默情趣的处女作。埃诺莉和玛丽安娜两姐妹生在一个英国乡绅家庭，姐姐善于用理智来控制情感，妹妹的情感却毫无节制，因此面对爱情时，她们做出了不同的反应。小说以这两位女主角曲折复杂的婚事风波为主线，通过"理智与情感"的幽默对比，提出了道德与行为的规范问题。此书和作者的《傲慢与偏见》堪称姐妹篇，同样以细腻的笔触和生动的对白叙述没有富裕嫁妆的少女恋爱结婚的故事。

三、选读作品赏析

Pride and prejudice

The story of Pride and Prejudice centers round the heroine Elizabeth Bennet and the hero Fitzwilliam Darcy and a minor couple, her sister Jane and his friend Charles Bingley. The uneventful vicissitudes of the lives of these characters, including teas and visits and walks and dances and conversations and other expected or unexpected happenings, finally lead to the happy unions of the two couples.

The title tells of a major concern of the novel: pride and prejudice. If to form good relationships is our main task in life, we must first have good judgment. Our first impressions, according to Jane Austen, are usually wrong, as is shown here by those of Elizabeth. In the process of judging others, Elizabeth finds out something about herself , her blindness, partiality, prejudice and absurdity. In time she discovers her own shortcomings. On the other hand, Darcy too learns about other people and himself. In the end false pride is humbled and prejudice dissolved.

Another theme is love and marriage. In the novel, three kinds of attitudes towards marriage are presented for manifestation: marriage merely for material wealth and social position; marriage just for beauty, attraction and passion regardless of economic condition or personal merits; and the ideal marriage for true love with a consideration of the partner's personal merit as well as his economic and social status. What jane Aasten tries to say is that it is wrong to marry just for money or for beauty, but it is also wrong to marny without consideration of economic conditions.

第五章　维多利亚时期的英国文学解读与作品赏析

从时间上讲，维多利亚文学时期恰好与维多利亚女王（1836——1901）执政期相吻合，这一时段是英国历史上最光辉灿烂的时段。经济政治实力空前强盛，文学、艺术、建筑和科技都有很大发展。文学中体现出的该时代精神风貌，既包括一整套高贵、体面、严肃、克制的道德体系，同时又深刻揭露出当时飞速发展扩张的社会中种种残酷的阴暗面，如泛滥的卖淫嫖娼、雇用童工现象，帝国主义无情剥削殖民地人民和工人阶级，等等。文学不但描绘着上流社会雍容华贵、尔虞我诈的奢侈享乐，还讲述着中产阶级虚荣、挣扎着向上攀爬的刻意体面生活，又刻画出下层人民食不果腹、艰辛困苦的悲惨境地。

一、主要文学特色

（1）小说成为最广泛阅读和最主流的文学形式。

（2）女性地位的改变带动了女性文学的发展。

（3）以萧伯纳和王尔德为代表的爱尔兰戏剧成熟。

（4）儿童文学的崛起，如刘易斯的《爱丽丝梦游仙境》。

（5）诗歌在技巧和主题上的突破为 20 世纪诗歌铺平道路。

二、主要作家与作品

维多利亚时期内，小说成为英语文学的主流形式。大多数作家都开始转向规模逐渐扩大的中产阶级，普通民众的品位喜好越来越比贵族资助者的更加具有诱惑力。查尔斯·狄更斯于 19 世纪 30 年代出现在文学舞台上，也采用了当时的连载出版风潮。狄更斯重视描绘出伦敦日常生活的景观，尤其是下层社会穷人的挣扎与拼搏，不过笔法相对诙谐幽默，哪个阶层的读者都能够接受。早期的作品《匹克威克外传》等都是喜剧的经典之作。到后期，他的作品如《双城记》《远大前程》等内容要严肃灰暗许多，但笔锋仍然未失讽刺夸张的特色。其他著名的有勃朗特姐妹的作品、萨克雷的讽刺小说《名利场》等。以托马斯·哈代为代表的一群小说家对乡村生活兴趣颇深，在作品中描绘出乡下地区迅速变迁的社会和经济环境以及对普通民众生活、心理的冲击与影响。这段时期重要的诗人包括丁尼生、罗伯特·勃朗宁和伊丽莎白·巴瑞特·勃朗宁夫妇，还有马修·阿诺德。

第一节 查尔斯·狄更斯

一、作家简介

查尔斯·狄更斯（1812—1870）是 19 世纪前期和维多利亚时代前期的英国现实主义代表作家。狄更斯特别注意描写生活在英国社会底层的"小人物"的生活遭遇，深刻地反映了当时英国复杂的社会现实，为英国批判现实主义文学的开拓和发展做出了卓越的贡献。马克思把他和萨克雷等称誉为英国的"一批杰出的小说家"。

二、主要作品介绍

（一）《雾都孤儿》

通过孤儿奥利弗·退斯特的故事，狄更斯对统治阶级的残酷与伪善进行了猛烈的抨击，并呼吁人们对孤苦无助的儿童给予同情和援助。奥利弗·退斯特是狄更斯塑造的第一个儿童形象。因为不幸，他来到了这个悲惨的世界，但却始终保持着纯洁、善良和文明的本性。作为小说的主人公，他起到了联系上层社会与底层罪犯的纽带作用。跟随他，读者可以看到两种社会的残酷、腐败和罪恶。

（二）《大卫·科波菲尔德》

这是以"成长小说"的形式写成的一部关于主人公大卫·科波菲尔德的故事。实际上是以狄更斯自己从童年到青年的成长经历为基础的故事。小说记载了狄更斯的一些鲜为人知的亲身经历和他深埋心底的感情纠葛。这部小说的结构与"灰姑娘"的故事有些相似。大卫——剥夺了继承权的王子——落入了一个残忍的继父之手，后被善良的教母特洛特伍德所搭救和帮助，最后找到了自己的公主阿基尼斯，并与她成婚。

（三）《荒凉山庄》

这部小说标志着作家在艺术手法的运用和社会批判方面已经成熟。《荒凉山庄》以其对腐朽的政治和司法制度以及道貌岸然的贵族阶级的批判而著称。狄更斯以他的讽刺天才在小说中塑造了一系列让人过目难忘的、来自不同社会阶层、不同职业和不同气质的人物，正是他们充斥着腐朽的英国。

三、选读作品赏析

Great Expectations

Great E. pectations is a novel of memory, a first-person story of a boy from his early childhood, through young manhood, with a brief summary of middle age. The story is revolved around the three stages of growth of Pip, the hero. The first time we see him. he is an orphan, living a natural, simple life in the country with his harsh sister and her honest, kind-hearted husband Joe Gargery, the blacksmith. One day, when Pip is again crying over his parents' graves after being again ill-treated by the sister, he meets an escaped prisoner. The simple, innocent and kind-hearted boy steals a file and a pork pie from home for the man. Later, Pip is told to go to a Miss Havisham's to help. There he is fascinated by his first glimpse of luxury, elegance and beauty. The beautiful yet cruel girl, Estella arouses in him the ambition to be a gentleman.

At the second stage, Pip is shown to be on the road to his great expectations Suddenly, he finds himself financed by some unknown source and sent to London for a gentleman's education. Mistaking Miss Havisham for his benefactress, Pip begins to cherish the idea that someday Miss Havisham will bestow the beautiful Estella on him. At the same time, life in London corrupts the young man. His moral values are deteriorated as his social graces improve. When Joe comes to see him in London, Pip is even ashamed of admitting their relationship. The great turning point in his life comes when his real benefactor Magwitch the convicted criminal to whom he had once given needed help, appears before him. Stricken by the discovery of the source of his windfall, he realizes that all his great expectations are built upon dirty money. He also realizes that by learning to be a gentleman, he has left behind all his natural simplicity, kindness and honesty. What is more, Estella, the star he has been trying to reach all along, turns out not really worth his while at all She is no princess, but daughter of Magwitch and a woman criminal, and she has now proved herself a vain, heartless, selfish snob. Pip falls into a long, serious illness, from which he is to recover a changed man.

The last stage is the shortest, dealing briefly with his life as a middle-aged man After a symbolic return to his home place, to the kind brother o and to biddy, the woman who had often comforted him when they were children, Pip finds himself no longer belonging there: Joe and Biddy are happily married. He leaves England and returns only eleven years later, a disillusioned but mature grown-up. One day, he goes to the site of the burned satis House of miss havisham he meets estella. now a widow set free at last after some years of unbearable treatment from her beastly gentleman husband. The two join their hands for the first time. Pips sudden rise from country laborer to city gentleman forces him to move from one social extreme to another while dealing with the strict rules and expectations that governed Victorian England. In form, Great Expectations fits a pattern popular in nineteenth-century European fiction: the bildungsroman, or novel depicting growth and personal development, generally a transition from boyhood to manhood such as that experienced by Pip.

Great Expectations is first of all a novel about great expectations, or more correctly here, dreams. Not only Pip, the hero, cherishes his great expectations or dreams of being someday a gentleman and marrying a rich, beautiful princess, all the other important characters have their expectations, too. For Miss Havisham, a rich world; he has always wanted to marry his ideal princess but finds her the daughter of a criminal; he does have unexpected fortune but it, instead of bringing him up in the society, drags him down to the underworld, and he does finally realize his wish by joining hands with his long-desired-for woman but their wedding bell will never ring happily because they both have to carry their painful memories into their future life. In a word, the happy tone of the fairy-tale has gone here, giving way to the sober reminiscence of a disillusioned, embittered grown-up. Nevertheless, it strengthens the force of social criticism and brings the cruel reality right to the front of the reader.

第二节　阿尔弗雷德·丁尼生

一、作家简介

阿尔弗雷德·丁尼生（1809—1892），作为一位桂冠诗人，是维多利亚时代最具代表性的诗人。在政治上，他尖锐地反映了科学与宗教信仰之间的冲突，提出了物种进化观点，认为社会也将一点一滴地逐步进化，渐臻完善。同时，丁尼生对当时女性问题也相当关注，作品中多次体现女性在男权社会争取自己的权利和爱情。在文学上，他的诗歌具备专业的完美性，意象丰富，语言节奏感强，尤其以优美的抒情、和谐的韵律和精湛的措辞著名。景、声、情完美地融合在一起，全无雕琢之痕。

二、主要作品简介

（一）《诗歌集》

这个诗集收录了著名的戏剧独白《尤利西斯》（见选读）和以亚瑟王及其圆桌骑士的古老传说为题材的组诗《亚瑟之死》。

（二）《公主》

《公主》是一部无韵体诗歌。在这里，丁尼生讨论了妇女在家庭和社会的权利和地位。丁尼生著名的抒情诗有《眼泪，莫名其妙的眼泪》《下来，噢，少女》《和畅而低柔》等。其中，有些诗还被作曲家配上了音乐。

（三）《悼念》

《悼念》是丁尼生为纪念亡友亚瑟·哈拉姆而作的挽歌，是他最伟大的作品。它也是一部诗体形式的日记，不仅表达了对挚友亚瑟·亨利·哈拉姆英年早逝的无限悲怀，而且也表达了处于社会急剧变化时代的大多数人对哲学和宗教的笃信与怀疑。这组诗以情感的真挚和艺术的优美著称。诗中似曾相识的感觉、美妙的音韵和图画般的描写使《悼念》成为英国文学中最瑰丽的挽歌之一。组诗由 132 首短诗组成，其中有一半是为悼念亡友亚瑟·哈拉姆而作的。

（四）《国王叙事诗》

《国王叙事诗》是丁尼生规模最大的组诗。全诗共 12 卷，以克尔特人关于亚瑟王与圆桌骑士的传奇故事为原型写成。尽管故事带有中世纪神秘、传奇的色彩，贯穿全诗的却是维多利亚时代的道德规范：对纯洁心灵的赞颂，对背叛与不忠的谴责。这组叙事诗以季节的周而复始为框架。组诗从春天亚瑟王的到来开始，历经夏天的繁荣——骑士和英雄们纷纷加入亚瑟的圆桌边、秋的衰落——以最后一次战役的失败为象征，以及冬的消亡敌军势力的增长、王国的崩溃、朋友、骑士、妻子和军师纷纷弃他而去。

三、选读作品赏析

"Break. Break. Break"

"Break，Break，Break" is a poem Tennyson wrote on the death of his friend arthur Hallam. The poet imagines to be standing near the cliff on the seashore and addressing to the sea waves which are lashing the rocks repeatedly. In the first stanza the poet says that the torment of his heart as the death of his friend is tremendous. There is a struggle like the struggle of the sea waves on the stormy shores. The question before him is how he can express adequately the thoughts which are rushing in his mind. In the second，stanza the poet says that life is full of joy for the fisherman's son and daughter who are laughing and shouting merrily. The poet，on the other hand，is entirely in a different mood. He is restless and grief-stricken at the death of his friend. The poet admires the innocent joy of these youngsters but he is sorry because he cannot share it.

The lad of the sailor is also happy and sings in his boat face to face with the magnificence of the sea. But such joy is not for the poet. In the third stanza the poet says that the majestic ships ply on their destination under the hill.

第三节　罗伯特·勃朗宁

一、作家简介

罗伯特·勃朗宁（1812—1889），维多利亚时期代表诗人和剧作家之一。罗伯特和著名女诗人伊丽莎白·巴莱特的爱情故事，是英国文学史乃至世界文学史上最美的爱情佳话之一。在艺术上，他最著名的是"戏剧独白"，一种他经常使用的技巧，目的是提高人们研究复杂的人物性格的兴趣。虽然戏剧独白并非勃朗宁首创，但是正因为勃朗宁，这种诗歌形式才得以成熟和完善。

二、主要作品简介

（一）《指环与书》

《指环与书》是一首 2 万行的无韵体长诗。该诗是根据法律文件中记录的 1698 年罗马谋杀案审判情况写成的。该诗由 12 段独白组成，由 9 位与案件有关的当事人、旁观者，或公众舆论的代表进行叙述。采用这种多视角叙述手法，其真正有趣和重要的是那些叙述者。

（二）《圣普拉西德教堂的主教吩咐后事》

《圣普拉西德教堂的主教吩咐后事》也是勃朗宁著名的作品之一。诗歌写一位 16 世纪的意大利主教在临终时吩咐他的几个私生子为他建立一座豪华富丽的坟墓。人之将死，其声亦真，这段临终"独白"，把主教贪婪伪善、爱慕虚荣、好胜逞强、多疑善妒的性格暴露无遗。

三、选读作品赏析

" *Meeting at Night* "

This is one of the few completely organized poems by the poet. In the poem, the speaker takes a little sailing trip, walks a mile on the beach, then across three fields, all under the cover of night, to reach a farmhouse where his lover awaits. The "startled little waves", the "slushy sand", the "sea- scented beach", the "three fields to cross etc.- merely stages on his advance to the anticipated climax of" two hearts beating each to each-, are details intended to stimulate in the readers a sense of urgency and expectancy. Every detail of sensuous images and constant action and movement contributes directly to the main impression the sensation of pleasurable excitement. During the lovers hurried trip over the water and across the land, his senses are also responsive to every sound and color around him. The "gray sea" and the black land under the feet, the "yellow half-moon large and low" up in the sky, and the fiery startled waves provide a most romantic setting for the coming meeting, and the "tap and the" quick sharp scratch And blue spurt of a lighted match，/ And a voice less loud... "anticipates the loud voice of" the two hearts beating each to each!

The poem gives us a unique first-person point of view，and actually shows how a persons passions can affect the way in which they view the world，suggesting the importance of emotions in establishing a "reality". Unlike most of the poet's poems，this simple poem has a rich，sensuous beauty that is easy to read.

第四节　伊丽莎白·巴莱特·勃朗宁

一、作家简介

伊丽莎白·巴莱特·勃朗宁（1806—1861）被公认为是英国最伟大的诗人之一。她的作品涉及广泛的议题和思想。勃朗宁夫人的诗歌主要有三方面的主题：（1）纯粹的爱情：《葡萄牙十四行诗集》是根据自己的亲身经历和感受创作出来的爱情诗集。诗歌语言委婉亲切，动人心弦，体现其细致唯美的写作风格。（2）人道主义精神：勃朗宁虽然出身于种植园主家庭，但她坚决反对奴隶制度，作品里处处体现着对黑人尤其是对女黑奴的同情，以及对奴隶制度的憎恶的人道主义精神。（3）女权主义精神：勃朗宁夫人关注维多利亚时代中产阶级妇女的需求和命运，思索着应该如何把妇女从枷锁中解脱出来，她以独特的女性视角审视女权主义这一社会性的问题。

二、主要作品简介

（一）《葡萄牙十四行诗》

《葡萄牙十四行诗》共4首，是女诗人专门献给自己的丈夫罗伯特的情诗，生动形象地表现了女诗人从疑虑到热恋的复杂爱情心理过程。诗人除了在每一首作品中进行连贯的感情表达外，在整部诗集中，也同样清晰地呈现这种起承转合的情感轨迹，从而使这一整部诗集成为勃朗宁夫人的爱情自传的诗体演绎。在表现上，诗人使用多种艺术手段使得单纯吟咏爱情地诗篇产生了厚重而多彩的魅力。诗人大胆使用复沓的方式，以相同诗情的反复咏唱增加诗歌的感染力，并且展开丰富想象，运用清新生动的比喻表达强烈情感。

（二）《奥罗拉·利》

《奥罗拉·利》是勃朗宁夫人的一首叙事诗。这是一首无韵诗，分为九部。以奥罗拉的视角用第一人称叙述。在前五部中，奥罗拉叙述了她的过去，从孩童时期到 27 岁。第六部到第九部中，叙述她现在的生活。在这首诗中，勃朗宁夫人表达了女性独立的女性主义观点，为女性思想自由和性别平等进行了辩护。勃朗宁夫人认为该诗是一部诗体小说，并把它称作自己最成熟的作品，反映了诗人最成熟的生活和艺术见解。

（三）《逃跑的奴隶》

《逃跑的奴隶》是勃朗宁夫人作为一名女性诗人反对奴隶制度，反对对黑人女奴的虐待与压迫的一部作品。作者运用女性的口吻构建了母亲与孩子之间的信条，这也正是人道主义者们所关心的话题。

三、选读作品赏析

"How Do I love thee"

This is a delicately crafted piece of verse which captures the love and affection of one person to another beautifully. It expresses the poet's intense love for her husband-to-Robert browning. So intense is her love for him, she says, that it rises to the spiritual level (lines 3 and 4). She loves him freely, without coercion; she loves him purely, without expectation of personal gain. She even loves him with an intensity of the suffering (passion: line 9) resembling that of Christ on the cross, and she loves him in the way that she loved saints as a child. Loving her husband with the "breath, smiles tears" of her life further emphasize this, as these three words represent three important aspects of life "breath" means the essence of her being, in other words her soul, while "smiles" and "tears" represents the "ups" and "downs" of life. By using these three different components of human life to describe her love for her husband she reinforces the idea that she is actively convincing herself that her relationship with her husband is perfect. Moreover, she expects to continue to love him after death.

The phrase I love thee is repeated many times throughout the poem which emphasizes the idea that her love seems genuine and heartfelt, imparting the sonnet with a sense of emotional fervor.

The poet uses a variety of repetitions and religious associations to accentuate the fact that their love exceeds the level of simple emotional exchange but is rather a Jane decides to obey Gods will and flees into the vast moorland, penniless. There, she almost starves herself to death but for the kindness of st. John rivers and his two sisters, who turn out to be Jane's cousins on her fathers side. There Jane finds refuge with the Rivers and nurses her wound by devoting herself to teaching children. There she also finds herself heiress to a handsome sum of money from her uncle. Cousin John a young clergyman who has made up his mind to sacrifice his own passion for Gods mission, asks Jane to go to India as his wife. Jane refuses this loveless proposal. She decides to go back to Thorn field, which is in complete ruin. She learns that the house had been set on fire, and Mr. Rochester, in order to save his wife, is seriously injured and blinded. Jane finds him in the secluded country house, Ferndean, a miserable and lonely man. She readily stays, and the two are happily married and lead a contented life ever after.

Ever since its publication, Jane Eyre has appealed to the general reading public. It is known as one of the most popular works of the working middle-class women. It's social criticism is found in its vivid description of life of a poor orphan left dependent on some selfish, cold-hearted people and her hard struggle to retain her dignity as a human being. The ill-treatment of and despise for the unfortunate lower class by the rich and the privileged are clearly shown. What is more, the brutality and hypocrisy of the english educational system are laid bare here in the example of Lowood School where children are exposed to unbearably harsh conditions and unreasonably rigid disciplines and are trained to be humble slaves only. On the other hand, the idle and vain life of the corrupted rich is also vividly depicted and sharply criticized.

Another factor for the popularity of the novel lies in the fact that it is the first governess novel in the history of English literature. Upon its first publication, the contemporary readers were fascinated as well as shocked by its titular heroine. Instead of the rich, gentle, frail, modest and virtuous beauties of the conventional heroine, here we have a small, plain, poor governess who begins her life all alone, with no body caring for her and nothing attractive. What she has is an intense feeling a ready sympathy and a strong sense of equality and independence. And she, in defiance of the social convention, dares to love her master, declares it openly, and finally marries him when he is in the most wretched situation. All this should certainly disqualify her as a heroine due to the then social prejudices. However, the young lady, for all her obscurity and inferiority, stands out as one of the most remarkable fictional heroines of the time. Her very unconventionality marks her as an entirely new woman.

Besides Jane's exceptional personalities, the book is also hailed as a representative work of feminist writings, works reflecting the experience and defending the interest of the weaker sex. In a way, it speaks not only for those unfortunate governesses like Jane but all the middle-class women and women of all classes Jane's declaration to Mr Rochester of her equality with him is really a declaration of the women of middle class and all classes. Such an independent and equal attitude was an astonishment and wonder to people of the day, but it is the first manifestation of the awakening of the exploited and maltreated women. Jane, small and weak as she is, becomes an amazon fighting for the emancipation of women.

In maintaining the conventional autobiographical form, the author uses two frames in the novel. The first is the exterior frame which depicts the objective picture of life as it is, with people of all kinds from the high to the low, from the rich to the poor, and from the clergy to the laymen, with different houses and natural scenery of different seasons and with the life of the heroine marked out by the change of geographical locations and environments and social relations. The other is an interior one which on the basis of the outer frame, tries to present a subjective picture of Jane, s thoughts, feelings and attitudes to the other people, through her dreams, her paintings and her meditations These two frames are not kept apart but are frequently interwoven; often the objective becomes the objectified subjective thoughts and feelings of the heroine.

第五节　艾米莉·勃朗特

一、作家简介

艾米莉·勃朗特（1818—1848），19 世纪英国作家与诗人，著名的勃朗特三姐妹之二，世界文学名著《呼啸山庄》的作者，而且这其实也是她一生中唯一一部小说，正是这部小说奠定了她在英国文学史以及世界文学史上的地位。此外，她还创作了 193 首诗，被认为是英国一位天才型的女作家。艾米莉·勃朗特一家居住在荒原附近，一向离群索居，四个兄弟姊妹便常以读书、写作诗歌，以及杜撰传奇故事来打发寂寞的时光。艾米莉表面沉默寡言，内心却热情奔放。作品中对极端爱情和人格的描写令人印象非常深刻。同时，她酷爱自己生长其间的荒原，最喜欢和大自然为友，从她的诗和作品中都可以看见她天人合一的宇宙观和人生观，被认为是神秘主义者。

二、主要作品简介

（一）《呼啸山庄》

《呼啸山庄》是一个爱情和复仇的故事，通过三十多年的时间跨度，叙述了恩肖和林敦两家两代人的感情纠葛，被誉为"最奇特的小说"，艾米莉·勃朗特也以她唯一的一部小说，奠定了她在英国文学史以及世界文学史上的地位。

（二）《贡达尔传奇》（*Gondal Saga*）

艾米丽在创作《呼啸山庄》之前的 10 年间，陆续写出了《贡达尔传奇》和大量的抒情诗。

贡达尔是艾米丽在 12 岁左右时和妹妹安妮作为游戏背景而创作的一个虚拟王国。在贡达尔王国里，各家庭之间矛盾重重、争权夺利，艾米丽以一个传奇式的故事为线索，叙述了皇族中两家人围绕着岛国王位进行竞争，以及女王与她的情人们所演出的一幕幕曲折离奇、缠绵悱恻的爱情故事。

三、选读作品赏析

An Excerpt from Wuthering Heights

The novel，Wuthering Heights，concerns two symmetrical families and an intruding stranger. The Earnshaw family ——a bluff prosperous Yorkshire-man, his wife, their son Hindley and their daughter Catherine——live in their handsome farmhouse Wuthering.

Heights up in the folds of the moors. The Linton family, richer and more civilized landed gentry——Mr. Linton, his wife, their son Edgar and their daughter Isabella——live down below in the valley at Thrushcross Grange. One day, Mr. Earnshaw brings home to the Heights a sallow, rugged found-ling he has found wandering in the streets of Liverpool, where he has been for business, whom he names Heathcliff. The children grow up together; Cather-ine comes to love Heathcliff while Hindley hates him from jealousy of his fa-ther's fondness for the waif. When the parents die, Hindley, in revenge, de-grades Heathcliff in every way he can; the lad grows brutal and morose. What is more Catherine, though fundamentally she cares for Heathcliff more than anyone else, is attracted to the handsome and mild Edgar Linton. Hurt by Catherine's vainglory Heathcliff runs away and returns three years later, rich and with the manners of a gentleman, concealing his dark, fierce heart, to find Catherine married to Edgar Between Edgar and Heathcliff, Catherine becomes distracted; she dies while giving birth to Edgar's daughter, little Catherine. Heathcliff, who has married Isabella, Edgars silly sister, in revenge, deeply grieves over Catherines death, thus hastening his revenge on his rivals. At Wuthering Heights, he gets Hindley into his clutches, winning his property from him by gambling and finally driving him to drink himself to death, leaving his son Hareton , a pauper at Wuthering Heights. Heathcliff also torments Is-abella to death. Then he manages to marry young Catherine to his own peevish ailing son Linton. Edgar dies of grief in 1801. Soon Heathcliffs son Linton dies too. Heathcliff is left in full possession of the properties of both Wuthering Heights and Thrushcross grange and the two children of his enemies to be tor-mented at his pleasure. But just at the climax of his revenge, events suddenly take another turn. Ever since her death, Heathcliff has been tortured by the memories of the first Catherine, and now, about 18 years later, he begins one day to actually see her ghost. He forgets his schemes of revenge, forgets even to sleep and eat with eyes fixed on his supernatural visitor, he slowly starves himself to death Meanwhile, the young Catherine is trying her best to change the savage, cruel Hareton and the two fall in love with each other. At Heathcliffs death, they retire to dwell happily at Thrush cross grange, while the spirits of Heathcliff and the first Catherine united at last, remain in possession of Wuthering Heights Wuthering Heights is a riddle which has meant so many things to so many people.

第六节　马修·阿诺德

一、作家简介

马修·阿诺德（1822—1888），英国近代诗人、教育家，评论家。在英国的教育史上，马修·阿诺德与其父托马斯·阿诺德均有重要影响。马修·阿诺德著有《报告集》，出版后即被指定为教师候选人的必读书。阿诺德的评论在维多利亚时代首屈一指，主张批评不应局限于文学，也应用于神学、历史、艺术、科学、社会与政治。关于诗的内容，阿诺德在《评华兹华斯》一文中主张，诗应该是诗人对于"生活的批判"，诗人应将道德观念应用在生活上。他肯定了诗的道德意义和教育意义，否定了歪曲生活、嘲笑生活与唯美主义的诗。

二、主要作品简介

（一）《评论荷马史诗译本》

《评论荷马史诗译本》发表于 1861 年，收录了阿诺德 1860 年 11—12 月在牛津大学任教时的公开课文本。阿诺德主要讨论了如何运用他的文学批评理论来分析荷马史诗及其翻译作品。他对不同版本的译本进行了比较和批评，指出在翻译荷马史诗时译者需要注意的诗人的四个基本特点。

（二）《文化与无政府状态》

《文化与无政府状态》于 1869 年出版，一定程度上也是对两年前通过的议会选举法修正法案中普及公民权内容的一个回应。当时第一个选举法修正法案被否决，改革团体组织的示威活动在海德公园举行，警察闻讯赶来与民众发生冲突。马修·阿诺德相信，唯有文化才是解决这种混乱的有效手段。阿诺德心目中的文化，不是僵化的精英文化传统，更绝非仅仅满口拉丁文，它是从属于任何阶级的任何个体自我修养的需要。在一个价值失衡的年代，阿诺德渴望文化取代日渐衰落的宗教与哲学的作用，以至于他会称"我们目前视为宗教和哲学的绝大部分东西将被诗歌取代"。

三、选读作品赏析

" *Dover beach*"

In this poem, the speaker looks over the shore at Dover and reflects on the scene before him. The first stanza opens with the description of a nightly scene at the seaside. The lyrical self calls his addressee to the window, to share the visual beauty of the scene. Then he calls her attention to the aural experience, which is somehow less beautiful. The lyrical self projects his own feelings of melancholy on to the sound, which causes an emotion of "sadness" in him.

The second stanza introduces the Greek author Sophocles'idea of "the turbid ebb and flow of human misery". A contrast is formed to the scenery of the previous stanza Sophocles apparently heard the similar sound at the "Aegean" sea and thus developed his ideas. Arnold then reconnects this idea to the present. Although there is a distance in time and space, the general feeling prevails.

In the third stanza, the sea is turned into the Sea of Faith, which is a metaphor for a time when religion could still be experienced without the doubt that the victorian age brought about through Darwinism, the Industrial Revolution, Imperialism, etc. Arnold illustrates this by using an image of clothes. When religion was still intact, the world was dressed. Now that this faith is gone, the world lies there stripped naked and Bleak.

The final stanza begins with a dramatic pledge by the lyrical self. He asks his love to be "true" to him. For the beautiful scenery that presents itself to them is really not what it seems to be. On the contrary, as he accentuates with a series of denials, this world does not contain any basic human values. These have disappeared, along with the light and religion and left humanity in darkness. We could just refer to the lyrical self and his love, but it could also be interpreted as the lyrical self-addressing humanity. The pleasant scenery turns into a "darkling plain", where only hostile, frightening sounds of fighting armies can be heard.

第七节　杰拉尔德·曼利·霍普金斯

一、作家简介

杰拉尔德·曼利·霍普金斯（1844—1889）是一名英国诗人、罗马天主教徒及耶稣会神父，其故后在 20 世纪的声誉，使他成为最负盛名的维多利亚诗人。霍普金斯在写作技巧上进行了多种变革，最为人所知的是他使用的"跳韵"（sprung rhythm），这种韵律更关注重音的出现而不是音节数量本身。霍普金斯的诗歌主题主要围绕着爱、政治和公民权利、宗教和道德以及大自然。尤其是诗人对大自然的热爱和细致观察反映在他的多首诗歌中。例如，《春天》《星夜》《茶隼》，等等。内容表现自然界万物的个性以及诗人对大自然的感怀，宗教色彩浓厚。

二、主要作品简介

（一）《德意志号的沉没》

这首长诗写于 1875—1876 年，但直至 1918 年才出版。这首诗描述了德意志号可怕的沉船事件。这些在这场事故中丧生的人们中有五个被迫离开德国的方济各会的修女，这首诗就是献给她们的。因为它的长度、主题和跳韵的使用，这首诗被认为是霍普金斯最杰出的作品。

（二）《诗集》

霍普金斯开始写的诗无人赏识，只是手稿在布里吉斯等少数几个友人间传诵，在他死后近 30 年始为布里吉斯收集并编成全集出版为诗集（1918），初版时仍不受欢迎。直到 1930 年再版时，他的独特风格和创新精神始为新的一代人所接受、赞赏，模仿者日益增多，影响渐趋深远。

三、选读作品赏析

" *The Windhover*"

The windhover is a bird with the rare ability to hover in the air, essentially flying in place while it scans the ground in search of prey. The poet describes how he saw one of these birds in the midst of its hovering. The bird strikes the poet as the darling of the morning, the crown prince of the kingdom of daylight, drawn by the dappled colors of dawn. It rides the air as if it were on horseback, moving with steady control like a rider whose hold on the rein is sure and firm. In the poet's imagination, the windhover sits high and proud, tightly reined in, wings quivering and tense. Its motion is controlled and suspended in an ecstatic moment of concentrated energy. Then, in the next moment, the bird is off again, now like an ice skater balancing forces as he makes a turn. The bird first matching the winds force in order to stay still, now "rebuffs the big wind" with its forward propulsion. At the same moment, the poet feels his own heart stir, or lurch forward out of "hiding", as it were- moved by "the mastery of" the bird's performance.

The opening of the sestet serves as both a further elaboration on the bird's movement and an injunction to the poet's own heart. The "beauty", "valor", and "act" "here buckle". Buckle is the verb here; it denotes either a fastening, a coming together of these different parts of a creature's being, or an acquiescent collapse, in which all parts subordinate themselves into some larger purpose or cause. In either case, a unification takes place. At the moment of this integration, a glorious fire issues forth, of the same order as the glory of Christ's life and crucifixion, though not as grand The confusing grammatical structures and sentence order in this sonnet contribute to its difficulty, but they also represent a masterful use of language. Hopkins blends and confuses adjectives, verbs, and subjects in order to echo his theme of smooth merging the birds perfect immersion in the air, and the fact that his self and his action areindividual, which a concerted religious life can expose. The subsequent image is of embers breaking open to reveal a smoldering interior. Hopkins words this image so as to relate the concept back to the Crucifixion. The verb "gash" (which doubles for "gush") suggests the wounding of Christ's body and the shedding of his" gold-vermilion" blood.

第八节　托马斯·哈代

一、作家简介

托马斯·哈代（1840—1928），英国诗人、小说家。他是横跨两个世纪的作家，早期和中期的创作以小说为主，继承和发扬了维多利亚时代的文学传统；晚年以其出色的诗歌开拓了英国 20 世纪的文学。以真实地再现生活和社会批判著称的哈代的作品，对维多利亚时期的腐朽、不公和伪善的社会体制，对资本主义的残酷剥削，对功利主义的商业气息以及非人的社会传统道德进行了辛辣的揭露和尖锐的批判。

二、主要作品简介

（一）《还乡》

这部小说讲述了一个年轻女子一心想逃出位于广袤荒凉的埃格登荒原上的沉闷、落后的农村生活和一个一心想改造这个荒原的男人的故事。富于野性的强大的埃格登荒原成了掌握和摧毁人类命运的原始自然力的象征。游斯苔莎、魏尔蒂夫和克利姆的悲剧是古老而原始的农村与现代城市文明之间矛盾的不可避免的结局。整部小说被一种压抑的沉闷的气氛所笼罩。

（二）《卡斯特桥市长》

束草工亨查德醉酒后在庙会上把妻女卖给过路的水手。当他酒醒后，妻女已不知去向。带着一颗内疚的心，他发誓 20 年不再饮酒。此后他勤奋努力，终于发家致富，成了卡斯特桥市市长。18 年后，妻子以为水手已死，就携女归来。亨查德与前妻重修旧好过着幸福生活。妻子过世后，女儿的身世也暴露了。亨查德从前的合伙人与他发生争吵后，反目成仇，成为他生意上和爱情上的对手，并四处撒布亨查德曾经出卖妻女的丑行。亨查德一时声名狼藉。亨查德又开始酗酒。当女儿也被当水手的生父领走之后，亨查德隐居埃格登荒原，最后在贫困、孤独中死去。

（三）《无名的裘德》

裘德是个可怜的孤儿，早年曾梦想上大学，毕业后成一名牧师。在美色的引诱下，他与一个自负的女子结了婚。后来，他与表妹苏·布莱德赫德相遇。表妹是个聪明能干、精力充沛的年轻教师，嫁给了一个年老的校长为妻。他俩堕入情网，并分别断绝了各自的婚姻关系，最后在一起共同生活了几年。由于他们的行为不能被当时的礼法接受，所以始终都没有结婚。两人都受到良心的谴责。孩子惨死的悲剧使他们的精神遭到毁灭性的打击。苏在自责和自卑中回到了原来丈夫的身边。裘德也被前妻带回，整日耽于杯中之物，后郁郁而终。

三、选读作品赏析

"The man he killed"

Superficially this is a simple, uncomplicated piece, but in fact, it is a very skilful poem heavily laden with irony and making interesting use of colloquialism. The title is slightly odd, as Hardy uses the third-person pronoun, he though the poem is narrated n the first person. The "he" of the title is evidently a soldier attempting to explain and perhaps justify his killing of another man in battle.

In the first stanza the narrator establishes the common ground between himself and his victim: in more favorable circumstances they could have shared hospitality together. This idea is in striking contrast to that in the second stanza: the circumstances in which the men did meet. "Ranged as infantry" suggests that the men are not natural foes but have been "ranged", that is set against each other (by someone else's decision) . The phrase as he at me indicates the similarity of their situations.

In the third stanza the narrator gives his reason for shooting the supposed enemy. The conversational style of the poem enables Hardy to repeat the word because implying hesitation, and therefore doubt, on the part of the narrator. He cannot at first easily think of a reason. When he does so, the assertion is utterly unconvincing. The speaker has already made clear the sense in which the men were foes: an artificial enmity created by others. "Of course" and "That's clear enough" are blatantly ironic: the enmity is not a matter of course, the claim is far from "clear" to the reader, and the pretence of assurance on the narrators part is destroyed by his admission beginning with Although.

The real reason for the victims enlistment in the army, like the narrators, is far rom being connected with patriotic idealism and belief in his country's cause. The soldiers joining was partly whimsical and partly the result of economic necessity: he was unemployed and had already sold off his possessions. He did not enlist for any other reason.

The narrator concludes with a repetition of the contrast between his treatment of the man he killed and how he might have shared hospitality with him in other circumstances or even been ready to extend charity to him. He prefaces this with the statement that war is "quaint and curious", as if to say, "a funny old thing". This tends to show war as innocuous and acceptable, but the events narrated in the poem, as well as the readers general knowledge of war, make it clear that conflict is far from quaint and curious and Hardy employs the terms with heavy irony, knowing full well how inaccurate such a description really is.

This is a rather bitter poem that provides an accurate description of the true nature of war. Increasingly, the decision to go to war is taken by the powers that are not representative of the emotions of citizens. The two men described in the poem had joined the war purely because they had no other option, not due to any deep conviction about the causes for it. As such, they are forced to fight for their lives and effectively commit cold-blooded murder in the name of something they do not even believe in. The poem orces the reader to closely examine the realities of war, and inspires disbelief in and anger at the prevailing system, which allows such events to occur.

第六章　现代时期的英国文学解读与作品赏析

一、主要文学特色

现代主义源于对资本主义的怀疑和对资本主义理想的幻灭。这使得作家和艺术家去探索新的方法来表达对世界和人性的理解。法国象征主义是现代主义的先驱。第一次世界大战加速了各种现代主义文学流派的兴起，到 20 世纪 20 年代各种流派汇合而形成一股强大的现代主义潮流。现代主义运动的主要人物有卡夫卡、毕加索、庞德、艾略特、乔伊斯以及沃尔夫。20 世纪 30 年代现代主义的发展在一定程度上受到抑制，但第二次世界大战之后，现代主义的变体（或叫后现代主义）在萨特的存在主义的刺激下重新抬头。然而，到 20 世纪 60 年代它们渐渐消失或者融入了其他的文学流派之中。

非理性哲学和心理分析是现代主义的理论基础。探索人与自然、人与社会、人与人以及人与自身之间扭曲的、疏远的、病态的、敌意的关系是现代主义文学的主题。现代主义的主要特征有：它以对过去义无反顾的、自觉的决裂为标志，抛弃过去的伦理、宗教和文化价值；它注重描写个人而非群体，强调主观而非客观；它非常关注个人的内心世界，赞同一种新的时间观，心理时间比物理时间显得更为重要，所以作品中过去、现在和未来是一个整体，混合在一起同时存在于某个个体的意识中；从很多方面来看，现代主义与现实主义都是截然相反的，它摒弃理性，而理性是现实主义的理论基础，它不关注外部的、客观的物质世界，而这些却是现实主义文学的创作源泉，现代主义提倡自由探索文学的新形式、新手法，摈弃了几乎所有传统的文学因素，如故事、情节、人物、按时间顺序的叙事等，而这些是现实主义文学所必不可少的，因此，现代主义作家的作品常被称为是反小说、反诗歌与反戏剧。

意识流文学是现代主义文学的重要分支之一，泛指注重描绘人物意识流动状态的文学作品。作家可以不必借助于客观的描述或传统的对话来描写人物内心的思绪和情感。英国现代派小说家詹姆斯乔伊斯和弗吉尼亚沃尔夫努力挖掘人类各种潜意识，是这种方法的支持者和实践者，开创了史无前例的意识流小说。同时，术语"内心独白"也被用来描述人物内心的意识活动。

二、主要作家与作品

萧伯纳，爱尔兰剧作家，文学评论家，1925 年诺贝尔文学奖得主，主要作品有《皮格马利翁》《华伦夫人的职业》《芭芭拉少校》等。阿尔弗雷德·爱德华·豪斯曼，英国学者、诗人，主要作品有诗集《什罗普郡少年》《最后的诗》等。约翰·高尔斯华绥，英国小说家、剧作家，英国批判现实主义作家，代表作为《福塞特世家》。威廉·巴特勒·叶芝，爱尔兰诗人、剧作家，代表作品有《茵纳斯弗利岛》《走过黄柳园》《第二次降临》等。T. S. 艾略特，诗人、评论家、剧作家，1948 诺贝尔文学奖得主，主要作品有《灰色星期四》《四个四重奏》《荒原》等。詹姆斯·乔伊斯，爱尔兰作家、诗人，主要作品有《都柏林人》《尤利西斯》等。戴·赫·劳伦斯，英国小说家，主要作品有《儿子与情人》《虹》《恋爱中的女人》等。威廉·戈尔丁，英国小说家，诗人，20世纪现实主义文学的代表人物，1983 年诺贝尔文学奖得主，代表作品为《蝇王》。塞缪尔·贝克特，20 世纪爱尔兰、法国作家，荒诞派戏剧的重要代表人物，1969 年诺贝尔文学奖得主，代表作品为《等待戈多》。狄兰·托马斯，英国诗人、作家，人称"疯狂的狄兰"，代表作品有《死亡与出场》《当我天生的五官都能看见》《请别柔声地对人生道晚安》等。特德·休斯，英国作家、桂冠诗人，代表作品有《栖息之鹰》《雨中鹰》等。谢默斯·希尼，爱尔兰作家、诗人、诗学专家，1995 年诺贝尔文学奖得主，主要作品有诗集《一位自然主义者之死》《通向黑暗之门》《在外过冬》等。下面介绍萧伯纳的《皮格马利翁》的主题和主要人物性格的分析；高尔斯华绥的代表作《福塞特世家》的主题和主要人物性格的分析；叶芝诗歌创作的特色，以及著名诗作如《茵纳斯弗利岛》《走过黄柳园》《第二次降临》等的赏析；艾略特诗歌创作的特色，以及他主要作品的主题、写作手法以及象征的运用；乔伊斯小说的写作技巧，如意识流手法，以及主要作品的主题和人物性格的分析；劳伦斯小说的特色和主要作品的主题与人物性格分析；戈尔丁的小说《蝇王》的主题和人物性格分析；贝克特的戏剧创作特色，以及他的主要作品《等待戈多》的主题和人物分析。

第一节　萧伯纳

一、作者简介

萧伯纳（Bernard shaw，1863—1950）受到尼采的哲学思想和马克思的《资本论》的影响，对社会主义产生了浓厚的兴趣，并力图通过民主的方法揭露资本主义的罪恶，教育广大民众，最终实现社会主义。他主张文学应该反映社会问题，强烈反对为艺术而艺术的信条。作为现实主义的剧作家，萧伯纳将现代社会问题作为其戏剧创作的主题，并希望以此指导社会改革。他的戏剧有强烈的喜剧效果，依靠对话和人物内心世界的展示来吸引观众。1925 年萧伯纳获得诺贝尔文学奖。

二、主要作品简介

（一）《华伦夫人的职业》

主人公薇薇发现母亲华伦夫人是欧洲几个城市里的一系列妓院的股东兼经理，由此而与母亲产生了矛盾。因不能原谅母亲的职业选择，薇薇终于与母亲决裂，并在伦敦找到份"诚实的"工作自食其力。在该剧中，萧伯纳揭示了卖淫的罪恶，并将其归咎于社会制度。另一方面，该剧也揭示了女主人公薇薇从幻灭走向现实的心路历程。

（二）《皮格马利翁》

语言学教授希金斯与皮克林上校打赌，要在 6 个月内把一个下层社会的女子培养成为上流社会的淑女。言语粗俗的卖花女伊丽莎·多利特成了这一赌局的试验品。经过刻苦学习，伊丽莎变得谈吐高雅、仪态端庄。最后在一次大型舞会上，赢得了众人的赞美，并被皇家语音专家认为是某国的公主。教授回家后，兴高采烈地向上校索要赌金，完全忽视了伊丽莎，伊丽莎一怒之下，愤然离去。此时若有所失的教授才感到伊丽莎已成为自己生活的一部分。希金斯把这个赌局简单地看作一项科学实验，忽视了实验对象的情感，以及身份改变后的归宿。该剧展示了伊丽莎从幻想到现实的精神之旅，从无知的黑暗走向了自我意识的光明，最终获得了独立的精神、坚强的个性和成熟的思想。

三、选读作品赏析

An Excerpt from Pygmalion

Pygmalion tells the story of Henry Higgins, a professor of phonetics (speech), who bets his friend that he can pass off a poor flower girl with a Cockney accent as a duchess by teaching her to speak with an upper class accent. This play represents Shaw's attempt to not just use words and language to create art and raise questions, but to force readers to examine the power and purpose of language itself. Reading Pygmalion, we come to learn that communication is about more than words, and everything from clothing to accents to physical bearing can affect the way people interact with each other. Like all of Shaws great dramatic creations, Pygmalion is a richly complex play. It combines a central story of the transformation of a young woman with elements of myth fairy tale and romance, while also combining an interesting plot with an exploration of social dentity, the power of science, relations between men and women, and other issues. Change is central to the plot and theme of the play. The importance of transformation in Pygmalion at first appears to rest upon the power Higgins expresses by achieving his goal. But where the real transformation occurs is in Eliza. Much more important than her new powers of speech, ultimately, is the independence she gains after the conclusion of Higgins's experiment.

Act Four is the most climatic of all acts as it is when Eliza has a realization of her worth as well as a sense of who she is and where her destiny lies. Eliza, Colonel Pickering and higgins have been out to a fashionable ball where Eliza has been a triumphant success. She has been passed off as a lady to such an extent that many of the people at the ball laughed in Higgins' face when he told them the truth about Eliza's origins. While the two men begin talking, Eliza sits alone. The men are tired and talk about how exacting the whole affair has been and are glad that now the tomfoolery is over. All this time, Eliza sits miserably and absolutely silent. The insensitive remarks of the men shock her. She has gone through a lot during the last six months. While it has been hard work for Higgins it has been much harder for Eliza herself. Both the men do not realize that the credit for the success of their experiment belongs as much to Eliza as it does to them.

It is at this moment that the Cinderella fairy tale is over. It is the hour of midnight a time for encountering the reality of the situation. Higgins trivializes Eliza's strenuous efforts and takes most of the credit for edifying her. This hurts her, as she has invested as much as they have in her edification. In the midst of this sudden deflation, Eliza awakens to the falsity of her Cinderella fantasies. A lesser dramatist would have hastily concluded the play after the triumphant test scene but delves deeper and confronts the reader with the problem of Eliza's dissatisfaction and unhappiness about being made a lady. He is more interested in what happens to the work of art after the creation of it has been presented to the public.

Eliza's awakening to social reality is expressed in her heartfelt cry of despair what's to become of me? For the first time she becomes aware of her loneliness and isolation as well as her inability to be a proper lady because she lacks the financial resources to be fully independent yet she cannot continue to live with Higgins. Mrs Pearce and Mrs. Higgins had earlier foreseen the problem of her future. Higgins' mother had in fact warned him about the disadvantages of imparting to Elizathe manners and criticism of social barriers and class distinctions and it upholds the ideal of equal opportunities of wealth and education for all, regardless of class and gender. It exposes the sham of genteel standards and examines the real difference between a lady and a flower girl, a gentleman and a dustman. It is a scathing criticism of the Victorian concept of the undeserving poor, who were accused of bringing their indigent state upon themselves due to vice.

Shaw believed firmly in the power of individuals to transform, to improve themselves. Drawing on a power Shaw called the Life Force, human beings could both evolve to the full extent of their capabilities and collectively turn to the task of transforming society. What Eliza learns by breaking free of Higgins's influence is an independence of thought Shaw believed was a crucial component of personal evolution Pygmalion is a refreshing mixture of comedy and satire. The play is vibrant and joyful. The dialogues sparkle with wit and humor.

第二节　豪斯曼

一、作者简介

阿尔弗雷德·爱德华·豪斯曼（1859—1936）的诗歌字斟句酌，格律严谨，音调优美，读来朗朗上口，不同于同时代诗人的风格，模仿英国民间歌谣，追求简朴平易，使用最简单的常用词汇使诗歌具有音乐的美感。诗的内容大多是哀叹青春易逝，美景不长，爱人负心，朋友多变，大自然冷漠无情，人生的追求虚幻如梦。他是同性恋者，诗中有深刻的悲观主义，但同时也表现出对苦难的普通大众的同情。

二、主要作品简介

青年时期，豪斯曼去到什罗普郡，这个地方给他留下了深刻的印象，1896年他自费出版了第一部诗集《什罗普郡少年》，用该地象征乡村田园的神秘和魅力，从此诗名日著。1922年出版《最后的诗》，获得更大的成功。逝世后，他的弟弟剧作家劳伦斯豪斯曼整理他的遗稿，辑成《集外诗作》，于1936年出版。

三、选读作品赏析

"When I Was One-and-Twenty"

The speaker begins his monologue by clearly expressing that at the age of twenty-one he was warned not to give his heart away by a wise man. He remembered exactly that the wise man suggested that he'd better give away the standard monetary currency of Crowns pounds and guineas and precious gems, such as pearls and rubies, rather than allow his "fancy", or love, to be restricted. At the end of the fist stanza, he admits that when he was twenty-one he was not likely to listen to the lessons taught by someone of experience. In the second stanza, the speaker tells us the second warning given by the wise man. Furthermore, we know the price for giving up the heart will be endless sorrow. In the last two lines, the speaker clearly expresses his agreement with the wise mans warnings, from which his pain of lost love was exposed. In the first stanza, the wise man, who knows the value of financial stability, has warned the young speaker of the poem that being poor is better than suffering the pain and despair of lost love. The implied information in the warning is that although you need money to buy food and shelter, it would be better to go without these necessities that keep you alive than to suffer in love. Heart is more precious than gems and should be protected even more carefully. The first stanza also implies a universal truth that the young usually do not listen to those older or wiser until they themselves suffer setbacks. From the second stanza, the poet makes us feel even more intensely that there is always an exchange in life and that one can never get something for nothing. By the end of the poem, we could clearly feel the speaker's agony. He begins his expression with "oh and repeats the phrase" is true, which suggests the intensity of the woe and sorrow felt, while continuing the poems musicality. The theme is typical of Housman's idea of mourning for the passing and uncertainty of the youth's love. Fortunately, through one years tragic love experience, the youth becomes mature and has a new perspective toward love and life. The rhyme scheme of the poem is ababacac, with short iambic meters. The poem transmits the tone of melancholy. The poet uses the style of English ballad and his verse is noted for its economy of words and directness of statement.

第三节　高尔斯华绥

一、作者简介

约翰·高尔斯华绥（1867—1933）是一个传统的作家。他的小说《有产业的人》获得广泛好评。他将小说家的视野带入戏剧，并探讨了由社会问题引起的伦理问题，颇具影响力。高尔斯华绥具有资产阶级自由主义改良倾向，对劳苦大众有深切的同情。艺术上，他深受维多利亚时代的小说家和大陆小说家的影响，通过讽刺，揭露了社会的不公正，以及对弱势群体的同情。

二、主要作品简介

《福塞特世家》，让高尔斯华绥名垂青史的是关于福赛特家族的三个三部曲，小说横跨 40 年的时空，今天依然被看作英国社会历史的有价值的记录。第一个三部曲包括《有产者》《骑虎》《出租》，第二个三部曲《现代喜剧》1929 年出版，第三个三部曲《尾声》于他死后的 1934 年出版。

三、选读作品赏析

An Excerpt from Chapter 13 of The Man of Property

James，the father，and Soames are discussing the house Soames builds for his wife Irene as well as the relationships between the couple. James wants to heal the relationship between his son and daughter-in-law and suggests that Soames take Irene to see the country house he is building for her. Then James and Soames part. Soames goes along in the train and James takes Irene down there to the house in a carriage. On their way, James tries to make Irene change her opinion and attitude towards her husband by saying that Soames is a good husband. But his effort turns out a futile attempt. At Soames' big house the three parties in the triangle Soames- Irene- Bosinney，are brought to face one another. Soames gets very angry and tries to make his revenge against his rival Bosinney by accusing him to have spent more money than stipulated. But his relentless action only makes Irene hate him even more. The excerpt ends with Soames indignation toward Irene's coldness to him.

This excerpt brings out the most essential information the book intends to convey. We get to know the definition of the spirit "Forsytism". Everything is measured in terms of property，including his wife Irene. He does not pay any attention to her feelings and thoughts，but considers her merely as a piece of his own property. Irene is not satisfied with their marriage and is drifting away from him. Soames can not stand the fact that his wife Irene is not his property in the real sense. So the tense relationship between husband and wife gets even worse. Irene is determined to leave her husband and Soames Forsytism is challenged by his wife.

第四节　叶芝

一、作者简介

威廉·巴特勒·叶芝（1865—1939）是一个温和的民族主义者，怀有民族骄傲感和对英国人压迫的憎恨。叶芝作为诗人、剧作家的奋斗目标是为爱尔兰观众描写爱尔兰，重塑一个独特的爱尔兰文学。叶芝的诗有两种趋向：关注人类生活、人际关系，关注个人的希望和抱负；或是乌托邦式的，关注预言，关注有限与无限、虚幻与永恒的关系。在诗歌风格上，叶芝早期的诗歌具有极强的韵律感和浪漫主义的传统，惯用丰富的修饰意象；中期则采用精确的意象，使诗歌通俗易懂、富有现实的表现力。他后期的诗歌加强了象征的使用每一个象征都是意义的核心。

二、主要作品简介

（一）《茵纳斯弗利岛》

茵纳斯弗利岛是一个湖中的水湾，在这里它指代隐士的住处。因为厌倦了现实生活，诗人向往一个理想的"天国"，希望像一个隐士那样安宁地生活，享受大自然的美丽。他认为治疗空虚的最好方法似乎就是回到过去简朴、安详的生活中去。该诗是叶芝最著名的抒情诗之一，结构紧凑，富于音乐感，包括三节五步抑扬格四行诗，每节的韵脚是 abab。

（二）《走过黄柳园》

这是一首关于人生本质问题的诗，带有浪漫的情调。爱情和生活就像长在树上的树叶和水坝上的绿草，它们有自己的生长规律。人们应该以一种顺其自然的方式来处理爱情和人生，不应掺杂过多的人为的干涉，因为这样只会违背自然规则。

（三）《第二次降临》

该诗写于 1919 年，当时整个世界，特别是欧洲正努力而缓慢地从第一次世界大战的阴影中恢复过来，爱尔兰处于动荡与流血冲突之中，西半球旧有的秩序被战争打乱。叶芝面对周遭形形色色的社会问题，为一个充满了罪恶、污染、混乱和颓废的世界发出悲叹，认为惨烈的战争似乎预示着旧有的基督教文明的终结，而一个可怕的时代即将来临。

三、选读作品赏析

" *The Lake isle of Innisfree*"

The poet declares that he will arise and go to Innisfree, where he will build a small cahin of clay and wattles made. He will have nine bean-rows and a beehive, and live alone in the glade. He says that he will have peace there, for peace drops from "the veils of morning to where the cricket sings". There is a glimmer at midnight, a purple glow at noon. And evening is full of linnet's wings. He declares again that he will arise and go for night and day he hears the lake water lapping "with low sounds by the shore". While he stands in the city, on the roadway, or on the pavements grey, he hears the sound within himself, in the deep heart's core. The poem is written mostly in hexameter with six stresses in each line, in a loosely iambic pattern. The last line of each four-line stanza shortens the line to tetrameter, with only four stresses. Each of the three stanzas has the same abab rhyme scheme.

This poem is one of Yeats'best-kmown lyrics. In Irish legends Innisfree is an inlet in the lake, and in this poem it is referring to a place for hermitage. Tired of the life of his day, Yeats desired to escape into an ideal "fairyland" where he could live peacefully as a hermit while enjoying the beauty of nature. He thought the best way to fulfill the emptiness of his age was to return to the simple and serene life of the past. Stylistically the poem is closely woven, easy, subtle and musical. The simply imagery of the quiet life the poet longs to lead brings the reader into his idyllic fantasy, until the penultimate line jolts the speaker back into the reality of his dull urban existence.

第五节 艾略特

一、作者简介

T. S. 艾略特（1888—1965）诗歌的主题是揭露西方文化的贫乏，揭示人与人之间沟通的衰竭，昭示人徘徊于意义和无意义之间所经受的幻灭感和挫折感，探询由宗教拯救而得到精神新生的途径。并置是艾略特诗歌的主要手法，结合反讽的手段，达到打动人心的效果。为了揭示人们的迷失感和无意义、无政府主义的混乱状态的整体面貌，他将那些来自古老神话、歌曲和经文片段，以及来自历史、宗教和现代生活的矛盾意象统统并置起来。他的诗歌有着丰富的古典的、圣经的和神话的典故，这是对读者的理解的一个挑战。艾略特还经常在他的诗集中用古老神话来表达人类在荒芜的世界里的挣扎和失败。都市的腐蚀、绝望与永恒的神话背景形成鲜明的对照。另外，音乐意象也在艾略特的诗歌中起了重要作用。

二、主要作品简介

（一）《灰色星期四》

这首诗表现了肉体和灵魂价值的冲突。主人公从厌世情绪到最终获得精神健康，使他能够去追寻存在于时间之中的永恒。这首诗不仅表明了艾略特对爱情的观点，而且也清楚地显示出他对英国国教的忠诚。

（二）《四个四重奏》

这是一部诗与乐完美结合的现代主义经典作品。这四首诗通过对基督教信条的具体化和重新阐释，旨在寻求永恒的因素。诗的主题是历史、诗意、爱情和信念。《四个四重奏》的哲学背景是西方传统的二元论思想，因此它呈现了有限与无限、瞬间与永恒、过去与未来、生与死等一系列二元论思想。《四个四重奏》同他早期作品的失望和痛苦完全不同，其特点体现在哲学上的和情感的宁静平和。

（三）《荒原》

《荒原》是现代英美诗歌的里程碑，是象征主义文学中最有代表性的作品，是艾略特最重要也是最有影响力的作品，被誉为 20 世纪英国诗歌划时代的经典和楷模，可以同华斯华兹的《抒情歌谣》媲美。因为在诗体和风格上的大胆革新，这首诗不仅全景式地展现了现代文明的物质紊乱和精神荒芜，也反映了战后整个一代人理想幻灭的普遍心境和绝望情绪。本诗的结构建立在时间对比的基础上，同时它也通过生与死、丰饶与贫瘠、爱与欲、理想与现实等意念的对比铺陈开来。

三、选读作品赏析

" *The Love Song of J. Alfred prufrock*"

This poem examines the tortured psyche of the prototypical modern man overeducated, eloquent, neurotic, and emotionally stilted. The poems speaker Prufrock, seems to be addressing a potential lover, with whom he would like to force the moment to its crisis by somehow consummating their relationship. In his mind he hears the comments others make about his inadequacies. He knows nearly everything about life and he doesn's dare an approach to the woman. Moving from a series of fairly concrete physical settings to a series of vague ocean images, the poem conveys Prufrock's emotional distance from the world as he comes to recognize his second-rate status. The poem is a variation of the dramatic monologue. Eliot modernizes the form by removing the implied listeners and focusing on Prufrock's interiority and isolation. The epigraph to this poem, from Dante's Inferno, describes Prufrock's ideal listener: one who is as lost as the speaker and will never betray to the world the content of Prufrock's confessions. For Prufrock, there is no such sympathetic person existing in the world.

The rhyme scheme of the poem is irregular but not random. In fact, it is a carefully structured amalgamation of poetic forms. The use of refrains is one of the most prominent formal characteristics of this work, which helps to describe the consciousness of a modern neurotic individual.

This poem displays the two most important characteristics of Eliot's early poetry. First, it is strongly influenced by the French Symbolists. The Symbolists privileged the same kind of individual Eliot creates with Prufrock: the moody, urban, isolated-yet sensitive thinker. The difference is that whereas the Symbolists would have been more likely to make their speaker himself a poet or artist, Eliot chooses to make Prufrock an unacknowledged poet, a sort of artist for the common man. The second defining characteristic of this poem is its use of fragmentation and juxtaposition. In this poem, the subjects undergoing fragmentation are mental focus and certain sets of imagery. Prufrock ends with the hero assigning himself a role in one of Shakespeare's plays which implies that there is still a continuity between Shakespeare's world and ours, that Hamlet is still relevant to us and that we are still part of a world that could produce something like Shakespeare's plays. It is implied that Eliot may now go on to create another Hamlet. The last line of the poem suggests that when the world intrudes, when human voices wake us, the dream is shattered "we drown". With this single line Eliot dismantles the romantic notion that poetic genius is all that is needed to triumph over the destructive, impersonal forces of the modern world. In fact, Eliot the poet is no better than his creation. He differs from Prufrock only by retaining a bit of hubris, which shows through from time to time.

第六节　乔伊斯

一、作者简介

詹姆斯·乔伊斯（1882—1941）是 20 世纪最重要的作家之一。他的作品都以爱尔兰，特别是都柏林为背景，主题都是爱尔兰人民和他们的生活。乔伊斯认为任何带来美感的事物都可以作为艺术主题，有创造力的艺术家应该关注美。至于如何领会美，乔伊斯沿用了阿奎那关于鉴赏美的三大要素理论，即整体、和谐及清晰。他认为文学艺术可以大致分为三种类型，即抒情型、叙事型和戏剧型，同时他也认为艺术家具有双重身份：一方面他是无意识的接受者；另一方面，他是有意识的转换者。在他看来，戏剧型艺术是最高形式的艺术，艺术家必须保持完全客观的立场才能达到最高的境界。乔伊斯认为，喜剧是最完美的艺术形式，所以他坚持在自己的作品中表现喜剧。

二、主要作品简介

（一）《都柏林人》

《都柏林人》被誉为是"一部爱尔兰的道德史"，从四个方面描写了爱尔兰人民的生活——童年、青年、成年以及公众生活。15 个故事由简单到复杂，每一篇都有一个完整的故事情节，来揭示人的心灵挫折和失败。这部作品代表了都柏林道德堕落的全过程，以灵魂的死亡为结局。麻痹和停滞是小说的中心主题。在乔伊斯看来，爱尔兰被英国征服不仅导致了政治上的奴役，更重要的是导致了精神和心理的奴役。现代主义的中心原则之一便是西方文化的麻痹，即无力进入一个新的生命视野和当代思想体系的停滞。逃离都柏林这个城市的束缚，逃离它幽闭、停滞不前的社会环境以及生命和青春的腐败也是这部小说集的主题。

（二）《一个青年艺术家的画像》

小说的题目暗示了这是一部带有自传色彩的人物性格分析小说，但它不是一部单纯的个体心灵成长史，而是与爱尔兰民族寻求自由的历史纠缠在一起。主人公斯蒂芬是一位敏感的青年，他被来自环境的过于强大的压力所塑造，但渐渐意识到这种压迫，并起来反抗它，最终找到自我。小说的结构是建立在斯蒂芬·迪达勒斯从少年到成人的三维成长过程（身体的、精神的和艺术的）基础上的。为了避免结构的松散，使小说更具有艺术的魅力，乔伊斯还运用了蒙太奇手法来组织小说。

（三）《尤利西斯》

《尤利西斯》是一部罕见的作品，因为它几乎没有传统长篇小说所必须具备的要素。故事通过人物的内心世界来展开。人物一天里的活动以及他们关注的事情看起来琐碎、无关紧要，甚至陈腐，然而，透过这些事件的表面，人物心理活动的自然流动、人物情绪的变化以及内心世界的冲动都以一种前所未有的直率、敏锐的方式得到了充分的表现。乔伊斯试图通过《尤利西斯》来说明一个事件中是如何包含着同类型的所有事件，一天中所发生的事情是如何概括着历史，从而来展示整个人类生活的微观世界。《尤利西斯》是一部反小说，其中的现代人既不是英雄也不是反面人物，而是琐碎的、世俗的；他们人格分裂、理想破灭、心灵肮脏、家庭破裂，在腐朽的世界中寻求人际关系的和谐和精神的维系。

三、选读作品赏析

"Araby" from Dubliners

The narrator of the story is a nameless boy who talks about life on North richmond Street. He always thinks about the former tenant——a priest. He lives with his uncle and aunt. The young boy dreams of Mangan's sister, whose image pursues him, even at night when he is trying to say his prayers. He hoped to see her everyday, but he seldom talks with her. Araby is a Dublin bazaar and one day the girl finally speaks to him and asks him if he will go to the bazaar. The boy is so excited that he promises to bring something for her from Araby. He reminds his uncle to return home early that day to give him some money, but his uncle is late. When the boy reaches the bazaar, it is nearly empty. He buys nothing for the girl and feels angry. When the lights go out, he stands in the bazaar and feels an epiphany.

Araby takes the form of a quest——a journey in search of something precious or even sacred, but the quest is ultimately in vain. In the story, Araby is the object of the search. Although the boy finally arrives at the bazaar, he is so late that he hasn't bought anything for the girl. Some critics have suggested that Mangan's sister represents Ireland itself, and that therefore the boy's quest is made on behalf of his native country. In the story, the bazaar seems to combine elements of the Catholic Church and England; Joyce blamed these two entities most for his country's paralysis. As the church has hypnotized its adherents, Araby has cast an Eastern enchantment over the boy. When the boy reaches Araby, it is empty - except for a woman and two men who speak with English accents. The woman speaks to the boy in a manner that is not encouraging and is clearly doing so out of a sense of duty. Thus, a mission on behalf of an idealized homeland (Mangan's sister is more or less a fantasy to him) is thwarted in turn by the Irish themselves (the uncle and his propensity to drink) the church, and England.

Joyce is such a consummate craftsman that he guides the readers through the story itself to consider its themes. The story is written from the first-person point-of-view, but it is the man that the boy grows into who recounts the story, because only a mature man is capable of recognizing and expressing such a sentiment. The story ends up with the boy's epiphany, which is negative. He realizes that in this world of darkness, everything is not so good as he imagines, including "Mangan's sister".

第七节　劳伦斯

一、作者简介

戴·赫·劳伦斯（1885—1930）是出身于工人家庭的重要小说家。他对资产阶级工业文明十分反感。在作品中，他对工业文明扭曲了男性与女性之间的自然关系进行了强烈谴责，抨击资产阶级文明扭曲了人性，压抑了人类本能的激情，消磨了人的意志，最终导致人性的丧失。他认为人们只有通过与自然保持和谐的关系，才能获得活力。劳伦斯强调个人心理的健康发展，认为任何心理上的压抑都可能导致精神疾病和人格的扭曲。在文学创作中，劳伦斯一直寻求理想的男女之间平衡而非统治的关系，因为这种关系可以维持人个性的完整和健全。劳伦斯的文学创作主要倾向于现实主义和自然主义，结合了若干戏剧性的场景和作者权威性的评述，这种倾向在他作品里细节的生动描绘中显而易见。在表现作品中人物的心理层面时，劳伦斯充分运用了诗歌的想象力和象征主义，通过描写自然意象作为诗意的象征来表现人物的感情状况和阐释人物所处的环境。

二、主要作品简介

（一）《儿子与情人》

《儿子与情人》是一部自传体小说，循着主人公从童年到成年的成长轨迹，塑造了一个艺术家类型的主人公保罗的形象。小说涵盖了劳伦斯许多颇具个性特色的主题：资产阶级工业招致的人性沦丧，人际关系的复杂性，人的情感的占有与被占有，以及主人公在寻求个性、实现自己艺术家之梦的过程中获得的精神解脱。

（二）《虹》

《虹》是一部社会批判小说，也是一部心理分析小说。劳伦斯以深刻细腻的笔触，从探索两性关系变化的角度，揭示了资本主义社会对人性的异化。劳伦斯认为工业文明必须对个人心灵的不健康发展、对夫妻性生活的曲解，以及对人类美满婚姻的可望而不可即负有责任。小说大量运用了象征、比喻和意象描写的手法。题目《虹》就是一个象征，它象征着一种自然和谐的两性关系和一种完美的人生理想。

（三）《恋爱中的女人》

《恋爱中的女人》探讨了两类爱情：戈珍和杰拉德之间毁灭性的爱及伯金和厄秀拉之间建设性的爱。杰拉德和戈珍都缺乏感情深度以及建立真诚的人际关系和亲情的能力，不能同其他的男性和女性建立正常的关系，他们的爱最终以火难和悲剧收场。而伯金和厄秀拉则通过坦诚相待，坚持个人独立，构筑了一个美满婚姻。《恋爱中的女人》也是一部由典型人物象征整个文明衰颓的代表性小说。杰拉德·克里奇作为一个冥顽不化的精神死亡者的形象出现，他代表着全套的资本主义伦理道德；而心灵优雅的伯金是象征人类热情的典型形象，他代表着自发的生命力量。

三、选读作品赏析

An Excerpt from Chapter 10 of Sons and Lovers

Paul sends a painting to an exhibition at Nottingham Castle. One morning the postman came to give them a letter, and Mrs. Morel gets very excited upon reading the letter. It turns out that Paul has won the first prize and that the painting has been sold for twenty guineas to Major Moreton. Paul and his mother rejoice at his success, and he tells her that she can use the money to buy Arthur out of the army. Morel comes home and exclaims at his son's success. which makes him think of william. Paul is invited to some dinner parties and tells his mother he needs an evening suit. She gives him a suit that was Williams. Paul's newfound success prompts discussions with his mother about class and happiness. She wants her son to ascend into the middle class, but he says that he doesn's belong to the middle class and he feels closest to the common people. Mrs Morel wants her son to be happy, which seems mostly to mean finding a good woman and beginning to settle down. Paul argues that he worries a normal life might bore him. Paul maintains his close relationship with his mother, allowing her to live vicariously through his experiences. He tells her everything that happens in his life, and she feels as though she is a participant. He even wants her to go along with him to introduce her to his new friends. When Paul wins the first prize in an exhibition, Morel says that William might have been as successful as Paul, had he only lived. This statement touches Mrs Morel deeply, and makes her feel strangely tired. When Paul tries on Williams suit, she thinks of William but is comforted by the thought of Paul. The notion that Mrs. Morel possesses Paul is particularly strong here, and this concept explains the reason for Paul's failure to develop a normal romantic relationship with another woman.

第八节 戈尔丁

一、作者简介

威廉·戈尔丁（1911—1993）的小说富含寓意，广泛融入古典文学、神话、基督教文化以及象征主义。作品的主题一般是与黑暗邪恶有关，同时也表达出一种昏暗的乐观主义。他运用现实主义的叙述方法编写寓言神话，承袭西方伦理学的传统，着力表现"人心的黑暗"这一主题。戈尔丁用他特有的沉思与冷静挖掘着人类千百年来从未停止过的互相残杀的根源，他的作品设置了人的原善与原恶、人性与兽性、理性与非理性、文明与野蛮等一系列矛盾冲突，冲突的结果展现出文明、理性的脆弱性和追求民主法治秩序的难度。1983年，戈尔丁获得了诺贝尔文学奖。

二、主要作品简介

《蝇王》是一部寓言式小说，借小孩的天真来探讨人性的恶这一严肃主题。故事发生在想象中的第三次世界大战，一群6岁至12岁的儿童在撤退途中因飞机失事被困在一座荒岛上。最初他们和睦相处，后来由于恶的本性便互相残杀，导致悲剧性的结果。人物、场景、故事、意象等都深具象征意义，那颗布满苍蝇的猪头则象征人心中的黑暗世界。这本小说突出了戈尔丁一直不停探讨的主题：人类天生的野蛮与文明的理性的斗争。文明的约束一旦放松，人类的原始本能就会暴露无遗。由于不敌大多数人的邪恶本性，少数坚持文明的儿童就成了无辜的牺牲品。

三、选读作品赏析

An Excerpt from Chapter 9 of Lord of the Flies

Ralph and Piggy find the other boys grouped together, laughing and eating. Jack sits on a great log, painted and garlanded as an idol. Jack orders the boys to give Ralph and Piggy some meat, and then orders a boy to give them a drink. Jack asks all of the boys who would like to join his tribe, and he will give them food and his hunters will protect hem. Ralph and Jack argue over who will be the chief. Ralph says that he has the conch, but Jack says that conch doesn't matter on this side of the island. Ralph warms them that a storm is coming. The littluns are frightened, so Jack orders them to do their pig dance. As the storm begins, Simon, having found the truth about the beast, rushes from the jungle, crying out about the dead body on the mountain. The boys rush after him, perceiving him to be the beast and killing him. Meanwhile, on the mountain, the storm blows the parachute and the body attached to it into the sea. That night, Simon's body washes out to sea.

Ralph finally loses his leadership over the other boys. All the boys desert Ralph in favor of Jack except Piggy, for Jack promises them meat without the responsibilities that Ralph has demanded. While Ralph has built shelters for the boys and is prepared for the storm, Jack has focused simply on hunting and entertaining the boys. When Ralph finds Jack, he is painted and garlanded, sitting on a log like an idol. This is a deliberately pagan image at variance with the ordered society from which Jack comes and the final manifestation of his descent from civilization. Jack totally disregards the rules established for the island, claiming that the conch yields no authority. Simon reveals the truth about the beast. The character whom most consider to be crazy is the first to discover the rational truth about the beast. However, Simon becomes a martyr for speaking the truth When he arrives to shatter the illusions the boys have about the beast, they perceive Simon to be the beast himself and kill him. This culmination of violence prevalent among Jacks band of hunters shows that they finally move from brutality against animals to brutality against each other.

第九节　贝克特

一、作者简介

塞缪尔·贝克特（1906—1989）是荒诞派戏剧的重要代表人物，创作的领域包括戏剧、小说和诗歌，尤以戏剧成就最高。贝克特在创作上深受乔伊斯、普鲁斯特和卡夫卡的影响，他的小说以惊人的诙谐和幽默表现了人生的荒诞、无意义和难以捉摸。贝克特戏剧方面的成就尤为突出，他一生共创作了 30 多个舞台剧本，其中最重要的三部作品是《等待戈多》《剧终》和《啊，美好的日子！》。文学风格上，贝克特从一开始就选择了一条远离现实主义传统的道路。他的作品很少涉及真实的社会生活场景和具体的社会问题，而是致力于揭示人类生存的困惑、焦虑、孤独以及现代社会中人们丧失自主意识后的悲哀。1969 年贝克特获得诺贝尔文学奖。

二、主要作品简介

《等待戈多》（1952）是一个两幕剧，没有冲突，只有一些乱无头绪的对话。主角是两个不明身份的流浪汉，他们在黄昏小路旁的枯树下等待着一个叫戈多的人。戈多是一种"虚无""死亡"的象征，代表了生活在惶恐不安的现代社会的人们对未来若有若无的期盼。该剧揭示了世界的荒谬丑恶和混乱无序，写出了在这样一个可怕的生存环境中，人们生活的痛苦与不幸。剧中的背景凄凉而恐怖，烘托了人们在世界中处于孤立无援、痛苦绝望的境地。

三、选读作品赏析

An Excerpt from Act I of Waiting for Godot

The play begins with two men or two tramps, Vladimir and Estragon, who meet by a tree on a country road. It is evening. They are clearly familiar with each other. They appear to have once been respectable but are now reduced to sleeping in ditches Vladimir idly adjusts his hat, while Estragon tries to take off his boot. They pass the time but can't move from the spot. They claim to be waiting for Godot. They think about the possibility of hanging themselves from the tree.

From Act I, we can see that Waiting for Godot has no real plot and the charactersare insubstantial. The language is sparse and meaningless. No grand themes appear in the play and no uplifting messages are contained within the dialogue. But Waiting for Godot has become a classic piece of twentieth-century drama, a modernist milestone. It has been described as a series of" meditations, not a statement of fact or theory.

Beckett gives us a sense of how it feels to be aimless and alienated. Most of the time the overwhelming feeling the audiences have is annoyance we simply want the action to move faster. Vladimir and Estragon revisit the same choice phrases, including the exchange: Let's go /We can't/ Why not? / We're waiting for Godot. The play appears to continually return to the same point. In addition, the musicality, pace, and rhythm of the words are more important than their literal meaning. The point of the play is its meaninglessness. The aimless waiting of the two main characters mirrors a contemporary lack of meaning, an inability to find answers to questions about existence and mortality.

Vladimir and Estragon are obsessed by the trivial things of life. They fail to think about the bigger issues that face them. They never face the most basic question of all- why are they waiting? The two men are trapped in a cyclical, empty universe, where nothing and no one seems to make sense. We identify with their boredom and their inability to move forward. They represent "everyman" -modern-day versions of the heroes of the medieval mystery plays.

第十节　托马斯

一、作者简介

狄兰·托马斯（1914—1953）的诗有一种古代行吟诗人的原始本质，同时还有一种现代心理学的意识。他以强烈的本能拥抱生命，在一种神秘的经验中将生与死、人与自然合为一体。他的诗中往往洋溢着一种神秘的原始力量。诗歌围绕生、欲、死三大主题；音韵充满活力而不失严谨；诗歌中的密集意象相互撞击，相互制约，表现自然的生长力和人性的律动，代表作品有《死亡与出场》《当我天生的五官都能看见》等。

二、选读作品赏析

"Do Not Go Gentle into that Good Night"

In the poem, the poet urges his ill father to fight his illness. Thomas declares that even in old age the old should violently resist their death. The poet urges his father to angrily hold on to his life. Wise men may know that death is natural but they too resist death violently because they realize that they have not made a sufficient impact on society with their wisdom. Honest men don't accept their death because they want to live on to give a better example to others. Men who lived mad and wild lives don't give in at the end. They enjoy the sunny side of life so long that they miss it and cry for it as they die. Men who lived serious lives are angry at death because they realize that they could have lived energetic and passionate lives instead. In the end, Thomas wishes that his father would give him his blessing but also curse him out of jealousy for continuing to live. The poem ends ambiguously hinting the acceptance of death by the father and the Son.

In this poem, Thomas depicts the inevitability of death through repetition and diction. The old man receives encouragement with pleads from his son to hold on to life Furthermore, the repetitious last lines serve to strengthen the speaker's thoughts. The final stanza combines the last lines from the odd and even-numbered stanzas for a final couplet. This portrays the ongoing war between life and death. In the end, the two last lines join together as the old man and his son accept that death is natural and it is a part of life. The references to " good men", " wild men", and " grave men" display the three basic stages of life birth, life, and death. How the speaker depicts that blind eyes could blaze like meteors and be gay refers to the bright light many often reported seeing in near-death experiences. In the line Do not go gentle into that good night, night replaces death in a metaphoric manner. The dying of the light refers to life as a light that shines to prove existence. If the light dies, then the life has ceased to exist. Written about his dying father, Thomas explores the personal experience of grief and death, and places it within a wider context. The subject matter is to ask the father not to accept death so easily, and this lends itself to the dichotomy of "day" and "night" which become somewhat symbolic for life and "death" in the poem. A son beseeches his elderly father to fight death. He gives examples of how "wise men", "good men", "wild men", and "grave men" "rage against the dying of the light", and begs his father to do the same. However, throughout the poem, we are subtly reminded that an old mans rage will be ineffectual in the face of death.

第十一节　休斯

一、作者简介

特德·休斯（1930—1998）的诗多以猛禽和暴力为主题。他认为，暴力统治着自然界和人类社会。因而他运用大胆的词汇和刺耳的节奏，通过急速旋转的想象来描写掠夺者与牺牲者。休斯从内部与外部两个世界来进行描写，有很强的象征性和寓言色彩，体现了一种人类学的深度。他的诗在真实与梦魇间保持着平衡，在人与其他事物间维系着张力。他的诗歌的活力和大刀阔斧的风格受到了众多追随者的模仿。

二、选读作品赏析

"Hawk Roosting"

In "Hawk Roosting" Ted Hughes attempts to speak with the voice of his animal subject——a hawk. It is the time for the hawk to rest after a day of hunting. The hawk like a king on his throne, perched high atop a tree. With its eyes closed, it appears to be sleeping in a vast wood but its body is still alive to instinct. It has none of mans falsifying dream. It is pure function; food is for consumption not thought. It has a mighty body, a powerful beak and vice-like talons. It often crushes its victims effortlessly. He fits perfectly into his environment. The high trees, the air that lifts him. the sun that warms him, and the earth that lies upward for his inspection are made so that he may function perfectly. Each single feather that covers his body is the masterpiece of countless millennia of evolution and adaptation. The death of its victims is regarded as fate. When he kills, he kills quickly.

The poem convinces us of the integrity of Hughes's vision. He defines nature within the framework of predator and prey; predators are irresistibly powerful and victims are powerless. In this poem we see everything through the hawks eyes in the first person Hughes writes in a cool, self-possessed, distanced language, which actually contributes to the poems effect of brutal hardness, as if each use were a robbery from some humane, rational context. The elegance and confidence with which they are used serve in place of any direct description of the hawk's physical splendor. The diction is prissy clipped, and the sentences get, shorter and shorter as the fanaticism clamps in. As for the theme, this poem is not so much to praise the hawk as to denigrate man. By saying there is no sophistry in my body, Hughes emphasizes that the hawk is not subject to self-doubt and it is a complete solipsist. The world is the world it sees and the creatures in the world exist to help the survival of the hawk. A predator has the total and complete control over its environments. It believes itself to be the supreme creation of God : My feet are locked upon the rough bark. /It took the whole of Creation / To produce my foot, my each feather/ Now I hold Creation in my foot. But man is unable to accept nature for what it is and always has the desire for casuistry, elaborate ratiocination, or self-deception.

第十二节　希尼

一、作者简介

谢默斯·希尼（1939—2013）是公认的当今世界最好的英语诗人和天才的

文学批评家。希尼的诗作纯朴自然，他以现代文明的视角冷静地挖掘、品味着爱尔兰民族精神。虽有学院派的背景，但他却绝无学院派的孤芳自赏。因其诗作具有抒情诗般的美和伦理深度，使日常生活中的奇迹和活生生的往事得以升华，希尼 1995 年获得诺贝尔文学奖。

二、主要作品简介

1966 年出版的第一部诗集《一位自然主义者之死》使他一举成名。1969 年，第二本诗集《通向黑暗之门》的发表，标志着诗人开始深入挖掘爱尔兰民族历史黑暗的土壤。基于爱尔兰的宗教政治冲突的诗集《在外过冬》（1972）寻求表现民族苦难境遇的意象和象征。此后发表的重要诗集有《北方》（1975）、《野外作业》（1979）、《苦路岛》（1984）、《山楂灯》（1987）、《幻觉》（1991）及《诗选》（1980）等。

三、选读作品赏析

"Follower"

The poem "Follower" is set on the farm where Seamus Heaney lived as a child. The poem is mainly about his father, who used to be an expert ploughman. Heaney was a nuisance to his father when he was ploughing because, as a little boy, Heaney was tripping, falling, yapping always behind. Heaney also makes it clear that when he was younger he wanted to be a farmer, like his father. But as he grows older he doesn't work in the fields. The poem brings visually alive the figure of a son "following in his fathers footsteps", and its reversal at the end, which says But today it is my father who keeps stumbling behind me, and will not go away. It carries double meanings: literally, the father is now old and clinging; metaphorically, the son, as a writer, is shackled with his farther. We can feel the distance between the father and the son. Not only do father and son have different skills, but also they are at the height of their powers at different times.

For Heaney, it is important to note down the generations of forgotten men and women whose names are lost, whose graves bear no tombstones, and whose lives are registered in no chronicle. In "Follower" his father at the plough is described moment by moment. The poem includes 6 stanzas of quatrains. From the first stanza to the fifth stanza, it pays homage to Heaney's father who is able to control powerful horses merely by means of a "clicking tongue" and "a single pluck Of reins". Surveying the land with mathematical precision, he is a Daedalus of the fields. Heaney also introduces himself as a clumsy disciple, following his father around the farm stumbling and falling. Heaney also shows the strong admiration for his father by stating that he hopes to become a skilled farmer like him. The last stanza conveys the poets sense of failure at ever being able to repeat his fathers skill. It expresses the pain and sadness which the poet feels as he explores his relationship with his father who becomes a shadowy presence and a past memory. In the poem, the observed and recollected facts of Seamus Heaney's early rural experience are conveyed in a language of great sensuous richness and directness. Some farming jargon and monosyllables, an effective simile and a metaphor are used to emphasize his fathers skill as a farmer. In addition, the onomatopoeia is used to indicate that the horses understood and obeyed his father, even when he made the slighted noise. In the last stanza, rhythmic control disintegrates and the feeling of the poem is suddenly complicated. Their positions are reversed. The poet is troubled by his memory: perhaps he feels guilty at not carrying on the tradition of farming, or feels he cannot live up to fathers example.

第七章　殖民主义时期的美国文学解读与作品赏析

自 1492 年哥伦布发现了美洲大陆以后，欧洲殖民者纷纷踏上这块神秘的土地。1620 年，102 名英国清教徒乘坐著名的五月花号（The Mayflower）来到美洲的普利茅斯建立殖民地，他们是第一批的新大陆移民，是未来 150 年后美国大多数人民的祖先。这批人的到来打开了北美洲的大门，也把他们的清教教义传播到了这片美洲大地，他们被称为清教徒之父，他们的到来标志着美国历史的开始。

一、清教主义对殖民主义时期美国文学的影响

作为美国文明与文化的主要源头，清教主义对美国文学的影响持久而深刻。清教主义，起源于英国，在北美殖民地得以实践与发展。清教徒在自己的祖国遭受迫害，对英国严酷的社会现实不满而移民到美国。他们坚信自己是上帝的选民，是上帝把他们从旧世界的罪过和堕落中拯救出来，送往北美这块福地。这种崇奉和笃信的态度使他们有一种崇高的使命感，也造就了他们自信、坚韧、禁欲的人格特征。作为美国的开拓者，他们的思想随着时间的推移，愈益显示出它的重要意义，对早期的美国文学产生了不可磨灭的影响。

（一）清教主义影响了文学作品的主题

秉承加尔文教义的清教主义强调对上帝的虔诚、敬畏与绝对服从，因此，表现在文学上就是对清教教义的宣传，如赞美上帝、描述人类的堕落以及歌颂圣人坚韧不拔的精神，从而证明上帝的伟大英明等。

（二）清教主义影响了文学作品的写作技巧

在写作技巧方面，清教徒作品的朴实无华给早期的美国文学留下了清晰的印记。早期文学作品的语言清新、简单、直接等特点都受到了清教主义的影响。

（三）清教主义影响了文学价值观

美国的价值观念在很多方面体现了清教主义。美国文学在很长一段时间内都呈现出说教的倾向，而娱乐作用则是次要的。从某种意义上说，清教主义束

缚了早期美国作家的自由创作，限制了其创作的空间。

二、殖民主义时期美国文学的主要特色

移民刚到新大陆时忙于生存斗争，所以开始时文学发展比较缓慢，文学作品的形式、内容和风格等都比较单一。

（1）最早发表的关于北美的作品是游记、日记之类的文字。这些作品主要描写他们跨洋渡海的经历，对新气候的适应，对新农作物的种植，及与当地印第安人的相处等。

（2）殖民主义时期另一重要的大众文学作品是以宣传清教主义思想为目的的布道文。布道文以其简洁明快、通俗易懂的语气感化说服教民，其中大量的比喻、平行、排比等手法的运用，使得其文学色彩异常浓厚。

（3）北美殖民地时期也产生了一些清教诗歌。说教性是清教诗歌的鲜明主题。诗歌篇幅较短、句式工整、言简意赅、声韵优美，因此成为清教徒比较热衷的一种体裁，并构成了美国文学史的源头。

三、殖民地时期的主要作家与作品

最早期的殖民地文学大多是宣传性作品，它们由早期的殖民者们在英国出版。最早描写殖民地生活的作品是队长约翰·史密斯（John smith）1608 年出版的《关于弗吉尼亚的真实叙述》（*A True Relation of virginid*）。人们争相传阅他写的那本小册子，因此他获得很好的声誉。约翰·史密斯一共出版了8 本书，记录、探讨了殖民者早期垦荒的历史。当时，比较知名的作家还有被誉为"美国历史之父"的威廉·布拉福德（William Bradford），其代表作品是《普利茅斯种植园史》（*History of plymouth plantation*）。

在殖民地时期有很多清教徒写诗，但大部分诗歌沉闷乏味，有两位教徒的诗达到了相当高的水平，真正称得上是诗作，其中一个名叫安妮·布拉德斯特里特（Ane Bradstreet），被称为殖民地时期的第一位诗人，代表作有《美洲新诞生的第十位缪斯》（*The Tenth Muse Lately sprung up in America*）、《沉思》（*Contemplations*）以及《致我亲爱的丈夫》（*To My Dear and loving Husband*）。另一个诗人名叫爱德华·泰勒（Edward Taylor），被认为是清教徒诗人中最杰出的一位，他的大部分诗歌直接以赞美诗为基础进行创作，其代表作为《家务》（*Huswifery*）。

第一节　布拉德斯特里特

一、作者简介

安妮·布拉德斯特里特是美国第一位重要的诗人。她与父母和丈夫于1630年乘船前往北美洲，他们都是创建马萨诸塞湾殖民地的清教徒。她的堂兄未经她的同意，就将她的诗带到英国，以《美洲新诞生的第十位缪斯》（*The Tenth Muse Lately sprung up in America*，1650）为题发表，具有讽刺意味的是，这些在她有生之年发表的唯一诗作今天被认为是其最乏味的作品。当代评论家及其作品的推崇者都更喜欢其反映日常生活的聪慧诗作以及她为她丈夫和孩子而写的充满温情和爱意的诗。布拉德斯特里特的诗以对其自身周围的观察为基础，主要关注宗教和家庭两大主题。她是一名清教徒，有坚定的清教徒信仰，但她也经常怀疑自己所相信的一切，质疑男权社会，甚至质疑上帝。布拉德斯特里特的文学天赋，她对家庭、爱情、女性地位和失去亲人的痛苦等普世性主题的探索，以及她与社会中有争议的朋友站在一起的勇气，都使她成为世界各地妇女和男人钦佩的楷模。

二、主要作品简介

（一）《美洲新诞生的第十位缪斯》

这是布拉德斯特里特生前正式出版的唯一一部诗集。她的诗歌带有浓厚的宗教气息，对上帝的崇拜，对天国的憧憬和描绘，对人类的认识，对死和永生的思虑，清教徒的虔诚和自我的剖析，构成了包括她的最动人的家庭诗等在内的诗作的基本内容。安妮努力地将自己的人生经历融入诗歌创作，既体现了诗人卓越的学识又创作了一些形象的比喻和动人的意象。美中不足的是诗人似乎难以驾驭双行押韵的偶句韵式，显得有些机械。此外，诗集中的不少诗篇涉及清教主义文化背景下的女性社会问题，以及安妮作为一名女诗人所面临的家庭和社会问题。

（二）《致我亲爱的丈夫》

这是作者去世6年后出版的第二本诗集《安妮·布拉德斯特里特诗集》（*Several Poems*，1678）中的一首代表作，是一曲爱的赞歌。该诗让读者窥见了诗人作为一个妻子和一名清教徒的内心世界。虔诚的清教徒只信上帝而别无所爱。但是，由于生活所迫，不少北美殖民地移民的清教观念发生了变化。他们已经不像移民前那么虔诚和狂热了。他们逐渐地开始把现实中的爱情以及其他世俗的乐趣当作上帝的恩赐。在《致我亲爱的丈夫》中，妻子对丈夫的恋情已经成为一位女性从现实通往天堂最接近的道路，诗人对丈夫的爱已经超越了她对上帝的爱。

三、选读作品赏析

"*To My Dear and Loving Husband*"

The poem depicts Anne Bradstreet's love to her husband. The phrase "loving husband" occurs in the title of the poem, which tells us that this is probably a poem about marital love. The speaker compares love to a powerful, unstoppable force, as an extraordinary gift that can never be repaid and as a means to achieve immortality. True love is so incredible that it can actually defy the laws of physics and make two people feel like they are one. From another point of view, Bradstreet persuasively presents her views on how to resolve the basic contradictions of puritan faith in other words how to live in this world while keeping an eve on heaven.

In the opening quatrain, her ability to reason, to construct an argument, commands center stage. Tuning to anaphora, a rhetorical device that consists of repeating a sequence of words at the beginnings of neighboring clauses, thereby lending them emphasis, she opens with a series of logical "If then" statements. Having established the value of her love through the power to reason in the first quatrain, she offers proof that its value is beyond compare in the second quatrain through the use of monetary metaphors and scriptural imagery. Interestingly, ending the eighth couplet on an unstressed rhyme ("recompense") creates a hesitancy that musically emphasizes the inadequacy she feels in finding a way to compensate, or "repay", her husband's love. She turns to heaven, something greater than herself, for his reward. The final couplet completes the poems theological argument by claiming that it is possible to realize rather than transcend, duality through achieving a balance between earthly and heavenly Love.

第二节　泰勒

一、作者简介

爱德华·泰勒生于英国农民家庭，是当初因不愿效忠英国国教、追求信仰自由而移居新大陆的清教徒中的一员。泰勒是一个坚定的加尔文派教徒，相信有一个全能的上帝，选定某些灵魂可以得救。这种得救可以通过毫无保留、毫不动摇的信仰实现，而不是通过善行。地狱的确存在，等待着那些未被选中的人。他的诗作中渗透着坚定的加尔文教思想，体现了宗教精神和诗歌艺术的高度结合。泰勒的诗歌灵感来自北美大地，而其艺术渊源则应追溯到英国玄学派。泰勒的诗作受英国著名玄学派诗人邓恩（John donne）和赫伯特（George Herbert）影响甚深。作为玄学派诗歌在北美大地最出色的继承者，泰勒擅长运用精心选择的暗喻和丰富而唯美的比喻，也采用日常生活中的寻常措辞和比喻。泰勒的代表作有两部，写于约 1685 年的《上帝对其选民有影响的决定》（*Gods Determinations Touching His Elec*）和写于 1682—1726 年的《内省录》（*Preparatory Meditation*）。他的诗歌被认为是诗歌的《圣经》，表达了他虔诚的清教思想。

二、主要作品简介

《家务》是泰勒最具有代表性的一首诗，是作者向上帝的祷告。在诗中，泰勒表达了他对上帝的绝对信仰，希望能与上帝更亲密接触，并由上帝来掌控自己的生命。他创造性地把清教徒的思想与富有激情的想象力融合在一起，《家务》这首诗以纺车来类比，通篇都是围绕织布的过程，使得全诗具有统一、鲜明的意象，同时，也很好地体现了玄学派诗歌擅用奇妙比喻的特点。

三、作品选读

" *Huswifery*"

This poem is a kind of prayer in which the poet asks God for grace. Huswifery develops out of an intricate comparison between cloth making and god's granting of grace. Such an extended comparison between two startlingly different things——a lowly household task and salvation is a type of metaphor called a "Huswifery". The conceit begins in the first stanza, as the poet compares himself to a spinning wheel. The "Holy Word" (the Bible) is like the distaff- a stick on which raw wool is placed before spinning The basic meaning of this complex comparison is that one cannot receive grace without having some knowledge of Scripture.

The poet s emotions are like the "Flyers" that twist and carry the raw wool; his soul is like the spool that gathers the thread from the wheel; his conversation, or social behavior, is like the reel to which the finished thread is transferred from the spinning wheel. The second stanza compares the poet to a loom, on which the thread or yarn is turned into cloth. God now appears as a weaver meshing the threads into cloth ("the Web"). Once the cloth is woven, it is to be cleansed by such sacraments or ordinances as communion (the "Fulling Mills"), dyed and decorated. In the last stanza Taylor asks that the colorful material be fashioned into beautiful robes to clothe his thoughts feelings, and behavior. If God will thus glorify the poet, say the final lines of the poem the poet will be able to glorify God through the beauty of his being.

第八章 独立革命时期的美国文学解读与作品赏析

18世纪的美国文学深受独立革命这一历史背景的影响，多为宣传和鼓动性的带有政治色彩的文字；同时，该时期的文学也深受启蒙运动的影响，相对殖民地时期的文学更加理性、乐观，并且努力摆脱清教主义的色彩。

一、独立革命时期文学的主要特色

18世纪初的殖民地文学仍然以清教主义思想和对新环境的憧憬与描绘为主，随着社会背景的变化，文学也发生着变化。18世纪中期至80年代初，启蒙主义思想盛行于美国，独立成为越来越多殖民地人民的呼声，文学成为宣传独立的有力武器。该时期北美殖民地文坛以其政治性著称，多为宣传和鼓动性文字，传达着反殖民统治的信息。政论文、演讲词散文、诗歌等大量涌现，其中有的鞭笞英国殖民统治，有的给予"保皇分子"（主张维持殖民统治）强烈的抨击，有的激励着革命者为赢得自由而浴血奋战。这些作品鲜有文学的美学特点，更多的是政治、社会、道德特色，它们为殖民地人们争取独立战争的胜利起到极大的激励作用。

1783年殖民地人民最终迎来了美国的独立。至19世纪初，美国文学开始寻找自己的民族身份，作家们开始打造具有美国特色的美国文学，从而美国的风格初露端倪。这一时段的文学具有两大主题：描写自然风光和独立革命。描绘美国本土的自然风景，这与18世纪的英国文学的主题一样，不同的是突显出了美国本土特色。同时，美国文学的民族特色也由以独立革命为背景和素材而创作出的小说、诗歌、戏剧等传达了出来。

二、独立革命时期作家概述

该时期著名的文学家、科学家、政治家富兰克林是18世纪美国启蒙运动的代表人物。他的《穷人理查德的年鉴》（*Poor Richard's almanac*）通过大量的格言警句宣传创业持家、待人处世的道德原则和勤奋致富的生活道路。他在独立战争期间撰写的《自传》（*Me Autobiography*）以亲身经历说明，在美国充满机遇，只要勤奋便能成功，他的经验对美国人的人生观、事业观和道德观产生了深远的影响。

弗吉尼亚的革命领袖帕特里克·亨利发表了《不自由，毋宁死》的文章，发出了："给我自由，否则让我去死！"的口号，激励着革命者去为赢得自由而浴血奋战。托马斯·潘恩在他的《常识》里提出了独立的口号。他的小册子《美洲危机》中的 16 篇战斗檄文更是激励着美国人民，为赢得战争的胜利起到了极大的鼓励作用。托马斯·杰弗逊在 1774 年就写出《英属美洲权利概述》的文章，抨击英国国会为美洲制定法律的武断行为。他的《独立宣言》更是一篇优秀的政论散文，成为独立战争的旗帜和动力。

在独立革命时期，美国的小说创作正处在起步阶段。威廉·希尔·布朗的《同情的力量》（1784）被认为是美国的第一部伦理和感情类小说；该小说与苏珊娜·罗森的《查洛特·坦普尔》（1785）共同打开了美国文学界小说创作的闸门。

诗歌在美国革命期间发挥着重要的作用。菲力普·弗瑞诺的慷慨激昂的爱国诗激励着大批爱国志士，他的爱国主义和充满战斗精神的诗篇，集中反映了独立革命时期的美国诗歌特征，他的许多歌咏自然的作品，也是美国浪漫主义诗歌的组成部分。

戏剧在美国发展较慢。托马斯·戈弗雷在 1767 年创作的《安息王》被誉为美国第一剧。而独立革命以后的由剧作家罗亚多·泰勒在 1787 年推出的《对比》和威廉·邓拉普在 1798 推出的《安德烈》标志着美国的戏剧开始步入成熟阶段，后者被认为是美国在这一时期最优秀的悲剧。

第一节　富兰克林

一、作者简介

本杰明·富兰克林（1706—1790）出身贫苦，但意志坚定，顽强奋斗，他从商、参政、写文章、也研究科学，是著名的文学家、科学家和政治家。他像是"从天上偷窃火种的第二个普罗米修斯"（康德语），成为那个时代中现代文明的引领者、美国人的象征。在商界，他从事出版事业，他创办的周报《半岛公报》（后取名为《周六晚报》）是当时美国当之无愧的第一大报，发行量遥遥领先。在 1732—1758 年期间，他自己创作并发行了《穷人理查德的年鉴》，这部流行谚语的集子，机智、风趣、幽默，很快成为该类作品中的最畅销书。在政界，富兰克林主张人权天赋、政治平等。作为殖民地的代表，他不断地建议英国政府采用民主的管理政策，当这些建议没有希望被采纳时，他开始积极支持独立事业，为大陆委员会献计献策，并且协助杰弗逊起草了《独立宣言》。他作为代表，同法国进行了艰难的谈判、协商，为美国在独立战争中获得法国在经济上和军事上的大量援助做出了巨大贡献。1787 年，他又作为议会代表，起草了美国的宪法。作为独立战争前唯一的杰出作家，他具有非凡的表达能力，语言真诚、简洁、流畅、幽默。他最好的作品收录在他自己的《自传》里，该书是他所生活的时代的最佳写照，是美国传记文学上的一个里程碑。作为科学家，他发明了避雷针、富兰克林电炉、双焦眼镜、微型印刷机、"阿莫尼卡"的乐器（由一些能发声的玻璃组成）等，他还首次使用了电流中"正电"和"负电"的专业术语。

二、主要作品简介

（一）《穷人理查德的年鉴》

也译为《穷人理查历书》，是一种箴言集，因为都是写在日历本上，所以叫作年鉴。该年鉴中包括日历、天气、诗歌、谚语（如：God helps those who help themselves. 自助者天助之。）和天文、占星等，还偶尔包括数学演习。这些格言通常带有节俭和礼貌的玩世不恭，也意在规范当时的社会习俗，并不是一种哲学文件。该书最早出版于 1732 年，随后继续出版了 25 年，给富兰克林本人带来很大的经济成就和知名度。

（二）《自传》

《自传》开创了美国传记文学。该书于 1771 年动笔，1788 年完成，记录了富兰克林前半生的生活经历。该书由四个部分组成：第一部分讲述其人生前 25 年读书、当印刷工、为报纸撰稿等的经历；第二部分描写其在科学研究上的努力和成果，以及在公共事业方面的经历；第三、四部分描述其中年至 51 岁间的生活经历。至于他后 33 年的生活，尤其在欧洲、美国政界的成就，作者只在后两个部分略有提及。

这部书中，富兰克林写出了"美国梦"，被全世界无数人尤其青年当成"人生指导"读物。用真诚简洁的语言，富兰克林把自己成功的经验和失败的教训娓娓道来，整部自传既无哗众取宠，又不盛气凌人，在通俗易懂的叙述中闪现睿智和哲理的火花，文字朴素幽默，叙事清楚简洁，使读者倍感亲切且易于接受。

三、选读作品赏析

An Excerpt from Chapter Vill of The Autobiography

The Autobiography of Benjamin Franklin is one of the best autobiographies in the world. it is a record of a man who has established himself in fame and wealth from a family of poverty and obscurity. This book was completed from four stages between 1771 and 1790: the first stage is for his early 25 years when doing printer's job and fortunately, trying to read and write; the second stage is about his scientific achievements and contribution in public affairs; the third stage is the rise and progress of his philosophical reputation; the last stage is about his political advocation. This excerpt is chosen from the first stage, and mainly talks about his moral perfection plan. Such awareness rises from his printers life while he reads, thinks and writes a lot and then the virtue becomes one of his focuses.

This excerpt shows him to be a representative of Enlightenment in America. He believes in reason, equality and freedom, especially the self-right to perfect oneself. He designs his moral perfection plan in a rational way. When it is useless to be only interested in and knowing the virtues, he decides to put it into action plan; when the virtues are ambiguous between each other, he turns to define and distinguish them when it is difficult to focus on all the thirteen virtues, he figures out the order to carry them out one by one; when he tries to make the plan efficient, he designs the chart to monitor each day and each week's failings to push himself to be better. It is this rational method that ensures the moral perfection to be realized. His words also reflect himself to be a puritan, not only for the endeavor for self-examination and self-improvement to be a perfect self-made man, but also from the virtues he upholds. The thirteen virtues, especially resolution, frugality, and industry are what the Puritanism stresses. It confirms the puritan belief that man is endowed by God with certain inalienable rights of liberty to purify and save oneself and to pursue the happiness. Franklin's moral perfection promotes his life's success- rising from rags to riches through hard work. Thus, it is also a real account of American dream and a good example for all the people.

As to the language feature in the excerpt, the puritan feature of simplicity directness and concision are very obvious. It has the clearness of order with one problem-solution to another; the plainness of its style in sharing his sparking experience; the homeliness of imagery, for example, weeding the garden efficiently with one bed following another, which is like acquiring the virtues one by one; the simplicity of diction and syntax with many loose sentences and the narrating tone; and directness and conciseness in expression to make the meaning understood in an easier way.

第二节　亨利

一、作者简介

帕特里克·亨利（1736—1799）美国革命家、演说家。基本上靠自学成才，1760 年取得律师资格，以机敏和演说技巧而出名；后曾为弗吉尼亚议会议员、并两次担任州长。他积极参加反抗英国殖民者、维护殖民地人民权利的斗争，在美国独立革命中有着不可替代的功绩。1775 年第二届弗吉尼亚代表大会上，提出应武装弗吉尼亚民兵、与英国作战，他的演讲以"不自由，毋宁死"的结束语闻名，鼓舞了弗吉尼亚的军心。建国后，他政治上趋于保守，1787 年拒绝出席费城制宪会议，翌年在弗吉尼亚代表大会上反对批准《美国宪法》。他坚持反对强大的联邦政府，拒绝了华盛顿让他担任国务卿的邀请，还拒绝担任最高法院的大法官等职位。亨利坚持个人信念，不追逐名利。在看到了法国革命的疯狂后，他的政治观点有所改变，最终成为联邦主义者。

二、主要作品简介

《不自由，毋宁死》（1775 年 3 月 23 日）这篇脍炙人口的演说在美国革命文献史上占有特殊地位。其时，北美殖民地正面临历史性抉择——要么拿起武器，争取独立；要么妥协让步，甘受奴役。亨利以敏锐的政治家眼光，饱满的爱国激情，以铁的事实驳斥了主和派的种种谬误，阐述了武装斗争的必要性和可能性。从此，"不自由，毋宁死"的口号激励了千百万北美人为自由独立而战，这篇演说也成为世界演说名篇。

三、选读作品赏析

"*Speech in the virginia Convention*"

This speech was given before the delegates of the colonies in the Virginia Convention with the purpose of convincing the delegates to take up fighting as their only alternative to gain freedom and peace. It is a patriotic and radical advocation for American independence and freedom. The speech achieves very good effect by several strategies.

Firstly, the speech is given by a careful logic. Starting with declaring his patriotism he illustrates the hope of peaceful freedom being an illusion and the necessity of a war being real. Next, he clarifies the doubt about weak power from the colonists to make wise the choice of a war. Finally he encourages his fellows to join the war and also gives his famous and inspiring slogan" Give me liberty or give me death.

Secondly, the tone of the speech is quite natural and also convincing by following an advancing pattern. Firstly the smooth and humble tone gets the audience's attention and interest. Then the critical and irritated tone pushes the audience to think deeply over the illusion of peaceful hope. Based on rational thinking, the tone begins to be more emphasizing and stressing on the point of fighting. Finally the intense and fierce tone for the advocation of war turns out to be a convinced and accepted choice. The speakers passion is shown and can affect the atmosphere of the convention.

Thirdly, the rhetorical devices contribute greatly to the success of the speech Rhetorical questions are applied a lot in paragraphs 2, 3 and 5 to arouse the audience's awakening from the illusion of hope and doubt. Parallelism is also well preferred to make emphasis, for example, the structure of "let us not deceive ourselves". we have done petitioned remonstrated/ supplicated.

Besides, there are metaphors to make the language more vivid and easy to understand. For example, bind and rivet. Chain implies the British's slavery and colonial rule upon them. And the famous slogan Give me liberty or give me death shows the antithesis and achieves a contrasted effect In the aspect of quotation, Patrick quotes many phrases from sacred and well-known books, such as "listen to the song of that siren till she transforms us into beasts", which is quoted from Homer's epic poem Odyssey with the intention to point out submission makes the colonists dehumanized having eyes, see not, and, having ears, hear not "in paragraph 3, which is quoted from Ezekiel; betrayed with a kiss", which is quoted from Luke to imply the betrayal from Britain.

In the sentence pattern, it combines the long and short sentences to attract the audience; it also uses many exclamation sentences at the end of the speech to recall the delegates to fight together.

Generally speaking, the speech is a well organized one to arouse the audience to feel, think and resolute the same as the speaker does. Therefore, it has powerfully encouraged people to fight against colonial rule and promoted the victory of American Independent war.

第三节　杰弗逊

一、作者简介

托马斯·杰弗逊（1743—1826）是位政治家、文学家、科学家、音乐家、语言学家。杰弗逊深受启蒙运动的影响，有强烈的人文主义精神，坚信自然权利，政治平等和自然利他主义。在政治上，他被誉为美国民主精神之父。他起草的《废止限嗣继承法规》，沉重打击了从英国带到美洲的封建主义残余。他还起草了《弗吉尼亚宗教自由法规》，并使这一法规在州议会获得通过，实现了政教分离。1789 年他担任美国第一位国务卿，后任副总统、第三任总统。执政期间他领导了反对亲英保守势力、争取资产阶级民主的斗争，为美国资本主义的迅速发展创造了条件。作为文学家，他的文风高雅，简洁明快。1776 年他主笔起草了《独立宣言》成为推动独立战争取得胜利的强有力的思想武器。此外，他的散文、信件和官方文件总共有五十卷。1819 年，他开始创建弗吉尼亚大学，他亲自担任第一任校长，这所大学也是他设计的著名建筑之一。

二、主要作品简介

《独立宣言》包括三个部分：第一部分阐明政治哲学——民主与自由的哲学；第二部分列举若干具体的不平等事例，以证明乔治三世破坏了美国的自由；第三部分郑重宣布独立，并宣誓支持该项宣言。《独立宣言》充分表达了殖民地人民反对专制统治、追求自由和民主的呼声，这一宣言也成为美国的建国原则、美国人民的信念和理想。

然而，这份伟大的文件却遗留着一个未解决的问题：奴隶问题。在它被大陆会议通过之前，佐治亚州和南卡罗来纳州代表们坚持删除其中的对英王乔治三世允许在殖民地存在奴隶制和奴隶买卖的有力谴责，并删除涉及奴隶制度的篇章，奴隶制得以合法地存在于新生的美国。而这剥夺了黑人奴隶的权利与自由，也限制了美国资本主义经济的发展。《独立宣言》强调的真理"人人生而平等"虽与当时遗留的奴隶问题形成强烈的反差，但仍不失成为美国正义的社会改革者们在面临不民主、不公正的统治时的最有力的思想武器。在各个社会的历史阶段，为了废除奴隶制，为了禁止种族隔离，为了妇女解放，社会改革者们都借用了这一有力口号，这足以见得"人人生而平等"这一真理的力量以及《独立宣言》的根本性地位。

三、选读作品赏析

Declaration of Independence

The Declaration of Independence states clearly the self-evident rights of life, liberty and pursuit of happiness and announces the colonies independence from tyrannical king is destruction on those rights. It is quite impressive by the declaration to analyze those rights and list twenty-nine events to prove King George Ill and British government's persecution on the colonies. Thus, it is full of convincing and inspiring power for American independence war.

Generally speaking, the whole document tends to be with a plainly noble style by using plain words to introduce sacred mission. It has appropriate and concise expression, many with rhyme to read.

As a national declaration, this document is aimed to be perfect in diction. There are many examples to show that. One people is used to avoid any argument about the colonies belonging to British people though having the same language and lifestyle, which may also greatly encourage the mind for national independence. The Laws of Nature and of Nature's Godreveals it is the god's willingness and order to get away from British rule; thus, the event of independent war turns to be official, sacred, and of glory. Indispensably necessary for the immediate Defense and Protection of our Subjects shows the necessity for independence war with no hesitation or wavering at.

第九章　浪漫主义时期的美国文学解读与作品赏析

美国浪漫主义文学始于 18 世纪末，止于内战爆发，其中华盛顿·欧文出版的《见闻札记》标志着其开端，惠特曼的《草叶集》是该时期的压卷之作。因其注重自然，强调抒发主观情感与发挥文学想象力，呈现出前所未有的繁荣景象，所以也被称为"美国的文艺复兴"。

一、主要文学特色

（一）衍生的美国浪漫主义作品

（1）强调文学的想象力和情感特质。

（2）倡导情感的自由表达和人物心理状态的展示。

（3）颂扬普通人和作为个体的人。

（4）迷恋历史和异国情调。

（二）本土的美国浪漫主义作品

（1）充满全国性"西部拓荒"的体验。

（2）自然/美国山水风光成为素材。

（3）清教主义下的道德说教特色。

（4）超验主义哲学的影响。

二、主要作家与作品

美国浪漫主义时期的小说富有独创性、多样性，有华盛顿·欧文的喜剧性寓言体小说，有爱伦·坡的歌德式惊险故事，有库柏的边疆历险故事，有麦尔维尔长篇叙事，有霍桑的心理罗曼史，有戴维斯的社会现实小说。美国浪漫主义作家在人性的理解上也各有不同。爱默生、梭罗等超验主义者认为人类在自然中是神圣的，因此人类是可以完善的；但霍桑和梅尔维尔则认为人在内心上都是罪人，因此需要道德力量来改善人性。《红字》一书就典型地反映了这个观点。此外，惠特曼的《草叶集》是美国 19 世纪最有影响的诗歌。

第一节　华盛顿·欧文

一、作者简介

华盛顿·欧文（1783—1859）被称为美国文学之父，其作品标志着美国文学从 18 世纪理性主义向 19 世纪浪漫主义的过渡。1820 年，其《见闻札记》以幽默风趣的笔调和富于幻想的浪漫色彩，描写了英国和美国古老的风俗习惯以及善良淳朴的旧式人物，开创了美国短篇小说的传统。

欧文的文笔优雅自然，清新精致，时常流露出温和的幽默。他厌恶资产阶级的浅薄与庸俗，对殖民主义者的无耻欺诈和残酷剥削以及他们屠杀印第安人的罪行进行讽刺和揭露，《纽约外史》体现了这一点。

此外，欧文是社会保守主义者，向往田园生活，对过去的荣耀和安宁的古老公社生活流露出留恋、哀婉叹息之情。他的很多作品取材于欧洲大陆的历史和传统，但也有以美国地理状况为背景的作品，因此也不乏美国式的浪漫气息和传奇色彩，比如《睡谷传奇》和《瑞普·凡·温克尔》。

二、主要作品简介

（一）《见闻札记》

《见闻札记》是欧文在遍游了欧洲的名胜古迹、城市与乡村后，写出的随笔和故事集，包括短篇小说、散文、杂感等 32 篇。它充满讽刺与异想、事实与虚构，描写了英美两国的古老风俗习惯以及活灵活现的各式人物，表达出喜好传统，反对新奇；喜好贵族统治，反对民主；喜好乡村，反对城市的思想。其中最为著名的是《瑞普·凡·温克尔》和《睡谷传奇》。

（二）《睡谷传奇》

《睡谷传奇》主要讲述纯朴的伊卡包德在与情敌布洛姆共同追求女孩卡特琳娜的过程中，他被一个圆乎乎的东西砸中后脑，他大受惊吓，却不知此物只是个南瓜，随后逃走。最终布洛姆和卡特琳娜结了婚，而伊卡包德再也没有露面。该作品讲述了当地的自然风光、神秘的传说，其语言流畅、情节悬疑、人物形象生动，并且充满幽默与夸张，表达了怀旧情感，以及物质文明与古老乡村的矛盾和冲突。

三、选读作品赏析

"An Excerpt from Winkle"

The novel is adapted from the German folk tale, but taking Hudson River as the background location, it also has the American feature. It uses a third persons perspective to carefully tell a story about Rip Van winkle, a "good-natured" man who was always eager to oblige the neighbors instead of his own family. Thus, his hard working wife scolded him a lot. Being a hen-peck man, he escaped from his home to be outside in the village or even ran into the mountain. It was there that changed his fate He met some strange Dutch men, got drunk and then fell asleep for. twenty years. When he woke up and returned to the village, he was met with a series of surprises. The most surprise was that his wife was already dead and he, like the new independent country got his freedom from the previous yoke.

The theme of the novel lies mainly in the conservative attitude to the past and to the change of society, which is a mental aversion to the revolution. The theme can be proved by many details. Firstly, when he went back to his village, he tried to seek for the previous leisure talking or drowsy tranquility, or the old friends, but all in vain.

Facing the unharmonious arguments for election and his friends being long gone, he felt his heart was overwhelmed by the fear, loneliness, and loss of identity. He understood and cared little about the talking of civil rights, war or independence. All he was concerned were his past, from which he could find his identity and his fun, which proves his reminiscence and no preference for the social change caused by the independent war.

Another theme is revealed by his escape from family responsibility and his wife's nagging into the mountain, a dream-like world. Irving gives very vivid and beautiful description of the scenery. It shows Rips and also the writers escape and conservation for realistic life and trouble. Some critic says that this is typical of American attitude in facing the reality by being immature, self-centered，careless，and imaginative.

The novel shows some conflicts with Puritanism. His wife is a hard-working puritan image，pursuing happiness with non-leisure lifestyle，which is totally contrary to Rips life value. Rip thinks life should be with less hard work，least material needs and mostspiritual enjoyment.

The novel is a representative work of Romanticism. One typical example is Irving's vivid and beautiful description of the natural scenery along Hudson River. Besides，there is an imaginary description of the folk tale and mysterious Dutch men，which is also the typical feature of Romanticism. Furthermore，Rip's obsession with the natural world is another romantic feature.

As to the main character in the novel：Rip，with mild，hen-peck，nostalgic and conservative characteristics，is fully described from appearance，behavior，conversation and thoughts，etc. His wife，a brave，hard-working，and puritanically disciplined woman，was only depicted by a third perspective with her husband s and neighbors comments. However her name "Dame"，meaning a noble woman，is ironically used by Irving to refer to her，a plain countrywoman.

As to the language style，it is typical of Irving's elegant writing，full of humor and witty，together with the vivid and detailed description. Besides，there is an ironical effect by choices of words and sentences. For example，sentences like what dog is ever brave enough to stand firm against the terrors of a woman's tongue and "Morning noon，and night，her tongue was endlessly going" shows the negative attitude toward Rips wife.

第二节　埃德加·爱伦·坡

一、作者简介

埃德加·爱伦·坡（1809—1849）的恐怖小说和推理小说尤为著名。他还被尊为西方侦探小说的开山鼻祖。其恐怖小说深受英国哥特式小说的影响，用词精当、情节惊险奇异，场景常为深渊、城堡、暗室、暴风雨或月光之下，其人物备受孤独、死亡与精神反常的折磨，且主要内容为混乱、死亡、怪诞和变态心理等，意境气氛渲染非常到位，代表作品如《厄舍大厦的倒塌》《威廉·威尔逊》。

爱伦·坡在诗歌领域也成就突出。他擅用象征主义，主张"纯诗"的艺术，极其注重诗歌的韵律节奏，并常将"死亡"作为主题，如《乌鸦》充满古怪奇特甚至病态的形象，对法国波德莱尔等象征派诗人产生了极大的影响。

二、主要作品简介

（一）《厄舍大厦的倒塌》

该作品是艾伦·坡的哥特式恐怖小说中的经典，其中传递"恐怖"的场景与情节主要有阴森的古屋、久病缠身的妹妹、精神异常的哥哥、妹妹被哥哥活埋后破棺而出并最终死在已经晕死的哥哥的怀抱里、挚友惊吓之余仓皇离开、古屋随后坍塌等。

故事采用第一人称，更易于将读者的情感带进作者设计好的情节中，恐怖的效果更为突出。艾伦·坡还抓住读者的恐惧心理，精心勾勒了恐惧、死亡、毁灭的画面，营造恐怖的气氛，描写心理的变态，而且用词考究，通篇字句和段落环环相扣，让读者好奇、紧张，甚至窒息般地一口气读完。

（二）《安娜贝尔·丽》

这是一首悼念爱人的挽歌，以"永恒的爱"作为主题。诗中叙事者和安娜贝尔·丽的爱情是如此炽烈而美好，以至于天上的六翼天使都心生嫉妒，并试图破坏他们的爱情。尽管安娜贝尔死去了，但他们的爱情却是永恒的，因为肉体可灭，而灵魂却永远在一起。这是一种海枯石烂、矢志不渝的爱情。这首诗中的韵律尤其优美，女主人的名字安娜贝尔·丽的名字被重复 7 次，与其他行末的词语押韵的同时，"Annabel Lee"这一发音也给人以无限美丽的联想，同时结合诗的主题——凄美的爱情，作品在音韵美、主题美上达到了完美的结合。

三、选读作品赏析

"To Helen"

Edgar Allan Poe wrote this poem in memory of his first true love with a beautiful women, mother of his classmate. Unfortunately, she died when Poe was young , The theme of this short poem was the beauty of a woman with whom fell deeply in love. Beauty, as Poe used the word in the poem, appeared to refer to the woman's soul as well as her body. At the beginning of the poem, he represented her as Helen of Troy - the quintessence of physical beauty; at the end of the poem, he represented her as Psyche that meant soul in Greek- the quintessence of spiritual beauty. That ultimate expression for beauty also showed Poe's pure and true feeling to his lover.

Poe believes a poem should be short and aim at beauty or any elevating excitement of the soul. In this poem, the image of beauty is well expressed by those following means: 1) Sensory images, the visual image fro "smile" "thy hyacinth hair" brilliant window-niche, etc; olfactory image from "perfumed sea", kinaesthetic image from "wanderer bore" "roam". 2) Rhetorical devices. There is hyperbole in the poem to praise the beauty which is in its most perfection so as to make the sea perfumed; simile in "like those Nicean barks" to compare his lover as a boat and imply her beauty owing the power to spiritually take him home; parallelism and metaphor in "Thy hyacinth hair thy classic face, Thy Naiad airs have brought me home" vividly depict how beautiful the woman is. 3) Symbolism is adopted. The images of two beautiful women, Helen and Psyche from Greek myth, are used to symbolize the physical beauty and spiritual beauty of poe lover.

Besides, Poe pays high attention to rhythm and defines true poem as the rhythmical creation of beauty. The rhythm and rhyme scheme in To Helen is irregular but musical in sound. The rhyme scheme in "To Helen" is ababb, ccdc, effef. It also has alliteration, such as "weary, way- won wanderer" " glory···Greece···grandeur".

Generally speaking, by using soothing, positive words and rhythms, Poe has created the fitting tone and atmosphere for the poem.

第三节　拉尔夫·瓦尔多·爱默生

一、作者简介

爱默生（1803—1882）是位散文家、诗人，超验主义哲学的主要倡导者。

他的作品体现出超验主义的哲学思想。（1）超灵与自然：超灵被认为是一种扬善抑恶、无所不在、无所不能的力量，它存在于自然与人类中，是心灵的最高现实存在，万物的精神统一。而自然是超灵的外衣，富有象征性和道德力量，他认为"自然界是精神的象征物"，他呼吁人们"回到自然中去，沉浸于它的影响，那么你会再次精神康健"。他的这种超灵观是对18世纪纯物质的牛顿宇宙观的反动，它还抨击了当时机械化的美国资本主义社会，因为它忽略了精神的健全。（2）自足与自助。爱默生强调个人主义，他坚信人作为个体的神圣性和无限可能性。人只要审视自己的内心和灵魂就可以用自己的力量改变世界，达到自我完善。他还认为人的直觉是一种比理性更为准确的认知方式，而大脑能通过直觉领悟超灵和某些绝对真理的存在，从而自信决断并自行其是。"相信你自己！""成就自己"等是他著名的口号。爱默生反对加尔文教关于堕落的人背负自身和祖辈的罪恶的理念，也批判了19世纪末兴盛的非人化的资本主义和工业化。爱默生的超验主义思想影响了梭罗、梅尔维尔、惠特曼、狄金森等大批美国作家，推动了美国文学在1835—1865年的繁荣。

二、主要作品简介

（一）《论自然》

《论自然》是宣传其超验主义哲学的代表作，包含引言和8个简短的章节，旨在阐述一整套关于宇宙和宇宙起源、现状及其最终命运的理论。爱默生提倡从不同视角——物质利益、审美对象、禁欲主义的指导者来考察自然。他认为自然是人的精神的化身，是人类异化的意识，快乐的自然是快乐的心境的反映，忧伤的自然是忧伤的心境的反映；还提出人类应回归自然，体会真实的自我，并摆脱外在的各种传统、习惯等的束缚而用单纯的眼光看待世界、去体会和发现隐藏在生活中的真谛。他对于物质与精神、现象与本质、知性与理性的观点与德国先验唯心主义遥相呼应。

（二）《论美国学者》

该演讲简要阐述了爱默生的人文主义哲学，认为真正的学者必须是"思想着的人"，而书籍是传递思想的途径，但要善用书籍，同时"思想着的人"重点应放在现在和进步上。爱默生也呼吁创造典型的美国风格，他激励美国人相信他们自己并全面治理自然，并要求他们既作为个体又作为民族来宣告自己的独立。由此，他鞭笞当时知识界机械的模仿、拘泥于传统以及学问与生活完全脱节等弊病，呼吁美国知识界摆脱欧洲的影响以争取完全的精神独立。这篇文章被看作美国学者挑战历史与旧世界的文化独立宣言。

三、选读作品赏析

" Nature"

This essay，"Nature"，is regarded as the Bible of New England Transcendentalism It consists of eight chapters nature，commodity，beauty，language，discipline idealism，spirit and prospects. The excerpt is from the first chapter.

In this excerpt，it firstly tells that the observation of stars can lead man to believe and adore their sublime and admonition，and the nature deserves people's reverence with its mysterious magnificence. Only few people can inwardly and outwardly observe themselves and the nature in order to comprehend the distinct but potential meaning out of them. Emerson is one of this wise men and he mentions himself to become a transparent eye. Then he or the eye can make himself transcend his superficial life to penetrate，witness and feel about the nature. As mentioned in the last paragraph，the nature is the color and symbol of spirit. Man should take a harmonious relationship with the nature. The final goal for man is to return to nature and find the true self.

The excerpt conveys Emerson's philosophy of transcendentalism in emphasizing the importance of spirit and nature，which constitute the whole universe. The language in it is philosophical，gentle and concise. It uses the first persons perspective to make the reader feel more sincere. The sentences are mostly speech-like and loose but convey the profound emotions. Symbolism is adopted by Emerson，too. Generally speaking，his vision of nature is the symbol. He refers to the past as "dry bones"，or "faded wardrobe" he thinks of the mind of the poet as an organic living tree；for Emerson nature is fully alive in response to mans sensitivities. In fact，the most remarkable image that suggests Emerson's symbolic method of perception is his ingenious use of a transparent eyeball which is a supreme reality of his mind，and also a spiritual unity of all Beings.

第四节　亨利·大卫·梭罗

一、作者简介

亨利·大卫·梭罗（1817—1862），是超验主义的代表人物。他深受爱默生影响，提倡回归本心，亲近自然。1845 年，在瓦尔登湖畔隐居两年，体验简朴和接近自然的生活，并以此为题材写成长篇散文《瓦尔登湖》（1854）。他也是一位废奴主义及自然主义者，有无政府主义倾向。他的代表作《论公民的不服从》（1849）对马丁·路德·金领导民权运动产生了巨大影响。梭罗才华横溢，一生共创作了二十多部一流的散文集，被称为自然随笔的创始者，其文章简练有力、朴实自然、富有思想性，注重使用地方语言，特别是双关语等，使自己的作品产生出一种"讽刺幽默"的意味。

二、主要作品简介

（一）《瓦尔登湖》

该作品由 18 篇文章组成，描绘了大自然的景象，以及他自建木屋、耕地、种豆、摘野菜、招待朋友等生活情况，形成了一幅与大自然水乳交融，并在田园生活中感知自然、重塑自我的神奇画面，引领读者进入一个澄明、恬美、素雅的世界。它抒发了梭罗的超验主义思想，体现了人与自然的和谐、自然简朴的生活类型与自力更生的谋生方式的乐趣，以及在节制物欲的前提下追求饱满的精神世界的必要性和实用性。他提倡将身体的物欲降低到最少，以便在读书、思考、观察自然与自我当中获得最大的精神财富和自由。

（二）《论公民的不服从》

该书创作于他在瓦尔登湖畔生活时，因未交税他被捕入狱，随后被无名人士付钱救出，愤怒之下他将个人的政治观点写成论文。文中，梭罗严谨地推理，最后得出结论，只有建立在个人主义、个人自由和个性解放基础上的国家，并充分尊重个人自由所组成的政府，才是国家和政府的正道；而强制的集体主义和专制教条式的强令所有国民"爱国"和"尊法"的行为，是最坏的政府行为。他还认为，一个公民如果认为法律是不公正的，就有义务拒绝服从它。梭罗的主张对甘地和马丁·路德·金等民主主义运动者提供了思想鼓舞和行动方向，"非暴力抵抗"就是其典型反映。

三、选读作品赏析

Walden

Walden is Thoreau's representative work which records his real life experience at Walden Pond. Thoreau expresses his meditation on the meaning of life and gives his. The excerpt is chosen from the second article and mainly talks about where he lived and what he lived for. In fact, he lived in a self-made cabin and his purpose in going to Walden is "to live deliberately, to confront the essentials and to exact the meaning of life". Thoreau combines the practical and the philosophical value in his Walden project The phrase "the essential facts of life" can refer both to material necessities like clothes food, houses and equipment, and also to the essence of human existence. He believes the richest life lies in simplest needs and wishes to choose his path of life independently and thoughtfully, subject to his own deliberation. Under the concern of humanity being spoiled by the industrial development and vanity-filling society, he recalls the simplest lifestyle with the least needs for material things but most needs for spiritual world. In order to do that, Thoreau emphasizes the importance of self-reliance, solitude meditation, and closeness to nature in transcending the "desperate" existence. Thoreau is close to the nature and makes himself part of the nature, which puts his transcendental view into practice.

The essay chooses a first person perspective to touch the readers mind easily and deeply. The language used in this excerpt is in a speech-like way with simple and plain words. It shows the typical feature of romanticism for its description of local landscape.

In describing that, Thoreau adopts multiple techniques, such as the different sensory description especially the visual and auditory sense, and the different angles like being panoramic, micro, moving and silent, close and distant. Besides, rhetorical devices are used, such as metaphor for comparing prejudice, tradition and delusion as alluvion covering the globe, which vividly and also sharply criticizes the social prejudiced view and tradition; paradox in "current slides away, but eternity remains" to convey his contemplation for nature; rhetorical questions like why should we knock under and go with the stream? Which remind people of figuring out reasons for following the majority's opinions and lifestyles, and in which it also uses "stream" as metaphor or symbol for the majority or even society. In fact, it has many images as symbol or metaphor to imply what the simple life he desires and the wrong social traditions or views are, such as "fam" "dawn" "rails" "the riches vein".

第五节　纳萨尼尔·霍桑

一、作者简介

纳萨尼尔·霍桑（1804—1864）的长篇小说《红字》（1850）使他名声大噪；随后的《七个尖角阁的房子》（1851）、《福谷传奇》（1852）、《玉石人像》（1860）也极为成功。霍桑的作品突出表现为描写社会和人性的阴暗面，且以表面温和但实质犀利的笔锋暴露了黑暗、讽刺了邪恶、揭示了真理。他受到加尔文教关于人的"原罪"和"内在堕落"理论的影响，着重探讨清教社会中人性的道德和罪恶及其与社会环境的关系等问题，主张通过善行和忏悔来洗刷罪恶、净化心灵，从而得到拯救。此外，霍桑的作品想象丰富、结构严谨；他除了进行心理分析与描写外，还运用了寓言以及象征主义手法，比如《红字》中"A"的众多象征意义，使作品发人深省。

二、主要作品简介

（一）《红字》

女主人公海丝特·白兰嫁给了与之并不相爱的学者奇灵渥斯。白兰先期移民美国，在孤独中白兰与牧师丁梅斯代尔相恋并生下女儿珠儿；由于她拒绝说出孩子的父亲，白兰被戴上标志"通奸"的红色字母 A 示众；奇灵渥斯随后来到美国，并查出牧师就是孩子的父亲。他以朋友的虚假身份不断报复、折磨牧师。最终，牧师放弃了与白兰私奔，并当着众人的面走上绞刑台，说出自己是孩子的父亲后憔悴而死。奇灵渥斯也因苦厄沉重而过世，白兰则以正直、善良的品行赢得了社会的承认与尊重。《红字》以 17 世纪北美新英格兰清教社会为背景，将历史事件和作家的想象结合起来，体现了小说的传奇性。故事以罪孽、理智和情感之间的冲突为主题，讽刺原罪对于人的社会地位、声誉等方面的毁灭性打击，暗示出作家对 17 世纪清教社会的评判。霍桑把基本道德和人类心理交融在一起，突出了道德寓言的特色；同时使用了心理分析、象征手法等，是美国浪漫主义小说的代表作。

（二）《七个尖角阁的房子》

全书借用家族诅咒这一古老的哥特传统，描写了品钦家族因祖上谋财害命而使后代遭到报应的故事。和《红字》一样，这部小说是关于罪孽行为的后果，且是延及几代的后果。这又一次证明了霍桑的想法：一代人的恶行会延续至下几代人，使其受到教训与惩罚。

三、选读作品赏析

Chapter 23 of The Scarlet Letter

The novel, The Scarlet Letter, is a story of sin and salvation. This excerpt is close to the ending part. It tells that Priest Dimmesdale, who committed adultery with Hester was tortured mentally and physically so much by his own belief in God and by the vicious plan of Chilling worth that he revealed his sin at the moment before his death.

The characters in this excerpt are Priest Dimmesdale, Hester, Doctor Chillingworth Hester's daughter Pearl. Their characteristics are fully depicted by Hawthorne lesdale is depicted as a successful and finally honorable priest due to the last exciting sermon. Committing adultery means destroying his career but the belief in God and the mental self-torture impels him to reveal the truth. The theme of sin and self salvation is well expressed on him. As to his lover Hester, a kind woman, she obeys the priest's willingness and endures the shameful scarlet letter for many years. She saves herself and wins the moral victory by her preserving work and relationship with the neighbors. Her husband Chillingworth is described as a real villain, the most sinful person, who constantly torments the sinning soul of the priest. He even tries to stop the priest's redemption before his death. Pearl is an innocent girl, who is the fruit of In expressing the theme and characteristics, the psychological approach contributes a lot. In this excerpt, Hawthorne excruciatingly analyzes the inward tensions of priest Dimmesdale when he is filled with remorse and keeps reviewing agonizingly his guilt in his mind.

Besides, Hawthorne is a master of symbolism. The most obvious symbol is the letter A, which symbolizes adultery; it also stands for Hester's being alone and away from the major social acceptance, and able to feed herself and daughter by being good at the art of embroidery. Other symbols are as follows the name Arthur Dimmesdale, short for "AD", can be the first two letters of "Adultery", and also the first two letters of Adam, who sinfully steals the forbidden fruit Pearl is seen as the shame to Chillingworth and sin for Dimmesdale and she actually is a living scarlet letter; Hester the heroine, sinful but gaining her salvation by hard work, symbolizes strength and Independence.

By detailed description and the use of symbolism, Hawthorne shows his concern for moral, emotional and psychological effects of sin on the people.

第六节　赫尔曼·麦尔维尔

一、作者简介

赫尔曼·麦尔维尔（1819—1894）的作品以海上生活为主题，其代表作品为《莫比·迪克》（1851）。麦尔维尔在政治上追求民主；宗教上，他深受加尔文教义的影响，认为人类天性邪恶；他支持"自助自立"，但质疑超验主义过于乐观的世界观，认为个人无力抗争社会。麦尔维尔还对人与自然的关系进行了深入思考，认为人类应该观察、探索自然，若狂妄地反抗自然，就会导致毁灭。通过象征的手法，麦尔维尔在《莫比·迪克》中将这一思想深刻地揭示了出来。

二、主要作品简介

（一）《巴特尔比》

这是麦尔维尔的文学名篇。巴特尔比是个抄写员，最初进入纽约市法律事务所时，他勤奋、能干；不过他拒绝做抄写以外的任何事情；过了一些日子以后，他连抄写工作也停下了，原因是"我不愿意"；他因此遭到解雇但拒绝离开事务所。最后巴特尔比因流浪罪被逮捕并死在狱中。小说描写了巴特尔比的缄默、孤僻和隐遁，以及他在社会困顿中的挣扎，反映了商品经济社会中人与人在思想感情上难以沟通的普遍现象。

（二）《自信者》

这是麦尔维尔的一部讽刺小说，探讨了人类轻信而又多疑的天性，还以假面舞会的形式探讨了人类主体的神秘性。在这部有着四十五章的小说中，麦尔维尔意图表达的是，随着假面舞会继续进行下去，普遍信心遭到攻击，不信任处于上风，而且欺诈四处猖獗。这些都是因为天生的人性弱点造成的。麦尔维尔以激烈而痛苦的反讽来抨击人性的弱点，透露出对超验主义的质疑。

三、选读作品赏析

An excerpt from Chapter 41 of Moby-Dick

Moby-Dick is Melvilles famous work is called the Shakespearean tragedy of man fighting against fates. This excerpt is from chapter 41, and mainly describes the widespread terror for Moby-Dick and how Captain Ahab loses one of his legs. Told by Ishmael, a crew on the ship, in a first person perspective, this excerpt conveys the weakness of human beings in front of the powerful whale. The narrator gives many examples and references to imply how powerful and evil the white whale is, which makes this excerpt seem to be a diary or journal.

Like Hawthorne, Melville is a master of symbolism. For instance, land is a symbol of safety while sea of adventure and danger. In this excerpt, the terror of Moby-Dick is fully introduced and analyzed. In fact, this white whale has different symbolic meanings for different people. To Ahab, the whale is either evil itself or the agent of an evil force hat controls the universe. He takes Moby-Dick as the target for all his pain, anger, and hatred. To Ishmael, Moby Dick is one of several different sperm whales that have rumors circulating about them in the whaling industry. It also represents the tremendous organic vitality of the universe, for it has a life force that surges onward irresistibly, impervious to the desires or wills of men. To superstitious sailors, Moby Dick seems immortal and omnipresent. Like a mysterious sea-faring God, it is impossible to be killed.

As to the reader, the whale can be viewed as a symbol of the physical limits that life imposes upon man. It may also be regarded as a symbol of nature, or an instrument of god's vengeance upon evil man.

This excerpt also shows Mclville's attitude about man s capacity in the nature which is so magnificent that men should realize themselves being weak and is doomed to yield up to the mercy of nature; otherwise men would end up in disasters, like captain Ahab losing his leg and finally losing his ship, crew and his own life.

第七节　亚伯拉罕·林肯

一、作者简介

亚伯拉罕·林肯（1809—1865）出身贫寒，在艰苦的劳作之余，通读了莎士比亚的全部著作以及其他大量历史和文学书籍，成为一个博学且充满智慧的人。1860 年他当选为美国第 16 任总统。大选揭晓后，南方种植园奴隶主制造分裂，发动了叛变。林肯坚决反对国家分裂，他废除了叛乱各州的奴隶制度，颁布了《宅地法》《解放黑人奴隶宣言》，并最终击败了南方分离势力，维护了美利坚联邦及人人生而平等的权利。林肯善于发表公众演说，著名的演讲有 1863 年 11 月 19 日在葛底斯堡阵亡将士公墓落成仪式上发表的演说，还有 1865 年 3 月 4 日第二次总统就职演说等。

二、主要作品简介

《葛底斯堡演说词》。该演说词是美国历史上引用最多的政治性演说。1863 年 7 月 1—3 日，葛底斯堡战役发生。南北双方留下超过七千具的战士遗骸，庄严有序地埋葬死者成为当地数千居民的首要之务。随后宾夕法尼亚州购下 17 英亩的土地作为墓园之用。1863 年 11 月 19 日，葛底斯堡国家公墓举行落成揭幕式。其中林肯的演讲修辞细腻周密，铿锵有力，极具感染力。林肯诉诸独立宣言所支持的"凡人生而平等"之原则，重新定义这场内战：不只是为联邦存续而奋斗，亦是"自由之新生"，真正将平等带给全体公民。其中"民有、民治、民享之政府"的观念深入人心。

三、选读作品赏析

" *The Gettysburg Address* "

"The Gettysburg Address" is the most famous speech of Abraham Lincoln and one of the most quoted speeches in the United States history. It was delivered at the dedication of the Soldiers' National Cemetery in gettysburg Pennsylvania, on November 19, 1863, ten month after the "Emancipation Proclamation", four and a half months after the Battle of Gettysburg. During the American Civil War, this battle is a devastating one with more than 7000 soldiers' death but it is the overwhelming change of the war in the favor of the Union.

In honor of the dead, the speech is made to encourage his fellowmen to fight for "a new birth of freedom" that would bring true equality to all of its citizens. The speech begins with "Four score and seven years ago", which refers to the events of the American Revolutionary War. By mentioning "testing", Lincoln implies the self-evident rights such as democracy, freedom and equality declared before by "The Declaration of Independence" to be tested. Another word "nation" is used by Lincoln for five times (four times when he referred to the American nation, and one time when he referred to "any nation so conceived and so dedicated"), but never the word "union" which might refer only to the North. He does not use the word "slavery" for it may allude to the 1789 Constitution, which implicitly recognizes slavery in the unequal three fifths compromise.

Lincoln also uses many uplifting words which are intended to honor the dead and encourage the alive, such as " liberty" " equal" " freedom" " dedicate" " consecrate devotion", etc. In fact, not only does he choose the careful diction, but also the excellent coherence devices. Firstly, repetition is well used for emphasis and also for rhythm, words like " nation" for five times, "dedicate" for five times, "consecrate" for two times, and "devotion" for two times. Secondly，synonyms are frequently used for emphasis，such as "dedicate" "consecrate" "devotion"；and antonyms like "endure" and "perish"，"live" and "died"，"forget" and "remember" are used for sharp contrast；parallel structures，like we cannot dedicate- we cannot consecrate- we cannot hallow-this ground. But it can never forget what we say here，but it can never be. And of the people，by the people，for the peopleo be. It is rather for us to forget what they did here. It is for us，the living，rather make the atmosphere of the speech strengthened and also its meaning stressed；pronouns，like "we" used for eleven times，"it" for six times，also serve to link the text and its semantics closely.

第八节　亨利·沃兹沃思·朗费罗

一、作者简介

亨利·沃兹沃思·朗费罗（1807—1882）是美国浪漫主义时期的诗人，受到德国浪漫主义思想的影响。1839 年他的第一部诗集《夜吟》出版，包括著名的《夜的赞歌》《生命颂》《群星之光》等音韵优美的抒情诗，为他赢得高度的社会关注。叙事诗《伊凡吉林》（1847）、《海华沙之歌》（1855）和《迈尔斯·斯坦狄什的求婚》（1858）是朗费罗的三部主要诗作，这些作品的发表使他声望日增。他一生创作了大量抒情诗、叙事诗，多从本乡本土或外国民间故事中取材，内容通俗易懂，文风凝练、飘逸、轻灵、活泼、温馨或凄婉，在美国和欧洲广受赞赏。

二、主要作品简介

（一）《生命颂》

诗集《夜吟》中的一首，也被译为《人生礼赞》。本诗四句一节，第一、二节开宗明义地指出"人生是实在的，人生不是虚无"。第三至六节指出，既然生活不是梦，那就要抓住现在去行动。第七、八两节以伟人的榜样来激励人们，要在"时间的沙滩上"留下脚印，给后来者以鼓舞，最后一节首尾呼应，在"不断去收获，不断去追求"的强音中结束全诗。该诗否定了悲观消沉、人生如梦的人生观，赞赏了积极乐观、不断进取的生活态度，并号召人们勇敢面对生活的挑战，学会等待与奋斗，使人生充实、圆满。诗中多处采用头韵，使全诗音韵自然、节奏明快，同时也铿锵有力、极富感染力。

（二）《海华沙之歌》

这是采用印第安人的传说而精心构思的一首四音步扬抑格的长诗，语言朴素自然、生动活泼，抒情细腻，韵调柔和。诗作主要歌颂了印第安人领袖海华沙一生克敌制胜的英雄业绩，以及他结束部落混战后致力于使各族繁荣富强的重要贡献。在描绘印第安人的生活时，诗人叙说了印第安人遭受种族主义者的残酷迫害。这是描写印第安人的第一部史诗，透露出印第安人的苦难，在当时是难能可贵的，也被称为美国伟大的史诗。

三、选读作品赏析

" A Psalm of Life"

This poem was written when Longfellow suffered from hypochondria because of his first wife's death. However, despite all the frustrations, Longfellow tried to encourage himself by writing this piece of optimistic work.

The poem is said to be the first English poem that was translated into Chinese. In the poem, Longfellow first criticizes the pessimistic attitudes like "life is but an empty dream" "grave is its goal" "enjoyment or sorrow is our destined end or way", etc. Then he enthusiastically points out that life is too short to be wasted, and we should "act in the living present" and "make our lives sublime".

The relationship of life and death is a constant theme for poets. Longfellow expresses his interpretation by this poem that life is hard and short, and human beings ought to act with courage and act with God to face the reality straightly so as to make otherwise meaningless life significant. At the time of acting and achieving, we should learn to be patient. This happened to coincide with John Milton's conclusion achieved when he was considering how his light is spent, They also serve who only stand and wait.

Generally speaking, the poem is written with gentleness, sweetness, and purity. It uses a first person perspective to draw close the distance between the poet and the reader and make the explanation more real and touching. It consists of 9 stanzas in trochaic tetrameters with a regular rhyme scheme abab, cd-cd, efef. On the other hand the poem is easy to understand with daily-used words and phrases, for example, "life is but an empty dream" "grave is not its goal" "life of great men... make our lives sublime", etc. what's more, it contains vivid similes and metaphors, such as "our heart. is beating like the muffled drums" And "the world's broad field of battle" in which the human world is compared to a battle field.

第九节　华尔特·惠特曼

一、作者简介

华尔特·惠特曼（1819—1892），是美国诗歌史上最为重要的人物之一。其诗集《草叶集》，是一部丰富的影响力深远的巨著。他的平等、民主思想充分体现在他的每一句诗行中。他也是一个民族主义者，对于美国的未来非常乐观，把美国喻为一个天天向前走的孩子，随着一天天过去将会变得越来越强大。在宗教上惠特曼是一个泛神论者。他的"heaven"总是指代布满星星和行星的天域，而非上帝所在的天国；他还用"复活"类比动植物的生命循环，即种子、发芽、生长、死亡和另一个种子再生的过程，而非"耶稣"的复活。他崇尚艺术的简单性，选用自由体诗作为诗歌的表达载体，使诗歌形式更为灵活多变便于运用口头英语畅快自如地表达情感。

二、主要作品简介

（一）《草叶集》

《草叶集》汇集了惠特曼终身成就的诗歌，其中非常著名的有《自我之歌》《有个天天向前走的孩子》《开拓者哟！开拓者!》等。惠特曼诗歌集以草叶命名，草叶象征着一切平凡、普通的事物，是生命力的象征，是发展与民主的象征。其中《自我之歌》就是自由、民主、平等和博爱之歌；《噢，船长！我的船长！》将内战中的美国比作一艘冲破风暴、胜利返航的巨轮，而亚伯拉罕·林肯就是那指挥若定、却在胜利之时被刺杀的船长。诗中叙述者对林肯的辞世悲痛万分，突显出他民主主义的立场。惠特曼在诗作中尝试运用自由体这种崭新的诗歌形式以及口头语言，因而《草叶集》堪称美国文学史的里程碑，代表着 19 世纪美国人民追求民主、平等的理想。

（二）《民主展望》

散文，收录于《草叶集》，其主题是民主和个人主义理想。他勾勒出一幅美国新文化的秩序图景，谴责内战后民主时期的腐败和物质财富的积累，预告了未来美国的伟大，宣称只有文化上的独立才能实现真正意义上的民族本土文学。文中也有对同性恋的歌颂，他认为对同志之爱的承认不仅是社会进步的标志，而且这种爱本身就是推动社会发展的进步力量。

三、选读作品赏析

"Hear America Sing"

This poem presents the reader with a picture of America singing the varied carols . People from different walks of life sing for their own honored occupations. It seems that the poet provides the reader with a harmonious and uplifting concert performed by his fellow Americans.

Whitman speaks highly of the working class of American people together with their work values and ethics. By depicting that everyone is singing together in a beautiful song, the poem means that all of the American people are creating and developing the industry of America, and they work together for the whole country. Nationalism can be seen from that. He exalts America to be a promising land where each person is united but also unique with their own singing, which also shows the individualism, democracy and freedom.

The poem has a positive, uplifting and passionate tone The poet chooses words like "Blithe and strong", "delicious sing" and "strong, melodious. songs" to appeal to the reader's imagination and feeling for such beautiful song from the strong, responsible and passionate American working people.

The verbs, such as " measures", " makes", "sits", "stands", "sewing", and "washing", obviously show the reader a moving and acting picture with quick pace. Thus, the reader is compelled to follow the poet to walk through each workplace and feel their enthusiastic spirits.

The poem is written with Whitman's free verse, without regular metrical pattern or the conventional rhyming system. The words in it are simple and some are in oral language. However, those simple words, combined together, form a moving picture of passion, thus showing the poet's capacity of excellence out of simplicity.

第十节　埃米莉·狄金森

一、作者简介

埃米莉·狄金森（1830—1886）一生创作了 1775 首诗。她的诗富于睿智和新奇的比喻。狄金森喜欢在诗中扮演不同的角色，如新娘、小孩、死者等。自然、成功、爱情、死亡与永生都是狄金森诗歌的重要主题。她的诗一般采用教会赞美诗的格律：每节四句，第三句八音节，第二、四句六音节，采用抑扬格，且第二、四句押韵。诗的篇幅一般短小，多数只有两至五节，经常破格地押"半韵"；她放弃了传统的标点，多采用破折号；她使用的名词多用大写，句子成分常被省略，有时甚至连动词也省掉；此外，她还喜欢运用倒装句。

二、主要作品简介

（一）《我是无名之辈》

这首诗采用了戏剧独白的形式，叙述者用第一人称，同无名之辈低声私语：一旦成为明星，那就被公众高度关注，再无隐私可言，突出了名声带来的困扰这一主题。叙述者庆幸自己仍然默默无闻，也劝告读者不要暴露，否则会被世界唾弃。自嘲与讥讽贯穿着整首诗。

（二）《成功的滋味最甜美》

这首诗探讨了谁能深切体会成功的滋味这一主题。成功的感觉对于失败者来说是最甜蜜的，就像人们受尽干渴煎熬时喝到花蜜水一样。那些耀武扬威的胜利者并不能深切体会到成功的含义；疆场上的士兵才能深切体会胜利是如何来之不易。通过比喻的形式，狄金森将诗的主题以及自己的肺腑之言淋漓尽致地表达了出来，她当时又何尝不是一个渴望体尝成功的失败者呢？她何尝不渴望自己的诗能被世人喜爱，并能被大量发表呢？

（三）《因为我不能停下等待死神》

死亡与生命是狄金森常用的主题，她认为死亡并不可怕。此外，死亡也不是终点，而是另一段生命的开始。该诗深刻地体现了似朋友般的死神带"我"走向"永生"。在这首诗中，死神是一位亲切的车夫，他停住等"我"上去，车里还坐着"永生"。"我"被死神的和蔼和礼貌所打动，决定放弃劳作和休息，一起踏上了死亡的路程。

（四）《我一直在爱》

爱情也是狄金森写诗时偏爱的主题。虽然她孑然一身独守渡船，但也有过两段爱情：第一段是与一位有妇之夫，爱情在开始前就结束了；第二段是与父亲的同辈人——一位法官的恋情，这位法官的妻子已逝，狄金森年近五十，面临爱人的求婚，她依然拒绝，为的是维护作为未婚女性的独立与自由。这首诗赞扬了叙述者所付出的永恒的爱，透露出"我"的痴情，对爱情的信心和忠贞不渝，哪怕是死亡也无法放弃爱情。通过这首诗，读者可以感受到狄金森的内心对爱情的向往与追求。

三、选读作品赏析

" *I am Nobody! Who Are You*"

This poem takes the form of dramatic monologue, and adopts the first person perspective to give the question and answer.

In Stanza 1, the narrator identifies herself or himself as "nobody" to get the topic introduced. Who are you? Are you nobody, too? this question is asked by this open naive, and innocent child-like "nobody". Then this "nobody" declares the view that the public may attack or destroy the nobodies. This stanza forms the foundation for the theme to be expressed in Stanza 2, which uses the metaphor of a frog's life- pleasing. the audience by keeping talking. The image of frog serves as a symbol, too. Since the frogs must croak and make a lot of noise so as to make themselves heard and noticed the celebrity is nothing different from the frog when they have to keep themselves exposed in public and do fake shows or else so as to make themselves noticed and admired by the public. Therefore, the theme of this poem is that being a celebrity means no privacy and pleasing the public; the real admirable life is a secluded and common One.

Dickson's poem is unique and conventional. In this poem, there is loose iambic trimeter with irregular rhyme scheme. In the first stanza, the ending words" you "too", and " know" are only in half- rhyme. She also uses rhythmic dashes to interrupt the flow, and exclamatory marks to show strong and stressed feelings.

Though the language in the short poem is simple and plain, the poet fully implies the intended theme. This poem is Dickinson's most famous and most defense of the kind of spiritual privacy she favored, implying that to be a Nobody is a luxury incomprehensible to a dreary somebody for they are too busy keeping their names in circulation. But to be somebody is not as fancy as it seems to be. Since Dickson only published fewer than ten poems out of her total 1800 ones, this poem may be her inner emotions reflection- to be nobody to get her private life and her own true heart.

第十章　现实主义时期的美国文学解读与作品赏析

1865—1914 年的美国文学在美国文学史上称为现实主义时期。这一时期的美国文学是对浪漫主义和感伤传统的反叛，注重反映生活的真实性，描写典型环境中的典型性格，揭露和批判社会的阴暗面，体现出人道主义关怀，同时为现代主义文学开拓了道路。

现实主义小说的真正开端是威廉·豪威尔斯和马克·吐温的创作。欧·亨利的短篇小说被称为"美国生活的幽默的百科全书"。亨利·詹姆斯被誉为美国意识流文学先驱。杰克伦敦的小说《铁蹄》是揭露"工资奴隶制的《汤姆叔叔的小屋》"。

一、主要特色

（一）地方色彩/乡土文学作品

（1）常常采用短篇小说的形式，也有少量诗歌。

（2）在艺术上的共同点是采用当地的方言，描绘本乡本土的传说、故事或现实生活，用幽默的笔法描写人物，具有浓重的地方色彩。

（二）现实主义作品

（1）追求艺术的真实模式，强调客观真实地反映生活，作家的思想倾向较为隐蔽。

（2）注重典型化方法的运用，力求在艺术描写中，通过细节的真实表现生活的本质和规律。

（3）强调外部环境对人物的影响以及探索人物内部的心理状况。

（4）具有批判性和改良性，特别注重社会底层社会及"小人物"的悲剧命运。

（5）提出开放式结局。

（三）自然主义作品

（1）取材于低层社会或是形势严峻的场景，描写垂死的或病态的"强者"。

（2）比先前的美国传统文学更具体地揭示了美国资本主义生产的社会心理本质，即生产过程作为"生产欲望和消费欲望"的社会化过程。

（3）充斥着命定论情愫，强调人的行为由环境和遗传因素决定、自然对人类的冷漠以及人在自然面前的无助。

（4）对素材持有非道德态度。

（5）受到了美国式幽默、来自尼采的超人哲学等的影响。

二、主要作家与作品

现实主义文学时期三位最重要的作家是豪威尔斯、马克·吐温和亨利·詹姆斯。马克·吐温以自己独特的幽默笔触和生动的口语和地方方言风格开创了美国的文学传统，代表作有《汤姆·索亚历险记》和《哈克贝里·费恩历险记》。亨利·詹姆斯是一位反映人类内心生活的现实主义作家。他晦涩的文体、开放性结局和内心独白等手法深深影响了后来的现代派作家，尤其是意识流文学。其主要作品有小说《一位女士的画像》《鸽翼》《专使》《金碗》，以及文学评论集《小说的艺术》。欧·亨利的作品构思新颖，语言诙谐，结局常常出人意料。他的主要作品有长篇小说《白菜与国王》，以及短篇小说集《四百万》《剪亮的灯盏》和《西部之心》。西奥多·德莱赛是一位以探索充满磨难的现实生活著称的美国自然主义作家。他的代表作品有《嘉莉妹妹》《欲望三部曲》和《美国的悲剧》。弗罗斯特被誉为自然诗人，诗歌语言质朴、清新、近乎口语化，但折射出真理的光辉。他的许多诗作都脍炙人口，比如《摘苹果后》《火与冰》《修墙》《未选择的路》等。薇拉·凯瑟的作品以擅长描写女性及美国早期移民的拓荒生活而闻名，著作如《哦，拓荒者!》及《我的安东妮亚》。舍伍德·安德森擅长描绘美国小镇人们的心理、情感状态，聚焦于下层阶级失败、堕落以及孤独的小人物，探讨人物的行为动机和受挫心理。他最著名的作品有短篇小说集《小镇畸人》《鸡蛋的胜利》和自传性小说《讲故事者的故事》。凯瑟琳·安·波特以中短篇小说创作为主，是公认的文体创新和技巧大师。其作品多设置为南方背景，运用大量意象和象征形象，通过独到的幽默展现现实生活的黑暗面。波特最为人知的短篇小说是《开花的犹大树》和《被抛弃的威瑟罗尔奶奶》。

第一节　马克·吐温

一、作者简介

马克·吐温（1835—1910）是萨缪尔·克莱门斯的笔名。马克·吐温以他独特的乡土文学、西部幽默、富有戏剧性的情节以及生动的口语和地方方言，开创了美国文学的传统。他幽默的笔触和口语体运用影响了安德森、海明威、艾略特、福克纳、塞林格等后世作家。同时，马克·吐温是美国批判现实主义文学的奠基人，他经历了美国从初期资本主义到帝国主义的发展过程，其思想和创作也表现为从轻快调笑到辛辣讽刺再到悲观厌世的发展阶段。

二、主要作品简介

(一)《汤姆·索亚历险记》

该小说也像《独立宣言》一样成为学校的经典读物，汤姆成为美国儿童的英雄人物。

小说通过主人公的一系列冒险经历，讽刺和批判了美国虚伪庸俗的社会习俗、伪善的宗教仪式和刻板迂腐的学校教育，以欢快的笔触刻画出了少年儿童自由活泼的心灵。

(二)《哈克贝利·费恩历险记》

这部小说事实上讲述了美国的历史和生活。与哈克一起，读者可以看到形形色色的人，并看到了剥去令人厌烦的细节后的人类特征。小说赞扬了男孩哈克贝利的机智和善良，谴责了宗教的虚伪和信徒的愚昧，同时，塑造了一位富有尊严的黑奴形象。

三、选读作品赏析

Chapter 19 of Adventures of Huckleberry Finn

In this chapter，Huck and Jim come upon two men fleeing some trouble. It turns out that the men both are professional con artists. The younger man claims himself an impoverished English duke and gets Huck and Jim to treat him like royalty. The old man then reveals his true identity as the dauphin. Huck and Jim then wait on the men and call them "Duke" and "Your Majesty" respectively.

The characters are fully portrayed on the basis of their words and action. Huck child as he is, shows natural intelligence and willingness to think through a situation on its own merits and his conclusions are surprisingly correct in their context. For example although he has discovered both the duke and king are liars, he caters to their requests. His pretended ignorance aims to keep on good terms with the duke and king lest these two bad guys would turn them into the slave-hunters. Twains use of dialects lays bare the duke's and the kings pretension and vanity. The two adults actually are blatant unnamed con artists, because they claim they descend from the royal lineage, even though they in reality fail to pronounce correctly the names of their ancestors.

Artistic techniques also find their way in this chapter. The most prominent one is the use of dramatic irony. The two battered men dress poorly, and do even worse for a living, not to mention their dialects. Yet, they are so hypocritical as to pretend they are of the royal blood. what's even worse, they request both Huck and Jim wait on them. In the last paragraph of this chapter, even Huck has realized the two men are lying, and hence dramatic irony is projected here. Obviously, throughout the excerpt, it takes little pains for a sophisticated reader to feel the tinge of dramatic irony.

Admittedly, the novel is written in the 1st person point of view. However, there are two voices in this excerpt. The one is the grown-up reminiscent Huck, while the other is the young, fleeing Huck. When the narrator comes to describe the goings-on, he tends to be the teen, naive and coming-of-age. Yet when it is the occasion for him to make comment, he proves to be penetrating and worldly, with reference to what he decides to do for their safety in the last paragraph of this excerpt.

Symbols are widely used in this excerpt. The first one is the Mississippi River. For Huck and Jim, the Mississippi River is the ultimate symbol of freedom. Alone on their raft, they do not have to answer to anyone. The river carries them toward freedom；for Jim，toward the free states；for Huck，away from his abusive father and the restrictive sivilizing of St. Petersburg. Much like the river itself，Huck and Jim are in flux willing to change their attitudes about each other with little prompting. The other one is the raft. In this part，the raft looks like a microcosm in which there are the grown-ups like the duke and the king and themselves. In this small world，they soon find that. they are not completely free from the evils and influences of the outside world，i. e hypocrisy of the civilized world.

第二节　欧·亨利

一、作者简介

欧·亨利有"美国的莫泊桑"之称。他的小说被誉为"美国生活的幽默百科全书"。欧·亨利选取的题材平凡且真实，在语言叙述方面多采用幽默讽刺的手法，在小说情节方面多采用结局意料之外却也在情理之中的"欧·亨利结尾"。

二、主要作品简介

(一)《警察与赞美诗》

作者用了一种轻松幽默的笔调描写了苏比这个流浪汉为达到自己可笑的目的而做出的可笑的尝试，更为可笑的是警察先生们对这些违法的举动并没有予以惩罚，反而显示出了种"宽容"，而当苏比打算重新做人时，"宽容"的警察却逮捕了什么也没干的他。故事方面讽刺了美国司法制度的黑暗，另一方面也流露出命运无情捉弄人的悲观情绪。

(二)《麦琪的礼物》

这个凝聚着社会现实生活无法解决的真实矛盾（爱情和财富）因作家深沉的文笔而倍增真实，更能引起读者的怜悯和同情，并将他们引入更深刻的思考中去。故事揭示了在那个唯金钱万能的社会中，他们的礼物不能算作是智慧的"麦琪的礼物"。但是，他们失去了财富，却加深了人世间最可宝贵的真挚的爱情。在爱情与财富的矛盾中他们为了前者牺牲了后者。

（三）《最后一片叶子》

作者通过对贫苦朋友之间友谊的描写，刻画出一个舍己为人而以自己的生命为代价创造真正杰作的画家形象，着力挖掘和赞美小人物的伟大人格和高尚品德，展示他们向往充满人性美的世界的美好愿望。

三、选读作品赏析

"The Cops and the Anthe"

The short story unfolds around a vagabond Soapy who is homeless and tries every means he can to get into jail for a shelter for the coming harsh winter. He therefore develops a series of tactics to encourage the police to classify him as a criminal and arrest him. For example, he eats in a restaurant but refuses to pay; he throws a brick to break a window; and he pretends to be drunk and violates the regulation of safety. Yet all these are of no avail. At last, the funniest thing is that when he decides to become a good person and give up the life as a vagabond, the cop puts him into jail for no good reason.

The short story is featured with four main devices, i. e. ironic coincidences, black humor, figures of speech and contrasts. First, the short story is full of ironic coincidences, which is mainly reflected at the series of strategies to catch the cop's attention. For example, when Soapy tries to offend a young woman of a pleasing guise, it never occurs to him that the woman is a prostitute and will never call for the cop. The victim of the umbrella theft relinquishes the item.

Without any grudge, blatant as he assumes to be Black humor is obviously reflected in Soapy's attitude to the prison. In the text there are descriptions of his attitude, such as "for years the hospitable Blackwells had been his winter quarters", "the Island seemed very far away, that would insure his winter quarters on the right little, tight little isle" and the persecuted young woman had but to beckon a finger and Soapy would be practically en route for his insular haven A large number of figures of speech are also used here, which include exaggeration personification, and metonymy. In fact, almost every figure of speech is ironic. The ambitions of Soapy" is an example of exaggeration. Personification is adopted when the author says "Jack Frost's card and minutest coin and himself were strangers Metonymy is displayed in" brass buttons.

The story is full of profound contrast. In the text, there are the descriptions of the environment, like glittering cafe, where are gathered together nightly the choicest products of the grape, the silkworm and the protoplasm, and "electric lights and cunningly displayed wares behind plate-glass made a shop window conspicuous". These descriptions expose the luxurious life of the ruling class and make a stark contrast to the lower-class people. Another contrast is the cop's attitude to different people. The cop tends to ignore the poor and caters to the rich, as is expressed in "the policeman hurried to assist a tall blonde in an opera cloak across the street in front of a street car that was approaching two blocks away". The weightiest one is that the cop arrests Soapy when he makes up his mind to start a decent life and when Soapy endeavors to be caught the cop does not get him. The ironic tone can be felt here.

第三节　亨利·詹姆斯

一、作者简介

亨利·詹姆斯（1843—1916）的小说作品多数属于世态小说。他的写作生涯可以分为三个时期。在第一个时期，他开始探索国际主题，此间的作品主要有《美国人》《贵妇画像》。第二个时期，他尝试创作带有浓重社会和政治倾向的小说。在第三个时期，国际主题再次回到他的创作中，主要有《鸽翼》《专使》《金碗》等。在小说技巧方面，他最有名的是评论作品集《小说的艺术》。他创造了"有限视角"的方法，以某个人物为"意识中心"，从他的"角度"铺展情节。他还将小说的现实艺术基础从外部世界转向了内心世界，被认为是意识流技巧的先驱。

二、主要作品简介

（一）《贵妇画像》

该小说采用国际主题作为其创作的中心素材，并使用隐喻手法，描写了一位天真、单纯的美国姑娘为追求自由和独立来到欧洲，最后其个性被她所追求的"自由"所毁掉的心路历程。这部小说中詹姆斯以深入的洞察力剖析欧美文化冲突，以人物之间关系的情节为中心，刻画这些人物关系中的权力关系，同时涉及其他道德方面的问题。这部小说可谓是詹姆斯的代表作，并将他的文学生涯推向顶峰。

（二）《拧紧螺丝》

这是一部描写心理的恐怖小说。小说讲述的是关于一个年轻的英国女子成为两个孩子——迈尔斯和弗罗拉的家庭教师，并且经受考验去营救迈尔斯和弗罗拉的故事。小说标题原意就是指一个向着同一个方向旋转的螺丝，在走到尽头之前，是不会改变方向的，就好像是剧中所有人物的命运一样；同时，整部作品从开始一直到结束，就悬疑迭出，令人紧张，也好像是越转越紧的螺丝一样。

（三）《鸽翼》

小说写一位英国记者为钱财追求一个患有不治之症的美国姑娘的故事。该小说是詹姆斯晚期创作的一部杰出的作品，它为读者展现了一个有着多重性格和丰满个性的人物——米莉·西奥尔。很显然，小说中如鸽子一样的人物是米莉·塞尔，她救赎着这世上可救赎的一切，她将丹什尔，也许还包括凯特，从对单纯物质和肉体的绝对追求中拯救出来。

三、选读作品赏析

An Excerpt from Chapter 1 of The Portrait of a Lady

The opening chapter paints a small afternoon tea party at gardencourt and the three major male characters. Mr. Touchett，Ralph Touchett and Lord Warburton are gossiping and joking over their tea. It is mentioned that Mrs. Touchett will soon be returning from her visit to America and that she plans to bring their niece with her for a stay in England.

None of them has met the girl，and according to the telegram sent by Mrs. Touchett，she is "quite independent". The chapter prepares the reader for the following unfolding of the theme：the clash between the typical European cultural backdrop and the young American culture.

第四节　西奥多·德莱赛

一、作者简介

西奥多·赫曼·阿尔伯特·德莱赛（1871—1945）是带有自然主义倾向的现实主义作家，是美国现代小说的先驱，被认为是同海明威、福克纳并列的美国现代小说的三巨头之一。德莱赛的作品充满长句，对细节有着极大的关注。

二、主要作品简介

（一）《嘉莉妹妹》

该作品描写了农村姑娘嘉莉来到大城市芝加哥寻找幸福，为摆脱贫困，出卖自己的贞操，先后与推销员和酒店经理同居，后又凭美貌与歌喉成为演员的故事。作品比较真实地揭露了 20 世纪初人们狂热地追求美国梦的悲剧事实，揭示了人类本能驱使人们享乐并导致最终幻灭的主题，说明了在以金钱为中心的美国资本主义社会里不可能有真正的幸福。

（二）《金融家》

这是《欲望三部曲》的第一部。作品通过对柯帕乌和市财政局长斯坦纳狼狈为奸、营私舞弊的描写，指出个人通过努力实现梦想的美好愿望与美国社会腐朽阴暗的制度之间的强烈反差，暴露了资本家剥削人民、投机欺诈、横行不法地积累财富的卑劣手段，猛烈抨击了资本主义的罪恶本质。

（三）《巨人》

这是继《金融家》后三部曲的第二部。在这一部里柯帕乌得到了巨大的财富，还有政治地位和特权。作品在揭露垄断资产阶级巧取豪夺、弱肉强食的发家过程中，批判了资本家投机欺诈、横行不法地积累财富的卑劣手段，猛烈抨击了资本主义社会金钱至上、道德沦丧的现状。

（四）《美国的悲剧》

德莱塞最长的小说《美国的悲剧》达到了他艺术创作的高峰。小说以纽约一起真实的谋杀案为题材，描写了主人公克莱特·格里菲斯受到社会上邪恶势力影响，逐渐蜕变，堕落为凶杀犯，最后自我毁灭的全过程。作品揭示了利己主义恶性膨胀的严重后果，更揭露了金钱至上的美国生活方式对人性的毒害。小说结尾的语句表明克莱特·格里菲斯的悲剧不仅是个人的悲剧，也是整个美国社会的一种悲剧。

三、选读作品赏析

Chapter 47 of Sister Carrie

Dreiser has been a controversial figure in American literary history. His works are powerful in their portrayal of the changing American life, but his style is considered crude. He shows a new way of presenting reality and inspired the writers of the 1920s with courage and insight. It is in Dreiser's works that American naturalism is said to have come of age.

This excerpt reveals social Darwinism that he embraces. Human beings are merely animals driven by greed and lust in a struggle for existence in which only the fittest, the most ruthless, survive. A mans success, for example, Carries, does not come from her moral soundness; rather, it is a product of random circumstances and her inborn desires. Besides, man lives in a rather indifferent world and society Random circumstances determine what you will make and will be. The caprice of fortunes may throw a virtuous man into a gutter. People in society are also indifferent. The rich will never go to great lengths to help the poor, as is in the case of Carrie and Lola. There is not even "good fellowship" between those people who are in equally piteous condition as is shown in those men of the large crowd.

On the whole, Dreiser's style is coarse and straightforward. His narrative is very unrefined, based on quantities of materials and detailed descriptions. Several techniques can be seen in his writing, though. First, he is good at employing the journalistic method of reiteration to burn a central impression into the reader's mind. For example, in this excerpt, two sentences run like this Not evil, but longing for that which is better, and Not evil, but goodness more often allures the feeling mind... The reiteration gives a central impression that men are not at fault; instead, it is men s desires and circumstances that mislead human beings. Second, Dreiser tends to use sharp contrast in his writing. On the street, rich men driving a wagon are posed as a contrast to the impoverished on the sidewalk. The wretched life of Hurstwood runs along with the luxurious one of Carrie and her friends.

第五节 罗伯特·李·弗罗斯特

一、作者简介

罗伯特·李·弗罗斯特（1874—1963）被称为美国的一个"非官方的桂冠诗人"，也常被称为"交替性的诗人"。在弗罗斯特的诗歌中，和平、有序是自然世界的重要特点。弗罗斯特把传统的诗体与具有鲜明特色的日常语言结合起来，从而获得幽默的效果。他的主要诗作有：《新罕布什尔》（1924）、《诗歌选集》（1931）、《又一片牧场》（1937）和《一棵作证的树》（1943）。

二、主要作品简介

（一）《一个男孩的意愿》

这是弗罗斯特的第一本诗集。这本诗集的最大特色是充满着浓烈却又内敛的情感，并展现了新英格兰人们生活的独特风味。尽管他仍采用了传统的诗歌形式，但不难发现他为创新所做的努力。他试图强调戏剧性的语调以及日常语言的节奏，借此来取代传统诗歌的旋律性，他还使用简单通俗的词语，将典型的新英格兰式的轻描淡写发扬光大。

（二）《波士顿以北》

这部诗集被称为是"孤独寂寞的人民生活的写照"，采取的主要形式是戏剧性的叙述和对话，作品展现了作者对于新英格兰人的性格以及形成这种性格的环境的一种深刻的洞察。在作品中，诗人的注意力主要是向外的而不是向内的。他描写了新英格兰人面对困境表现出的种种不同的反应，其目的并不在于记录地方的风俗民情，而在于引发普遍性的意义的外延。

（三）《新罕布什尔》（New Hampshire）

这部诗集是弗罗斯特诗歌事业的新起点，并使得弗罗斯特第一次摘得普利策奖的殊荣。在这本诗集中，他尝试用幽默、诙谐、随意的笔触批判社会现象，尤其针对那种对大公司、商业化和物质化的美国式的颂扬与美化。

三、选读作品赏析

"Fire and Ice"

The speaker considers the age-old question of whether the world will end in fire or in ice. This is similar to another age-old question whether it would be preferable to freeze to death or burn to death. The speaker determines that either option would achieve its purpose sufficiently well.

An extremely compact little lyric, "Fire and Ice" combines humor, fury detachment, forthrightness, and reserve in an airtight package. Not a syllable is wasted. We can attribute part of the poems effect to the contrast between the simple, clipped precision of its vocabulary and the vague gravity of its subject "Fire and Ice" follows an invented form, an irregular mix of iambic tetrameter and dimeter, and the rhyme scheme (which is A-B-A, A-B-C, B-C-B) follows the pattern of terea roma. Each line ends either with an "-ire", "ice", or "-ate" rhyme. Each line contains either four or eight syllables. Each line can be read naturally as iambic although this is not strictly the case for several lines.

On line 7, Frost employs a strong enjambment, incomplete syntax at the end of a line, to great effect. The delay of meaning creates a tension which arises from the mixed message produced both by the pause of the line-end, and the suggestion to continue provided by the incomplete meaning. In this way, Frost holds the attention of his readers and encourages them to read on and to find what power ice does have The author bases the poem on two obvious images. He likens the elemental force of fire with the emotion of desire, and ice with hate. This poem, in terms of the images can be said a counterpart of Dante's masterpiece Inferno. In the nine rings of Hell, a visitor can see sinners of desire are tormented by fire and the betrayers are punished by ice. Besides, the nine lines of the poem can be interpreted as a parallel with the nine rings of Hell, and the rhyme scheme, ABA-ABC-BCB is also similar to the one Dante invents for Inferno.

第六节　薇拉·凯瑟

一、作者简介

薇拉·凯瑟（1873—1947）选取最具美国本土特色的中西部拓荒运动和拓荒者来作为其创作主题。她的作品还流露出强烈的女性意识，并塑造了一系列草原上女开拓者的形象。同时，她主张一切艺术的提高过程全在于单纯化的过程，倡导写"不带家具"的小说反对叠床架屋式的细节描写。美国评论家斯威尔·盖斯马尔称薇拉·凯瑟为"荒野上的贵妇人"，并认为凯瑟"是工业社会中的一位重农作家，是不断物质化文明中的一位精神美的捍卫者"。《哦，拓荒者!》和《我的安东妮亚》是美国重要的乡土文学作品。

二、主要作品简介

（一）《哦，拓荒者!》

这是薇拉·凯瑟最有特色的一部作品，描写的是女主人公亚历山德拉生命中一段最为重要的奋斗经历。凯瑟通过自己笔下的人物，表达了人类精神和自然欲望，反映了人们在创造和积累物质财富过程中的价值观、道德观以及宗教、文化等方面与人类社会发展进程之间的关系和变化，有褒贬地表现了人性中最具本质意义的内涵。

（二）《我的安东妮亚》

这部作品被公认为薇拉·凯瑟最优秀的小说。它以朴实无华的文字，清新扑面的边疆景致以及独具特色的叙事风格，成为 20 世纪美国文学中的经典。该作品通过对美国中西部边疆地区开拓者的生活描写，真实地反映了移民拓荒者如何处理新旧文化冲突，以及人与人之间的关系，塑造了许多富有魅力的开拓者形象。

三、选读作品赏析

"Neighbor Rosicky"

Neighbor Rosicky is the account of an admirable life and the portrait of an idealized person, worthy of emulation. It has a minimum of plot and a maximum of characterization. The story resembles the "Novel Demeuble", or "Unfurnished novel" which Cather invented to strip the narrative of excessive characters and incidents in order to concentrate on a central character. Reduced to the bare facts the narrative in the present consists only of Rosicky's medical diagnosis, his developing friendship with Polly, and his death. The message for the reader is that one should try to have an equally admirable character, to accept life with amusement and interest rather than to complain of ill fortune or to compete with ruthless cruelty to get ahead of others.

A prominent characteristic of the story is the effective use of the third person point of view limited. First, the story is full of Anton Rosicky's reflections on his past lives which are triggered by the casual circumstances of his daily life. In Part III, Rosicky's reflection shows his tailoring in London and New York City when he first came to America. It displays the harsh living conditions for a poor man to live in the city. Yet once again, in Part V, come his recollections of the detectable London days. These parts are charged with the contrast between his difficult beginnings and the tranquil life he has accomplished, as well as a conflict between the first generation of immigrants and their children. Another equally significant perspective is that of Doctor Ed Burleigh's. It is through his recollection that the reader can see the Rosicky familys kindness and hospitality shown in their home after delivering a neighbors baby. Then in Part VI (Last Paragraph), he stops at the country graveyard and gets an epiphany the graveyards for the country people are open and natural while those of the cities are closed. It is through his mind that we see Neighbor Rosicky's life proves "complete and beautiful" Unlike her contemporaries and those figures from the generation which succeed hers most especially Faulkner, Fitzgerald, and Hemingway - Cather's fiction creates a personal intimacy between writer and reader which both creates a deep bond and feels authentic, special.

As in all of Cather's writing the style is clear, spare, and uncluttered, an art that conceals its artistry. Her style stands midway between the journalistic style whose omniscient objectivity accumulates more fact than any character could notice，and the psychological style whose use of subjective point of view stories distorts objective reality. She selects facts from experience on the basis of feeling and then presenting the experience in a lucid，objective style.

第七节　舍伍德·安德森

一、作者简介

舍伍德·安德森（1876—1941）是第一次世界大战后美国文学史上第一位"心理小说家"。他擅长描绘美国小镇人们的心理、情感状态，聚焦于下层阶级失败、堕落以及孤独的小人物，探讨人物的行为动机和受挫心理。他的创作主要以短篇小说为主，《小城畸人》被视为美国文学史中第一部表现"荒原"这一时代主题的作品。安德森在美国现在文学史上享有非常特殊的地位，威廉·福克纳将他奉为"我们这一代作家的父亲"，而马尔科姆·考利也称他为"作家的作家，是他那一代讲故事者对后一代的风格和视野都造成影响的唯一一位"。

二、主要作品简介

（一）《小镇畸人》

这是安德森最成功也是最著名的一部作品。它由 25 个互相关联又相对独立的故事组成，以年轻记者乔治·威拉德贯串全书。作品塑造了美国亥俄州一个小城里的一系列平凡而真实的人物形象，如单纯的牧师、芳华虚度的女店员、抑郁的旅馆老板娘、神秘的医生、丑陋的电报员、30 岁未婚的女教师等。在思想上，作者把城乡文化的冲突集中在人物内心深处，从而创造出美国文学史上全新的畸人形象。在艺术上，他找到了适合自己个性的、与古老传统小说形式迥异的"新的松散"形式，即是对小说表达主体心灵自由的追求，而这正是现代派文学的基本特征之一。

（二）《鸡蛋的胜利》

作品以诙谐的笔触，从一个孩子的视角向人们展示了美国中西部一个普通家庭既悲惨又滑稽的处境。在这里，那只鸡蛋实际上象征着命运和人生。作者的父亲企图改变命运，就像他企图征服那只鸡蛋那样。但是最终还是要失败，遭到他人的耻笑和命运无情的打击。这不仅仅是一个家庭的人生悲剧，更是普通大众在盲目欲望的支配下被毁灭的悲剧。

三、选读作品赏析

"The egg"

"The Egg" is a humorous account by a child of his father from the countryside who later becomes infected with the American spirit, i. e. wealth and social position, the ideals of the 1920's. In this story, plot gives way to the experimentation in form, i. e. theme, character, tone, and setting over actions and events. On the whole, the story does not follow a conventional linear sequence of events that eventually build to a climax. This sequence is replaced by a disrupted one, with much authorial intervention Yet, characterization is constructed natural and vivid. First the narrator child as he is, sounds naive yet some bit insightful. He finds the change in father's outlook and the inscrutabilities in raising a chicken. He also imagines the two "roads" on fathers head to be a path leading to comfort and pleasure. However, a kind of worldly tone also runs throughout the story. When it comes to the baby carriage brought along, he wisely comments that all possessions are valuable for those poor people. Father is depicted as quiet in nature yet ambitious under the influence of the outer world. When he is a farmhand, he enjoys what his life is. He then becomes quite motivated by the dreams to be another epitome of from-rags-to-riches man, yet he turns quiet and disappointed Even when he runs the restaurant and wants to humor a guest, what he does looks so awkward and unnatural. Mother is presented as a woman of not many words yet of action. She encourages father and me to be a successful man. When they come to a new place to start a new business, she tries hard to support her husband. She turns to be a source of strength when father becomes totally frustrated and furious at his failure to humor a guest.

The narrator is posed as a vibrant, immediate presence in the story. In Paragraph 5 the author leads the reader to the detailed descriptions of the life of a chick and the challenges for a chick to live. The next paragraph then, renders clear that he, as a speaker, has digressed and should come back to the topic. The narrators presence is once again rendered prominent when it goes Did I say that we embarked in the restaurant business in the town of Bidwell, Ohio? I exaggerated a little. The last par also features a dominant narrator. Even before he explains father's awkward entertainment of a guest, he says to the reader, "At any rate an egg ruined his new impulse in life", the outcome of the event. In this way, his role as a narrator is Highlighted.

The use of images is another characteristic of the story. The leading symbols are the egg, the chicken and the grotesques. The egg is loaded with multiple references: the American spirit, the ruthless realities of life, and exploitation. Another image is the chicken. It stands for the people who are living in this world, tempered by the realities of life yet full of aspirations for a brighter future. The grotesques, sad to say, are those people who are doomed to fail and fall out of pace with the world. They are an unfortunate lot, just like the narrator's family.

Spiritual epiphany can also be found in this story. In the last chapter the father is portrayed to experience an epiphany, as is shown in the sentence, When he got into the presence of other something happened to him, he laid the egg gently on the table. At this moment, it seems father has realized the egg means destiny for him, and all his endeavors are in vain, and yet, this is life. His fury and disappointment vanish and cry. And with the comfort from his wife, it seems that he finally regains tranquility and will have another try in the future.

第八节　凯瑟琳·安·波特

一、作者简介

凯瑟琳·安·波特（1890—1980）以中短篇小说创作为主。她的代表作是《开花的犹大树和其他》（1930）。波特拒绝女权主义者的头衔，在她的作品中，她试图将女性人物放置于宗教和南方神话的环境中。她是公认的文体创新和技巧大师，运用大量意象和象征形象、跨时空蒙太奇、梦幻、内心独白、象征意象多重意识流艺术手法，来增强作品的艺术感染力。

二、主要作品简介

（一）《开花的犹大树》

《开花的犹大树》是她文学成就中一个辉煌的作品，它建立了波特在文学领域的崇高地位。在这篇小说中，波特向读者展现了丰富的象征艺术。波特在描述这些人物时，并没有直接表达自己的真实感情，而是留给读者小说中人物身上许多不被解释的细节，这些细节是有关象征意义的至关重要的线索。通过微妙地运用象征艺术，波特不仅深化了小说的主题——背叛，也使故事的风格更加优美。

（二）《被抛弃的威瑟罗尔奶奶》

这是一篇意识流短篇小说，讲述了威瑟罗尔奶奶躺在病床上，处于弥留之际的一系列内心思想活动。临终前，威瑟罗尔奶奶的人生经历犹如电影画面一般浮现在她的眼前：当年婚礼之日被抛弃、含辛茹苦抚养孩子们成人，等等。最后在恐惧和悔恨中，威瑟罗尔奶奶去世了。

（三）《愚人船》

波特自称这是她写的最费力的一篇小说。它写 1931 年希特勒政权以前从墨西哥开往德国的一艘客轮上形形色色的人物，描绘了一幅大难临头的世界图景。作者试图表明，"恶"总是在"善"的妥协与默契下得逞。人的天性是脆弱的，人有毁灭别人和自我的本能。

三、选读作品赏析

"The Jilting of Granny Weatherall"

This story unfolds around the dying moment of Granny Weatherall. Before Granny dies, the most significant episodes come to her mind, muddling with the present environs she is in. She recalls that after her husband John's death she struggles for a living to raise all the children. What also comes back to her is the first time for her to get married and that the groom George never comes to the church. Granny Weatherall is a tenacious, loving, responsible and religious woman. Despite the difficulties in life after John, she death, she manages to pull through, as a farm-woman and midwife and nurse. At the same time, she's an ardent advocate of Catholicism. Although she's worked hard as a farm-woman and is loving and caring as a mother, something unknown to others is always gnawing at her heart, that is, her being jilted. Her pain at this comes from her fear of committing adultery in that the doctrines of Catholicism approve only one marriage. She is so anxious and scared at the thought of death and her being sent to Hell that she looks a sign from God who does not give anything and jilts her. On the whole all her psychic activities revolve around the idea of Hell.

The dominant technique used here is the stream-of-consciousness. Its use juxtaposizes what is going on around and what is going on in a characters mind. This xtaposition further disrupts the conventional linear sequence of events. For example she remembers lighting the lamps when her children were young. She recalls how they stood close to her, moving away once the frightening dark had been dissipated. At this point, her exclamation is given, God, for all my life, I thank Thee. Without Thee, my God, I could never have done it. Hail, Mary, full of grace. This is her instant thought in mind which is used to reveal what abominable life they have suffered and her stalwartfaith in God. In the last part, when all her children cluster around her sickbed, her muddled state of mind is further shown in the use of stream-of-consciousness. When she seems to have seen a lightning, she mentally addresses Cornelia. When she feels Jimmy's thumb and beads, the following text goes like, So, my dear Lord, this is my death and I wasn't even thinking about it. I want to send six bottles of wine to Sister borgia Symbolism is adopted to make the story thought-provoking. The Color Blue is Blue symbolizes the various stages of Granny Weatherall's life. The color is introduced when granny recalls her glory days of running a tidy, organized household.

She visualizes the neatness of the white jars labeled in blue letters that identify their contents, such as coffee, tea, and sugar. This blue symbolizes the time at which Granny's youthful energy enabled her to act as head of the household. Blue recurs when Granny remembers the way her children watched her light the lamps at night, leaving her once the flame "settled in a blue curve." This blue symbolizes the transitional moment in Granny's life during which her children, after drawing comfort from her strength, stopped needing her and were able to go off into the world on their own. A hidden blue exists underneath a picture of John: a photographer made Granny's husband s eyes black, instead of the blue they were in real life. This blue-turned-black lizes a stage in granny's life that seemed to last for the duration of her marriage.

第十一章 现代主义时期的美国文学解读与作品赏析

20世纪初，以德国为中心兴起了一场通称为"表现主义"的国际性文艺运动，它涉及文学艺术的各个领域，强调作品应关注人的主观世界，他们不重视对外在客观事物的描写，而要求表现事物的内在实质。1908年立体主义出现于法国。立体主义的艺术家要求在画面上肢解物体的形象，然后再加以主观的拼凑、组合，以求在平面上表现出二维和三维空间，甚至表现出肉眼看不见的结构和时间，并以此来表达对物体最为完整的形象。

一、主要特色

（一）美国意象派运动

（1）直接处理无论是主观的还是客观的"事物"。

（2）使用普通语言，但是用准确的字眼，避免有音无意、用作装饰的诗歌惯用词汇。

（3）至于节奏，创作要依照乐句的排列，而不是依照节拍器的机械重复。

（4）意象要在一瞬间呈现出作者的理智和情感，意象主义诗歌必须准确地表现出事物的视觉意象。

（二）"迷惘的一代"

（1）作品具有鲜明的文化反叛性，挑战清教伦理和以资本主义理性为基础的美国文化传统。

（2）通过对话和行动来表现人物的个性和内心世界。

（3）打破现实主义小说以故事、人物、背景为创作基本要素，以情节为主体的传统结构框架，以碎片式结构、意识流、"蒙太奇"和多视角叙述等为基本特征。

（三）美国戏剧的表现主义

（1）使用不同的创作手法，力图将现实主义和浪漫主义或象征主义等方法融合在一起进行创作。

（2）运用反戏剧的叙述模式，将剧作者的主观意念人物化，以及人物的无个性化或抽象化。

（3）通过象征、暗示、隐喻、自由联想，以及语言的音乐性曲折地表达作者复杂微妙的情绪和感受，进而去表现理念世界的美和无限性。

（4）反映人与社会、人与自然、人与人、人与自我之间的矛盾与冲突，突出人的"异化"和社会危机。

二、主要作家与作品

埃兹拉·庞德是意象派诗歌的创始人，其主要诗作有《神州集》和《诗章》。庞德的诗歌受到了中国和日本诗歌的影响，充满了密集的意象，对美国现代文学产生了极大的影响。艾略特是后期意象派诗歌的代表，其主要作品《荒原》被认为是现代主义诗歌的代表作。威廉斯的诗风明朗，意象鲜明，细节逼真，语言精练，具有明显的美国本土特色。他的《春天与一切》诗集中的《红色手推车》极负盛名。兰斯顿·休斯是美国现代优秀黑人诗人，也是"哈莱姆文艺复兴"的杰出代表。其代表诗作为《黑人谈河流》。肯明斯是现代派著名的诗人。受立体主义的影响，他利用书写变异手法来创作诗歌，使其担负新的美感使命。

美国现代主义小说也在不断推陈出新，涌现出了一大批影响整个现代主义文学以及后世作家的人物。海明威创造了"冰山原则"——简洁的文字、鲜明的形象、丰富的情感和深刻的思想。他的小说《老人与海》获得了1954年诺贝尔文学奖。菲茨杰拉德是"迷惘的一代"的典型代表作家，也是"爵士时代"的代言人。他的小说《了不起的盖茨比》反映了20年代"美国梦"的破灭。福克纳是美国南部文学的代表人物。他运用"意识流"来揭示人物的内心世界，表达了他对南方传统文化与历史的留恋。

20世纪前半叶的美国戏剧也得到了极大发展。尤金·奥尼尔是美国第一位伟大的剧作家。他把自然主义、象征主义、表现主义和意识流的手法运用于美国戏剧的创作中。他的最大的成就是关于人们对自己身份认同问题的探索。威廉斯的戏剧表达了对为环境所困神经焦虑的人物的同情。在创作方式上，他力求广泛采用象征主义、表现主义、浪漫主义，兼及现实主义的各种艺术手法。

第一节　埃兹拉·庞德

一、作者简介

埃兹拉·庞德（1885—1972）是美国意象主义的主要倡导者，并在诗歌创作方面引领了美国诗歌的发展。他阐述了意象主义的三条原则：（1）直接处理"事物"，不论是主观的还是客观的；（2）决不使用任何无助于表达意思的词语；（3）至于节奏，应按照短语的自然音乐性的节奏，而不是格律的节奏来进行创作。他鼎力提携新秀，对著名作家如乔伊斯、艾略特、弗罗斯特和威廉斯等都有很大影响。他的意象派作品汲取了某些日本诗歌和中国古典文化的精华，极大地开拓了美国诗歌的创作领域。同时，庞德还是 1948 年诺贝尔文学奖的得主。

二、主要作品简介

（一）《神州集》

这本诗集是美国意象派运动初期的重要作品，是庞德在厄内斯特·费诺罗萨遗稿的基础上选译的 19 首中国古典诗歌。在《神州集》中，庞德保留或创造了密集的意象，以增强诗歌的张力。同时，他在翻译中省略了原诗中大量的文化因素。评论家认为，《神州集》是庞德史诗性巨著《诗章》的底稿，其诗歌技巧、诗学特点和文化因素对庞德个人的文学生涯乃至美国现代文学都产生了巨大的影响。

（二）《诗章》

这本诗集是庞德主要的一部长诗，以"诗章"的形式分批发表。这是一首现代史诗，包括世界文学、艺术、建筑、神话、经济学、历史名人传记等方面的内容，以反映人类的成就并描绘一个由一些思想正确、有行动能力的人物所领导的美好的文化。这部长诗晦涩难懂，而且涉及 16 世纪的意大利建筑、普罗旺斯的诗歌、孔子哲学、中古的经济史等。

三、选读作品赏析

" *In a station of the metro*"

The poem depicts a moment in the underground metro station in Paris in 1912. When the author gets out of the metro train, he sees some beautiful faces in large crowds and he thinks they are as lovely as flowers on a tree branch. In respect of form, this poem is a variation on the Japanese form of the haiku, a very short poem divided into three sections with a certain number of syllables in each section. Although written in a succinct and straightforward style, this short piece illustrates Pound's imagistic motif to the full in that the entire poem deals with images alone.

In Line 1, one image overshadows the rest : apparition. Previously referring to a ghostly figure, something unusual and bizarre; here it enables Pound to convey the expression of shock and awe once he steps into the metro station. It's almost as if he discovers the faces in the crowd surprisingly. More importantly, he may have not seen. the faces clearly and sees only a blur that he interprets as a vision of attractiveness. This image meantime is an illustration of pure beauty or images of flawless human beings The second line renders another two images that give strongly expressive touches to the whole poem, that is, the "petals" and the "bough". Petals are vibrant flowers that have different colors and represent beauty when blossomed, which he identifies as the faces in the crowd. Additionally, petals are flowers that come in various shades sizes, shapes, and so forth, akin to human beings. Therefore, Pound perhaps envisioned . the people in the crowd as beautiful for the diversity they embody. Yet the adoption of "a wet, black bough" carries an implication of mortality. Anyway, the petals and the dark boughs will never last long, as long as there will be too much sunshine.

In all, the poem is incredibly short, but profound and takes the meaning of the short poem to its purest form. The juxtaposition of these three images is so captivating that it makes the poem move beyond the literal sense. When Pound takes them and morphs them together, a greater visual effect has been achieved. The beauty of the human faces has been put in a stark contrast with the transience of existence.

第二节　威廉·卡洛斯·威廉斯

一、作者简介

威廉·卡洛斯·威廉斯（1883—1963）强调美国本土风格，写美国题材的诗歌。他的诗歌具有鲜明的绘画和视觉特质。和他同时代的诗人不同，威廉斯坚持使用口语、简明清晰的描述性意象和松散的短句。他抛弃了诗歌的传统格律，开创了"可变音步"，即"新音律"。1963 年他去世后，他的诗集《来自布鲁盖尔的画像及其他》获得了普利策诗歌奖。威廉斯是意象派诗人群体中的核心成员。他的诗歌创作与艺术观念对 20 世纪中叶的一些重要诗人，诸如艾伦·金斯堡、罗伯特·洛威尔等产生了显而易见的影响。

二、主要作品简介

（一）《春天与一切》

这是威廉斯于 1923 年出版的一部重要诗集。在这部诗集中，威廉斯尝试将大段散文嵌入诗歌，以夹叙夹议的方式阐述自己独特的诗学体悟。诗集中最负有盛名的作品包括《红色手推车》和《去传染病院的路上》。

（二）《佩特森》

这是威廉斯的长篇叙事诗，共五卷，每卷分三部分，以新泽西州一座小城的历史和社会生活为背景，诗文混杂，引录了不少地方史资料，结构颇为特殊，反映美国的文化和现代人的风貌，是当代美国哲理诗的代表作之一。

三、选读作品赏析

"The Red Wheelbarrow"

The poem represents an early stage in Williams'development as a poet. It focuses on the objective representation of objects, in line with the Imagist philosophy that was ten years old at the time of the poem's publication. The poem is written in a brief and free verse form.

In terms of its sounds, quite apart from its images or its vocabulary, williams intricately tunes the poem. The first and second stanzas are linked by the long "o", in so and "barrow" and by the short "uh" in "much", "upon" and "a". "L" and "r" interlace the core stanzas (the second and third) i these two sounds, however, are not in the first and fourth stanzas. This simple device distinguishes the framing stanzas from the central stanzas. One result of this distinction is that the central stanzas are mellifluous, the frame stanzas choppy. Then again, however, the honeyed and the choppy are linked in the third and fourth stanzas. They are joined by means of a parallel construction; the long vowels in "glazed with rain" match those in beside the white In the last stanza, another loop is closed when the sounds "ch" and "enz" in the last word of the poem echo the sounds in the initial line, so much depends to begin with, the poem is a good example of enjambment to slow down the reader creating a "meditative" poem. The poem is composed of one sentence broken up at various intervals, and it is truthful to say that so much depends upon each line of the poem, if a reader wants to get the idea of the whole poem. The frequent postponement of information builds up suspense and drags the reader all through the whole poem. In his process, the readers dedication and imagination will be fully required. For example the first stop at "depends" (Line 1) makes the reader wonder what will come next in Line 2. Yet, another delay appears in Line 2 in that it fails to tell the reader on what premium does "so much" relies. Finally, the readers imagination is drawn to the second stanza, which points out the long-delayed premium, though the reader does not get it until the second line of this stanza.

The poem is characterized by its pictorial style. This effect is achieved first through the use of images of color "Red", "white" and "glazed rain" are the most visual compelling words. The colors stand out because of their contrast with each other: the bright red wheelbarrow contrasts with the rain, which is further distinct from the white chickens. Second, the juxtaposition of static images and dynamic images, natural images and manmade images render the poem vivid and pictorial. For instance, the wheelbarrow and rain stand static, while the chickens are moving and changing. When a reader comes to them, the contrast will be impressed upon his mind.

第三节　兰斯顿·休斯

一、作者简介

兰斯顿·休斯（1902—1967）被誉为"哈莱姆桂冠诗人"。修斯认为自我塑造是黑人改善自我形象、提高社会地位的必经途径，这成了他诗歌创作的重要内容。他还非常注重对美国主流文化传统进行逆向挖掘，力图从文化深层修正主流文化。休斯大胆地将黑人方言、土语以及布鲁斯音乐引入他的诗歌创作。在写作技巧方面，修斯一直乐于采用蒙太奇、多重声音等手法，并以此表现某种客观的真实，从而增强了诗歌意义的多维性。

二、主要作品简介

（一）《黑人谈河流》

诗人选取在黑人民族文明史上起过重要作用的四条河流来概括黑人民族悠久的历史。幼发拉底河代表古代巴比伦文明；尼罗河代表古代埃及文明；刚果河代表非洲文明；密西西比河代表美国文明。短短四句诗，浓缩了黑人民族六千多年的历史，概括了黑人民族从幼发拉底河到密西西比河的沧桑经历。从这首诗中，我们还可以看出，尽管在诗人生活的代种族歧视的恶习在美国还没有根除，诗人却没有因此悲观失望，而是为自己身为黑人种族的一员充满了自豪之情。

（二）《萎靡的布鲁斯》

这首诗用第一人称描述了一个夜晚在哈莱姆街道上听布鲁斯歌手演唱时的场景。诗人通过选词、重复句子、引用布鲁斯歌词来表达悲哀之情和布鲁斯歌曲舒缓的节奏，从而使读者感受到布鲁斯歌手的情绪。诗中布鲁斯歌手身体的活力同低沉的音调形成反差，揭示出歌手内心的张力。整首诗表露出了歌手疲惫、孤独的心情，以及他通过布鲁斯音乐拒绝现状，力图维持尊严的复杂心情。

（三）《延迟的梦之蒙太奇》

与他的其他作品集不同，这本诗集虽然也由一系列的诗组成，但诗人却用一个总的诗名以贯之，并且将这些诗按照一首诗的格式不间断排列。这样，不同主题、不同风格的诗被粘贴成一个庞大的诗章，这是蒙太奇手法在休斯诗歌的宏观构架中的运用。

三、选读作品赏析

" *Dreams*"

The poem revolves around the subject matter "dreams" which is also a recurrent subject all through Langston Hughes'literary career. Thematically, the speaker stresses that dreams will motivate man to a better life. Man should carry a dream when he is living otherwise, his life will paralyze and freeze. The poem is imbued with plain and terse words, and simple sentence patterns. This style fits into the oral tradition and sounds like a simple ballad. It is more likely for the reader to memorize and sing it another person.

Structurally, this poem borrows from Blues, the musical form and genre; the method of repetition is shown in the reiteration of "Hold fast to dreams" in Line 1 and Line 5. Besides, the lines 1, 2, 4, 5, 6 and 8, all are comprised of four syllables. They balance the rhythm for the whole poem and rhyme roughly. In this way the poem is more suitable for oral transmission. The 3rd line and 7th one contain more syllables than others, each of which helps to prolong the whole line and build up kind of climax for the four lines.

As is mentioned by Hughes, although the tones for Blues are normally sad melancholy and depressing, the way it is performed is amusing and entertaining. The incorporation of Blues patterns can light up the sobriety of the theme and drum people to shift from a morose attitude to a more active and sanguine one.

第四节　E. E. 肯明斯

一、作者简介

E. E. 肯明斯（1894—1962）是美国 20 世纪现代主义诗歌中备受争议的人物。有人称他为"打字机键盘上的小丑"，认为他的诗歌缺乏思想深度，指责他的诗是肢解了诗歌语言的"假实验"。但有些文学批评家却认为他是"最有成就的城市诗人之一"，是现代主义诗歌的杰作代表人物。肯明斯深受超验主义的影响，把自然看成实实在在的、和谐的"超灵"。他也注重事物的感性特征，认为万物都是这个和谐自然的一部分。同时，他也强调人在大千世界的唯一性和特殊性，认为人类灵魂可以与上帝进行直接交流。在表现技巧上，肯明斯倡导"立体主义"，利用书写变异手法，自由组合或分解文字的拼法和印刷格式，使它们担负新的美感使命，从而加强文字的表现力，来传达自己的情感。

二、主要作品简介

（一）《正是春天》

这是肯明斯早期的一篇作品，出现于第一部诗集《郁金香与烟囱》（1923）中，描写在春天来临之际，孩子追求童真般的欢乐与幸福，对春天来临感到无比喜悦。在诗中，肯明斯将"Betty"和"Isabel"两个名字拼在一起，生动地再现了两个小女孩手拉着手蹦蹦跳跳的欢快情景。他用"mud-luscious"和"puddle-wonderful"这类儿童语言来展现初春大地上泥水闪闪发光、迷人的小水洼处处可见的场景。此外，他还多处使用空格给予读者进行思考和想象的空间。

（二）《L（a）》

在这首诗中，作者将"a leaf falls（一片树叶飘落了）"一句话插入"loneliness（孤独）"这一个词之中。在这首诗中，肯明斯通过模拟树叶的下落，把"loneliness"（孤独）一词拆开，分撒在下落的树叶中，从视觉角度上让读者看到，就连 loneliness 也被下落的树叶给打乱了。这一视觉效果传达给读者的是一种奇特的认识——孤独之外的孤独之感。

（三）《蚱蜢》

这首诗初看起来参差不齐。但深入细读，读者会发现它是通过书写变异、标点符号以及大小写字母等手段，并使用合词、分词、词间空格等巧妙安排来创造蚱蜢这一意象，给读者塑造一种混乱的视觉效果，再现蚱蜢充满活力、又蹦又跳的形象。

三、选读作品赏析

"Your Little Voice"

This piece is a free verse dwelling on the contrast between the speakers memory and the present. In the past, when the speaker heard the nice voice of the girl he loved, he felt giddy but now, when he recalls her voice, he feels devastated at her death. In some sense, however, her voice links his memory of the past and the reality he is in. Despite her death his love for her lives.

The first feature of the poem is its use of fragmentation and jumbled mass. For instance, the parts about his response to the girls voice are full of fragmentized expressions. Lines 5 to 8 are a sheer fragment in that they are a nominal construction following the preposition with. They have no direct connection with the previous sentence, nor do they have any with the following one. Yet it is equally obvious that within the fragment, a lot of images are jumbled up. The merry flowers and flames are stuffed into one construction that runs on, without any effective punctuation. Similarly Lines 9 to 11are also so fragmentized that a reader may wonder whether the act of looking up is simultaneous with that of dancing. Compared with the former half, Lines 12 to 24 are more clear-cut. Although there is no punctuation, the different elements of a sentence can be made out. The shift implies that the man was in such an exalted state when he heard the girls voice while they conversed on the line and that he is calmer when she is dead and he is recollecting.

Apostrophe is applied to shorten the distance between the speaker and the reader. In the poem, the speaker sounds like addressing the girl he loves and since written down for a reader, the addressed will normally feel like he is holding a dialogue with the addresser, which brings a more intimate connection with the speaker. In this way, there will be more engagement on the part of the reader. Besides, your voice appears twice first in the first line and then in the last line. They act in concert to yield a cyclical effect. Her little voice, so to speak, resounds when the speaker thinks of the past and it is also her voice that lingers on when the speaker comes to the present. On his level, her voice comes to bridge the authors memory and the reality. And it is proof of the famous adage love conquers all.

第五节　厄内斯特·海明威

一、作者简介

厄内斯特·海明威（1899—1961）是"迷惘的一代"作家中最著名的代表。海明威自己以及他笔下的主人公都是英雄主义的代表。尽管处于一个冷酷的世界，他们都能勇敢地面对现实。在重压之下，他们也总能以优雅的方式生活。海明威文笔简洁，内涵却高度丰富。他的这种文体被喻为"冰山"原则。海明威作品中显著的艺术特色是反讽，揭示出人生本身是个巨大的反讽，每个人都必须以乐观的态度对待人生中的反讽。海明威叙事时不动声色，语气不带感情色彩。这种平淡而克制的陈述，很多时候真实而富有戏剧性。

二、主要作品简介

（一）《在我们的时代里》

这是一个短篇小说集，包括 15 篇故事，其中大部分与中西部生活相关，但也有一些描写发生在欧洲的战争以及斗牛的小插曲。这个短篇小说集在海明威的作品中占有重要地位，因为这是第一次有一位受到精神和肉体双重创伤的海明威式的英雄尼克·亚当斯站在聚光灯下，学会在重压之下以优雅的方式生活。

（二）《太阳照常升起》

1926 年，他发表了第一部长篇小说《太阳照常升起》。小说扉页上写着斯泰因曾经对海明威等作家说过的一句话："你们都是迷惘的一代。"随着小说的出版与成功，"迷惘的代"便成为那一代作家的代名词。《太阳照常升起》以第一次世界大战之后流落在欧洲的青年男女为描写对象，反映了他们憎恨战争、心情苦闷迷惘而又找不到出路的思想情绪。

（三）《永别了，武器》

这是一部以一战为背景的小说，讲述了美国青年弗雷德里克·亨利在意大利北部战区担任救护车驾驶员，与英国护士凯瑟琳·巴克莱相识、相恋与分离的故事。小说标题的第一重意思是告别武器，反对战争，表达出对战争的厌恶之情。它的另一层含意是亨利永别了自己的真爱。在创作风格上，海明威运用情景交融的环境描写，纯粹用动作和形象表现情绪，电文式的对话、简洁而真切的内心独白、简约洗练的文体和日常用语等。

（四）《丧钟为谁而鸣》

书名来自约翰·邓恩的一篇布道词。故事讲述的是美国青年罗伯特·乔丹志愿参加西班牙政府军，历经爱情与职责的冲突和生与死的考验，在炸完桥撤退的时候，独自留下阻击敌人，最终为西班牙人民献出生命的故事。海明威通过主人公的内心独白，淋漓尽致地探讨了生与死、爱情与职责、个人幸福与人类命运等问题，展现了他笔下的具有男子汉气概的英雄人物。

（五）《老人与海》

这其实是一则关于人与自然之间斗争的寓言。围绕一位老年古巴渔夫圣地亚哥与一条巨大的马林鱼在离岸很远的湾流中搏斗而展开，强调人的高贵勇气和坚忍品德。它奠定了海明威在世界文学中的突出地位，这部小说相继获得了1953 年美国普利策奖和 1954 年诺贝尔文学奖。

三、选读作品赏析

"Indian Camp"

"Indian Camp" is a story of initiation in which young Nick Adams accompanies his father, a physician, on, a call to an Indian camp, where the father delivers a baby by cesarean section using only his jackknife. It is constructed in three parts: the first places.

Nick and his father on a dark lake; the second takes place in the squalid and cramped shanty amid terrifying action and the third shows Nick and his father back on the lake bathed in sunlight.

This story introduces the reader to the Hemingway style, clipped, pared down exact a style that would make the writer famous and much imitated. The plot of the story is minimal (a simple night's experience), the images are few, and the modifiers scarcely in evidence. However, each word has been chosen with a poet's care. It is a new kind of writing in prose; each word carries weight and seems endowed with a meaning beyond itself.

The story unfolds around a childs reaction to different events, including childbirth and death. When they come into the patient's cabin, they hear the woman screaming Nick seems upset. It is possible that he links it with death. During the operation on the woman, the father inquires Nick about his feeling of being an internee, and Nick just looks away and is afraid of seeing his father's doing. Here Nick also seems to equate childbirth with death, something ominous. When in the kitchen, he accidentally sees the death of the woman's husband. This initiates him into the bloody and ruthless reality of real death. Hemingway uses the innocence and simplicity of a child to reveal the fact that every human being can not escape the capture of death. And in the last part where the father and Nick talk about death, it seems that Nick comes to realize the peremptoriness of death.

In the story, characterization is built on the solid basis of characters' action, mostly and 370 dialogues. The last part of the story is mainly comprised of the dialogue between the father and Nick. From this dialogue we see the consequences the experience has on Nick. He is possessed with the idea of death. He inquires about the reason why people to commit suicide and he is told some people do kill themselves. At this point, he shifts to ask about Uncle George. It indicates that he is anxious that Uncle will also kill himself. His fear of death is displayed most expressively.

Contrast is another feature of the story. The violence and pain of the birth contrast sharply with the ease of the suicide of the pregnant woman's husband. From Nick's experience, child delivery is closely related with death. Her labor tums successful only after she has been cut open and sewed up. The husband, when waiting during the operation, kills himself for he can't stand the whole mess. This construction of plot makes most explicit the theme that death wraps everything and comes easy to everyone. "Indian Camp".

第六节　菲茨杰拉德

一、作者简介

弗兰西斯·司各特·菲茨杰拉德（1896—1940）是 20 世纪 20 年代"爵士

时代"的发言人和"迷惘的一代"的代表作家之一。1925 年他杰出的代表作《了不起的盖茨比》问世。该书奠定了他在现代美国文学史上的地位。他的创作深入反映了注重金钱和享乐的"喧嚣的二十年代"和"爵士时代"的时代潮流。一方面他自己随波逐流，沉湎于物质享乐，另一方面却能以冷静批判的笔触反思社会现实以及"美国梦"的追寻及幻灭。菲茨杰拉德使用有限视角和双重视野讲述故事，使作者能够以旁观者的态度冷静观察。象征手法的运用是菲茨杰拉德小说的另一个艺术特色。通过这种手法，作者能更好地展现主题思想。艾略特在给菲茨杰拉德的信中说："实际上，我认为它（指《了不起的盖茨比》）是亨利·詹姆斯以来美国小说跨出的第一步。"

二、主要作品简介

（一）《人间天堂》

这是菲茨杰拉德的第一部长篇小说。它的问世奠定了菲茨杰拉德作为"爵士时代"的代表作家的地位。它描述了一群 20 世纪 20 年代美国青年放荡不羁的生活。《人间天堂》准确地抓住了时代的脉搏。在写作技巧方面，小说运用了不同的艺术形式，如诗歌、戏剧、意识流等。

（二）《了不起的盖茨比》

小说的背景设定在现代化的美国中上阶层社会的白人圈内，通过卡拉韦的叙述展开。小说揭示了美国梦的幻灭，显示了在进入物质空前富足繁荣和经济大发展的时代，人们在追求物质利益至上的拜金主义和及时行乐中，陷入越来越深的精神危机。此外，小说中西区和东区象征着盖茨比和汤姆两股势力之间的对立，即新富阶层与富贵世家之间的对立。

（三）《夜色温柔》

小说讲述了在 20 世纪 20 年代的欧洲大陆，一个出身寒微却才华横溢的青年对富有理想梦幻般的追求以及如何遭到挫败而最终变得颓废消沉的故事。这是菲茨杰拉德的一部带有自我体验的文学作品，情节曲折，寓意深刻，是战后美国中上层阶级精神生活的真实写照。

三、选读作品赏析

An Excerpt from Chapter 3 of The Great Gatsby

The novel develops around the parallel between the disillusionment of

Gatsby's dream and that of American dream. Gatsby, a poor young man, comes to the East Coast and makes a fortune in order to win Daisys heart. However, what befalls on him in the end is that he finds the girl void of the idealizations he imagines. What runs deep is that the idealized aspects of life have already been shattered into pieces in the society of the 1920s. Mans dreams are of no avail when materialism prevails.

Fitzgerald has delayed the introduction of the novels most important figure-Gatsby himself- until the middle part of Chapter 3. The reader has seen Gatsby from a distance, heard other characters talk about him, and listened to Nicks thoughts about him, but has not actually met him (nor has Nick). Despite the later introduction, this chapter continues to heighten the sense of mystery and enigma that surrounds Gatsby, as the low profile he maintains seems curiously out of place with his lavish expenditures. From this chapter on his mysterious conversation with Jordan Baker becomes the motivating question of the novel.

Many aspects of Gatsby's world are intriguing because they are slightly amiss-for instance, he seems to throw parties at which he knows none of his guests. His accent seems affected, and his habit of calling people old sport is hard to place. Host as he is the pompous party, he stands outside the throng of pleasure-seekers Chapter 3 also focuses on the gap between perception and reality. At the party, as he looks through Gatsby's books, Owl Eyes states that Gatsby has captured the effect of theater, a kind of mingling of honesty and dishonesty that characterizes Gatsby's approach to this dimension of his life. Owl Eyes suggests that Gatsby's whole life is merely a show, believing that even his books might not be real. Besides, the party itself is a kind of elaborate theatrical presentation, because many of the inhabitants of East Egg and West Egg use an outward show of opulence to cover up their inner corruption and moral decay.

Another characteristic is the third person point of view limited. The novel is developed from the perspective of Nick Caraway, a person involved in the story. what's equally important is that he is an observant participant of the story. He is a man with much conscience and caution. As can be seen from the novel, he prefers a world that enjoys a serious and righteous outlook. And because he is a veteran, he is also a bit disillusioned and cynical. As a result, being involved in the events that make the whole story, he holds a detached and critical attitude to other people. Unlike the jubilant and callous people around, he judges people and their behavior on grounds of his moral Tandards.

Each of the four important geographical locations in the novel- West Egg, East Egg, the valley of ashes, and New York City--corresponds to a particular theme or type of character encountered in the story. West Egg is like Gatsby, full of garish extravagance, symbolizing the emergence of the new rich alongside the established aristocracy of the Twenties. East Egg is like the Buchanans, wealthy, possessing high social status, and powerful, symbolizing the old upper class that continued to dominate the American social landscape. The valley of ashes is like George Wilson, desolate desperate, and utterly without hope, symbolizing the moral decay of American society hidden by the glittering surface of upper-class extravagance. New York City is simply chaos, an abundant swell of variety and life, associated with the quality of distortion that Nick perceives in the East. Setting is extremely important to The Great Gatsby, as it reinforces the themes and character traits that drive the novels critical events Apart from geographic locations, symbols are also prevailing in the novel. The most important ones are the green light at the end of Daisy's dock and the eyes of Doctor T. J Eckleburg. To Gatsby the green light is the embodiment of his dream for the future, and it beckons to him in the night like a vision of the fulfillment of his ideals. The eyes of Doctor T. J. Eckleburg work in the same fashion, although their meaning is less fixed.

Until George Wilson decides that they are the eyes of God, representing a moral imperative on which he must act, the eyes are simply an unsettling, unexplained image as they stare down over the valley of ashes. The eyes of Doctor T. J. Eckleburg thus emphasize the lack of a fixed relationship between symbols and what they symbolize: the eyes could mean anything to any observer, but they tend to make observers feel as though they are the ones being scrutinized. They seem to stare down at the world blankly, without the need for meaning that drives the human characters of the novel.

第七节 威廉·福克纳

一、作者简介

威廉·福克纳（1897—1962）是南方文艺复兴的领军人物。他用小说题材描写他熟悉的家乡，并以家乡为原型虚构出约克纳帕塔法县，并以此为背景，创作了反映内战后南方的物质与精神衰败的系列小说。这个小说群的核心是康普生家族、沙多里斯家族、斯图本家族，以及麦卡斯林家族的兴衰历史。它所反映的实质就是美国南方社会将近一个世纪以来各个阶级之间的矛盾、斗争和演变。1949 年冬，福克纳被授予诺贝尔文学奖金。福克纳的语言生动，象征，特别是圣经典故丰富。他对叙事结构的创新和创作技巧的实验体现在他试图以小说中不同人物的不同视角来进行叙述，创造性地运用意识流技巧和时间错置等手法。

二、主要作品简介

（一）《喧哗与骚动》

这部作品的书名出自莎士比亚的名剧《麦克白》："人生就像一个白痴所讲的故事，充满了喧哗与骚动，却没有丝毫意义。"小说描写了杰弗生镇康普生一家由望族到没落的过程，以及各家庭成员的遭遇和精神状态。这是意识流小说的代表作品之一。而多视角的叙事手法，也奠定了它在文学史上的地位。

（二）《押沙龙，押沙龙》

这部作品的书名源自《圣经》典故。书中描述的亲子之间的爱与恨、兄妹之间的暧昧感情等，具有《圣经》故事的色彩。该小说以托马斯·塞德潘发家和败落为缩影，反映了美国南北战争前后南方各州向现代社会转化的历史。这部小说的表现手法与《喧哗与骚动》相似，通过罗莎、康普生先生和昆丁等人的叙述来表现塞德潘家的盛衰史，不同的是所叙述的故事要复杂得多。

（三）《熊》

在小说《熊》中，福克纳运用新颖的富有想象力和创造力的隐喻表达，提供了新奇独特的审美体验，同时生动地展现了现代工业社会人与自然之间的生态伦理关系，表现了福克纳强烈的生态忧患意识。

三、选读作品赏析

"A Rose for Emily"

A Rose for Emily begins with the announcement of the death of Miss Emily Grierson, an alienated spinster living in the South in the late nineteenth or early twentieth century. The narrator, who speaks in the "we" voice and appears to represent the people of the town, recounts the story of Emily's life as a lonely and impoverished woman left penniless by her father, who drove away suitors from his overprotected daughter. Emily was left when her father died with a large, dilapidated house, into which the townspeople have never been invited, and there is an almost lurid interest among them when they are finally able to enter the house upon Emily's death. At that point they discover the truth about the extent of Emily's problems: she has kept the body of her lover. A northerner named homer barron locked in a bedroom since she killed him years before, and she has continued to sleep with him.

"A Rose for Emily" unfold around quite a few conflicts, of which the dominant ones are the conflict between Emily and her townsfolk, that between Emily and Homer Barron. First of all, the tension between Emily and Homer is obvious. They are of different background and position, with the one being an aristocratic lady from an ancient family, and the other being a Yankee laborer. They are different in temperament.

Emily lives a pride, lonely and quiet life that is required of a lady, while Homer frequents Clubs, loves men and enjoys fun in his life. The deadly conflict between these two is their attitude to love. It is obvious that Emily falls in love with Homer and takes a public ride with him, though it is indecent for a lady to be seen alone with a single man Homers attitude to their affair looks so causal and even irresponsible. The other dominant conflict occurs between Emily and her community. To some extent. Emily is a spokesperson of individualism and her neighborhood stands for communal spirit. When Emily fails to pay taxes, the officials call a meeting and assign a deputation to her house.

The townspeople whisper gossip when Emily is seen taking a ride with

Homer, and some ladies interfere and bring her blood-kin under her roof. When they learn that Emily orders a mans toilet and outfit of mens clothing they become "really glad" on because of their disgust at her haughty cousins. Yet, people become a little disappointed because, when Barron is gone, there is not a great sensation. Throughout the story Emily has to be confronted with the probing and judgmental speculations of the Townspeople.

The story carries different levels of interpretations. First, it is a tale of the decline of the griersons. Emily, as the last of the Griersons, is shaped by his father into a traditional mold of aristocracy. Yet, after the Civil war, when the old values are challenged and new ones emerge, some of her privileges are challenged and denied Besides, the story is an allegory of the collision between the northern culture and the old traditional southern culture. Homer follows the trend of the emergent materialistic values. He leads his group to construct the road, makes quick acquaintances with the townspeople and haunts the Elks ′ Club with younger men. Emily, however, lives in a way as is expected of a lady. The third theme of the story is the conflict between the past and the present. When the present is muddled with the memories of the past glory, a man will be pushed into a dilemma and will not likely to adjust to the present and the future that is built on it. He will be a sacrifice that is offered on the altar of the fading past The story adopts a peculiar point of view. By confining himself to the pronoun we, the narrator gives the reader the impression that the whole town is bearing witness to the behavior of a heroine, about whom they have ambivalent attitudes ambiguously expressed. The ambiguity derives in part from the community's lack of access to facts, stimulating the narrator to draw on his own and the communal imagination to fill out the picture, creating a collage of images. The narration gives the impression of coming out of a communal consciousness, creating the effect of a peculiar omniscience. If Faulkner had Emily tell the story, the reader would not have seen this or understood how the town is also a character in the story. When a main character is the arrator, the story is told from a particular perspective, and in this case, we would probably be even more sympathetic towards Emily than we are through the narrators version.

For its manipulation of time, the story departs from the traditional writing. On the whole, it is a blending of flashback and chronological order. Part I shows us that Miss Emily dies and her refusal to pay taxes in 1926. Part li comes to explain to the stink of her house and people's solution. Part II relates her affair with Homer and purchase of arsenic. Part Iv tells the arrangement of her marriage and the sudden disappearance of Homer. Part V picks up the end where Part I has left people's visiting the house of the deceased and the finding of the dead body of Homer. This way of construction gives the reader much room for imagination and reconstruction of the story-line.

A pattern of motifs that interact, contrasting with or paralleling one another sometimes symbolically, sometimes ironically, flows naturally from the reservoir of communal elements in the narrators saturated consciousness as he tells the story: the funeral, the cemetery, the garages, cars, cotton gins, taxes, the law, the market basket and other elements of black existence the house. its front and back doors its cellar and upper rooms, the window where Emily sits, the idol image that becomes a fallen monument, images that evoke the Civil War, images of gold, of decay, the color yellow dust, shadows, corpses and bodies like corpses, the smells, the breaking down of doors, the poison, and the images of hair. Of the symbols, rose is the predominant one. First, as a traditional symbol of love and passion, "rose" in the title can mean everlasting love. To Emily, we know, the rose ironically refers to the dead body of Homer Barron, which is sealed with death and hence last for ever to testify her love. In this sense, rose is closely related to the idea of death. Only with death can love last forever. Besides, "rose" means the authors compassion. It is used as a salute to a woman who in her life is always handed thorns.

第八节　尤金·奥尼尔

一、作者简介

尤金·奥尼尔（1888—1953）是美国现代戏剧的奠基人。他早期的剧作大多以大海为主题，真实再现了海员的艰苦生活和他们对大海和陆地的复杂感情。奥尼尔喜欢尝试新的题材和表现手法：《琼斯皇帝》（1920）和《毛猿》（1922）运用了表现主义手法；《奇异的插曲》（1928）有大量的意识流成分；《上帝的儿女都有翅膀》（1924）和《大神布朗》（1926）则利用面具揭示出人物的双重性格和内心的挣扎。奥尼尔对不同的文化成分十分敏感《马可百万》（1928）对中国文化进行了美国式的塑造；《悲悼》（1931）将古希腊题材移植到了新英格兰。他后期的作品《送冰的人来了》（1939）和《长夜漫漫路迢迢》（1913）是悲剧杰作。"由于他剧作中所表现的力量、热忱与深挚的感情——它们完全符合悲剧的原始概念"，奥尼尔 1936 年获得诺贝尔文学奖。

二、主要作品简介

（一）《琼斯皇帝》

这是一部表现主义的剧作。它描写一个岛上的黑人首领琼斯的悲剧故事。在描写琼斯精神恍惚和下意识的行动，以及在这种情况下出现各种幻象的时候，作者充分运用了表现主义手法。这部剧作还包含着象征主义、浪漫主义、神秘主义和情节剧的多种特征。

（二）《送冰的人来了》

剧中描绘了十几个长年寄居于霍普旅店的生活失败者。他们整天蜗居在霍普酒店里无所事事。每个人都为自己的过去编造谎言，并把希望完全放在不可能实现的明天的"白日梦"上。通过该剧，奥尼尔旨在揭示现实的毁灭是不可避免的。在奥尼尔的作品中，这部戏最为深刻地揭示了生活中的绝望。丰富的象征意义与伊丽莎白时代式的双重情节为该作品赢得了声誉。

（三）《长夜漫漫路迢迢》

这是一部半自传性的戏剧，描写了一家四口存在的种种矛盾和人心的异化，象征着奥尼尔致力发现真理、寻求认同的生奋斗历程。奥尼尔以自然主义的精神创作了这部戏剧，通过一个悲剧家庭的种种矛盾反映了现实，而这个悲剧的家庭在某种程度上正是社会的缩影。

三、选读作品赏析

An Excerpt from Act 2，Scene II of Long Day's Journey into Night

This scene is structured on the conflicts among family members. The first one is Mary's obsession with drugs and the others'indignant acquiescence with her. without her addiction, they hardly have any real communication nor will they, especially the sons and the father, behave so stoic when Mary becomes agitated and starts to complain.

Another conflict in the play is the characters'uncanny inability to communicate despite their constant fighting. Even when the men stand in ally to resist passively Marys squeamishness, they themselves hardly have a cordial conversation. They tend to criticize or taunt each other. In the play, the younger confront the older generation in terms of their outlook. The older generation, the father and mother, still feebly clings to religion and the grace of God. They sometimes pray to God. However, Jamie and Edmund take on the philosophy of the new world. They sound skeptical. Edmund reads extensively, and he is well versed in the German philosopher Nietzsche and poet such as Baudelaire. They don't have unquestionable faith in religion. The last contention appears between the family s memory of the past and the present. All of them are so drawn to the good of the past that they themselves are dissatisfied with the present life. The ugliness of life drives them to either drugs or alcohol. And they also find consolation from arguing with their blood-kin.

Accordingly, there are different interpretations of the theme of the story. Breakdown of communication is a very apparent theme. We are forced to listen to the same arguments again and again because nothing ever gets resolved. The Tyrones fight, but often hide the most important feelings. There is a deep tendency towards denial in the family. Edmund tries to deny that his mother has returned to morphine. Mary denies Edmunds consumption. Although the four Tyrones live under the same roof this summer, there is a deep sense of isolation. Although Tyrone professes admits he is not an ardent believer, he seems to have kept his faith in God. Yet, his two sons have long since abandoned the Catholic religion. Tyrone's religion also spills over into his taste in art. He considers Edmund's favorite writers to be morbid and degenerate. Mary's loss of faith also recurs as an issue. Although she still believes, she thinks she has fallen so far from God that she no longer has the right to pray.

Forgiveness is the other pivotal theme of the play. Although old pains cannot be forgotten and the Tyrones are, in a way, a doomed family, Edmund is able to make peace with his past and move on to what we know will be a brilliant career. His ability to do so is based in part on his capacity for forgiveness and understanding. The four Tyrones are deeply, disturbingly human.

第十二章　第二次世界大战后的美国文学解读与作品赏析

第二次世界大战之后，美国文学进入第三次繁荣时期。20世纪50年代在"冷战"、麦卡锡主义和朝鲜战争的背景下，文坛趋于沉寂；六七十年代，经过越南战争、民权运动、学生运动、女权运动、水门案件，文坛又开始活跃起来，各种流派相继出现，形成了50年代新旧交替、60年代的实验主义精神浸润、70年代至20世纪末多元化发展的鲜明特色。

一、二战后的美国文学流派及文学特点

（一）新一代小说家的崛起

战后出现的第一股文学浪潮是战争小说，战争一结束，便有一批以二战为题材的作品问世。这些战争小说的许多作者都是从太平洋战场和满目疮痍的欧洲归来的军人或记者，他们根据亲身经历和所见所闻为创作蓝本，讲述军旅生活，勾勒历史事件，阐述各自的体验和感受。就创作手法而言，作家们大多继承现实主义的传统，力求真实客观地再现二战这一特定的历史时期。反战和写实成为此类作品的一个特点。

第二次世界大战结束后，一批犹太作家相继走上美国文坛。他们属于第二代美国犹太移民，生在美国或在美国长大，并且有机会接受高等教育。年轻一代的犹太人受到本民族文化传统的熏陶和影响，但他们同时面临来自美国现代文明的压力和挑战，必须接受美国的同化。50年代以来，不少犹太作家注意淡化犹太特征，强调作品反映的是整个美国社会中普通人的处境。犹太作家成功地用英语写作，使犹太小说取得突破性进展，从边缘进入美国主流文学。

20世纪美国黑人小说的思想内容显示出一条鲜明的发展轨迹。前期的图默、赖特等作家创作的"抗议小说"，主要揭露美国社会的种族压迫和种族歧视，揭示种族歧视给黑人心灵造成的损害；中期的艾里森、沃克等作家创作的小说侧重反映在现代社会中黑人个性和自我本质的失落，探索如何实现黑人个性的独立和黑人妇女的解放；后期的哈利、莫里森等作家创作的小说努力追寻

美国黑人的文化之根，呼唤黑人民族文化意识的觉醒。50 年代美国经济稳步发展，生活水平提高，讲究消费和物质享受成为时尚。生活上的实惠原则和文化上的贵族新倾向使青年一代处于沉默和麻木不仁的状态。但是，这种沉寂并没有能维持很久。率先打破坚冰的是塞林格，以及被称为"垮掉的一代"的一批青年作家，他们追求个性自由，表达对现状的不满和反叛心声，终于掀起一场反正统文化运动。

（二）流派纷呈的诗歌

20 世纪 40 年代末 50 年代初，在美国西海岸城市旧金山，聚集着一群诗人、作家。他们对艾略特的"新批评"派诗风非常反感，通过一些小杂志和油印的小册子，他们发表了很多"不合时宜"的作品，阐述自己的艺术观。50 年代中期，由于金斯伯格、凯鲁亚克等人的加入"垮掉派"基本形成。

崛起于 20 世纪 50 年代初，黑山派是当代最有影响的诗歌流派之一。20 世纪 50 年代初，在马萨诸塞州黑山学院任教的查·奥尔逊、罗·邓肯、罗·克里利等人创办《黑山评论》杂志，提倡与 40 年代流行的传统格律体相反的"放射体"诗歌，逐步形成一个流派奥尔逊认为诗是把诗人的"能"传递给读者的东西，因此诗是"能的结构"和"能的放射"；要以顺应呼吸的"音乐片语"代替传统诗律中的节拍；形式只是内容的延伸；一个意念必须直接导向另一个意念，提倡快速写作。黑山派诗人还倡导诗歌朗诵。他们强调诗歌的自发性和口语化，采用美国口语和俚语，反对艾略特等人精雕细刻、广征博引的学院派诗风。

二战后的美国社会处于动荡不安的时期，传统的学院派诗歌对人们的创造束缚很大。很多诗人因为所处的社会环境和创作环境，处于一种心灵、情绪无处发泄的状态。于是各种诗歌流派如当年的嬉皮士一样，迅速出现并成长。鲍威尔经过痛苦的反思，将现实、文化中所体现的种种矛盾，融入内心，"坦白地倾诉个性的丧失"。鲍威尔和伯里曼两个互为竞争的自白派高人，使自白派成为千山群峰中的一个较高的山峰。

（三）戏剧的全面繁荣

第二次世界大战后，美国各种社会问题日益突出，人们对社会和人生普遍丧失了信心，尤其是在部分知识分子中间产生了一种精神危机感。荒诞派作家正是基于这种认识，用自己的作品对资本主义世界表达了不满和抗议。荒诞派戏剧在内容上表现对世界的不可理喻，人生的荒诞不经；在艺术手法上则打破了传统的戏剧结构，在作品中以反理性的结构、不合逻辑的情节、性格破碎的人物、机械重复的戏剧动作和荒诞的对话从总体上凸显世界荒诞的根本主题。

二、二战之后的主要作家与作品

在战争小说中，较好的是诺曼·梅勒（Norman mailer）的《裸者和死者》（*The Naked and the Dead*，1948）和詹姆斯·琼斯（James Jones）的《从这里到永恒》（*From Here to Eternity*，1951）。两部书的共同点是通过战争，写小兵、下级军官与军事机构的矛盾，即人的个性与扼杀个性的权力机构之间的冲突。这些小说已经触及战后整个一代文学最突出的一个主题。在犹太小说中，最杰出的是美国犹太作家索尔·贝娄（Saul bellow）的《荡来荡去的人》（*Dangling Man*，1945），小说采用日记体形式，客观记录了主人公约瑟夫在家闲荡、与家人和朋友无缘无故地争吵的生活，以及他内心进行的一场深刻的自我分析。

在黑人小说中，理查德·赖特（Richard Wright）和拉尔夫·艾里森（Ralph ellison）是两个主要代表人物。赖特的《土生子》（*The Native son*，1940）把对美国社会制度的控诉包含在一个描写黑人青年犯罪故事的寓言里，不仅是赖特最优秀的代表作，而且被认为是黑人文学中的里程碑。艾里森的代表作《看不见的人》（*Invisible Man*，1952）与赖特式"抗议小说"不同，着重探讨的是"寻找自我"这样一个具有普遍意义的命题。反正统小说的第一个代表作就是 J. D. Salinger 的成名作《麦田里的守望者》（*The Catcher in the Rye*，1951），讲述一个少年圣诞节期间在纽约市游荡的故事，满足了反对文化上精神庸俗化的青年一代的需要。

垮掉派中真正的大诗人是艾伦·金斯伯格（Allen Ginsberg），《嚎叫》（*How*，1955）是金斯伯格本人和整个垮掉派文学的代表作，这首诗无论在其描写的内容还是在其展示的美学风格上，都是打破常规、惊世骇俗的，它超越了文学艺术领域，影响了美国的社会历史进程关于黑山派诗歌，毫无疑问，查尔斯·奥尔逊（Charles olson）是这群诗人的领袖，他不仅是这派诗人活动的组织者，也以独特的诗歌理论与实际的诗歌创作成为大家尊崇的对象，其代表作是《马克西姆斯诗抄》（*The maximums poems*，1953—1975），这是一部苦心经营近 30 年的哲理诗史。自白派诗歌的代表人物是罗伯特·洛厄尔（Robert lowel），《人生研究》（*Life studies*，1959）是一部里程碑式的诗集，它的发表使洛厄尔成了"战后美国是各种最强劲、最有原创力的声音"。安妮·塞克斯顿（Anne exon）即使在自白派诗人中间，也是最大胆狂放的一个。从第一部诗集《去精神病院，病情部分好转》（*To*

Bedlam and Part Way Back, 1960）开始，她就在诗中赤裸裸地坦白自己。自白派中最富才情也最年轻的诗人是西尔维亚·普拉斯（Silvis plath），她最著名的作品都是在她死后结集出版的。

田纳西·威廉斯（Tennessee Williams）称得上是二战结束时期所出现的最杰出的美国剧作家。他于1948年及1955年分别以他的《欲望街车》（*A Streetcar Named Desire*）及《热铁皮屋顶上的猫》（*Cat on a Hot Tin Roof*）赢得普利策戏剧奖。除此之外，《玻璃动物园》（*The Glass Menagerie*）在1945年以及《大蜥蜴之夜》（*The Night of the iguana*）在1961年拿下纽约戏剧评论奖（New York Drama Critics，Circle award）。阿瑟·米勒（Arthur milller）的名字常常与威廉斯连在一起，这两位剧作家是40年代后期以来美国戏剧的主要代表人物。相比之下，米勒更倾向于直面现在，反映人们所关注的社会问题。他以剧作《推销员之死》（*Death of a Salesman*，1949）和《熔炉》（*The Crucible*，1953）而闻名。

第一节　索尔·贝娄

一、作者简介

贝娄（1915—2005）被认为是美国当代最负盛名的作家之一。他的创作思想和创作方法代表了当代世界文学多元交融的走向。在作品中描写了"异化世界"和"寻找自我"，塑造了一系列充满矛盾的"反英雄"，深刻地展示了当代社会中个人与社会、自我与现实之间难以调和的矛盾，阐明了人的价值与尊严在异化的生存条件和环境中所面临的重重困境表明了现代人的生存状态和生存心理以及对现代社会的思考。贝娄在创作艺术上的杰出成就为叙事艺术的发展做出了突出的贡献。他创立了一种独特的"贝娄风格"，它的特点是自由、风趣，寓庄于谐，既富于同情，又带有嘲讽，喜剧性的嘲笑和严肃的思考相结合，幽默中流露悲怆，诚恳中蕴含超脱。文体既口语化，又高雅精致，能随着人物性格与环境不同而变化。在表现手法上，贝娄既继承了西方古典文学遗产，又融合了希伯来文化的传统既吸收了现实主义的某些长处，又运用了现代主义的某些手法，善于把内心活动和外在世界，把现实描绘和历史回忆巧妙地交织在一起，使我们得以同时看到主人公的内心世界和他置身的现实世界。

二、主要作品简介

（一）《晃来晃去的人》

《晃来晃去的人》是贝娄的第一部小说，用日记的形式展现了主人公约瑟夫辞去工作等待应征入伍这段时间内的心理状态。他开始思考人生问题，渐渐对友谊的价值、家庭的意义、生活的目的等都产生怀疑，并发现自己与自己所处的那个社会格格不入，和妻子、兄弟、朋友都合不来。他不知道自己究竟是谁，找不到自己在社会中的位置，最终成了一个晃来晃去的人，一个被"挂"起来的人。最后他横下心来提前入伍，即使在战场上丧命，他也不会遗憾，因为困惑地活着并不比死亡强多少。

从约瑟夫这个游离于社会之外的"局外人"身上，读者不难看到作者受到了以法国哲学家萨特为代表的存在主义哲学的影响，约瑟夫这个"局外人"也自然使人联想到卡缪的小说《局外人》中莫尔索这个人物形象。在这部小说中，我们不再有旧日小说中的高、大、全形象，也没有王子与公主最后结合的喜剧结尾。我们只有莫名其妙地开头，不知所云地结尾。主人公在伟大的理想和卑微的现实间晃来晃去，无意义地消磨着每一天。

（二）《只争朝夕》

故事讲述了一个失去工作、与妻儿分居、被父亲抛弃、被朋友欺骗的中年男子汤米威尔赫姆在一天内的生活遭遇。这一天里，威尔赫姆一生的苦难达到了顶点，感情与金钱损失殆尽的威尔赫姆在一个陌生人的葬礼上放声大哭。小说仅仅记述了威尔赫姆的一天的活动，但通过主人公的回忆、联想以及人物间的对话将他大半辈子的经历一一展现在读者面前。在贝娄的精心安排下，主人公在精神上进行了一场彻底的"流浪"——焦虑、抑郁烦躁，在社会上也处于一种"无根"的状态——没有金钱、事业、亲情、爱情、友情，与整个社会格格不入，这在很大程度上反映了相当一部分美国犹太移民在现实社会中的真实境遇——无根基地漂泊。

三、选读作品赏析

Seize the Day

The excerpt focuses on Tommy's encounters and conversations with Dr.

Tamkin who is a seemingly fraudulent and questionable "psychologist". Throughout this chapter Tamkin provides Tommy with lies and truths. These "truths" will eventually allow him to break free from his "drowning state". However, at the present he has not quite accomplished such a feat. The chapter ends with the image of drowning. Tommy is brought back to the external world of money by thinking of his seemingly failing investments. Through the conversation between Tommy and Tamkin, Bellow reveals the predicament of modern man.

In Seize the Day, Tommy is an idealist surrounded by the pressures of the outside world. He is isolated and, thus, is forced to turn inward. The urban landscape is the symbol that furthers his isolation, for he is always "alone in a crowd". Bellow wants the reader to understand this isolation and thus has almost the entire novel take place within Wilhelms head. We experience the back and forth of uncertainty, the wavering of watery thoughts, the sadness and frustration of being that person that is alone in the crowd.

第二节　阿瑟·米勒

一、作者简介

阿瑟·米勒（1915—2005）是 20 世纪 40 年代后期以来美国戏剧的主要代表人物之一，被誉为"美国戏剧的良心"。米勒作为一位严肃的剧作家，特别关注戏剧作品的社会功能与道德教谕作用。米勒对美国现代戏剧的贡献表现在他写出了普通人的悲剧。米勒从普通人身上看到了悲剧因素，强调普通人生活中同样有悲壮的一面，有着可歌可泣的一面。米勒塑造了推销员、农民、警察、码头工人等一批中下层人的悲剧形象。他努力在自己创作的现代悲剧中探索这些普通人的心灵，表现他们丰富的精神世界。

二、主要作品简介

（一）《都是我的儿子》

这是一出易卜生式的社会道德剧。故事讲述一位飞机零件制造商乔·凯勒，在战时的生产压力下，明知可能造成重大事故，危及他人性命，仍向陆军航空队交付了一批不合格的飞机引擎气缸。乔·凯勒的罪行，在于交付了一批不合格的飞机引擎气缸盖，犯下伪证罪，自己敢做不敢当，宁让他人承担责任。但罪行并不是这出戏的重点。这出戏的重点是，一个男人没能理解社会契约的条件。这个问题不仅是乔·凯勒一个人的，因为在这部戏中，可以说，几乎没有哪个人物毫无自私自利之心。这部戏的成功来源于米勒"懂得世故人情"的能力，用角色来表现混乱的价值观、错误的野心、背叛、拒不承认、深刻幻灭的能力。

（二）《推销员之死》

这是他所有剧作中成就最高、上演最多、影响最大的作品。男主人公威利·诺曼是一个推销员，他和所有美国人一样相信自己的工作是有价值和意义的，只要勤奋工作，终会有所成就，他也相信他的两个儿子是了不起的人，会大有出息，但由于环境和自身的原因到他年老体衰的时候，并没有达到他预期的那种成功和辉煌，反而最终失去了他赖以生存的工作，不得不靠每周向人借50美元度日。作品用心理现实代替了外在现实，使剧作在结构上有了更大的自由度，大多数场景都由威利的回忆和心理意象来进行转换和调度，使作品在现实、回忆和想象中自由切换，具有舞台艺术独特的魅力。两幕故事虽然发生在一天两晚之间，观众却看到威利的一生和比夫兄弟的成长史，看到20世纪三四十年代美国都市民众的普通生活的画面，这主要得益于作者对舞台区域的灵活分割和倒叙手法的运用。

三、选读作品赏析

An Excerpt from Act ll of The Death of a Salesman

The excerpt is close to the end of the play. The play begins in the present as willy is hown in the grips of a crisis. The source of this conflict is not totally shown to the audience，but Miller tells us what we need to understand through a series of flash back.

We soon discover that Willys lack of self-worth derives from experiences related to his son Biff，to his waning career as a salesman and to his inability to make life wonderful for his wife Linda.

The excerpt starts from the final confrontation between Willy and Biff. Biff forces Willy to face the reality, which is the conflict between them. From Biffs crying, we can see that he confesses his love for his father. Motivated to buy back Biffs respect, willy committed suicide to provide the insurance money that he thought would finally allow Biff to be magnificent. He kills himself, dying "as a father, not as a salesman". There is no doubt of willy's deep love with his family. Willy has too much emotional capital tied up in his dreams of Biffs magnificence. He prefers to sacrifice his life, rather than illusions. Willy Loman symbolizes the common mans struggle under the pressure of the American Dream of success, a dream that every person strives for. He is a convict of American Dream, and also his son Biff. Biff is a living reminder of willys broken dream.

第三节　杰罗姆·大卫·塞林格

一、作者简介

杰罗姆·大卫·塞林格（1919—2010），美国"二战"以后最重要的作家之一。塞林格的文学声誉建立在他数量不多但影响极大的作品上。《麦田里的守望者》（1951）是其最著名的代表作，一经出版，立刻成为畅销书。该书主要表现了二战后青少年思想上和精神上的混乱、迷茫和苦闷。塞林格的后期创作明显地表现出他对东方哲学的兴趣。他对社会的描写越来越淡漠，思想也像他的生活一样处于归隐的状态。

二、主要作品简介

（一）《麦田里的守望者》

这部小说出版于 1951 年，是 20 世纪美国文学的经典作品之一，也是塞林格唯一的长篇小说。《麦田里的守望者》出版后引起了美国青少年极大的兴趣和强烈的共鸣。主人公霍尔顿是一个出身于中产阶级家庭的孩子。他对学校生活极为腻烦，对老师、同学和功课都看不顺眼，被认为是垮掉派的代表。整部小说以主人公霍尔顿·考尔菲德的口吻叙述，回忆他被学校开除之后在纽约城闲逛的一天两夜。霍尔顿的反感、孤独和逃离构成了他形象中的不同层面，表现出这个少年丰富的内心世界。小说采用"意识流"的写作手法，使用大量的口语和俚语，使读者更能激起共鸣和思索。

《麦田里的守望者》细腻地描写了年轻人成长过程中的心路历程。它强烈的现实性使这部作品具有打动人的强大力量，使每一个读者尤其是青少年读者都在霍尔顿身上看到了自己的影像。

（二）《九故事》

这是世界公认的当代经典短篇小说集。虽然该书由九个故事构成，但并不是九个短篇的简单聚合，而是一个精心构建的整体。塞林格用九个，而不是八个或者十个故事来构成这部小说集，显然是怀有深意的。阿拉伯数字从 1 到 9 之后，接下来就是零。零是数的起点，也是终点。同样也是事物的起点与终点。然而数字的组合使它们失去了本来的面目，以至于给人的感觉是它们可以变成无限多，可以有无限的变化。但再多的变化，最后仍旧会归于零，整个世界就是这样，从无到有，包罗万象，最后一切又都会化为无。

三、选读作品赏析

An EXcerpt from Chapter 21 of The Catcher in the rye

In this chapter, Holden wants to visit Phoebe at the family apartment, in the middle of the night, without his parents' knowledge. Using his key to enter, Holden sneaks to Phoebe's room only to realize that she now is sleeping in D. B, room because he is away in Hollywood; Holden peruses items on her desk, by lamplight, until he wakens Phoebe. She reveals that their parents are out for the evening and will return very late . As they talk, Phoebe guesses that Holden has been expelled and concludes that their father will kill him. Upset, she hides her head under a pillow. Holden goes to the living room for cigarettes.

Through the conversation, Phoebe clearly brings out the best in Holden. He says that he actually feels good for a change. He is glad to be home and is resigned to the fact that if his parents find him, he will just have to accept it. In fact, it almost appears that he wants to be caught, given the fact that he is smoking and willing to take a chance on waking up his mother who is a light sleeper. Before Holden wakes Phoebe, he goes about the room looking at her clothes and things with affection and pride. As he reflects on these accouterments of childhood, he seems to be preparing himself for the ordeal of putting his youth behind him, and foreshadowing the quasi-religious calling he sees for himself in the next chapter.

Phoebe's significance in the novel is crucial. Despite her youth, she sometimes seems to be holdens best friend. He can confide in her and share his dreams, Like a real friend, she does not always agree. She often sees right through her brother, detecting early on that he has been kicked out of Pencey Prep. Her advice frequently is superior to what Holden plans to do. Phoebe is also Holdens most trusted connection to family and home. On the other hand, she has trouble understanding Holdens darker side. She wonders why he is so self-destructive and why he doesn't just succeed in school the way she does. She may not quite grasp what he means by being the "catcher in the rye".

第四节　伊丽莎白·毕肖普

一、作者简介

伊丽莎白·毕肖普（1911—1979）是美国 20 世纪最重要的、最有影响力的女诗人之一。美国文学艺术学院院士，桂冠诗人，曾获普利策奖和全国图书奖，近年来声望日隆，她的诗歌富有想象力和音乐节奏感，并借助语言的精确表达和形式的完美，把道德寓意和新思想结合起来，表达了坚持正义的信心和诗人的责任感。毕肖普诗风严谨，在写实中寓含深意。在她的诗中，语言、技巧、意象都和谐地糅合在一起，产生了极高的艺术效果。毕肖普一生创作的作品并不多，但这并不意味着她的表达乏力。在平淡的一生中，值得人们动情的时刻本来就不多。家庭、旅行、恋人、朋友等都是毕肖普一生关注的主题。在人生各种经历的交织过程中，迸发出了诸多可能性，而对某种可能性的极致的描绘，成为她许多诗歌的原型。

二、主要作品简介

（一）《北方·南方》

这是毕肖普 1946 年出版的第一部诗歌集，诗集标题的地理意味暗示出她生活的空间坐标，也象征着她艺术中回环往复的情感极限。《北方·南方》一经出版，立刻受到广泛欢迎。诗集中收录的很多诗都被看作年轻诗人的身心难以在这个世界上安放，毕肖普的迷失主题在诗集的很多意象中都有明显的体现。该诗集代表了诗人心路历程的第一阶段。此时的毕肖普塑造了一系列脍炙人口的超现实形象。通过荠草、玩具马、纪念碑及冰山等诗歌意象，诗人巧妙地传达了身处纽约大都市的茫然失措。通过把内心挣扎转嫁于这些分裂的人物身上，毕肖普获得了某种程度的支配感，有效地抵制了童年创伤给她带来的"崩溃性焦虑"。

（二）《地理Ⅲ》

这是毕肖普的封笔之作。全书仅收录九首诗，却被公认为是诗人最好的诗集。在《地理Ⅲ》中，毕肖普的诗歌创作逐渐转向更为个性化的风格，在回忆中对人生和自我进行思索和剖析。毕肖普的童年非常不幸，但她一直小心翼翼地不去触碰那段遭遇，直到侨居巴西 15 年之后，事业的成功和情感的慰藉才使她克服心理的不安全感和不确定性，直面年幼时的不幸。《地理Ⅲ》是一部自传性作品。通过回忆人生各阶段的经历，毕肖普审视了相应阶段的自我状态：从童年时懵懂自我的觉醒到对自由生活和自我的追求，及至中年时期流放的自我的审视和晚年时期对现实自我的思索。

三、选读作品赏析

" *The Fish* "

In this poem, the speaker catches a huge fish while fishing in a little rented boat. She studies her catch for a while as, holding it up half out of water beside the boat. The fish is pretty old and gnarly-looking, with barnacles and algae growing on it, and it also has five fishing hooks with the lines still partially attached hanging from its jaw. The speaker considered how tough this fish must be and how much he probably had to fight. She begins to respect the fish. The poem takes its final turn when the oil spillage in the boat makes a rainbow and the speaker, overcome with emotion by the fish and the scene, lets the fish go.

One of the themes of the poem is how to choose. We know pretty early on in "The Fish" that having caught the fish, the speaker has to decide whether to keep it or release it. Either decision, of course, has consequences. If the speaker keeps the fish, the fish will die (and become dinner). If the speaker lets him go, what will happen? Well, from the outcome of the poem, it seems that the speaker feels quite satisfied and fulfilled with her decision to release the fish.

Another theme is the relationship between man and natural. The cool thing about this struggle, though, is that there is very little struggle at all speaker catches. the fish (though the fish doesn's fight), then holds the fish out of the water for a bit (the fish is still not fighting), and ultimately lets him go. So while the scenario allows for the age-old man vs. wild battle, there is no real violence. The struggle happens within the speaker, and ultimately ends peacefully.

第五节　罗伯特·洛威尔

一、作者简介

罗伯特·洛威尔（1917—1977）是美国当代最有影响的诗人之一，自白派的代表人物，素以超复杂的抒情诗、丰富的语言运用及社会批评而著称。洛威尔的诗在表达当代世界风云变幻方面，无论是客观描写还是表达主观感受都有较强的表现力。他的诗以独特的方式全面表达了生活在当代美国社会的痛苦经历，无论是描写公共事务还是个人情感都带有一种张力，充满冲突的意象与不和谐的音调，认为这个荒凉的世界需要宗教上的神秘主义来帮助人们解脱。其神秘性既体现在对信仰的忠诚上，又同时体现在适度的怀疑上。洛威尔的后期诗歌较为舒缓，常以对话体及口语形式出现。

二、主要作品简介

（一）《威利爵爷的城堡》

这本诗集 1946 年出版，共包含 42 首诗作，是洛威尔早期的代表作。这个集子得到了一致好评，批评家和读者都把它的出现当作一个重要的文学事件，文学刊物登载了占显著地位的评论，老一辈诗人艾略特和威廉姆斯也给予较高的评价。1947 年此书获得了普利策诗歌奖，奠定了洛威尔作为当代主要诗人的地位。

《威利爵爷的城堡》是诗人成名之作。这里的诗篇大多具有深远的历史背景，浓厚的宗教色彩和强烈的社会意义。贯串全书的主题思想是探讨在战争、财富、罪恶阴影笼罩下的现代社会里，美国引以为自豪的文明遇到了什么难题，以及基督教拯救灵魂的教义有无实现的可能。诗人以天主教信念为依托，通过大量的寓言神话，对清教徒历史上的业绩及其罪恶负担进行了深入的剖析，对崇尚金钱和武力的美国社会发出了猛烈的抨击。

（二）《生活研究》

这是洛威尔第二个时期的代表作。其诗风发生了很大的变化，开始由原来的险怪变得平易。原有的格律被打破了，严整的句法也变得松弛起来。最主要的是，他在直截了当地叙述自己的生活，挖掘自己的内心世界。他的个人生活在这些诗里暴露无遗。正是因为这个缘故，他的这些诗被称为"自白诗"，后来又和具有相当创作趋向的贝里曼、普拉斯和塞克斯顿等人被合称为"自白派"。

《生活研究》不仅是洛威尔创作生涯的转折，也是战后美国诗歌的一个重要的里程碑。诗人在一组组的自由诗行中毫无隐讳、不加修饰地陈述着他的童年：对父母的反叛，对自我身份的寻求，宗教信仰的改变，不幸的婚姻，神经病症的发作，对新英格兰既恨又爱的感情，对文化遗产既想吸收又要拒绝等。其复杂心理一幕接着一幕，一个思路引向一个思路，这些影像都呈现在诗人与读者的眼前，像浮世绘一样纷纭多端，像纪录影片一样翔实可信。洛威尔在社会的冲击和内心的压力下创作的诗篇，给美国诗歌带来了一种新的自传色彩，一种新的迫切感，一种极为坦率而真诚的语言。

三、选读作品赏析

"Skunk hour"

"Skunk Hour", from Life Studies, is Lowell's response to Elizabeth Bishop's "The Armadillo". It's well known that the two poets were very close friends. The poem starts with the speaker reflecting on a coastal town in Maine. His observations track an elderly wealthy woman who seems to have a ton of property，but who is quite alone in her old years. Then he starts to describe the things that have begun to go wrong with the place Then the speaker shifts the focus to himself. He remembers a drive he took through the town one night and what he saw as well as how he felt. It all seems pretty gloomy, and he admits to being depressed and feeling kind of crazy. What he observes after he lets us in on his mental state seems to be affected by how he's feeling, and as the poem progresses it gets pretty bleak.

In this poem, one of the themes is madness. The speaker said it himself! His "mind's not right" and it becomes clearer as "Skunk hour" progresses. Another theme is isolation. The speaker of "Skunk Hour" is stuck on an island, so his human interaction is limited to who's stuck there with him and his neighbors aren't his best friends. When night rolls around, he drives around looking for signs of human life, and finds nothing but skunks.

This poem is told through the lens of someone who is mentally ill. The speaker even admits, "My minds not right". So it shouldn't surprise us that the words and phrases in this poem have shifting, sneaky, and sometimes funny, double meanings. In some instances the other meaning is important to the poem, and in others, it appears as though Lowell was just having a bit of fun. Either way, this poems chock full of them and they add an extra dimension to what's going on.

第六节　西奥多·罗特克

一、作者简介

西奥多·罗特克（1908—1963）是美国当代"中间代诗人"的杰出代表，受浪漫派诗人华兹华斯、惠特曼等影响较多，但他主要是一个自然主义诗人，他擅长于糅合传统技艺与现代风格，采用严谨写实的诗风和舒卷自如的韵律节奏，通过对人的自然超然的精神魅力的展现，来抒写自我的内心世界和情感。罗特克的诗风严谨，技巧娴熟，在节奏上运用自如，诗歌里常常有玄秘与超现实主义意象，对未知的内心世界的深入挖掘，对潜藏在黑暗污浊里真与美的歌颂。同时他的诗歌个性突出，敏感真挚，感情强烈。他在发掘内心世界上给人以玄妙的空间，这种空间状态所引起的共鸣是超越时间和地域的，罗特克在诗歌里对内心题材的挖掘是让人惊叹的，自我与自然沟通交流如此微妙，内在世界与外在世界的沟通如此流畅，在自我与非我之间的转化如此娴熟。诗人给读者营造了一个理想与现实世界的完美结合体。这是否正是诗人内在世界的通灵？当我们去细细品味诗歌中的情感与节奏时，这种想法也就油然而生了。没有谁会怀疑这种通灵的感悟，也没有谁会质疑他的匠心独运。这是罗特克独有的世界，一个完美的内心世界，一个纯粹的通灵的世界。

二、主要作品简介

（一）《失落的儿子》

这是罗特克的第二部诗集，是诗人真正走向成熟的标志，很多批评家认为这是他最优秀的诗集。这本诗集中的 14 首"温室诗"就是主人公温室情结的集中体现。诗中的插枝、根窖、野草、兰花、青苔、康乃馨等植物仿佛都被赋予了人的感情。主人公出生于花农之家，在温室之间长大，自幼与花草苗木感情深厚，后因父亲早逝而远离这种田园生活，成为"失落的儿子"。

"失落的儿子"是西奥多·罗特克系列作品的中心人物，主人公自小生活在父亲培育的花房之间，对于父亲，他有着既敬佩又怨恨的复杂感情。然而，父亲的早逝使他产生巨大的失落感和愧疚感，同时远离了伴他成长的温室生活，精神长期失落，成了一个"失落的儿子"。由于童年曾与大自然共同呼吸、对话，很多年后他的内心深处仍有着一种温室情结。主人公的心理创伤与精神困惑是其心灵回归的起因，而回到从前、回到无意识深处是进行自我抚慰、自我调整和疗伤的一剂良药。结合诗人生平，我们不难发现罗特克本人亦即"失落的儿子"的原型。

（二）《苏醒》

《苏醒》是罗特克 1953 年发表的一首十九行诗，诗中直截了当地展现了意识与无意识之间的对话，开始的两节就清楚地表明了他如何在这两个世界之间穿行。运用严谨而松缓的维拉内拉诗歌形式，罗特克想告诉我们，他称之为"睡眠"的这种半意识、丧失自我和理性意图的状态在其创作过程中是多么不可或缺。这种睡眠不是简单地坠入一些模糊的、浪漫的梦幻中，而是如标题所强调的是一种"苏醒"。诗人"醒来"就看见"睡眠"，声明他的意识是分裂的，一半意识足够清醒，能记录并注意到另一半意识所呈现的东西，仿佛想象在"梦想着"

其连接、韵律、突转和关联。罗特克用诗的形式，讲授枯燥的人生哲学，既深刻优美又生动感人。整首诗的调子是积极乐观的，反映出诗人面对生活的压力、命运的挑战不屈不挠，努力抗争的精神和豁达开朗的气质，绝没有与他同时代的许多诗人的诗歌里那种茫然失落的气氛。罗特克把对人生的理解用诗的语言表达出来，让人在欣赏诗的优美和浪漫的同时，获得心灵的启迪和升华。

三、选读作品赏析

"*My Papa's Wat*"

This poem was selected from The Lost Son (1948), a collection of the autobiographical poems about his childhood days together with his father. After a whole day's labor and drinking of some whiskey, the father was dancing with his little son Although the father's steps were clumsy and the son was too short, they all enjoyed the crazy waltz round the house in spite of the mothers frowning. The rough hand touched the boy with all the affection a father can afford; while the boy was so attached to that until he was too tired to go on. The poem presented a living scene of a happy family of the laboring class.

This poem is about a moment in the life of a family: father and son romping around in the kitchen, with mom looking on. there's controversy about the family in this poem-some readers think this is a perfectly happy family scene, while others view the family as torn apart by alcohol and abuse. I think that while there may be fear and love mixed together in this family, there aren't many dark secrets hiding in this poem except for the inevitability of death splitting the family up. Even though the son in "My Papas Waltz" is dizzy, and keeps getting his ear scraped by his dads belt, he clings to his father. This shows that he really looks up to and loves his father.

In this poem, this father and son pair is not really waltzing, but romping. Still, the poem maintains a steady, three beat per line waltz the whole way through. As you read think about what this dance symbolizes in the relationship between the father and son love, but also power and fear. Behind the joy of romping, and the father-son love in this poem, there's a hint of violence. While there is no indication of overt abuse, there are hints of violent tension throughout the poem which contrast strongly with our expectations of a waltz with dad.

第七节　艾伦·金斯伯格

一、作者简介

艾伦·金斯伯格（1926—1997），美国"垮掉一代"代表诗人，20世纪世界著名诗人之一。他在20世纪50年代便以其反主流文化、惊世骇俗的长诗《嚎叫》一举成名。1974年获美国全国图书奖，入选美国艺术文学院院士，1995年获美国普利策诗歌奖最后提名。金斯伯格的诗作明显受到布莱克、庞德、威廉斯和惠特曼的影响。他冲破了以艾略特为首的美国诗坛学院派的藩篱，主张"一切都可以入诗"，"诗歌语言应来自口语，能吟唱、朗读"，对美国当代诗歌借助于音乐朗诵走向大众化有深远影响。他的写作及生活方式催生了美国20世纪60年代开始的反战、黑人民权运动、生态环境保护、妇女解放及性革命，给美国40年来文学、音乐、政治以及抗议运动注入了新的精神，其影响持续至今。

二、主要作品简介

（一）《嚎叫》

1955年在旧金山的一次朗诵会上，艾伦·金斯伯格以其《嚎叫》获得轰动性成功。《嚎叫》这首诗由三个部分及后面的《脚注》组成。第一部分最长也最有力。诗人开篇就大声疾呼，直指美国社会，痛斥、抗议贯穿其中，折射出美国社会的物欲横流、物质至上，人们空虚、浮躁难耐。第二部分据说是金斯伯格有一次在吸毒后凝望住所对面的弗朗西斯·德雷克爵士旅馆的塔楼时，联想到《圣经》中的凶神"摩洛克"，在"半梦半醒"间获得的灵感。诗人认为，当时整个美国社会就是一个精神病院。诗人以严厉的姿态面对美国社会的黑暗，却无能为力，茫然无助。第三部分表达了诗人对关在精神病院的卡尔·所罗门的爱意与同情。在诗中，所罗门成了一种永恒精神的象征，与他的相处不仅反映了金斯伯格对诸如他的母亲等持不同政见的美国诗人、艺术家们的遭遇的同情，还对美国社会的丑恶进行了鞭挞。《嚎叫》一诗问世后，由于很多人批评它的"消极颓废",为回答这种批评,金斯伯格不久发表了《嚎叫的脚注》,本意将它作为全诗第四部分,后接受建议,将其单独成篇,转"消极"为"积极",转"悲观抱怨"为"乐观憧憬",称颂一切"神圣"。诗中连续使用了 15 个"神圣",寄托了诗人的希望。

(二)《祈祷》

确立金斯伯格在美国文学上的地位的两篇诗作,一是《嚎叫》,另一篇便是 1961 年发表的《祈祷》。金斯伯格借用犹太教哀悼祈祷文悼念母亲,虽然略有改变,但基本遵循其形式。全诗可依次分为五个小部分,即序曲(Proem)、叙述(Narrative),其中包括赞歌(Hwmn)、挽歌(Lament)之一、挽歌之二、悼文及赋格曲(Litany and fugue)。

全诗中穿插着诗人对母亲脱离生活引起的愤怒,母亲精神错乱时对他的遗弃,他对母亲漫不经心的行为习惯的厌恶,对母亲对他的性诱惑态度的迷恋,母亲精神崩溃期间他对母亲的负罪感。诗人借写给母亲的挽歌,反映社会的黑暗与丑恶,通过描写母亲生活,反映了他们两代人的困惑,尤其是"垮掉的一代"在精神上所受的苦难与困惑;母亲得到解脱,而他们还不知道何时才能脱离精神上的苦海,还在人生的道路上徘徊,感到无比迷茫,不知道生活目的,看不到生活的希望;因此对人生的意义,对生死悲苦产生了冥想:是在现实生活中忍受肉体和精神的磨难,还是一了百了?提出了"是生还是死?"这一古老而永恒的主题。

三、选读作品赏析

An Excerpt from "Howl"

This is the first section of "Howl". "Howl", the representative poem of the Beat Generation, was first read by ginsberg to his "Beat" friends in 1955 and came out with other poems in a collection, Howl and Other Poems in England in 1956. The original poem consists of three sections, each constituted of a single but extremely long sentence of about a hundred lines, formed by paralleled phrases, each beginning with the same word, for instance, "who" in the first section, "Moloch" in the second section. and "I'm" in the third.

This poem, a torrent of deliberate voluble curses written in blank verse, is a work revolting against conventional morality，culture，and the main-stream of society but，to the surprise of most people，it presented a positive assessment of all the eccentric behaviors of the Beat Generation，such as drug addiction，abusing sex，communal living or homosexuality，for the poem is aimed at the presentation of the destruction of the best minds of the generation by materialist society after World War I．The lines sometimes run to an enormous length，but sometimes the phrases in a line are disconnected．They just accumulated as narrative shrieks to shock the reader．The language in the poem is considered somewhat too obscene．However，Ginsberg purposely made use of obscene words just to wake up people to face the horrible reality of American modern society．As a representative writer of the Beat Generation，ginsberg described modern American society by looking at himself and narrating his personal experiences，by using "I" at the beginning of the poem，to tone up the facility of the Words．

第八节　西尔维娅·普拉斯

一、作者简介

西尔维娅·普拉斯（1932—1963）是继艾米莉·狄金森和伊丽莎白·毕肖普之后最重要的美国女诗人，美国自白派诗人的代表。1963 年她最后一次自杀成功时，年仅 31 岁。普拉斯的杰出成就是不可模仿的，她用一种精神直觉来直接抵达作品的深处，她挖掘丰富的自我和情感因素，用全部的生命力量进行创作，直至内心出现幻象。普拉斯的诗歌穿梭于"自白、自我、自杀"之间，并将罗伯特·洛威尔所开创的一代诗风推到了顶点，实现了 W. B. 叶芝所谓的 20 世纪诗歌将是"心灵发出的叫喊"的夙愿。普拉斯的诗显而易见具有某种类似于疯癫状态的狂躁气质，它们不仅有许许多多突兀的、出人意料而又光芒四射的意象和意味难以穷尽的象征、隐喻，而且诗的语言也往往打破逻辑和时空的顺序而随意识自由地驰骋于两个截然不同的世界，成为超越理性束缚和心理屏障的精神载体。她的意识在摆脱理性的限制而濒于疯狂之际，往往能直接洞穿生命的内核，妄言妄语成为最灿烂夺目的诗章。

二、主要作品简介

（一）《钟形罩》

《钟形罩》是由美国自白派著名女诗人西尔维娅·普拉斯在去世前 3 周发表的自传体小说，也是她唯一的一部小说体裁的作品。因忠实地记录了一个女人在男权社会令人窒息的"钟形罩"中孤独、绝望与挣扎的心灵历程而风靡 20 世纪 60 年代的美国校园。

《钟形罩》以普拉丝自己早年的生活经历为蓝本，表达了一个初入社会的少女角色选择的冲突和内心的抑郁与挣扎。小说分为三个部分，第一部分描写女大学生埃斯特·格林伍德在纽约的人生经历，第二部分描写埃斯特对故乡传统生活的厌恶、精神崩溃和自杀经历，第三部分描写埃斯特接受精神治疗，等待复原。小说取名" bell jar"（钟形罩），本是指医院中存放胎儿标本的罐子，这些胎儿通常是因为母亲吸毒嗑药或基因突变而导致畸形早死。因此，"钟形罩"是一个具有惊惧与死亡意象的隐喻，透过罐中的尸体标本象征人生的夭折、窒息、束缚、变形。对普拉丝而言，人就像困在罐中的婴儿，一丝不挂、面无表情；这个世界就像那装满福尔马林液体、寒酸发臭的钟形罐子，就像一场噩梦。

（二）《爸爸》

《爸爸》这首诗就是在普拉斯自杀前 3 个月时写出的，是普拉斯的公认代表作。"爸爸"这一人物形象的选择对诗人来说极富象征意义，诗人正是通过对"爸爸"的讨伐来颠覆几千年来的父权、夫权与男权的社会秩序。诗人以自白体诗歌所惯用的独白方式叙述了一名被赋予多重身份的人物形象"爸爸"：父亲、丈夫和男性代表；通过独白，叙述者"我"因而也不断地相应变换着自己的角色：女儿、妻子和女性代表。尽管形象与角色不断地错位与更换，但诗人还是以其高超的艺术手法刻画出一个"是父非父"的人物形象。

该诗的前八节主要描述"爸爸"，后八节逐渐过渡到"丈夫"。表面上看来，这两个人物形象似乎是一个人，但是由"我"的叙述可以得知，她所尊崇的对象"爸爸"已永久逝去，而拥有着他的形象的活着的却是一个"吸血鬼"。整个"吸血鬼"形象的替代与转变是与对爸爸和丈夫的爱恨交织在一起的。全诗的高潮出现在杀死"吸血鬼"的同时，诗人宣告的不仅是恋父情结的了结，更是对让人伤怀的爱情与婚姻的彻底弃绝。她不仅要摆脱自己的噩梦，更是要找回普天之下妻子的主权和主体意识。在诗的结尾，我和"爸爸"的安息是紧张孤寂后最终的宁静，"我"不仅摆脱了痛苦的噩梦，也宣告了男权社会下女性的觉醒。

三、选读作品赏析

" *Mirror*"

Sylvia Plath's "Mirror" is one of her masterpieces. The first stanza describes the mirror, which seems to be like one of those people who doesn't tell white lies-it's truthful and exact, but not cruel. Jump into the second stanza, and the stakes have changed. The mirror is no longer a mirror, but a lake, which also shows reflections. And we get to see a whole new character: a woman. We saw faces in the first stanza, but now we focus on one face in particular. This woman, we find out, isn't very happy with her reflection in the lake, so she tries to find a kinder reflection under the light of a candle or the moon. When the lake reflects her faithfully anyway, she cries and gets upset. In the last two lines of this poem, we see why this woman is so upset: in her watery reflection, her past is drowning, and a horrible future is rising to meet her.

In this poem, this mirror tells us repeatedly about how accurate and unbiased it is in showing appearances- which doesn't work out so well for the aging woman in the second stanza, who seems very concerned with the way that she looks. This poem explores the importance and transience of appearances. This poem looks at what is important to a female character from the point of view of a speaker claiming to be unbiased. Our speaker, a mirror, reveals a woman concerned about her appearance and aging. The mirror may change into a lake, but it doesn't seem to age as time passes unlike the woman who sees herself aging in her reflection in its waters. We don't find out that youth and old age are involved in this poem until the last few lines, but throughout the poem we get hints that time is passing, he poem revolves around water, which is both a reflecting surface and an actual lake. So, water, in this poem, is both clear and mysterious. In talking about mirrors the sense of sight is pretty important. So, of course, colors and darkness figure into this poem. From silver to pink to moonlight, this poem uses colors and light to give the reader images as they read about a mirror.

第九节　罗伯特·海顿

一、作者简介

罗伯特·海顿（1913—1980），是非洲裔美国诗人，终生以教书为业。作为一个黑人，海顿注重从历史和文化的角度对美国黑人历史上遭到的不公正待遇，特别是奴隶贸易和蓄奴制，给予伦理道德上的批评与谴责。但是，海顿的诗歌获得了第一届世界黑人艺术节的最佳英语诗歌奖后，他却遭到了猛烈的攻击和批判。年轻一代的黑人作家攻击海顿作为一个黑人，不是为黑人写作，却把精力放在个人经验和社会历史文化上了，是又一个"汤姆大叔"，是黑人作家中的叛徒，是"被美国主义主流文学污染的"。海顿创作的旺盛时代是在二战以后，20世纪上半叶经历的两次世界大战给人类造成了巨大的创伤。人们开始思考和反思人类自身的问题。人类为什么会这样惨绝人寰地互相杀戮，人类自身到底是怎样的，现代社会又将往何处去？海顿的诗歌注重从历史和文化的角度出发去关注社会现象。因此，海顿诗歌的象征体系之中还可以看到他对整个社会文明及人类未来的困惑和担忧。

二、主要作品简介

《海顿诗选》是海顿1985年发表的一部诗集，除了包括著名的诗篇《冬日的星期天》和《鞭打》之外，这部诗集还包括了其他一些震撼人心的作品。尽管海顿的诗中描写了大量非裔美国人的历史和文化，但他的诗并没有告诉读者如何去思考，如何去感受。相反，他小心地精雕细琢出海浪的意象，细心的读者可以通过这些意象在不同寻常的，或美丽或令人难受的领域来回走动。海顿的诗使读者想起那些压迫者，比如《大西洋中央航线》中著名的"阿姆斯达号事件"以及《夜晚、死亡、密西西比》中一位老三K党成员，他因为太脆弱以至于不能亲临他为之自豪的儿子的死刑。尽管海顿获得了无数的奖项，但直到生命尽头他也并不为一些读者所熟知。幸运的是，自从《海顿诗选》在他去世后发表以来，海顿的名望逐渐得以提高。

三、选读作品赏析

" *Those Winter Sundays*"

Robert Hayden wrote some awesome poems about African-American history and his experiences of being a black man in America, but "Those Winter Sundays" is not about race at all. It's a small but powerful poem about a father-child relationship and all the mixed feelings that come with it: love, admiration, fear, misunderstanding, and even hate. We'd even go as far as saying that it's a universal poem -it transcends race class and nation.

At its heart, "Those Winter Sundays" is about love, the deep and serious familial love between a parent and a child. The type of love gets you up at the crack of dawn even when you're exhausted from a long week of hard work. This love is quiet and brave; it's not showy; there are no hugs and kisses and snuggles. That means unfortunately, that it can easily slip by unnoticed. Besides love, this poem is also about fathers sacrifice. The father wakes up early, works hard, and provides for his family.

Seriously, he works (in and outside of the home) seven days a week for his family.

"Those Winter Sundays" is very much concerned with the temperature. First it's cold. The temperature outside and inside the house reflects on the speaker's relationship with his father. In other words, the temperature is a symbol or representation of the speaker's inner feelings and relationships. The weather is cold, and the young speakers relationship with his father is indifferent and emotionally cold. His father has created literal warmth in the house, but not emotional warmth. The speaker doesn's understand his dad s literal warmth as his expression of love.

参 考 文 献

[1] 张佩，方映，范成功．英美文学［M］．天津：天津大学出版社．2011.

[2] 孙川慧，胡玲，刘丽．英美文学经典选读1［M］．重庆：重庆大学出版社．2017.

[3] 张小平．英美文学阅读与批评［M］．苏州：苏州大学出版社．2015.

[4] 陈红．英美文学精粹赏析［M］．北京：人民邮电出版社．2018.

[5] 段晓霞．英美文学意义与人文思想研究［M］．长春：吉林出版集团股份有限公司．2018.

[6] 谭丽娜．英美文学人文精神与现实意义研究［M］．长春：吉林出版集团股份有限公司．2018.

[7] 张莹波，李静．英美文学选读［M］．南京：东南大学出版社．2018.

[8] 龙毛忠．英美文学精华导读［M］．3版．上海：华东理工大学出版社．2016.

[9] 江滨，张佩．英美文学修订版［M］．天津：天津大学出版社．2017.

[10] 周定之．英美文学作品赏析［M］．长沙：湖南师范大学出版社．2002.

[11] 赵秀兰．英美文学作品赏析［M］．兰州：敦煌文艺出版社．2010.

[12] 刘赢南，张杰，谭宏伟，等．英美文学经典作品赏析［M］．北京：北京理工大学出版社．2014.

[13] 郑茗元，岳丽萍．英美文学经典作品赏析与导读［M］．广州：世界图书出版广东有限公司．2015.

[14] 郑野，李雯．英美文学经典作品赏析与导读［M］．广州：世界图书出版广东有限公司．2015.

[15] 胡宗锋．英美文学精要问答及作品赏析［M］．西安：西安出版社．2002.

[16] 陶丽丽，吕艳，李方木．英美文学经典作品赏析［M］．徐州：中国矿业大学出版社．2017.

［17］陈悦，张巧娟．英美文学史与作品赏析［M］．长春：吉林大学出版社．2015.

［18］江艳．英美文学史及作品赏析［M］．北京：中国广播电视出版社．2005.

［19］胡宗锋．英美文学精要问答及作品赏析［M］．西安：西安出版社．2009.

［20］徐庆宏．英美文学教学与人文思想渗透［J］．好家长．2019（12）：251.

［21］肖芳，肖福兰．英美文学课的"翻转课堂"［J］．人文之友．2019（8）：93－94.

［22］徐庆宏．英美文学欣赏的课程改革［J］．校园英语．2019（5）：23.

［23］冯一哲．教学英美文学的意义与策略［J］．科技风．2019（17）：51，70.

［24］胡瑞．英美文学与大学英语教学［J］．散文百家．2018（12）：2－3.

［25］张芳芳．英美文学的修辞手法分析［J］．报刊荟萃（下）．2018（7）：284.

［26］吴丹．英美文学中的情感渗透［J］．求知导刊．2018（16）：54.

［27］孙晓梅．浅谈英美文学的改进［J］．西部皮革．2016，38（6）：227－228.

［28］刘冰．浅谈英美文学翻译中的美学价值［J］．大众文艺．2019（5）：177－178.

［29］张寿颖．认知诗学视野下的英美文学教学［J］．读书文摘（中）．2019（2）：125.

［30］林璐延．茅盾英美文学译介概述［J］．海外英语．2017（22）：134－135.

［31］朱子琳．英美文学的特点及文化内涵探析［J］．北极光．2019（2）：15－16.

［32］朱薇．英文电影和英美文学之间的关系分析［J］．白城师范学院学报．2019，（C1）：73－75，88.

［33］张凤丽．英美文学中的哥特传统［J］．课程教育研究．2019（4）：249－250.